9/11/92

D1357048

Arrivals
and Departures

LESLIE THOMAS

Arrivals and Departures

A Novel

METHUEN

First published in Great Britain in 1992 by Methuen London,
an imprint of Reed Consumer Books Ltd
Michelin House, 81 Fulham Road, London sw3 6RB
and Auckland, Melbourne, Singapore and Toronto

The extract on page vii from 'Little Gidding' in *Four Quartets* by T. S. Eliot is
reproduced by kind permission of the publishers Faber and Faber Ltd.

ISBN 0 413 66520 8
A CIP catalogue record for this book
is available from the British Library

Phototypeset by Intype, London
Printed and bound in Great Britain
by Richard Clays, St Ives plc

For my friends Denis and Liz Riley,
with thanks

. . . the end of all our exploring
Will be to arrive where we started
And know the place for the first time.

T. S. ELIOT

One

On that June evening, at ten o'clock, the airport appeared from the incoming plane curiously like the eastern city it had left not many hours before; low buildings, flat roofs, white walls, light languid in the late day. The London sun had gone down ahead of the aircraft in a dusty orange cloud, the level land below was darkening and the vast reservoirs on the western side of the runways dimly reflected the sky.

Edward Richardson was going home again. Every week, sometimes more often, he flew home from some far place, the change in times and climates, lands and people, all part of his life. He was a tall but solid man with a tired face. At forty-three he had done so much travelling, so much flying. He was becoming unclear where he was going.

As commercial manager of the airline he was well known on the plane and at Heathrow. Landing formalities were quick and the terminal was quiet, almost idle. He went briefly into his office, two hundred yards distant, then boarded the bus for the staff car park, collected his car and with the window down drove towards home. There was a touch of pungency from the airport sludge farm.

Adele was already in bed. She often had early-morning meetings. She stirred sleepily. 'How was it?'

'Bahrain? Oh, it was all right – in the end. The usual insurmountable problems. But we shuffled them around until they didn't look so bad.'

'There was a call from Gohm, Brent and Byas Travel

Management. They really want you, Edward. They're very keen. They're ringing back tomorrow.'

Richardson sighed. '*I* don't want Gohm, Brent and Byas. In any case I have to go to Istanbul tomorrow. There was a message when I arrived at Heathrow.'

She half sat up in her bed. She had left the side light burning and it shone on the curve of her cheek. Adele had always had a strong face and the illumination was unflattering. 'Istanbul?' she said frowning. 'But surely that's on the way back from Bahrain.'

'It is, more or less.' He sat on the end of his bed and took off his jacket. They had not kissed. 'But for a start the flight didn't call there and even for me they won't divert. You should know that. And additionally, I didn't get the Istanbul message until I was back at Heathrow.'

'Jesus, that's typical. So you have to go most of the way back again.'

'It's the job.'

'I don't know how you stand it. Or me.' She corrected the double meaning. 'How I stand it.'

He took off his shoes and put on a pair of light suede slippers. 'Nor do I,' he confessed. 'I'm going up to take a look at the stars.'

'I thought you might.'

'The night's clear. I know, I've just been up there.' He pulled on a sweater. 'Ray Francis, the manager in Istanbul, has gone off with a local woman.'

'Some bimbo? I suppose they have bimbos in Turkey like everywhere else.'

'This bimbo is a university professor. Francis was always original. I've got to find him or sort it out somehow. I may be back in the evening.'

'Oh good,' she said flatly.

She extinguished the bed light as he was going out of the door. He thought how poor their marriage had become. It was strangely as though it were someone else's marriage,

2

viewed from a safe distance. Each of them watched its disintegration as if fascinated, the slight crumbling here, the insidious rot and the powdering there, but with neither making any move to stop or save themselves. Sometimes he felt that if she would only hold out her hands to prevent another piece falling away, then he would help her. Between them they might save it. But then they might regret the attempt; they might be left standing, holding up only a ruin.

Softly he walked along the corridor. The house was old and close. It held the warmth of the summer night. One of the lattice windows had been left open at the end and a climbing rose tapped like a reminder against the frame. He passed his son Toby's room and heard him mildly snoring.

There was a brief flight of stairs up to another room, once a half-landing, which he used as a study. He switched on the lamp at the desk and its glow circled the walls. There were two cases of books, the titles gleaming from their spines and a series of prints of celestial charts, copies of the ancient maps of the universe, and a burnished astrolabe. Even now, in the low luminescence, the colours glowed finely, and his hand went out and touched one of the frames. He began to smile. He mounted a second short flight of oak steps and opened a silent door. It swung to reveal a telescope on its mounting, a tipped chair beneath it, and a glass dome eighteen feet wide, above, ribbed into sections but displaying the sky, the stars and the beginnings of a moon.

He settled into the tubular steel chair and, with a touch of the controls, swung the telescope towards the southern sky. As he did so he activated another switch and music, eerie, spacious music, filled the dome. He turned the volume down so that it seeped gently and mysteriously into the room; Walton's theme from the Antarctic of chill and winds and lonely emptiness.

Now he traversed the telescope across the deepness of the southern sky. There was the summer triangle, Vega in Lyra the Harp, Deneb in Cygnus the Swan, Altair at the centre

3

of Aquila with the Wild Duck far out on the fringe and
Arcturus, the brightest star in the Northern hemisphere.
He watched them playing tag across infinity. The music
surrounded him, the stars held his gaze. He felt himself
relax into happiness.

A burned-out earth satellite swooped across his view.
Richardson let it go past with a sniff of annoyance. He
concentrated on the southern firmament, as he always did,
for to the north the lights of Heathrow glowed, itself like
some planet landed upon the world.

He was there for more than an hour. His eyes became
tired. The music had changed several times. He turned the
switch off and rubbed his eyes. Just below him the village
of Bedmansworth was silent as the stars. There was one
light in the short street and another in the church (a pre-
caution since a burglary during which the money from the
Footballs for Africa Fund had been stolen) but the night
itself was fine enough for him to distinguish the shapes of
the houses, the two inns, the tower and arrow of the church
and the end of the row of shops.

Bedmansworth had been a village for centuries and was
noted on the 'Actual Survey of the County of Midlesex', a
copy of which hung in the drawing-room downstairs, drawn
by John Ogilby, cartographer to Charles the Second, in
1675, who noted also with a single thatched cottage, the
hamlet of Hetherow in the Hundred of Elthorne.

In the pale night he could see, beyond the roofs, fields,
indistinct as cobwebs, real meadows once, that had stretched
from the fringes of London to Uxbridge, to Windsor, to
Hounslow Heath, then the territory of the highwayman but
now covered by the tarmac flat-tops of the Heathrow runways and the metropolis of its buildings.

The road through the village was as dim as a secret
passage. He picked out the sleeping outlines of the houses,
knowing each family who lived there: the Swan Inn, where
Jim Turner held the licence, and the other smaller pub, the

Straw Man, once a drovers' inn on the sheep and cattle trails from Wales to the markets of London. There was a squat row of roadside cottages, their backs to him, that had been there since farm labourers were paid threepence a day. Old village families still lived in them, most of the men employed at the airport.

Richardson was about to lower the chair again when he detected a small movement below, then heard the yawning call of a cat and saw it strolling along the middle of the road, deliberate as a drunk, keeping to the white lines. The cat knew it was safe because there would be no traffic at that time; the highway, which a hundred years before had been a cart track to the villages of Sheepcoat and Powdermill and thence to the Bath Road and London, now went nowhere. It looped around a small green with the Straw Man at its head. There was a patch of grass, a public seat and a stump which was said to be all that remained of a gibbet where they hanged highwaymen, three of whom had been called Tom, Dick and Harry, thus giving a phrase to the English language.

The cat had trundled from his view when he caught a remote whine, like that of an insect in the night. A light, isolated and small, was jolting in the dark distance. He knew what it was even as it approached. One vehicle only was likely to come on that route to nowhere at that hour. It spluttered on the corner and then bobbed into his vision, a thin motor cycle with a heavy figure astride it; Bernard Threadle, the self-appointed guardian of the village, the vigilante. Richardson pictured the round, set and devoted face under a heavy helmet on each side of which was emblazoned a winged letter 'B'. Bernard wore a heavy protective coat and leggings and carried a torch which he hinted could double as a truncheon. His goggles fitted over rimless glasses that were familiar by day as he served behind the counter of Weaver's, the Bedmansworth chemist's shop. His earnestness in applying the scarlet flying-B transfers to the sides of his helmet had not prevented him applying one upside down and back to front, one winging forward, the other winging away.

He covered the countryside in the dark hours; once before midnight, once at two o'clock and then the dawn patrol, rising from his bed for each mission. His soft face hardened into an expression of assurance and his eyes shone surely behind his spectacles as he boasted: 'I *never* sleep.' Bernard had never as yet apprehended any nocturnal felons although he himself had twice been stopped and questioned by the police.

It was two fifteen. Richardson nodded at the stars, extricated himself from the tight tubular chair, and crouched his way to the door. There were duplicate controls on the wall. He touched the switch lightly, as if that would ensure that the instrument itself would slide back smoothly. With another switch he closed the aperture of the covering dome. Then he extinguished the light and clambered back down the steps into the house, into reality.

In those early hours the airport was wet and empty, the planes lying against the buildings like sleeping animals in stalls. Lights shone whitely within the terminals. An Indian youth began his day's labour as a cleaner, checking toilet rolls and walking into lavatory cubicles to lift the seats from the pans. As he did so he repeated 'Smile please,' a joke he had learned from his Irish predecessor.

Music floated in the long void but the woman behind the refreshment counter had heard it many times before, a never-ending melody. It was interrupted by a warning: 'This is a security announcement. Do not leave baggage unattended. It may be removed and destroyed.'

At that hour there were few travellers: a knot of young people hunched tiredly in one corner, a man asleep, his arms across one of the refreshment-area tables, his snores enough to rustle a paper napkin close to his nose. A wandering security man surveyed him for a moment but moved on. 'Why don't you stop him snoring?' the tea-counter woman called. 'Ruddy row.' The paper napkin flew off the table. 'Look at that,' she said.

The first of the morning's incoming flights rumbled across the roof. 'Ruddy row,' she repeated.

The security man slouched towards her and, without being asked, she poured him a cup of tea. His eyelids drooped. He had another job in the day. Outside a taxi pulled up. A traffic warden watched it as if it might possibly commit an offence.

'Here they come,' grumbled the security man. 'Now they'll all start coming.'

'Yes, they'll all start now,' said the woman pointlessly.

'They'll all be coming.'

A uniformed woman customs officer came smartly through the sliding doors.

'She's early,' she added with a touch of interest.

'Keen,' nodded the security man over his weary teacup. His eyelids dropped further. 'Wish I was.'

'I don't,' responded the woman. 'Where does it get you?'

The customs officer went briskly through the inner doors and began to set out her desk. Her glance went to the glass corridor along which processions of fatigued, hapless and herded passengers, worried and relieved at the same time, would soon be shuffling.

The first dayshift of immigration officials arrived and the woman in the flower shop rolled up the blind. The stock had been replenished overnight and a scent as strong as a garden or a funeral greeted her as she eased open the glass door. The shop was strategically placed opposite the Arrivals doors. Men, stirred by kindness, love, or conscience, were the best customers.

Pallid porters in beige uniforms stood leaning unexpectantly on barrows:

'How's your missus?' called one.

7

'Still there,' answered another.

'Wish mine was,' said a third.

Thick wedges of newspapers were taken into the book-shop, the half-asleep assistant knocking over the best-selling-paperback stand as she did so. She quickly righted the frame, putting back the titles haphazardly.

It was full daylight outside now. Passengers were begin-ning to flow into the Departures hall and out of the Arrivals doors. Planes appeared in the sky, their incandescent land-ing lights blazing even against the early sun, one, two, three, stretched far out, a fourth flickering into view, nearing journey's end, at the start of another ordinary airport day.

On the flight from Los Angeles, travelling Club Class, Mrs Pearl Collingwood squeezed her eyes to focus on the English fields below. 'Pretty small,' she muttered. 'Not much of it at all.'

'It's a small country,' pointed out her daughter. She was a soft-faced woman with dark hair and strong brown eyes. She leaned to look over the older woman's shoulder. 'I've always wondered why you never came before.'

'Never any time,' answered the old lady. Her face was patterned with lace wrinkles, her eyes deep, dark and lively and there was an uplift at the corners of her mouth.

The Boeing 747 tagged onto the course of the Thames, flying straight along the river's bends on an easterly approach, having made a wide, elliptical, stacking circuit over Sussex and Kent. 'Small houses,' sniffed Pearl Colling-wood.

'Mother,' said Rona reprovingly. 'We're still a long way up. At least there's no fog. You always thought there would be fog.'

'Now, *that* I was looking forward to, fog,' grunted the old lady. 'It just don't seem right without the fog.'

'We'll have them fix some,' promised her daughter. 'Anyway, you've seen fog. There's plenty in San Francisco.'

8

'London fog,' insisted her mother.

'Why don't you put your glasses on?' suggested the younger woman, as if they might make fog appear.

The old lady sniffed. 'They're for long distance,' she observed without turning from the window. 'But not this long.'

She fumbled ineffectually with her handbag. Rona found the spectacles and, taking them from their tortoiseshell case, handed them to her. Her mother nodded her thanks. 'You're a good girl, Rona,' she said adding, almost to herself: 'I'm glad you're around.'

The captain of the aircraft conversationally informed them that they were on their final approach and would be landing in six minutes. The exactness did not impress Pearl. 'Six minutes,' she muttered, her wrinkles moving in a pattern. 'How can he be so sure?'

Rona patted the brown, knuckled hand. 'He's just letting everybody know that he's got everything under control,' she whispered.

'I certainly hope so,' returned the old lady. She was once more peering critically from her window. 'Those fields do look small,' she reaffirmed. 'Just see how bitty they are.'

'And very green,' pointed out Rona.

'All that rain,' her mother replied.

Rona leaned over and touched the buckle of her mother's clipped seat-belt. Her mother had only once been to Europe, twenty-five years before when her husband was alive. They had travelled to Paris and Rome and then returned to California. Apart from a vacation in Mexico she had not left the United States since. At seventy-seven she had seemed unlikely ever to want to do so. Until an afternoon a month before when she had telephoned her daughter: 'Get yourself packed. We're going to London.'

At first Rona had thought it was because of her divorce. She had been so low and drained, it seemed that it was her mother's idea of a diversion. But Pearl denied it.

9

'*I* want to go,' she had stated firmly. 'I'm going whether you come or not. I can get by.'

'It's not just for me, then?' said her daughter. 'Not because of my marriage.'

'Your *ex*-marriage,' the old lady corrected bluntly. 'Not at all. Nothing to do with it.'

Rona said: 'I could do with a break.'

'Show me a pleasant divorce,' said her mother. 'So you do want to come.'

'Yes, of course, I'd love to. Can we have dinner at the Ritz?' She gave a small laugh into the telephone.

'Sure. We'll go to the Ritz and the Savoy. And Buckingham Palace.'

'It's not going to be too tiring?'

'For me?'

Rona smiled again. 'Yes.'

'Not for me,' confirmed Pearl. 'Start getting packed.'

Georgina Hayles was fatigued; weary of the long flight and the people on it. Most of her working life was spent seeing only the tops of their heads as she moved swiftly up and down with her professional sway, touching the shoulders of seats as she went, as though to propel herself by means of them. The passengers in their little niches were only fully revealed as she bent to serve them or speak to them. With their nerves and their quibbles, their complaints and their stupidity, she sometimes wondered whether she was somehow doomed to wait upon mass transportations of fools and inadequates. A drunk had been sick over her hair on the previous flight. All she wanted now was to get home, get into bed, and, having slept, put into effect the long-considered decision to escape, dangerous though it might be.

The aircraft was about to touch down. Bright, early sun shimmered on the wet grass and reflected on the wings and tailfins of planes standing outside maintenance hangars, making them shine like banners. Rona held her mother's wrist but the old lady was peering from her window. 'He made it,' she announced loudly as the tyres squealed on the runway. 'He got it down.' The big aircraft landed like a pelican on a lake. The engines reversed. The captain said: 'Welcome to London. The local time is seven o'clock.' He added: 'In the morning. The temperature is fifty-eight degrees Fahrenheit. We hope you had a good flight.'

'Pretty good,' replied the old lady as if speaking for all the passengers. 'Even though it took long enough.'

A pier floated to the side of the plane and the door opened, letting in a stream of cool air. 'I don't feel too good,' mentioned Pearl Collingwood suddenly. 'But I'll be okay.'

Her daughter's face clouded. She caught the stewardess's eye. 'My mother is feeling unwell,' she said. 'It's been a long trip.'

Georgina glanced at the old lady. 'I expect it has for her,' she said. At least she had not collapsed in mid-air. 'I'll get some help. She should have a wheelchair.'

'I don't want any chair,' said Pearl her head coming up briskly. Her mouth knitted. 'I'm not going to arrive in London in any chair. I'll be okay. Don't worry.'

Rona 'Perhaps we could get off first,' suggested Rona to the stewardess.

'Yes, of course.' She went briskly to the exit and spoke to the cabin services director. He glanced back into the cabin towards the old lady, left the door and walked down the aisle. 'We'll get you off first, madam,' he said. He glanced at Rona. 'There's a chair if you need it. It's quite a walk.'

Rona leaned towards her mother. 'I think you ought to use a chair,' she suggested firmly. 'It's a long way.'

'I'll take it easy,' insisted the old lady. A smile wrinkled briefly. 'I hate being pushed around.'

Her daughter gave a look like a shrug to the director who still appeared anxious, but nodded. He walked back and picked up the telephone at the now open door and ordered a wheelchair anyway. 'Get her off quickly,' he said to Georgina out of the side of his mouth.

The wheelchair was swift in arriving; it was standing outside the door when Rona and her mother disembarked. A pink-faced man was peering from behind it, his very expression an invitation to Pearl Collingwood to occupy the conveyance. She refused sharply, shaking her head and muttering: 'I'll use my usual feet.' With her daughter supporting her arm she took her first steps in England. The wheelchair and its attendant sedately followed ten yards to the rear, keeping pace with them, the pink man at the apparent ready to scoop up the elderly American if she should fall. The trio's pace was slow and other hurrying passengers caught up and overtook them, a race for Immigration, trolley lines, baggage claim and Customs. Pearl Collingwood waited, letting the rush go by. The man with the wheelchair paused, smiling rosily, giving it a minute push of invitation towards her. 'Don't need it,' she called back. 'Take it away!'

Rona apologetically acknowledged the man who showed no sign of going away. She took her mother's elbow once more and they proceeded carefully with the attendant and the chair keeping pace. 'Is he still there?' asked the old lady sneakily, inclining towards her daughter.

'He is,' confirmed Rona. 'Are you sure you wouldn't like a ride?'

'No way,' responded her mother firmly. 'I'm *not* arriving in England on wheels.' She turned and glared at the attendant who blinked mildly back at her. She said nothing, but waved a feathery hand dismissively and strode out with the determination of a staunch but tiring explorer on the last testing lap of a difficult journey.

They reached the Immigration area and Rona saw with a surge of dismay the long, scarcely shuffling lines of incoming passengers. She half turned towards the wheelchair man. Her mother, her wrinkles mazed into a puzzle, regarded the queues, her mouth working. 'Don't they want us in their country?' she grumbled.

Cockney

'If you use the chair you can go straight to the front,' the pink man pointed out pleasantly.

Pearl Collingwood remained truculent, although wavering. 'So you have to be dying first,' she grimaced. She turned to her daughter. '*You* sit in the thing,' she suggested. Rona laughed and the attendant laughed too. He pushed the chair forwards and after a final hesitation the old lady sat in it with an ill grace. 'Okay, driver, let's go,' she said. But her glance back at the man was grateful. 'But step on it,' she added.

Posher

The immigration officer was sympathetic. 'It's been a long journey, has it,' he said as he took Mrs Collingwood's passport.

'Oh me, I'm used to it. I'm flying about all the time.' She waved his sympathy aside.

'Don't overdo it,' he advised, returning the document to her.

She continued the journey by wheelchair, giving the impression that she might be someone important. Rona gave a wry and relieved smile. Her mother knew when she was beaten, although she did not like anyone else to know. The attendant helped them at the baggage collection and through the Customs channel. Rona pushed their cases on a trolley. Mrs Collingwood insisted on going by way of the Red Route, although they had nothing to declare. The turbaned customs officer was cooperative. American 'Just wanted to see you were on the ball,' the old lady informed him. 'We could be drug barons.'

'We know the drug barons,' answered the Sikh mildly. He waved the small group through. 'What sort of Englishman was that?' said Mrs Collingwood cautiously.

The invalid chair was propelled through a moving mass of other passengers, most of them pushing wire trolleys piled with luggage, some tiredly holding onto the vehicles as if they might lend support. The trundling advance rolled through the Arrivals exit to be faced with walls of faces, some expectant, some blank and clutching below their chins names in capital letters on squares of cardboard: 'Mr Jenkins', 'Mr Ali', 'Mr and Mrs Snodding', 'Bennett of Guinness', 'Christian Brothers', and others. It was an odd identity parade in reverse, not lost on Mrs Collingwood. 'Looks like they rounded up the usual suspects,' she muttered.

'There's our driver,' said Rona. A man in a grey uniform and sharply peaked cap was holding a discreet notice which said: 'Mrs Pearl Collingwood from Los Angeles.'

'Now somebody else can transport us,' she said to the pushing attendant. 'How much do I owe?'

cockney

'Nothing, madam,' he replied soberly. 'No payment. Nice to help somebody with a bit of spirit. Some people give up too easy if you ask me.' He looked thoughtful as though unsure whether or not to confide in her. 'In any case, this is a special journey. Like a celebration. We've just taken over these.' He patted the conveyance.

'Taken them over?' It was Rona's question but her mother looked up sharply. 'There's been a revolution in wheel-chairs?' she asked.

He grinned. 'You could say that. We used to work for the airport but they made us redundant. So six of us got together and bid for the wheelchair contract and we *got it*. We operate all the chairs in Heathrow now. We charge the airport for each case we handle. From today.' He said it like a man who had just bought an airline. They wished him luck and he pushed off, zigzagging through the people with their luggage trolleys.

'Always knew we should give that guy our business,' said Mrs Collingwood. She examined the capped and uniformed figure who had spotted them. '*He* looks real English,' she concluded.

'I expect he is,' agreed her daughter. The man, sober-faced as his suit, lifted his cap. 'Mrs Collingwood and Mrs

Essex

Train,' he recited. 'I'm from the Excelsior Hotel. My name is Arthur.' He took the handle of the luggage trolley from Rona. 'If you would not mind waiting one moment, the car will be here. He was just circling.' He looked anxiously at the older woman. 'Not too weary, madam?'

'I feel bad,' said Mrs Collingwood, holding onto the handle of the trolley with Arthur.

'Still?' Rona asked anxiously.

'Sure, still. I'm sick. I feel it.'

Arthur was diffident. 'Perhaps madam is tired after the flight,' he suggested to both women at once. 'It will only take forty minutes into London.'

Mrs Collingwood eyed him. 'I know the difference,' she told him. 'Tired is tired and sick is sick. And I'm sick.'

He glanced again at Rona. 'Would madam like a doctor?' he asked.

'Not right now,' the old lady put in firmly. 'When we get to the city. You may have to break the speed limit.'

'It's nearly all motorway,' he answered inconsequentially. They were outside the building now. 'Here he is,' he added.

'He's quit circling,' said Mrs Collingwood. 'Maybe he thinks he's a flier.'

The driver, a tall, stooped man with a creased chin, left the car and announced himself. 'I'm Charles, ladies,' he said. 'Welcome to London.'

'The lady is not feeling well, Charles,' said Arthur, his eyebrows rising. He nodded at Mrs Collingwood. Charles was at once concerned. 'Nothing serious, I hope,' he said inclining his folded chin towards her. 'Perhaps we're feeling fatigued.'

'You may be, but I'm not,' reaffirmed Mrs Collingwood. 'I'm sick.'

'I think we must get going,' suggested Rona. 'We'll get a doctor when we reach the hotel.' She looked anxiously at her mother. 'Maybe we shouldn't have come,' she said.

'We're here now,' said the old lady. For a sick woman

15

she sounded oddly forthright, but Rona was often puzzled by her mother. She patted the thin hand as soon as they were settled in the car. 'We'll soon be there,' she assured. 'Then we'll get you a check-up.'

The big car turned out of the airport and drove swiftly but quietly towards the motorway. Mrs Collingwood now became silent but peered from the window intently. 'Very flat,' she commented eventually, drily. 'No hills, no ocean.'

'The hills and ocean are in other parts of the country,' her daughter replied firmly.

Mrs Collingwood's face wrinkled into a grin. 'But I like it,' she conceded. 'The British seem glad to see us.'

They were on the motorway heading east when she complained of being ill again. 'I've got to get out of this car,' she told Rona. 'I need to rest.'

Rona was aware of how difficult Pearl could be; but now she was anxious. 'My mother feels ill again,' she said over the driver's shoulder. 'I think maybe we'll have to stop somewhere.'

Charles stared at Arthur. 'Hillingdon Hospital,' he said decisively. 'That's nearest.' They regarded each other with abrupt concern. 'Not in the car,' muttered Arthur like a prayer. 'Not this car,' whispered Charles. 'It's new.'

'No hospitals!' bellowed Mrs Collingwood from behind. 'Did I hear you say a hospital?' I didn't come to England to go to hospital. I can do that in California. I have insurance.'

Stoically Charles pulled the car onto the hard shoulder. 'What would madam's instructions be?' he inquired of Rona.

The answer came from Pearl. 'I want to go *there*,' she declared pointing from the car window. 'See – right there.'

'Where, madam?' blinked Arthur, craning to look around the driver.

'That's a church,' said Charles.

'I know. I know a church when I see it,' retorted the old lady. 'But there's got to be houses, hotels. That's where I want to go.'

Rona regarded her with astonishment matched only by that of the two men. 'You want to go *there*?' she asked.

'Right there. And right now. I'm sick.'

'What's there?' Rona asked the two men.

'Don't rightly know, miss,' said Charles helplessly. 'There's a few villages around here. We could see if you like.'

'I like,' put in the old lady. 'I want to go there. I need to rest.'

'Yes, please,' Rona nodded haplessly at the driver. 'I'll call the Excelsior and tell them what happened.'

Charles eased the car forward from the hard shoulder. 'There's an exit a mile further on,' he said. Arthur half turned and looked back with concern. 'There are other hotels around here,' he offered. 'Plenty of them. And motels around the airport.'

'I want to go to the place with the church,' Mrs Collingwood told him uncompromisingly. Her creased eyelids slid up and he backed away from her scrutiny. 'I may need to die there.'

'Next exit,' Arthur muttered to Charles.

Rona was more than aware that her mother had a strong streak of eccentricity. In Mexico, on her seventieth birthday, she had ridden a striped donkey along the main street of Tijuana. Once she had nudged a man she disliked into a swimming-pool at a politician's party. Rona remembered how she and her former husband Jeff had stood immobilised while the man surfaced and splashed like a walrus, spouting water and bellowing: 'You didn't know I could swim, did you? You pushed me and you didn't know whether I could swim!'

'I sure didn't,' her mother had replied grandly.

There had been other incidents: the explosion of some homemade moonshine which she had concealed below her bed; her interruption of a shocked preacher at a man's funeral with muttered corrections about the deceased's past;

17

the absent-minded lighting up of a cigarette in church; croaky singing during a chamber-music recital. Now Rona looked sideways at the older lady who was staring from the window as if to make sure that they were truly going to go in the direction she required. Her mother returned the examination with pain crossing her face. 'I don't feel much better,' she complained.

They had reached the exit and Charles turned the car off and crossed the bridge back over the motorway. 'This is foreign country to me,' he confided to Arthur.

'Go straight,' suggested Arthur.

The guess was sound. The road narrowed and then split into a series of lanes but by this time the square tower of the church was near. The hedges on either side were ragged and coated with dried mud and dust, there were short fields, electricity pylons, shaggy horses and muddy cows, rusty corrugated-iron fences and pigs, then an open space sown with crops.

'Turnips,' said Arthur informatively. 'This is big turnip country.'

'Bedmansworth,' read Charles as a sign appeared at the side of the road. 'Never heard of it.'

The route turned quickly and they found themselves moving the length of the churchyard wall. 'Slow down,' called Mrs Collingwood. 'Take it easy.'

Rona asked: 'Are you feeling better?'

'It comes and goes,' responded the old lady doggedly. 'Where can we stop?'

'Here's the pub,' said Arthur. 'The inn. The Swan.'

'We'll stay here,' said Mrs Collingwood. 'This will be fine.'

'They may not have accommodation,' pointed out Arthur doubtfully. 'A lot of these places don't.'

Charles pulled up in front of the open door. There were flowers in a basket by the entrance and more in window-boxes suspended over the street. Arthur half turned and spoke to Rona. 'Would you like me to inquire, Mrs Train?'

'This will be fine,' asserted Rona's mother, her head nodding vigorously. The younger woman stilled her with a touch. 'We'll need to see if they have rooms,' she said. She looked at Arthur. 'I'll come with you,' she said. 'I'd better explain.'

Charles was left in the car with Mrs Collingwood. 'I hope you'll be better soon, madam,' he said inadequately.

'I make quick recoveries,' she assured him. She eyed him conspiratorially. 'You'll need to make an excuse to the hotel,' she said. 'What's it called?'

'The Excelsior, madam,' he replied a touch loftily.

'Right. You'd better say I died.'

His eyebrows went up. His creased chin swung around. 'Madam?' he said in a shocked tone.

'Tell them I died,' she repeated with a wink. 'I died on the way from the airport. They won't blame you, will they?'

'No, madam,' he said weakly. He was relieved to see Arthur emerging from the inn and giving him the thumbs-up sign. Rona followed with a woman in a flowered blouse. Rona opened the rear door. 'Mother, they have a room. In fact they have two.' She turned to the other woman. 'I can't tell you how relieved I am. I think she had better see a doctor.' She said to her mother: 'This is Mrs Turner, she's the . . .'

'Landlady,' provided Mrs Turner. 'I'm Dilys. Everybody calls me Dilys.'

With undisguised relief Charles was hurriedly taking the luggage from the boot. Arthur relieved him of one of the smaller cases and stood ready to assist Mrs Collingwood from the rear of the car. 'It's okay,' the old lady said reassuringly. 'Already I feel much better.'

She half closed her eyes as they went into the dim bar. There was a youth with his hair in a pigtail frowning over a comic book behind the bar and a grey-haired woman polishing beer glasses. She looked up curiously as they entered and wished them good morning in a country voice that surprised the London men.

'It's good. It's real good,' enthused Mrs Collingwood. She was helped up the turning stairs. 'This place must be older than me.'

'Seventeen sixty,' said Dilys. 'Mind how you go.' She called over her shoulder: 'Randy, bring up the cases. Now.'

They reached the landing and Dilys opened a thick door. They walked into a long, beamed room with three windows and a large quilted bed. 'It's our best room,' she said.

'It's wonderful,' said Rona. 'Isn't it, Mother? Wonderful.'

The boy called Randy puffed up the narrow stairs with the cases. 'What a neat idea,' said Pearl Collingwood looking at his pigtail. 'The Chinese used to do that.' She moved towards the nearest window. The lattice was open and while her daughter, the landlady and the boy watched curiously, she opened it wider and sniffed out over a garden set with summer flowers, with a square lawn and a bench. She could see the grey stone back of the church and some great yews. There were red roofs beyond. A roar came from the direction of the airport. 'I'm afraid it's noisy when the wind is in the wrong direction,' apologised Dilys. 'When it's the other way we occasionally get a whiff from the sewage farm.'

'It's just fine,' Mrs Collingwood assured her without turning round. Her daughter was regarding her with great uncertainty. But Mrs Collingwood was smiling out across the garden, to the church and beyond. 'Just fine,' she repeated almost to herself.

Two

At ten o'clock that morning the Boston flight came home and half an hour later Bramwell Broad was at the crews' Immigration desk, halfway along a line of stewards and stewardesses. Even after the journey they remained well pressed and sharp seamed, but for the most part low eyed and unspeaking. The queue's easy process through the formalities was observed with envy by American passengers shuffling tiredly in the extended chains of non-European arrivals. Bramwell was a long rather than a tall man with a rink of bald tanned skin on the top and front of his head, fringed by fair, short hair. His face was humorous, inclined to the sardonic, and his eyes drifted. He made a tired face at the neat, blonde stewardess behind him. They had not met on the flight.

Bramwell told harmless lies; juggled with his age which was thirty-five, and often amended his marital status. According to his story, he had been given his name after Bramwell Booth, founder of the Salvation Army, while an inmate of an orphanage, which was touching but fiction. His real name was Sidney and he had not been fully orphaned until he had attained his thirties. To his friends and to Lettie, his young Filipino wife, he was Bram.

Staff immigration procedure was perfunctory but as Broad passed his passport across the desk, a photograph of a comely young woman naked to the knees slipped out. The checking officer handed it back as if it had been a receipt or a business card. 'My mother,' Broad said smiling.

'Hurry home to her,' advised the official flatly. He sighed as though he had glimpsed a world he could not know and phlegmatically reached for the next passport in the mundane line. The stewardess who owned it had glanced over Broad's shoulder as he was concealing the frank picture. 'Like the socks,' she remarked quietly.

When they climbed onto the crew bus for the car park he found her standing next to him. All the seats were occupied. 'It's nice to carry around pictures of your family,' she said.

'Then you never forget,' he said piously. 'What's your name?'

'Barbara Poppins,' she said. Then to forestall him: 'No relation.'

She glanced out at the airport traffic. They were held up at the entrance to the tunnel. The air was misty with fumes.

He could not recall having seen her in Boston. Her fair hair curled about a round face. There were rings of weariness below her eyes and a touch of pink at the end of her nose. 'I didn't see you on the stopover,' he said.

'I went to bed,' she shrugged. 'I nearly always do, unless I have a friend in the crew and we go out somewhere. Room service and television, that's me.'

Once on the ground people who flew aeroplanes to the distant places of the earth usually lapsed into everyday domestic talk for, despite their wanderings, or perhaps because of them, they were domestic people. 'Do you have to go far?' he asked.

'The Grand Union Canal,' she said. He eyed her oddly. 'It's no distance. I live on a houseboat. You?'

'Fifteen minutes,' he answered. 'Bedmansworth.'

The bus had edged through the tunnel. Another airport bus was crawling in the opposite direction full of crew. Somebody waved quickly and a steward seated by the window responded. 'That was Bertie Sweet,' he said to the steward next to him. 'Remember Bertie Sweet, don't you?' His friend said he remembered. 'Two-faced,' he sniffed.

Once out of the tunnel the bus turned left, mounted the short hill and heavily negotiated two roundabouts. On the main road beyond the perimeter fence, morning traffic was thick, going towards Hammersmith and London. On the other side an Air India Boeing took off for Bombay.

They left the bus in the staff car park and Broad stood fumbling with his Vauxhall keys at the door of a silver Mercedes until Barbara had walked out of sight towards the end of the long rank of cars. In a few moments she drove by in a red Sierra and stopped. 'Having trouble?' she asked.

'There must be something wrong with the door-lock,' he said leaning against the Mercedes. 'Can't get the key to fit.'

'Try the Vauxhall,' she suggested, revving her own car.

'That's what I *have* been trying,' he flustered. He inserted the key into the commonplace car's lock and pretended to turn it only with difficulty.

'There,' she said when he had achieved it. 'It fits after all.' Concorde took off from the parallel runway, its white belly flying away like a discus. Its roar stemmed their conversation. When it had almost gone Broad checked his watch.

'On time,' Barbara said nodding at the white fleck in the sky. She smiled at Bramwell. 'Goodbye then. Love to your mother.' She drove away and his eyes followed the car until it turned at the distant gate. He muttered after the vanished Concorde for its noise had prevented him suggesting that they should meet again. Sighing, he climbed into the Vauxhall, started the reluctant engine and, as he backed out, poked his tongue at the Mercedes.

He drove home leaving the main route and going into the flat and damaged half-country that surrounded Heathrow; Airportland, the strange, ragged place of shabby farms, ugly fields, clogged streams, rubbish tips, donkeys, houses, cows and sheep, stone deaf to the shattering roar of aeroplanes.

Bedwell Park Mansions Estate was halfway between

Bedfont and Stanwell, on the borders of the village of Bedmansworth. Its detached houses, alike as cogs, staggered over the flat tops of two hills. At that time of the day its roads were almost empty of inhabitants; men and most of the wives were at work, children in school. In one tilted garden a parked pram was apparently ready to roll down the sloping lawn, and from the front window a young woman stared out like a resentful prisoner. She looked at his car as though it were an event, and Bramwell wondered who she was and what she did all the lonely day. He drove down one gentle, neo-Georgian hill and up another until he reached his own house. His neighbour, Mrs Hilditch, watched him from her window. They rarely spoke. Her husband was in Thailand and seldom came home.

Three years before, when he had first brought Lettie to England, his newly-purchased wife would have wanted to haul him off to bed at once, no matter how weary he was, squealing with laughter, pulling his clothes off as they stumbled upstairs, her breasts nosing from her robe as if to see what all the excitement was about. But these days they usually waited until evening.

She opened the Georgian-style door; she was in a bright native sarong, which she often wore for his returns home, a touch of the Tropics in Middlesex. One of her Doris Day tapes was playing and she had Radio One tuned in at the same time. Discord did not worry her for she had been brought up amidst the unremitting cacophony of Manila. She smiled and said what she always said: 'Welcome to our house. I have waited for you alone.' They embraced and kissed extravagantly. It was as though he had been voyaging far away in an outrigger.

It was long into the afternoon before Pearl Collingwood stirred from her weary sleep and, lying in the large old bed, gazed, at first inquisitively, at the black and bowed beams of the ceiling. 'I'm here,' she eventually assured herself. 'I

24

got to England.' The old lady lay back with a crackly smile. There was a knock at the door, a second knock, for it was the first which had roused her. She called and a thin, hurrying woman came in, the woman who had been polishing glasses when they arrived.

She was wearing a pinafore. 'I'm Mrs Durie,' she announced floating a tray on one hand, around the bed. 'I'm Dilys's mother. You like tea, don't you? Some of them don't.' She glanced in a concerned way at the woman now propped up in the bed. 'Americans, I mean.'

'I love it,' Mrs Collingwood assured her amiably. 'When I'm in England I *always* have tea. I feel much better now.'

'It's Prince George's birthday today,' confided Mrs Durie easing the cosy from the pot. She leaned forward solicitously. 'I'm glad you feel better. Shall I pour?'

'Sure, do, please,' said the American. She watched the tea curving strongly into the cup. 'Prince George,' she echoed. 'Well, well. Will there be celebrations?'

The inquiry patently took Mrs Durie by surprise. 'Oh, he's dead,' she said. 'Dead since nineteen thirty-six. January twentieth. It's just his birthday.'

Mrs Collingwood accepted the enlightenment with a smile and a nod. She tasted the tea to which Mrs Durie had added milk and sugar and decided she liked it. 'You know a whole lot about history?' she ventured. 'You study it?'

'British royal families,' corrected the Englishwoman. 'Only about them. Prince George became King George the Fifth, you know. I ought to go on television by rights.'

She fussed out of the room needlessly dusting a chairback with a flick of a napkin. Sipping the tea, Pearl Collingwood watched the filtered sun on the lace curtains. The window was a little open and she could hear afternoon birds. There was another knock and her daughter came in. 'Oh fine, you've got your tea. They seem really nice people. Is it too strong, Mother?' She regarded the old lady quizzically: 'You seem much better.'

'The tea is just fine,' responded the old lady 'And so am I.' She lifted the cup. 'Here's to King George the Fifth.' She added uncertainly: 'It's his birthday. Or was.'

Accustomed to her parent's swift turns of conversation, Rona merely said: 'I'll ring the hotel. I'll tell them we'll check in tomorrow.'

'You don't need to do that,' said the old lady assertively, waving her tea cup. 'We're staying right here.'

'*Here!*' Rona exclaimed. Pearl pretended not to notice her daughter's astonishment. 'But . . . Mother . . . we can't . . . we're supposed to be visiting London. This isn't London.'

'I know that perfectly well,' said the older woman primly, stretching to peer towards the window. The curtains moved in the air, a truck rattled below, children's voices called. 'But this will be just fine. I want to stay here. *I* like it.'

Gradually Rona sat on the side of the bed. 'But they may not be able to accommodate us for long . . .'

'And why not? It's a hotel, isn't it?'

'It's an *inn*, Mother. A pub. And what do I tell the hotel in London?'

'Tell them I'm dead,' replied the old woman briskly. 'Say I passed on at the airport. People are always dying at airports. Maybe they'll refund our deposit. They *have* to give a refund if I've died.'

Rona began to laugh through her fingers. 'You're quite sure of this?' she said touching the old lady's brown hand. 'We're at least fifteen miles from London here.'

Pearl Collingwood swirled the tea around her cup. 'London won't go away,' she insisted. 'Will you let me have some more of this tea.'

Her daughter laughed outright. She poured the tea and her mother added the sugar and milk. 'You're crazy,' Rona said.

'Always have been,' agreed her mother, her chin firm. 'Always will be. Too late to change now.'

Still intrigued and smiling, Rona went to the window.

Summer light drifted through the dusty trees indenting the street with the shapes of its shadowy old houses. A brewer's truck was delivering barrels outside the Swan, the men rolling them with muscular care down the ramp, calling instructions and warnings to each other. Her mother got out of bed and went to the bathroom. She was wearing a long lace nightgown. Her lively head appeared around the door. 'You can get to places from here,' she said encouragingly. 'We can *go* places. We can still visit.'

Her head withdrew, the door closed again, and Rona returned to her view from the window. Her life had been bitter of late. Her husband had left her for a woman eleven years older. Not many men did that. She had returned to their home in San Francisco one afternoon to find his businesslike note and had sat for two hours in a chair while the room grew dark around her. She remained motionless, knowing at the conclusion of what had seemed an ordinary day that she had not only lost a man she had relied upon and loved, but that she had lost herself also. As she sat there it was almost as though she could see herself drifting out of sight. Now this place, this distant half-village, with planes going to and from the world, roaring above its roofs, might be as good as anywhere to be. What was the difference?

She could hear her mother running the bathwater; she called out to her and then returned to her own room. She had slept for two hours that afternoon but the edgy weariness of the journey still lay on her. She bathed again, dressed and went to knock on her mother's door. Pearl Collingwood called and Rona found her sitting next to the window, looking out.

'Six o'clock,' Pearl said looking over her shoulder. 'Time to meet the natives.'

They went down the elbowed staircase. The room below was deserted except for a man in a plum-coloured pullover behind the bar, reading a newspaper propped against the beer handles. His rough face accentuated his eyes, light as boiled sweets. He greeted them genially and placed two glasses of sherry on the bar. 'Dilys tells me that you've decided to stay with us for a while,' he said. 'Why not? It's not so crowded as London.' A plane sounded overhead and his eyes went up. 'Although London's quieter.'

They laughed and thanked him and sat behind a thick round table near the bar. Mrs Collingwood tapped it firmly as though testing its strength or age. 'Plenty of room here,' she said surveying the heavy chairs and tables. Rona followed her eyes around; some of the corners were dark as cupboards. On the wall were old cider bottles, a bug-eyed fish in a case, some pictures and prints, faint and discoloured, a dartboard surmounted by a shelf on which a trophy in the shape of an aeroplane stood.

'Monday,' explained the landlord waving his hand as if introducing the unoccupied chairs. 'They watch telly. And the darts team's playing away. I'm the captain but I have to be in the bar tonight. That's the Heathrow and District Cup we've just won. My name's Jim, by the way.'

'Dilys is your wife,' said Rona.

'Right you are. And . . .' His eyes flicked for a fraction to the ceiling. '. . . Dilys's mother is my mother-in-law.'

'Mrs Durie. She's hot on royalty,' said the old lady. 'She told me about Prince George's birthday. He became King George the Fifth.'

'Knows them all. She knows King Kong's birthday,' he sighed. 'Then we've got a boy, you saw him, I think. Randolph, Randy he's called. Wears a pigtail like a Chinese. He's useless. Like a lot of kids these days. No job and no intention of getting one if he can help it.'

'He doesn't contribute,' said Pearl as if she understood.

'Only to the unemployment figures,' he said.

Mrs Collingwood began studying a shabby framed map a little askew on the wall behind the bar. She stood up, put on her glasses and read slowly aloud: 'The County of Middlesex.'

Jim Turner paused in mid-pull of the beer handle then filled the half-pint tankard. 'Last me the night, that will,' he assured them. 'Right till closing time.' He turned to look at the map and he too studied it intently as if he had scarcely noticed it before. Setting down his tankard he wiped the bar cloth over the framed glass. 'No such place now,' he informed them. 'Middlesex doesn't exist though everybody still calls it that.' He peered closer. 'Nineteen forty-nine, it says. Since then they've done away with a lot of places, changed the boundaries. Put bits of this with bits of that. Some places just vanished.' He fluttered his hand across the map as if to make it disappear.

'The Thames River is still there,' pointed out Mrs Collingwood.

Jim examined the map uncertainly but then followed the meander of the river with his finger. 'That's something they couldn't alter,' he said. 'They would have if they could, I expect.' With some searching he found their own location. 'Here *we* are,' he said. 'Bedmansworth. London Airport wasn't like it is now. It was just prefabs, Nissen huts, tents in those days. Tents! Can you credit it.' His hand took in the central area of the map. 'All Indian country now, this is, Southall, Hayes . . . all around.'

'Boondocks, you mean?' queried the old lady. 'Backwoods?' Her daughter thought she knew what he meant. 'Indians?' she asked.

'Indians from India,' responded Jim sombrely. 'Not like the Indians you've got in America, feathers and that. This is Tandoori Junction. They're getting everywhere.'

'We saw them sweeping the airport,' nodded Mrs Collingwood.

Two people came through the open door. Bramwell Broad blinked in the dimness of the bar. Lettie followed him swaying her hips and smiling. Jim introduced them to the

Americans. 'Lettie's from the East,' he said, nodding his head in the right direction.

'I am from the Philippines,' supplemented Lettie.

'It's all the East to me,' replied Jim as he pulled a beer for Bramwell. 'The vicar says the church points east to west.' He nodded again. 'The Philippines is somewhere beyond Bedfont.'

'Would you mind if I asked what you're drinking?' asked Rona.

'We want to try the local drinks,' her mother agreed vigorously.

Indicating Broad's tankard, Jim said: 'We call this bitter.'

Bramwell lifted the beer to the light and said: 'Cooking bitter.' He nodded towards his wife. 'Lettie drinks Ribena.'

'It looks like wine,' suggested Pearl. 'Is it?'

'Sort of,' said the landlord. 'She gets through gallons of it over the course of a year.' A telephone rang and he turned and went through the curtain at the back of the bar.

'And what brought you to England?' Mrs Collingwood asked Lettie kindly.

'My husband,' said Lettie seriously. She indicated Bramwell. 'He paid and I came.'

Dilys reappeared from behind the curtain holding a square of cardboard. 'Menu for tonight,' she announced.

She handed the card, embellished with childishly large handwriting, to Rona. 'Or there's a nice steak,' Jim ventured coming through the curtain. 'Although you probably get fed up with steaks over there.'

Two women came in followed closely by three small men. 'Oh God,' muttered Jim. His tone changed: 'Good evening, Mrs Kitchen.'

'We'd like our corner,' announced Mrs Kitchen briskly rubbing her hands. She was bell shaped with a narrowing head like the handle. Almost challengingly she regarded the people in the bar. Her companions stood nodding like dogs.

'Right you are,' agreed Jim. 'It's reserved especially. Usual drinks? One half of bitter and four lemonades.'

Firmly checking the faces of her party, she answered: 'Correct.' Full of purpose she swung her ungainly form around the tables and chairs towards a niche at the distant end of the room. Her plaid-skirted hip pushed one table aside and she moved a solid chair with one sweep of her moccasined foot. Her companions sat themselves obediently around the wooden table, their eyes on Mrs Kitchen. 'We'd like some light,' she called towards the bar. Grimacing, Jim put down a switch and a cowled light glimmered over the niche. Mrs Kitchen placed a cardboard file before her. Jim took a tray of drinks to them. 'Here we are then,' he said carefully placing the glasses. 'Half a pint and four lemonades. Hope none of you are driving.'

Two of the men obediently shook their heads but Mrs Kitchen paid no attention. Muttering Jim went away and Mrs Kitchen opened the file with slow importance. 'I've called this emergency action committee meeting,' she growled, fiercely looking at each anxious face around the table, 'to report on an unauthorised erection.'

It had rained in the night. It sounded heavier, and a touch frightening, when you were living in a tent. Anthony and Annabelle Burridge had lain awake as it rattled fiercely on the canvas. It was prolonged and both knew what that meant. Groaning by torchlight, he had rolled from bed, tugged his macintosh over his pyjamas, and gone out into the soaked night to loosen the guy ropes. Twice during the three months it had been their home, the tent had fallen down on them like a sail of a ship.

Seven o'clock, however, saw the rain move sulkily away and the sky clear apologetically. Anthony had been for his run, his trainers spraying through the wet grass; he leapt mud flats and scattered clouds reflected in puddles. Cows grazed below the silvery electric pylons; big rooks squawked

31

as they flew; a cockerel sounded from a shabby farm. The country here was made for jogging; it was as flat as any in England, so level it had been used as a basis for the first Ordnance Survey of the Kingdom in 1750. Flights were lifting steadily from Heathrow, each plane like a deliberately shot arrow into the frothy sky. Up they went, one after the other and, from the other horizon, they approached in the same spaced sequence.

Back at the tent, Anthony drank some coffee and, now in his City clothes, striped trousers, dark coat, and bowler hat, he set out for the underground which would take him into central London. Travelling daily on the line from Heathrow he had become used to the awed gazes of recently landed foreigners in robes and strange hats taking in his City mode of dress. He often sat on the tube, among piles of backpacks, regarded with mystified respect by young Australians and Americans straight off the plane. Older Americans took the bowler and stripes to be the usual and universal London uniform although he had heard with amused satisfaction an occasional whisper of 'Get that' as he unfolded his *Times*.

Annabelle would clear up in the tent, wash the cups in a bucket of stream water and fasten the doorflap. She would walk sturdily in her big summer dress, into the village to catch the bus for Slough where she had a secretarial job with an air freight company.

They remained deeply in debt, but their sense of shipwreck was less now, the sudden shock of being penniless: both their jobs gone, hers following his, having to quit their suburban house, the car repossessed. The sound system, video, television and the expensive dining-room suite not to mention the jacuzzi, the mobile telephones, the home fax, the deep freeze, and the tropical fish in their exotic tank, had all been reclaimed by a surly finance company. The rest of their furniture – apart from their bed – and their expendable chattels had been sold for what they could get

32

and they had walked upright out of the house thanking God they had no children, no dog, no cat.

Disaster had, however, provided the opportunity to test a hypothesis, a game they had played in better days – that it would be possible to live in a suburban tent. They now lived in one, a relic of Annabelle's time as an enthusiastic Brown Owl. It had been in their garage awaiting the next Brownie camp.

They pitched the tent on rough land near Heathrow surrounded by meadows of mud with a few cows, millions of turnips and cabbages, tangled sheep munching below grid wires that sang in the Middlesex wind and advertisement hoardings that rattled with a sound like kettle drums. They shared a field with a disjointed horse they named Freebie that had been abandoned by some gypsies. Anthony and Annabelle had tried to curry-comb Freebie and had wondered why his legs appeared to be attached to the wrong corners of his body.

They were glad of the site which they rented from a smallholder called Mr Best for three pounds a week. It was summer and they heard frogs in the morning and owls at night. Sometimes the horse stood at the back of the tent while they were in their bed, breathing like a furnace or emitting anal wind, depending on which way he was facing. Sun and rain seeped through narrow gaps in the seams of the tent, needles of yellow light, trembling gobbets of water.

Tony had found some wooden pallets outside the airport perimeter fence apparently tipped from a turning lorry, and from these he had inexpertly fashioned a raised floor.

The tent was almost as spacious as their main room had been in Norbiton but now it had to serve as a whole house. Behind a canvas screen at the back was a chemical lavatory stamped 'A. Coy. 34th RASC Suez'.

It had been difficult to fit their Norbiton bed into the tent but they were determined to continue sleeping together in it. Clothes – and Tony was pedantic about his – were on hangers suspended from a dress-shop frame. They read by lantern light.

A canvas screen separated the bed area from the living space where there were two deck chairs, an orange-box bookcase of paperbacks, and a sofa that twanged like an untuned harp. They had a plastic table on which they played Scrabble and ate their meals which Annabelle prepared on a wood fire.

In the City of London, where he worked on a commission basis for a troubled broker, Anthony told his colleagues that he and Annabelle had moved to the country for the quality of the life.

His weekday path to the Terminal Four underground station took him along the route of ancient lanes, hedged byways now diminished, as though hiding from the progressive invasion of the airport, and along the side of the concrete-banked Longford River with its enclosed swans. On some mornings he would be greeted by a man who occupied, with a conspicuous defiance, a bench outside a house which had formerly been grand but was now cowering directly below the flight path for Runway Two. Its old windows reflected the rising and descending planes that rattled its doors and frames.

Today the seated figure seemed unusually hunched, as though by a weight of worry, and Anthony Burridge interrupted his own brisk step: 'Good morning. How's Sergeant Morris?'

The man scarcely moved, looked up only fractionally, but the reply was uncompromising: 'Old, sir.' He nodded backwards towards the house. 'Like this place, St Sepulchre's, sir. Old and fucking shaky.'

He appeared prepared to add to the condemnation but an Iberia flight crossing their heads froze conversation. When it had gone, leaving its signature of smoke wriggling low in the sky, the elderly sergeant continued, with a general upward nod. 'Just like that, see. Shaking the house down.

What a place to have a home for old folks, I mean, I ask you. Mind you most of the old fools shake so much anyway a bit more won't matter. And they're deaf too, deaf as stones a lot of them.'

An outward flight gathered strength and then came snorting down the runway. 'Perhaps it's just as well,' shouted Anthony. The shadow passed across them like a hand.

Cokey

'That's why it's cheap,' admitted Morris in the moment of comparative quiet. 'Being here. It's all right if you're mutt and jeff and you've got the shakes, because it's all the same. But *I'm* not bloody deaf.' He pummelled his ear with his fist. 'I might be before long, mind you.' It was the turn of his nostrils now. 'And just smell that muck, that petrol. Clogs your lungs.' He nodded grimly with the back of his head towards the house again. 'There's a few in there that won't survive till Christmas, believe me, sir.' His tone changed: 'Would you like a paper? Save you buying one.'

He reached below his backside. There was a pile of crushed newspapers on the bench. He detached one and attempted to smooth it. '*Telegraph*? Here, have the *Telegraph*. They'll never notice.'

'They come from St Sepulchre's?' asked Anthony carefully as he hesitated but then took the profferred newspaper.

'On the hallstand,' confirmed the sergeant winking and becoming a touch jovial. 'Brought them out because I thought the seat might be damp. Poured last night, didn't it.'

'But . . . surely someone will miss it?'

Morris took the point. 'Better not have the *Telegraph*,' he decided taking it back and replacing it on the pile. 'She'll miss her rotten crossword and then there'll be all hell let loose.' He selected another newspaper. 'Here, take the *Mirror*. Barmy as a lark, he is. I'll give him yesterday's to read again. He won't notice.'

'I'll get a paper at the station,' decided Tony.

'Oh, all right.' He replaced the *Daily Mirror* under his

35

buttocks. 'Off to the City, are you? I like your titfer. The sun shines on it. I can see you coming up the road. I look forward to it.'

He surveyed the grey-green monotonous countryside before him. Another plane ascended over his shoulder. 'I envy you, I do, son,' he burst out like a confession. 'Going off like you do every day, seeing women and buses and everything. When I think of Dunkirk and Alamein, and now this.' He shrugged.

'At Dunkirk and Alamein, were you?' Tony said. He resisted the need to check his watch.

The veined eyelids came up. 'Not me, but I had a cousin who was. We're an old army family. My grandad was in India. Belonged to a famous regiment, he did, the Seventeenth Slashers. Me, I was a cook.'

Three

Small shop fronts were strung like shabby washing along the main road before the large, and necessarily squat, Heathrow hotels. Few drivers in the unending heavy daytime traffic took note of them, but 'Exhaust and Tyre' was one which Edward Richardson had frequently observed with wry fatigue when going home from a distant flight. There was 'Elaine (Hair) of Hounslow and Rome' in company with the cheap premises of finance companies, do-it-yourself and tool hire shops, 'Knox Brothers', aptly stone masons, and the ominous 'Impact Driving School'. There were flagged areas of used and suspiciously shiny cars; steamy launderettes and cafés, newsagents and Indian all-night corner shops.

In that part of Airportland, brick streets, crescents with scarred trees, and cul-de-sacs, patterned out behind the shops; backwaters and byways where children were born to shout, where lip-reading came naturally, women wiped kerosene from window panes, and bottles rattled like the playing of xylophones in public houses; the country of low flying aircraft.

As Edward drove he began to think of Adele. He tried to fix the point when they began to go wrong, where the enjoyment of a marriage had descended to indifference, the sharing of a house with a stranger. Women often said that they knew the moment when they began to love someone, first sight, second sight, or whenever. Men could not often remember details like that. And who could tell when a marriage showed the first sign of rot?

They had met twenty-two years before when both were working at Heathrow. It was one of the first bomb-warning alarms and they had found themselves standing next to each other on the pavement outside the airport church, the emergency assembly point for all staff. They were there for more than an hour and when they returned to the terminal, no bomb having exploded or been located, Adele found that most of the expensive perfumes in the shop which she managed had been stolen.

At that time she had been engaged to a rising business executive, Peter Rose, who, over the intervening years, had gone through a succession of successes. His doings often appeared in the financial pages of the newspapers and in the gossip columns; his marriages, his mansion, his money. Adele had grown to regret leaving him – Edward Richardson was aware of that as he continued the hard and slow climb up the difficult ladder of airline promotion – and she had sacrificed her job so that they could have some home life and Toby, born sixteen years before. The house at Bedmansworth called 'Vinards' had been owned by her parents and she was the only child. It was natural that they should live there. Adele had taken up social services work as a volunteer and was now a paid regional organiser. It required much of her time at odd hours, in the same way as his own profession.

But, he continued to wonder, as he drove in traffic that gave ample opportunity for thought, who could tell where a relationship began to waver? Rarely the participants. It may have been some habit, some quirk, some everyday disagreement; a word even, or perhaps a long, almost unnoticed erosion of feeling. One day he and Adele, embarking on a long-promised, much-postponed vacation had travelled on the same aircraft as Peter Rose and his second wife who were going on their honeymoon. The second wife was stupid and beautiful. She displayed a great glinting ring. They had met awkwardly at Heathrow. Mr and Mrs Peter Rose had settled into the First Class section of the plane; Mr and Mrs Edward Richardson had flown Economy, the only seats left available to staff on an almost full flight. He thought perhaps that was the moment it began to go wrong.

The traffic was different on this road. No one ever seemed to leave for the airport in time. Everyone rushed as if speed, the great plus of air travel, had to begin at their doorsteps; drivers raced along the spur roads, cutting through the surrounding routes along the motorway as if some dread voice issued from the steadily whirling dish on the central radar tower, a voice demanding: 'Hurry! Hurry!' And the more they rushed and the more they manoeuvred, the slower the progress, traffic blocks and jams, cars and drivers straining to get forward, a grand prix race in slow motion.

The return was different. From the Heathrow car parks, through the exits, the procession was sedate as if the crossing of oceans and continents had removed all the urgency. Taxis which had been waiting in the rank for two hours headed at last for London, their drivers commenting over their shoulders to homecomers on the weather, recent sport, and the descent of everyday decency, with news concerning the Royal Family and exchange rates for arriving strangers.

Soldiers hung with camouflage and guns stood around an armoured car on the grass below the model of Concorde at the entrance to the long northern tunnel. Richardson remembered there had been notification of a security exercise that day. They were posed, astride and so stationary that they appeared like a silhouetted statue group, just as representative of travel in the 1990s as Concorde. The armoured car had the snout of its gun pointing unerringly towards the exit tunnel: 'Welcome to London.'

This morning Richardson had a meeting, then lunch and afterwards the flight to Istanbul. He would not be back that evening although he had told Adele he might. What she could never comprehend was that, although he had spent all his working life in the airline business, he retained a sense of novelty and excitement – what she called his Biggles complex – with it all, the tennis-ball size of the world, the airiness of passing from city to city, frontier to frontier, climate to climate, with oceans, deserts, ice-caps, great mountains, reduced to interesting and remote tableaux. Journey begat journey and flight followed flight but he still kept, unembarrassed, that grain of the excitement – the uncertainty, the risk, the fear, of the first time he was airborne.

His job was more encompassing than most in an industry of compartments; he was responsible for his company's services, the comfort it provided or lack of it, the efficiency, resilience, attitudes of its crews, particularly its cabin crews, their problems, the satisfaction of its passengers, confined for hours in a flying tunnel. It was also his function to persuade them that his airline was best, that it would transport them, feed them, care for them and calm their fears. It was his lot to listen patiently to complaints about in-flight movies, the dearth of chamber music on the audio system, the accents of the cabin staff – to allay fears that the flight would be late or never get there at all, the tail having fallen off. Disturbing, perhaps extraterrestrial, lights were seen to travel so mysteriously alongside the aircraft, and the explanation that they were on the tips of the wings was often unaccepted. He had read complaints that the engines were too loud, that the ground was too far out of sight, that none of the windows would open, that children should be sent to play outside.

That morning's meeting was a routine discussion on medical facilities aboard aircraft, the training of crew in advanced first aid, instructions to pilots on diverting in urgent cases, and the covert propping up and disguise of inconveniently dead bodies.

No passenger ever passed away in mid-air whatever his

appearance to the contrary; crowded planes were sensitive areas and no place to die. A recently dead man looked much like a sleeping man and a carefully rigged blanket camouflaged the truth. Edward Richardson had once had to deal with complaints from a woman who awoke to find a moribund stranger slumped across her. A steward had been cautioned for taping a glass of scotch to a deceased hand, a subterfuge referred to, in the report, as scotch-taping. The non-recognition of death whilst airborne was acknowledged throughout all airlines, occasioned by the massive legal complications arising from it happening in foreign airspace, over frontiers, above oceans, between tray meals.

Richardson went to his own airport office and left his travelling bureau, a laptop desk in a black leather case, and his overnight bag there. He always travelled light, if possible without check-in baggage. Five per cent of all airline luggage went astray.

His office window peered over the top tier of a car park and then onto Number One Runway. From habit he looked out to see what business was taking place. The hourly British Airways shuttle was poised to leave for Edinburgh; a bulkier plane had just galloped along the runway like a getaway horse: Cathay Pacific, twelve hours non-stop to Hong Kong. There were three planes in the taxi-way queue, the shamrock, like a white hand, of Aer Lingus, another British Airways flight and the KLM City Hopper on the 'coffee break' trip to Amsterdam.

He remembered an air traffic controllers' strike when no planes could land or leave, and he had gazed out with disbelief at the huge place, the familiar, animated amphitheatre, lying empty and windswept as a prairie.

On his office walls were photographs which showed Heathrow Airport in 1948, like an army camp, ranks of saggy tents, passengers stepping across guy ropes, a brave Union Jack flying so that no one should be in any doubt in which country they had arrived, interiors showing desks on rough floors like stalls in a country show.

He put his case on the desk. From the adjoining storeroom he could hear Harriet, his secretary, making coffee.

'Harri,' he called. ' 'Morning. I have to go to Istanbul.'

'I saw,' she called back. 'They rush you around like a dodgem car, don't they.'

She came in, tall and narrow, so much so that the tray she carried looked like an aircraft's wings, her big cockpit glasses adding to the illusion. She blinked through them. 'You'd think they might have caught you in Bahrain, then you could have gone straight there.' She put the tray on the desk, a coffee pot, two cups and a small plate of biscuits. Her arms, extended, were thin as rods, her dress without a curve.

'It's the job,' he said. Why did women repeat each others' complaints? It was almost as if she had been discussing it with Adele. 'I'll be back tomorrow. Trouble in the office there.'

'That Ray Francis has gone off with a Turkish delight,' she said promptly. 'I heard. The flight is at fifteen hundred, you're at the Imperial Hotel, Paddy Bush will meet you.' She leaned forward confidingly: 'I've got a new bike.'

Her face was flushed and pleased as he looked up from his coffee. 'Oh, good. I'm glad,' he said. 'Is it the one you wanted?'

'It's a Muddy Fox mountain bike. I'm going to come to work on it tomorrow.'

'Watch yourself in the tunnel.'

'I'm not worried. There's others.' He knew she wanted to ask him something. 'Would you mind if I came in cycling shorts? Just for the summer.'

He laughed. 'As long as the British Airports Authority doesn't,' he said. 'You'd better check. They've probably got regulations forbidding it.'

'I'll change when I get here,' she promised seriously.

42

'Obviously I won't wear them all day. But I'd like to go for a decent spin before coming in.'

She took her coffee back to her own desk on the far side of the room. A landing aircraft crossed the roof. Richardson went through the papers on his desk. 'You've got the medical meeting at eleven,' Harriet reminded. 'And Mr Grainger at twelve thirty.'

He sighed: 'Yes, I know. I'm just sorting out the stuff.'

'Mr Francis went off with somebody before.'

'He was on leave then. This time he's supposed to be in charge of the station.'

'I wouldn't mind going to Istanbul,' she said.

'Why don't you? You could fly for ten per cent.'

She looked affronted. 'Cycle, I mean,' she said. She nodded at the ceiling as another plane crossed the building. 'Not in one of those things.'

'You'd be tired when you got there,' he pointed out good humouredly. Sometimes he had difficulty in equating her girlishness with the excellence of her work.

'I suppose I would,' she conceded. 'And then there'd be all the way back. It would take months. I think I'll stick to Suffolk.'

Richardson rose and put his papers in his case. 'Suffolk's flatter,' he smiled at her. 'Almost as smooth as flying.'

He went through the door and down the stairs, checking through the punch-in security system, and out into the noise and the smell, a mixture of dust, gasoline and, today, a whiff from the sludge farm, the everyday scent of the airport.

Traffic curled around the knotted roads as busily as in any city. There were signs, indicators, warnings, traffic lights, pedestrian crossings and one-way pointers. He passed the chapel, well visited, although not as much so as the preflight insurance bureaux, and the statue of Alcock and Brown, the first Atlantic aviators looking out from their plinth at the amazing and eventful new world they had begun. Entering a box of a building, he fed his name and identification number into another security system.

The six other participants of the meeting were already seated when he arrived but he glanced at the wall clock and saw that he was before time so did not apologise. There were two medical men, one a doctor he had met before in dramatic circumstances, one a salesman supplying emergency medical equipment, and four commercial managers from other airlines. He knew everyone except the equipment expert.

The doctor, Horace Snow, a Scot, nodded recognition. They had met when two drug smugglers had died in a plane delayed an hour by hydraulic failure on the runway during a fierce July heatwave the year before. The men had literally exploded when the cocaine-filled condoms concealed within their bodies had burst as the temperature in the cabin rose.

'Not so exciting today,' Snow whispered as Richardson sat down next to him. 'Methods of dealing with unexpected births at thirty thousand feet – the complications legal and practical of a surprise extra passenger. Do you issue another ticket?'

The room was another which gave broad views of the activity on the runways. Edward could never resist a glance at a departing airliner. Air New Zealand was arriving from Auckland; Alitalia was ready to take off for Milan. The eyes of the other airline men were straying in the same direction. Snow, the chairman of the meeting, observed laconically in his mild Scots: 'The sun's a trifle strong this morning.' He rose and pulled the lattice curtains.

'The fascination never seems to leave you flying people,' he observed to Edward Richardson as they walked out after the meeting. 'You stare at aeroplanes like children.' They went towards Snow's office and surgery. 'Sailors are like that. Sailors can never resist a ship. Looking at her, recognising who she is, where she's bound. God, years ago there was an old chap who was my patient.' He grinned from

44

memory as they walked. 'A sea captain. He required that he be wheeled down to the sea, with his nurse, a man behind the chair, and me, so that he could take one more look at it before he died. He passed away right there on the front at Brighton. Watching the waves. It was a terrible day, cold, pouring, blowing, the gulls could scarcely fly, and the sea coming up right over the top chucking shingle across the road. He loved it. Died sniffing the ozone.' He laughed and shook his head as he walked. 'The rest of us very nearly died too. Come in and have a dram.'

The surgery was adjacent to Snow's office and through the glass door Richardson could see an Indian youth sitting on a bed while a nurse examined his leg. Snow said: 'Won't be a minute' and went into the surgery. Richardson looked around the walls of the office. There were scores of Tchaikovsky's music, *Swan Lake, Eugene Onegin, Romeo and Juliet*; a Victorian photograph of a man with burning eyes and another, a modern studio picture of a poised and handsome woman in evening dress and holding a sheaf of music.

Snow returned. 'One of the cleaners,' he said nodding towards the surgery. 'Only started yesterday. In India last week. Slipped on the toilet floor. He's very bright. It's a shame they have to start off in the lavatories.' He paused. 'Looking at my relics?'

He went to his drinks cabinet. His movements were slower than his speech. He was short and old-fashioned looking with a dusty suit and a handkerchief sagging from his top pocket. 'What will you have?' he asked. 'Scotch? Going to Istanbul you may need a scotch.'

'I also have a meeting with Hardy Grainger,' sighed Richardson. 'So it had better be a small one. With water, thanks.'

'Istanbul and Grainger,' mused Snow passing him the glass. He poured a larger one for himself. 'It's my afternoon off,' he said adding: 'Istanbul and Grainger is a heady combination.'

45

They lifted their glasses. 'Istanbul,' mused the doctor. 'I only get as far as Fulham these days. That's where I live. Not bad for the airport, even if I never fly anywhere.' He drank his scotch quickly and poured another. Richardson declined. 'I attend the Tchaikovsky Festival in Moscow every year and that's about it,' said Snow. 'It's my holiday.'

'You're a fervent admirer,' observed Richardson nodding at the music scores and the framed photograph of the fierce man.

'Tchai,' said Snow fondly. 'That's him. Ah, Tchai . . . there never was another to touch him. Not for romance.' He moved to the photograph of the woman. She had a fine neck and her dress fell from beautiful shoulders. 'Freda Carlsen,' he mused. 'Violinist. One of the greatest when it came to Tchai. To hear her play the concerto . . .' He made the pretence of running a bow across his crooked arm. 'A foretaste of paradise.'

'You know her personally?'

'I was married to her,' replied Snow sadly. 'She said she would marry me for one year only. And she did exactly that. She went away with someone else, the timpanist of the City of Minneapolis Orchestra. A strange pair, violin and drums. They died in a boating accident a few years ago. . . . In a lake in Norway.'

'A sad story,' said Richardson awkwardly.

'It still is for me,' said the doctor. The nurse came to the glass door and smiled professionally at Richardson. 'Do you want to see this young man, Doctor?' she asked. 'He's going off for the rest of the day but he'll be at work tomorrow.'

Snow excused himself and went into the other room. Richardson saw him pat the Indian on the shoulder as the boy left. 'Makes you wonder what they think of it all,' he said when he returned. He shook his head. 'Cleaning out the bogs of a cold country.'

Hardy Grainger's secretary Moira had the perpetual expression of someone expecting the worst, and still worse to follow. She made short darts around her outer office, her eyes mouselike, her voice hushed. It was said that she had put aside the chance of a good marriage because it would have meant leaving Grainger.

'He's had a morning,' she said warningly to Edward Richardson. Her eyes came up with all their worry. 'Although he's coped very well. So far.'

'Let's hope he keeps coping,' Richardson smiled at her. He sat in the middle of a row of three chairs and picked up *Skyport*, the Heathrow newspaper. There was an interview with the catering manager of Terminal Two; the new contractors reported the initial success of the wheelchair concession; a stewardess wished to share her canal barge home with another and a masseuse was advertising her whereabouts 'Near Stains'. His eyebrows went up. Moira said: 'It's very good, that *Skyport* don't you think, Mr Richardson? Tells you everything that's going on.'

'It seems to,' he agreed. The phone rang on the desk and Moira picked it up. 'He'll see you now,' she said with an air of cautious relief.

'Is he still coping?'

'So far today he's been managing well. But he's had a morning, as I said.'

She went at a walking fidget before him, opened the door, and announced him, an unnecessary formality. Grainger appeared to be trying to stare through the top of his desk. His slow eyes came up. 'Sit down, Edward,' he sighed. 'It's been a morning.'

Richardson said he expected it had. The desk top was bare of papers. Grainger almost sulked as he picked up a file from his basket. 'What's this bloody fool Francis been up to for God's sake?'

'Running off with a Turkish lady,' replied Richardson succinctly. He did not know anyone who liked Grainger.

'I know that.' The words were almost snapped. He glared

47

at the paper he had taken from the file. 'What the hell's Batman got to do with it?'

'I don't know,' replied Richardson honestly. 'I only heard about the business last night. When I got back from Bahrain.' He made it a separate last sentence but Grainger did not comment. He was staring at the report.

'Oh, it's where she lives. Batman is a town in Turkey.' As if anxious to prove it he went to a giant world map which occupied a whole wall and eventually pointed. 'There it is. Silly name for a town.' He glanced over his shoulder and seemed disappointed that Richardson had not risen to confirm his discovery. He returned to the desk. 'Whatever's wrong with the fellow?' he asked.

Richardson said he did not know but that he was going to Istanbul that afternoon to find out. 'I'll be back tomorrow, I hope with a clearer picture.'

'Can't imagine Francis with a Turk,' said Grainger. He looked up. 'Does his wife know, do you think?'

'I've no idea. She's in Cheltenham, I believe. But she may be not unfamiliar with the general pattern.'

Grainger sighed. 'How do we get people like this in charge of an overseas station in the first place?'

'Francis is an excellent manager,' Richardson pointed out. 'He's just inclined to . . .'

'Put himself about?'

'I was going to say "fall in love". He's serious about it.'

'And I'm serious about our representation there.'

'Of course.'

Grainger rose from behind the desk. 'Let me know what happens,' he said.

'Of course,' repeated Richardson. He went towards the door.

'There,' said Grainger as though not to be denied. He found Turkey on the map. 'Batman, see.' Richardson saw. 'It's miles from Istanbul,' continued Grainger. 'How did he manage to meet a woman from there?'

Edward Richardson was still trying to sort out the logic in the question when Grainger surprisingly shook his hand fiercely. 'Bahrain to London to Istanbul,' muttered Grainger thoughtfully as though checking a timetable. 'You haven't been head-hunted have you, Edward?' he inquired earnestly. His dull eyes looked directly into Richardson's.

'I've had interest,' admitted Richardson carefully. 'But I haven't responded to it.'

'Good, good. We couldn't afford to lose you.' He modified it. 'People like you. Loyalty is a great thing. And there's your pension.'

Richardson could not avoid a laugh. 'There's always that,' he agreed.

Grainger walked from the door with him. Moira looked startled and began unnecessarily tidying her desk. 'Let me know as soon as you can,' said Grainger. He put his hand familiarly on Richardson's arm. 'Try and sort that idiot out. Love, indeed!'

The Boeing crossed from Europe into Asia Minor with a tempestuous sunset flung across the Bosphorus, the sea below brooding red, the lights of Istanbul beginning to show. The airliner went inland a little towards mountains already black, and then turned again towards the sea, the city and the airport.

Edward Richardson had often thought that there were few places on earth that did not look better from the air. That late afternoon he had been treated to a god's-eye view of Greek islands, white stones in burning blue, before that the Italian coast sculpted to the shape of a sea horse; and now the extravagant evening of the Golden Horn. Cities, even flat, gridded cities like Los Angeles, were given a grand aspect from a height; slums became neat, dockyards were transformed into havens, concrete highways were cut into ribbons. He had seen the mud delta of a river spread like a dancer's shining skirt, villages of shacks clinging

49

romantically to the sides of evening hills, red-light districts blinking like fairyland. From above a desert, its dangers obviated, looked benign as a carpet; the intimidating icecap sparkled like candy; mountains became mounds and oceans shallow and stormless.

In a contrary way he had often felt disappointed, cheated even, when the final approach of a flight missed out the spread of a city: the squares and bridges of London, unseen on the landing from the west, Charles de Gaulle from the north with no vision of Paris, the long drop to Kennedy across Jamaica Bay, the city reduced to packing cases piled on the horizon. But Istanbul provided the perfect landing.

Paddy Bush met him at Yesilkoy Airport. He had a car and driver waiting and they drove through the dusty evening towards Istanbul. 'Where is Ray Francis?' he asked Bush.

'God only knows. He's gone, that's all I know.'

The driver, who wore a fez and a maroon suit, interrupted. 'We go along coast road. Along Sea of Marmara.'

'Yes. Thank you, Mustapha,' said Bush.

'Past Castle of the Seven Towers.'

'Good. Yes. Thanks.' He grimaced at Edward. 'He is normally a tourist guide.'

'Best in Istanbul,' said Mustapha over his shoulder. 'See, the Sea of Marmara by night.'

Bush raised his eyebrows.

'On our left,' said Mustapha.

He appeared to have finished. Richardson said: 'How is the operation going?'

'Well, we're managing but it's not easy when the station manager walks out. He took the keys of the safe for a start.'

'Oh?'

Bush looked sideways at him. 'No. It's not like that. There isn't anything valuable in there anyway and Francis wouldn't do that.'

'I didn't think he would.'

'But we've had to get a locksmith to open it. He took all

50

day. Said he was a former burglar but I doubt it. He wasn't quick enough. All the documents, receipt books and suchlike are in there. We were lost without them.'

'The Castle of the Seven Towers,' interrupted Mustapha. 'See also Tower of Marble. Nice eh?'

'Very nice,' muttered Richardson.

'He's very useful to us,' warned Bush. 'We use him all the time.'

'Up there famous Topkapi Gate, Topkapi Museum.'

'Yes, thanks.'

They turned from the sea into the city. The lights in the streets shone on the roofs of the slow traffic, people crowding the pavements. There were street cafés and deep alleys full of activity.

'Ataturk Bulvari,' Mustapha informed them. 'Ataturk Boulevard. Name after Ataturk.'

'Ray Francis always had a theory that this was the nearest place to London for making a good disappearance,' said Bush.

Edward looked at him wryly. 'What did he mean by that?'

'Well, it's a totally foreign city. It's not like Rome or Athens, it's the East. So if you don't want anyone to find you, even if your picture is in the papers, this is the place.'

'You haven't had . . .'

'Inquiries from the press? No. Not yet.'

'God, we can do without that. Imagine the British tabloids. "Airways chief goes off with belly dancer".'

'She's a professor.'

'I know. But that wouldn't stop them. "Brit's Turkish Delight" – can't you see it? "Weeping wife in Cheltenham while air executive is in the kasbah".'

'Grainger would go through the roof.'

'He's heading that way anyhow. I saw him before I left.'

Mustapha appeared to have become sulky at their monopolising the conversation. They arrived at the hotel and he got out to open the doors saying only: 'Imperial Hotel. Hotel Imperial.'

They thanked him and he seemed mollified. 'Go on tour tomorrow,' he suggested. 'Elephant Path, Chicken That Would Not Fry Street, Mosque at St Sophia?'

'Mr Richardson has to return to London tomorrow,' said Bush.

'Another time,' said Edward.

'I been visit London,' said Mustapha. 'Regent Park, Buck Palace. Very nice.' He paused. 'Now I go get Mr Francis.'

They stood astonished on the pavement. A braided hotel porter hovered, holding Richardson's hand baggage. 'Mr Francis?' queried Bush. 'You're going to fetch him?'

'He tell me.'

'Where is he?' asked Richardson.

'Over bridge,' smiled Mustapha pointing and pleased at their interest. 'By historic Tower of Galata.'

'And you're bringing him here?'

'To Hotel Imperial,' confirmed the driver. 'Imperial Hotel.'

Richardson said quietly. 'Perhaps we'd better go with him.' Bush touched his sleeve.

'No,' confirmed Mustapha quickly. 'Mr Francis want to come here. Back in no time, half hour.'

He left them summarily, climbed into the car and drove off into the traffic. Slowly Richardson retrieved his hand-baggage from the porter, saying he would check in later. 'Well, what do you make of that?' he said to Bush.

'He'll come back with him,' said Bush confidingly. 'We'd better go and have a drink and wait.'

They went into the big, marble hotel. The bar was full of men drinking coffee at low tables. Smoke drifted heavily. Bush ordered two gins and they sat almost concealed by an ornamental palm.

'What did Grainger say about it?' asked Bush.

Richardson sniffed. 'The usual barely controlled spleen,'

he said. 'Although, this time he's got some justification. I'm not all that pleased with Ray Francis myself. I was in Bahrain yesterday.'

'Do you think there's going to be redundancies?' asked Bush as if he had been waiting for the opening. 'We never hear anything out here, except from crews and people passing through.'

'They're probably looking at it,' shrugged Richardson. 'But then they always are.'

'I'll bet my life that Grainger will still be there, recession or not,' probed Bush.

'He probably will,' said Richardson. 'He asked me today whether anyone else was head-hunting me and I told him I wasn't interested in going anywhere else. Which probably means I'm first for the chop.' He paused and nudged Bush as he saw Ray Francis come through the door. 'Well, the second anyway,' he said.

Francis was a pale, anxious man with hair so fine and fair that from a distance he appeared bald. His normal tentativeness had been replaced by a temporary and unconvincing bravado. 'Ah,' he said as he advanced on them. 'Waiting in ambush.'

'We'd have to get up early in the morning to ambush you, Ray,' said Richardson. They shook hands all round. Bush diplomatically excused himself. He was halfway to the door when he returned. 'Have you got the safe keys?' he asked Francis.

The fair man looked startled. 'Oh, yes. Of course.' He produced two keys from his pocket and handed them to Bush. 'I suppose that's been inconvenient,' he said lamely. Bush said: 'A little,' and left.

'Nobody's very pleased with me, I suppose,' said Francis miserably sitting down in the chair which Bush had vacated. A waiter approached and he ordered a beer, then changed it for a Coca-Cola.

'You can suppose that,' confirmed Richardson. 'What happened?'

'I fell in love,' sighed Francis. 'Again.'

'Can't you fall in love without pissing off with the safe keys, just for a start.'

'I know. And now *you've* had to come out. There's been all sorts of trouble.' He became abruptly afraid. 'Nobody's told my wife, have they?'

'Not as far as I know. I thought *you* might tell her.'

'Oh, no. But thank goodness for that. She'd be furious.'

'She's still going to be.'

The Coca-Cola arrived and Francis sipped it. 'There'll be no need,' he said. 'I've left Gloria. Or she's left me rather.'

'Gloria? That's a funny name for a Turk, isn't it?'

'Turk? Who said she's a Turk? Somebody's obviously got the story all arse-about-face.'

'Well, you weren't around to correct them.'

'She's at the University of Ankara. She's a professor of psychology there. But she comes from Barnsley.'

'Barnsley?'

'Yes, why not? Professors can come from Barnsley.'

'Listen, Ray,' said Richardson impatiently. 'Wherever she's from, you can't just clear off and leave Bush and everyone else in the lurch.'

'Did Bush tell on me?'

'No, he didn't. He's not the school sneak. He covered up for you as long as he could. But we've had two flights a day into Istanbul this past week. People tend to wonder where the station manager is, for Christ's sake.'

'Will I get the axe?'

'That's not up to me, you know that. But this isn't the first time. There was that burgomaster's daughter in Germany. . . .'

'Gerda,' nodded Francis. 'I do pick some names, don't

I.' He looked sorrowfully at Richardson. 'I'll go in tomorrow,' he said. 'If they sack me, they sack me.'

'The trouble is you're so bloody good at the job,' grunted Richardson. 'When you're there.'

'I let my heart lead me.'

'I wouldn't have said it was your heart.'

'Well, that as well. What do you think will happen?'

'I don't know. Grainger is furious, but then he always is. What I imagine will happen is that you'll be brought home for a while. Bush can take over in Istanbul – he's got used to it.'

Francis looked relieved. 'Thanks,' he said genuinely. 'I'm very grateful. It's not the sack I mind so much, but I don't want the wife to know. I don't know what I'd do without her.'

The lych-gate creaked like a cleric clearing his throat. The sound pleased Pearl Collingwood and she shut and opened it again to hear it repeated. She enjoyed believing that it had been like that for several centuries.

From where she stood, the side of the porch and the west window of the church were framed by the iron-black wood of the gate; she had to walk below the arch before the full view came to her. She smiled her pleasure at seeing it, like someone recognising family traits in a distant relative. She was wearing a light summer dress and a straw hat. She had bought it in Maidenhead when she and Rona had gone there to have tea by the river.

Bedmansworth Church had a look of long prosperity. It had flourished in the age of manors and estates. The lord of that land had ridden to London to send Guy Fawkes to his gallows death from the Gunpowder Treason Plot. Rich merchants and owners of great houses had been prominent in the parish right to the end of Victoria's reign.

It was built of figured brick and had a four-square tower surmounted by a vane in the form of a golden ball above which was a splendid golden arrow, like a near miss from a large angel.

Pearl walked up the path and at once realised that its paving was formed by broken gravestones worn smooth by years of feet. Bending closer and adjusting her spectacles, she could make out rubbed names and dates, or segments of them. '*Agnes Jones. . . . Ap . . . . John Martinda. . . . 30th August . . . in the year of Our Lo . . . 179. . . . To the good memory of Timothy . . . . Mary Taylor . . . a spinst. . . . of this par. . . .* ' She recited them quietly to herself, the words of a jigsaw made up of former inhabitants of the village. She felt sorry that their memorials had fallen but not even chased stone was meant to last forever and she liked the notion of those one-time people being together there, neighbours still as they had been in the hamlet of long ago, their loves and sins and quarrels trodden by their successors.

It was mid-morning; a blackbird sang in the dark yews of the churchyard, there were fresh wet flowers on a grave by the far wall, a dog relieved itself against a leaning cross, and a light blue skein of smoke curled from behind a ruined vault. Mrs Collingwood sniffed and advanced. Peering around the mouldy wall of the vault she saw a silvery man in striped shirtsleeves with a vicar's bib strapped around him, as though he were about to wash dishes. He was smoking a cigarette, his face composed in an expression of secret bliss. It changed swiftly when he saw her. The cigarette was squashed and thrust into his trouser pocket. The aura of smoke hung about his grey head.

'That's a sure way of catching yourself on fire,' pointed out Mrs Collingwood with a worried stare at his trousers.

'You're quite right,' he agreed. He smiled with her. 'If I am to be consumed by flames I would prefer it to be later rather than sooner.'

'I guess that goes for all of us.' She patted the roof of the vault and held out her long hand. 'I'm Pearl Collingwood. I'm visiting from Los Angeles with my daughter.'

56

'And I am Henry Prentice,' he said. 'I'm the vicar here.
I heard you were in Bedmansworth. My wife forbids me to
smoke and some of my parishioners don't like it either. So I
have to sin like this.' He glanced guiltily at the vault.
'Hiding behind the dead.'

Pearl sighed. 'Don't they just bug you,' she sympathised.
'People who don't smoke. My doctor and my daughter
between them stopped me, or they tried. Now I have to do
it under the bedclothes, which *is* dangerous.'

They exchanged covert glances. 'Would you like one
now?' the vicar inquired kindly.

'I just would,' affirmed the old lady her eyes brightening.
'It's a fine morning for a smoke.'

Slyly, and first looking around, he opened a wooden trap-
door in the wall of the church. Within were two watering
cans and a pair of grass shears. From one of the watering
cans he took an unopened packet of Silk Cut. 'Low tar,' he
said like an absolution. 'Although *that* always sounds to me
like a disreputable sailor.' He took the wrapping from the
packet with difficulty, complaining: 'You have to break and
enter these things nowadays.' He offered the packet to her
and she took a cigarette. He selected one for himself, choos-
ing as though they were not all the same. He produced a
box of matches. 'I'm allowed matches,' he said as he lit up
for them both.

The blackbird, like some tell-tale, increased its song. They
puffed, the secrecy seeming to increase the enjoyment.

'When I was at school,' mentioned Henry Prentice, 'a
smoke was called a drag.'

'We called it a puff,' she said. She intook heavily. 'God,
this is good.'

'Yes, a drag,' he mused. 'Nowadays if you see a headline
saying: "Vicar in Drag" it means he's a transvestite.'

'Life gets so complicated,' Pearl agreed. She pushed aside
her own emitted smoke to read the names on the vault. 'It's
like a little house,' she said.

'It's the Malcomb-Ferringford family tomb,' he said patting the warming stones fondly. 'They did a lot of good in this parish when it was not a general virtue with the landed gentry.'

'And they're still proving useful,' acknowledged the American woman also touching the stone. She regarded him conspiratorially. 'Do you have any other hideaways for dragging?'

'In the winter I crawl behind the organ,' he told her releasing a small smoke-ringed confessional grin. 'I blow into the pipes, through the holes, and it sort of wanders about in there. The organist is an abolitionist and I've derived a certain measure of enjoyment from observing his nose twitch while he's playing. But generally, when the weather is suitable, I conceal myself here.' He laughed jollily. 'One evening, at just about dusk, a young couple crept into the churchyard. I was standing here with my secret cigarette. They were cuddling on one side of the Malcomb-Ferringfords and I was puffing on this side. Then the girl saw the smoke drifting up from the tomb. Ghosts! They tore off like fury.'

'Do you think Our Lord would have smoked?' asked Mrs Collingwood soberly. 'Say it had been available.'

'It's the one temptation He was spared but I like to think that He might,' Henry Prentice mused. 'It is after all a contemplative occupation. It's pleasant to think of Him having a quiet puff by the wayside.'

'Out there forty days in the wilderness,' she reflected. They had finished their cigarettes. The vicar hid the butts in the watering can and they walked into the alternating sunlight and the warm shadows of the trees. 'It's a fine church,' she said looking at the stout tower.

'One of the finest in Middlesex. We still call ourselves Middlesex although we don't officially exist. We're not far from Whitehall in distance but we're a long way in other matters.'

A silver-bellied plane came noisily and low from behind the tower.

'When they use this particular flight path, which fortunately is not all the time, everything shakes in the church,' said Henry Prentice. 'I've seen the communion wine swishing about and plaster falling from the memorial tablets on the wall.'

The plane had quickly gone. Pearl smiled: 'It's just like standing in the middle of a history book here.' She surveyed the graves. 'These people who knew this place.'

'And they would recognise it now, I'm sure,' he said. 'Despite Heathrow, despite everything, it hasn't changed that much. Only the surroundings have changed. Mind, it took a determined effort by the present inhabitants and the other villagers around here to prevent the airport swallowing it up.'

They strolled along the path with its broken memorial slabs. Pearl studied them once again. 'Some fell down, some crumbled,' he explained. 'Inferior stone I suppose and lately, of course, there's been pollution from the airport and the motorway and the industrial estates.' He rubbed his shoe against a segment of masonry. 'And some were damaged in the war.'

'The Nazis bombed the church?'

'I don't think they were aiming for it. It was a landmine actually,' he told her. 'Drifted down quite gently. It was daylight and apparently the villagers saw it dangling from its parachute. It exploded against the churchyard wall and only just missed the tower.' He pointed. 'Right over there it fell. You can't tell now. After all it was half a century ago. Some Americans and Poles who were based here came over and helped to rebuild the wall. It's all in the parish records. It makes interesting reading. They couldn't do much about the wrecked headstones. Then others fell to pieces, even stone is not immutable, and we have some vandalism, like everyone else.'

59

'Difficult to think of vandalism here,' said Pearl Colling-wood. She looked about her at the speckles of sunshine flickering through the quiet churchyard trees. The blackbird was still tuning his notes. The factory roar of the airport was in the background but she was already accustomed to that.

'We had an offertory box recently stolen from the church,' the vicar said seriously. 'That's why normally the church is, regrettably, kept locked. There was a lectern, a full golden eagle lectern taken from another church not far away.'

Pearl suddenly asked: 'Where were the Americans in camp? The fellows who rebuilt the wall.'

'I'm not sure,' he said. 'The Poles were at Ruislip. There's a memorial there. There were a good many bases in this area.' He made a diversion. 'Here, let me show you another headstone that has come in useful. It's actually outside the wall.'

They walked through a wooden side gate. 'There,' said the vicar. 'Hubert Belling died eighteen twenty-eight.'

'Why was he put out here in the cold?'

'Suicide. Took his own life because he was too old to play cricket any longer, so it is said. It's in the parish records.'

The headstone was brown, almost bronzed, and pitted, but the incised name was discernible. Henry Prentice said: 'In those days, in some places, suicides were buried outside the churchyard wall. Still, he's as warm as those inside. And the cricket pitch was, still is in fact, just over there.' He nodded to the sloping meadow that fell away from the churchyard to a line of oaks. 'Local lads come up in the evenings and use his headstone as a wicket.'

'To throw the ball at?'

'Indeed. They bowl for hours on end here. See the lumps it has taken out of the stone. But I think he would have liked that.'

Indian

'Homelea',
Anglia Road,
Hounslow,
Middlesex,
England,
Great Britain

23rd June

My Dear Father and My Dear Mother,

Well here I am in Good Old Blighty. The Brits all say that it is summer but I am cold. Everybody smiles and they are always telling me what hot weather it is and it must make me feel at home!!!

I am homesick. I am missing our home and Benji. There are many dogs here but people train them to bark at Indians and Pakistanis (so at least we are getting the same treatment as them). Uncle Sammi and Marika and the children are in good shape but their shop which is part of our house, address as above, is on a road where the motor vehicles are passing very fast at day and night. I have my room but I have not yet learned to sleep in it.

I am now working at London Airport. It is not a major appointment, you will understand, but it will lead me higher, I am sure. I am a facilities operative, which is important because I am part of the working of the airport. I have made friends with the airport porters who are teaching me English slang etc. They are always taking the peas, as they say. I start work very early in the morning because they always put Indians and beginners on the first shifts. Yesterday I had a bad moment because I slid on the floor and I had to go to the doctor. The medical set-up here is very good and there was nothing to pay (I was afraid it would take all my money) and the doctor and nurse were first class. The nurse said they had nothing better to do at that time which shows the fine state of health in this country. I remember how long we had to line up for the doctor in the village every two weeks or more.

My injuries were small and today I am back on my duty as a

61

facilities operative. I will work hard and one day I may be in command of the whole sodding show, as the porters say.

Goodbye for now.

Your loving and obedient son,

Nazar

Four

Wearing a cream slip Rona sat on the edge of her bed and regarded the trees lying like tracery against the window. It overlooked the back garden of the Swan and she could smell lilac and hear a couple laughing quietly as they sat on the bench below. She stood and walked to the window, carefully peering out. They were sitting below the lilac. They were not as young as she had imagined. Why had she thought that from the fact that they laughed? As she watched two children, a boy and a girl, appeared and sat one side of the couple. The woman produced a bag of potato crisps and gave it to the children to share. She continued talking to the man and they laughed again.

Suddenly even more lonely, she went back and sat on the bed once more. She eased herself back onto the pillows and raised her leg so that the silk slip rolled down her thigh.

By far the worst thing about it all was that she had imagined they were happy. How was it possible not to tell? It was. There had been a case which was handled by the law firm in San Francisco for which she worked, an attempted insurance murder by a husband on his wife of twenty years. And she had thought he deeply loved her. She and Jeff had even discussed and wondered at that case the same week as he left. Even now she could see them sitting in the evening on the terrace with its far-off view of the Oakland Bridge and talking about it. An unremarkable cameo in an ordinary week – except in the context of what had happened after-wards.

She had found that she could recall all the things they had done those last seven days. Two nights they had been at home together, once they had been to dinner with friends in Chinatown, once to see a play at Sausalito, and the other night he had played squash and she had gone to her sketching class. It was not often that they spent so much of the week together, and that was another strange aspect of it. She had often thought since that perhaps he was spending time with her in order to tell her but that they had been having such a quiet, comfortable and enjoyable time, that he had never been able to do it. While they were at home those evenings she had cooked dinner and they had watched television. Nothing different about that – except it was the last week of their lives together.

On Friday he had suggested that they go upstate for the weekend and early the following morning they had driven up to Mount St Helena at the head of the Napa Valley. Here, at Silverado, an abandoned silver mine, the writer Robert Louis Stevenson and his American bride Fanny had spent their honeymoon, more than a century before. There was a stone marking the place, put there by enthusiasts. Rona and Jeff had looked out over the same awesome view of tree-topped valleys. She had spent the time painting. She still had the small picture she had painted that weekend. There remained signs of the old mine workings up there and the mountain wind sighed powerfully across the slopes. They had walked hand-in-hand down to the road and driven back to the timber cabin in the grounds of the hotel to spend their last night lying against each other.

It was she, Rona, who had suggested the trip to Silverado. It was only a year after he had gone that she learned that Robert Louis Stevenson had married a woman eleven years his senior. Jeff left on the Monday morning to spend the rest of his life with someone that number of years older. A man at a crossroads might seek signs, pointers to a decision, and Rona had often wondered if this had been a sign for him.

It was the ninetieth anniversary of the postponement of the Coronation of King Edward the Seventh and Queen Alexandra. Mrs Durie had checked it in her *Royal Family Almanac* before she took up the early morning teas. Pearl Collingwood inquired further that evening as she and Rona were having dinner in their special corner of the bar.

'Not the *best* king we've ever had,' conceded Mrs Durie, clearing the dessert dishes. 'Nothing ever went right with him. They had to put off the Coronation until August because he wasn't well.' She leaned towards them suggestively. 'His trouble was other women . . . ladies. Gave them babies. Kept doing it. But the Queen was beautiful. She suffered, and everybody knew, but she was real royal material no mistake. Never a complaint.'

'Remarkable,' acknowledged Mrs Collingwood.

'Remarkable,' agreed her daughter.

As usual the bar began filling at this time. The joking man with the wistfully smiling Filipino wife was making customers laugh.

'Rona,' whispered Mrs Collingwood. She adopted a confiding angle, copied from Mrs Durie. 'I feel sorry for that girl.'

'Mother,' warned Rona glancing towards the bar. 'Please don't start becoming involved in other people's lives.'

'I'm just getting settled in,' her mother reproved. 'Getting the feel of the place.'

The younger woman regarded her with puzzled amusement. 'You've got to know more people here in a week than I know in my own home town.'

'Because I'm *interested*,' insisted the old lady. 'Interested in people.' A couple came through the door, the young man taking off his bowler hat with a flourish. His hair was curled

65

and fair. His wife was broad and homely, with a brown, pleasant face.

Anthony and Annabelle Burridge exchanged greetings at the bar. 'How's London?' inquired Jim Turner from behind his bar. He placed their drinks.

'Glad to get out of it, as usual. Glad to get home.'

'They live in a tent,' Mrs Collingwood confided a little smugly to Rona.

'Oh, now you're kidding.'

'I *am not* kidding. They live in a tent, on that bitty hill, back of Bedmansworth, because their whole world fell down. You know how it happens, jobs go, house goes.'

'You've met them?'

'Well not exactly, not yet. But I know all about them.'

Rona put out her hand and touched her mother's wrist. The old lady's hand, brown and frail as a tealeaf, turned and held hers. 'Mother,' said the younger woman smiling seriously into the lined face. 'What are we doing here?'

'*Being* here,' shrugged Mrs Collingwood. 'I like it.'

'You've started smoking again,' frowned Rona. 'I know.'

'I'm just helping the Reverend come to terms with his addiction,' replied her mother. Her voice dropped. 'But don't tell a soul.'

'I just can't believe how you've got *into* this place. You just drop in here. You were sick, I know, but you seem fine now. In no time it's like you've been living here all your life. You know *all* these people. This couple live in a tent . . . the parson smokes . . . What next?'

'That young man, Bramwell, is a woman chaser,' provided Mrs Collingwood grimly. 'Another King Edward the Seventh.'

Rona laughed. 'I give up,' she said. They were still holding hands and she gave the old fingers a squeeze. 'Don't you seriously want to move on now? We came to visit, remember. To see things.'

66

'We *are* visiting,' pointed out the old lady. 'The best kind of visiting. Getting to know people.'

'You are certain you don't want to go to London?'

'We can go tomorrow,' Pearl informed her decisively.

'Oh?'

'There's a trip, an outing they call it, to London. The darts team are going. Jim is the captain and Dilys is going too. There's tea somewhere-or-other, where they make special cakes. Then we're all going to a show. We've got afternoon tickets for a flop. Then we all ride back. The coach leaves here – right outside – at one o'clock. There's time for sightseeing.' She regarded her daughter with direct challenge. 'I've put our names on the list.'

Rona released her hand and put her own fingers over her face to muffle her laughter. 'You're wonderful,' she said truthfully.

'I know,' asserted her mother. 'And I am going to be even more wonderful.' She rose elegantly. 'Let's go and meet the folks who live on the hill – in a tent.'

They left their corner. Half a dozen more customers had arrived in the bar and were sitting at the dark wooden tables. Jim was busy with his beer handles and bottles. Dilys came through the curtain at the back to help. The door was open letting in the evening light and air. Conversation and casual laughter drifted out into the quiet street. Pearl Collingwood greeted the Burridges like old friends, leaving Rona to add a secondary smile. Anthony Burridge bought them each a drink.

'You haven't met,' said Bramwell. 'This is Mrs Collingwood from America and her daughter . . .'

'Rona,' said Rona. 'Rona Train.'

'This is Tony and Annabelle,' said Bramwell. 'Burridge.'

'My grandfather lived in a tent,' offered Mrs Collingwood at once. 'Before he struck gold that's where he lived. In a tent. Then the gold ran out so he went into insurance.'

Rona discovered herself looking around the salient of

67

friendly and inquisitive English faces. It was almost as though she were looking for someone in that place where she knew no one. Her mother had made everyone smile. She began to feel a touch of gladness that it was happening like this. Her own unhappiness might, after all, have only increased had they been touring as they had intended. Sitting in buses and trains was a solitary thing even with a companion; too much time to think, to wonder, to regret and live over. Her mother was lifting half a pint of bitter, scrutinising the beer through the bevels of the tankard. Rona sipped her gin and tonic and watched her with concern and amusement.

The eight o'clock summer light issuing through the open door was suddenly shadowed. Outlined in the aperture was a Martian form which stumbled solidly into the room. Bernard Threadle habitually missed the step. He was festooned with motor cycle clothing: boots ballooning from his trousers, a shining helmet embellished with wings, one set pointing backwards, goggles pushed up from sweating eyes. His upper body was encased in a crackling leather parcel held together by a thick belt.

' 'Evening everyone,' he gasped as he removed his helmet to reveal a red and rotund face. 'Anything to report?' He loosened the wide belt and his form sagged.

'Anything to report?' echoed Bramwell looking around. Heads shook seriously.

'Nothing, Bernard,' Jim reported.

'Just checking,' muttered Bernard his eyes flicking about. He glanced at Bramwell. 'Somebody's got to.'

Jim Turner leaned from his side of the bar. 'Drinking, Bernard?' he inquired soberly. 'Or are you on duty?'

'On duty,' reported Bernard stiffly. 'But that doesn't stop me having a drink. I'm not official, after all.' He looked at the faces for confirmation. Several nodded agreement and Pearl nodded with them. Rona was watching entranced.

'Double scotch, then?' suggested the landlord.

68

'Sweet sherry,' corrected Bernard primly. He was holding his helmet below his arm in the stance of an armoured knight prepared to joust, and he awkwardly transferred it below the other elbow and began to rummage in his copious leather pocket. He produced a small mallet, a screwdriver, a nylon stocking, and several pencils. Anthony forestalled him and paid for the sherry.

'You watch out the police don't stop you, Bernard,' Bramwell warned. He nodded at the contents of the pocket spread across the polished surface of the bar. 'Housebreaking implements by night. Serious offence. And a nylon stocking. Where did you get that?'

Bernard collected his dainty glass and lifted it in the direction of Anthony. 'Found it in the hedge up the road,' he informed Bramwell continuing darkly: 'You never know with these things. Where is the other one, I ask myself. Anyway it would take more than the local fuzz to question me.' He winked enormously at Pearl Collingwood who returned the wink. 'I've got too much on that little lot, I'll tell you.'

'These American ladies are staying with us,' introduced Jim leaning over the bar. 'Mrs Collingwood and Mrs Train.' 'We certainly are,' confirmed Rona's mother still surveying Bernard's apparel.

The vigilante wiped his meaty hand on his leather trouser-leg before offering it to them in turn. 'The US of A,' sighed Bernard. His eyes rolled. 'I'd like to get my hands on that. Now, *that's* a place for crime. Just let me loose in Chicago.'

'You ride a motor cycle?' inquired Mrs Collingwood unnecessarily, still engrossed in his appendages.

'Sharp little Honda,' he told her, privately. 'Not powerful, I admit, not as bikes go, but *sneaky*. I can get places on that where no big brute would even try. That's where I have the advantage over the police.'

Annabelle Burridge suddenly, as if it were time to do

69

so, explained: 'Bernard keeps an eye on things, don't you, Bernard.'

Bernard did not appear grateful. 'I was about to tell these visiting US of A ladies of my patrols,' he said. 'And I hope you've locked your tent up, Mr Burridge.' His glance went to Anthony as if the matter were better discussed with a man.

'Locked and barred, mate,' Anthony assured him lifting his glass.

'There's travellers around,' said Bernard. 'I'm monitoring their movements.' He said like a translator to the Americans: 'Gypsies.'

Rona and her mother glanced at each other, both sets of eyebrows minutely raised, a sign they had enjoyed using since Rona's girlhood. The lemon light through the door was dimmed again. Stooping into the bar Edward Richardson wished everyone a good evening. He smiled at the Americans. There are moments, Rona thought many occasions later, when you face someone for the first time and you unerringly know that they are going to be important to you, that they are going to play a part in your life. And this was one of those times.

At the end of his long but narrow lawn, between the flower-beds behind the house, Edward had implanted a single golf hole. The grass was short and consistent there and kept level as a coat, and the lawn opened out into an onion shape so that there was room to use a putter from varying distances. The amusement was a remnant of the game he had given up through lack of time years before. Now he embellished the routine by imagining that the central hole was the sun and attempting to strike a succession of golf balls into the positions of the planets in the solar system.

The garden ended in a threadbare field, the sort of field, never now aspiring to be the meadow, that lay in the unkempt countryside about Heathrow. His horizon was near, a gentle rising of the land, studded by a few hawthorns above which lay a drift of smoke. Anthony and Annabelle Burridge had lit their campfire.

Adele came out into the garden. She had been out all day and she had bathed and changed. 'While you were sorting out the Istanbul drama, a Mrs Kitchen called for you,' she said. 'She left a letter.'

'Mrs Kitchen? Who's she?' He took the envelope from her.

'Bedmansworth Residents, she said,' Adele told him. 'She lives in one of those dreadful brick boxes on the new estate.'

'Bedwell Park Mansions,' he said. He had opened the letter and was reading it in disbelief. 'I don't believe this,' he said. 'This woman, the bloody Residents' Association, says that I've got to take down my observatory! According to them it contravenes some damn covenant. What a cheek! What nonsense.'

She took the letter from him and read it.

'I checked,' he said. 'I checked with the planning department. It's only a greenhouse after all.'

'On the roof,' she pointed out. He could not help feeling she was pleased.

'What are you going to do about it?' she asked.

'I'm going to ask her what the hell she's talking about.'

Adele said: 'She quotes a covenant from nineteen thirty-seven. Sometimes these things get lost – until somebody turns them up.'

'Thanks. That's very encouraging.'

'Sorry, I'm only telling you what I know from my own professional experience. The social services are often coming across odd things that suddenly resurrect themselves.'

'I'm not concerned,' he said bitterly. 'She's obviously just one of those self-appointed busybodies.' They walked from the garden through into the dining-room. She had set only two places.

'Toby's out with Lizzie,' she said. They sat down at the

table as they had done for twenty years. She served the salad bowl and he poured two glasses of white wine.

'The woman's mad,' he grunted. 'That sort really gets up my nose. God, she probably hasn't been here five minutes.'

'I have to live with them all the time,' she shrugged. 'They're always on committees.'

'I don't know why you bother,' he said. It was a well-worn argument.

'Because it's my job. You do remember I have a job?'

'I remember.'

'I should never have left my job at the airport.'

'There's no guaranteeing any job at the airport.'

'Not even yours?'

'Not even mine.'

'I don't know why you don't just give them the two fingers and go and work for Gohm, Brent and Byas.' She regarded him thoughtfully. 'It might make a difference to our lives.'

They had grilled lamb chops, potatoes and ratatouille. The discussion, none of it new to them, ceased. They ate moodily.

'It would make a difference to mine,' he said eventually. 'One I don't want.'

'You must be crazy. The minute they can do without you, out you'll go.'

'The same could happen with Gohm, Brent and Byas.'

Adele knew the argument was terminated, for the present.

'I went to St Sepulchre's yesterday,' she said neutrally. 'While you were in Istanbul. The old people's home. We're trying to place one of our cases there.'

'Odd situation for a place like that,' he said, glad also at the change of subject. Sometimes they both needed to back off. Neither had anywhere else to go. Peter Rose had faded from her thoughts into another marriage. She had read it in one of the columns. 'Right on top of the runways.'

'They were given the house for nothing,' she said. 'So

they took it. It's a condition that they can't change the name which is unfortunate for elderly people. They sit at the windows and watch the planes landing and taking off. It's sobering to see it. They had homes, jobs, responsibilities once. Now they have to be amused until they die.' She pursed her lips. 'It's like seeing the future.'

'The future is not yet,' he said. 'Have another glass of wine.'

'The Burridges have invited us to a barbecue,' she said. 'Do you want to go? It's in aid of the church. They're trying to recover some of the money stolen from the offertory box.'

'Ah, the famous Footballs for Africa Fund,' he mused. 'Why not?'

'As long as it doesn't rain. It will be crowded in that tent.'

They knew they were just making conversation. They were both relieved when they heard the front door opening and shutting. 'Toby,' said Adele. 'He's got something he wants to ask us.'

'He's not getting married?'

'Not at sixteen, I hope.'

Richardson half turned in his chair towards the door as the boy came into the room. Toby kissed his mother on the side of her hair.

'How is Liz?' she asked.

'Oh all right,' shrugged Toby. He was square and short with untidy fair hair, his face serious. 'She's into older men now, so she says. She wants to marry Richard Branson.'

'I'll get you something to eat,' said Adele. She seemed anxious to leave the room but Toby delayed her: 'No, not yet, Mum. I want to ask you something.' He pulled out a dining chair. They watched him cautiously. He was their only child. Richardson suddenly realised he could scarcely remember his growing up. 'It's not about Liz,' Toby said. He glanced at each in turn. 'So don't worry.'

Richardson continued eating. 'It all sounds a bit portentous,' he said.

'Well, it *is*, to me,' remarked Toby. 'I want to leave the college. I want to get out of it. I'm not learning any of the things I want to learn, only maths, economics, all that stuff, I'm no good at them anyway. I want to get a job.'

'So do a few million others,' pointed out his father. Adele glanced at him quickly. 'What job are you thinking about?' she asked.

Toby swallowed and looked first at his mother and then, challengingly, at his father. 'Antiques,' he said firmly.

No one spoke. 'Antiques,' said his mother eventually. She looked at her husband. 'Antiques,' said Richardson.

'Antiques,' repeated Toby doggedly. 'I *like* old things.' He smiled miserably. 'Like Liz really, I suppose.' He stared at the table. 'Richard ruddy Branson,' he muttered with sadness and scorn. 'Virgin Airlines should be just right for her.'

It was cloudy, not a night for watching the stars. Adele was already in bed, propped up against her pillows reading a multi-paged report. She had a committee at nine. Edward came from the bathroom. 'Antiques,' he repeated gently shaking his head. 'Why didn't *I* think of that?'

'Maybe there weren't any in your day,' she suggested over the edge of the page. Her shoulders were plump below the straps of her nightdress.

'Well, it's different, you've got to give him that,' he said. 'But he's got to learn the trade properly from somebody who knows what they're about.'

'He's going to see the man at Windsor. That shop's been there centuries, I've looked in.' They were both relieved to have it to discuss. It was like meeting in No Man's Land.

Richardson took off his dressing-gown and prepared to climb into his own bed. They had abandoned their double bed. The excuse had been his arrivals from late flights, his astronomy and his and her frequent early leaving of the house. Now, going to bed was as compartmentalised as the rest of their lives, lying just too far apart.

He went to the window and touched aside the curtain. A glow was coming from the other side of the field beyond their garden. 'The Burridges are up,' he said over his shoulder. 'The campfire is still burning.'

'What an extraordinary thing to do,' she said without looking up from her papers.

'Living in a tent? Well they're obviously enjoying it,' he said. 'It's given that marriage a new twist.'

'*That* marriage can't have been going very long,' she observed over the edge of the page.

'They seem to enjoy both,' he said. 'Marriage and camping.'

'Until winter comes,' she forecast.

He turned from the window and said: 'As it does.' Both were tempted but neither wanted to quarrel now. He kissed her on the cheek and got into his bed. 'The Burridges were in the Swan tonight,' he said. 'Two Americans were in there. An incredible old lady and her daughter.'

'I heard,' said Adele. 'They've decided to visit England out of Bedmansworth. The Swan's bound to be cheaper than the Savoy. What's the daughter like?'

'Nice, educated, American,' he said.

'Is that an official category in the airline business?'

'Not necessarily. I thought it summed her up. Mid-thirties, I'd say. Smart, probably divorced. She's called Rona.'

Mr Old's name had always been Benjamin Old. 'I didn't change it because I'm in the antique business,' he often said. 'I was Old when I was born.' The shop had been opened by his grandfather before the First World War and the original black and curly gold lettering still embellished the front window. In those days Victoriana was derided; now it formed the main part of the trade. Uncertain items were casually referred to as 'turn of the century' and even pre-war radio sets and old telephones, popular with sub-urban householders, were stocked. The bell at the door sounded with a Dickensian tinkle as Toby entered at noon. The elderly owner was seated on a high stool eating a Chinese take-away from the counter.

'Have to eat when you can in this business,' he said, rice cascading from his fork. 'You never know when there's going to be some terrific excitement. About this time of the day there's always a lull. It comes just after the morning lull and just before the afternoon lull.' He scraped together some chicken remnants and ate them. 'So it's a job in antiques you want.'

Mr Old pushed his plate aside. He lifted it and examined the base although only casually. 'Why antiques? No money in it, you know. All that stuff about old dears coming through the door lugging Captain Kidd's treasure chest is baloney. Do you know anything? Do you know what that is?' He pointed to a dusty Georgian tantalus.

'Three bottles in a rack,' suggested Toby.

'Good observation,' Mr Old conceded. 'Actually, it used to be a trick to frustrate the servants. You kept the booze in the decanters and then locked in the wooden bit to stop the butler tippling, see. It's like that bit there, see, standing under the fake Rubens. The Rubens is late Margaret That-cher period. That thing's called a dumb waiter, another device to defeat nasty Victorian servants. They used to put the food and stuff on that so that they didn't have to have somebody serving who was going to earwig on their conver-sation. How much do you want a week? How about fifty pounds?'

Toby swallowed but replied: 'How about seventy-five?'

'All right. Glad you can haggle.' He was spooning up cashew nuts. 'Fancy a spring roll?'

'Yes, please,' said Toby diplomatically.

'Not much good,' summed up Mr Old handing the roll

76

across in his fingers. 'God knows what they put in them but it's not as fresh as spring.' He leaned forward conspiratorially, so much so that he almost tipped from the stool. 'But I buy my grub there because I know they've got some lovely Chinese blue and white in the back of the take-away. He's shown it to me. Lovely. Not a hair crack in it. I'll buy that one day. If his grub doesn't poison me.'

He cackled. Some of the rice had fallen on his waistcoat and he carefully picked it off and put it into his mouth. 'Waste not want not,' he said. 'Good motto for this business. All right, I'll take you on. Seventy-five a week. Another tenner if you work on your day off.'

'Thank you,' Toby said happily. 'That's brilliant.'

'Brilliant,' cautioned Mr Old, 'is not a word to use in this shop. Too shiny, touch of the repros.'

'No, of course not, Mr Old.'

'Don't be sorry. Just learn. We'll start you off right now, studying silver marks. You know that silver is marked with a stamp for the city of manufacture, a letter for the name of the year it was made, and sometimes the initials of the silversmith? No? Well, Hester Bateman was a famous English silversmith. See if you can see her mark on that pile of old knives and forks and spoons over there. While you're cleaning them.'

The Reverend Henry Prentice was sweeping rubbish from along the churchyard wall when Richardson emerged from his house. 'Thirsty work, Vicar?' Richardson suggested.

'I wouldn't mind one, Edward,' said Prentice. 'It might make me feel more Christian.'

He left the broom propped against the wall and they went into the Straw Man, Bedmansworth's second inn, adjacent to the small oval green. Although Prentice was not very tall they both needed to crouch through a low and narrow door, built three centuries before when people were much smaller. Mrs Mangold, who had kept the licence for twelve years since the death of her husband, was behind the bar, so confined that it always reminded the clergyman of a pulpit, her grey hair in a bun perched above a miniature beaming face. 'You're the first tonight, Vicar,' she told them, her eyes like bright insects behind her glasses. 'Good evening, Mr Richardson.'

She knew the vicar would have a Guinness. 'I'm having a scotch,' said Richardson. 'I need a little Dutch courage. I am off to see our formidable Mrs Kitchen.'

Prentice blew a bow wave across the black surface of the Guinness as though trying to cool it. 'Who's Mrs Kitchen when she's home?' asked Mrs Mangold. 'I thought I knew everybody.'

'Chairman of the Residents' Association,' he said. 'She's only just moved in here.'

'Ah, yes, I know,' nodded the clergyman. He looked in a concerned way at Richardson. 'Formidable. No sooner had she come into the parish than she began taking things over. As far as the Residents' Association was concerned, it was a *coup d'état*, a *putsch*. She and her husband and a few cronies hijacked the committee and that was that. You know how people around here don't bother turning up for things. I'm surprised some of them get to their own funerals.'

'She wants me to pull down my observatory.'

'That's terrible,' said Mrs Mangold looking upset. 'Your nice glass dome.'

'On what grounds?' asked the vicar frowning.

'A covenant, so she says. I'm not worried, she's just trying it on.' He finished the scotch and refused the vicar's offer of a refill. 'I needed one,' he smiled. 'But two might make me truculent.'

He and the clergyman walked out into the evening. Mrs Mangold called: 'Good luck, Mr Richardson.' The vicar picked up his broom and began sweeping where he had left off. The village street was empty except for two parked cars. A cat had placed itself on the wall and sat prospecting for

78

graveyard mice. An airliner droned low and slow overhead, just passing by. An insect whine sounded in the distance and, without speaking, the two men waited until the fragile motor cycle bearing the bulky Bernard Threadle turned the corner. He made an attempt to wave to them, thought better of it, and clumsily circumnavigated the green island in front of the Straw Man before cruising back.

Wobbling alongside them, as though combating a difficult wind, he put his booted foot on the kerb and attempted to lift the visor of his winged helmet but remained trapped within the window. He gave it a second desperate push and it rose. The framed, artless face was revealed.

'All quiet, Vicar./All quiet, Mr Richardson?'?

The first was a statement, the second an inquiry. They exchanged glances. 'Yes, it's very quiet indeed, Bernard,' confirmed the vicar checking along the clear and dusty street. The only noise was the mild coughing of the vigil-ante's own motor cycle until it was joined and drowned by a DC10 of Air Lanka, climbing for Colombo. It took a long time to rise over the house-tops. 'As quiet as it ever is,' he added.

Bernard studied Richardson. 'Nothing to report,' added Richardson. 'Not yet.'

Bernard blinked. 'You think there may be, sir?'

'There could be sounds of a fracas from the direction of Bedwell Park Mansions,' Richardson told him. The vicar grinned thoughtfully at the handle of his broom.

'I'll keep alert for it,' said Bernard. He revolved his atten-tion to the clergyman. 'I don't suppose the official police have any news of the robbery in the church? "The Footballs for America".'

'Africa, Bernard,' corrected the vicar mildly. 'Americans don't need footballs.'

Bernard's enclosed face frowned. 'Africa it was. My mis-take. But they've found nothing.'

'There have been no arrests,' confirmed the vicar.

The vigilante tutted his head, swaying. 'Not a clue,' he sighed.

He revved his machine, pulled down his visor and with a stilted wave of his gloved hand, set off on his patrol once more.

'He means well,' said the vicar shaking his head. 'I only wish the poor fellow's face in that helmet didn't look so much like a turkey in an oven.'

They laughed, shook hands and parted. Richardson walked on purposefully. He had never had need to walk through Bedwell Park Mansions before. From a distance it appeared as a conglomerated place and it was now revealed, as he walked, as functional and square, rectangular detached house faces, the same windows, the same roofs. Only the colours of the doors and the odd embellishment, a wagon wheel here, a private lamppost there, a short flagmast in a front garden, distinguished one dwelling from another. The newly laid gardens had known no opportunity for individuality. Evening cars were canted in drives, and faces looked out at him from picture windows, but there were few people outside; a man metallically tapping below the bonnet of a Toyota, another peering glumly at some meagre roses, and a lost-looking child sitting on a step.

Mrs Kitchen's house was called 'Halifax Villa'. She was eponymously at her stove in her kitchen for she came to answer the chimes with flour on her hands. She wiped them on her apron in the manner of one about to do business.

He guessed she was in her fifties and she had spread. Her baggy chest rolled below a woollen jumper, her legs were bare and sturdy, so were her arms. The skin on her face, however, was smooth as milk and pale except for two doll-pink blotches on her cheeks.

They faced each other in silence. Eventually Mrs Kitchen said: 'Yes?'

'Mrs Kitchen?' he inquired. 'This *is* Halifax Villa, I take it? I'm Edward Richardson.'

'Oh, you are.' She attacked first. 'Well, I'm glad you've come into the open. You'd better come in.'

He stepped into the hall. On the floor was a rag rug, the sort made on dull winter evenings, a telephone on a stand with a framed print of two shire-horses ploughing a field above it. 'Halifax Villa's an unusual name,' he mentioned conversationally as she led him into a sitting-room furnished with tassled blue chairs and a red sofa. 'Do you come from Halifax?'

'It's named after the building society,' she told him bluntly. 'We've paid out our last penny on this house. That is why we don't want the neighbourhood spoiled.' She regarded him. 'You're very tall,' she said as if it might be cured. She invited him to sit down.

They sat looking at each other. Then he said: 'It *doesn't* need planning permission.'

'Right,' she said, accepting the challenge. 'Let's get down to business. The Residents' Association requires you to dismantle, take down, or whatever, but remove that unauthorised erection on your house. It's contrary to the nineteen thirty-seven covenant.'

'I've never been party to any covenant. This is the first I've ever heard of it. That dome comes under the same heading as a greenhouse. It needed no planning permission.'

'Ah, but it *does*,' she said so strongly that he suddenly feared she might be right. 'They are two separate and different erections, greenhouses and observatories. This one, for a start, is on top of your house and can be clearly seen. The covenant requires that such additions should not be made to residences in this village.'

Richardson felt himself bristle. 'I will need to see written evidence of that.' He kept his tone even.

'Our Action Committee will provide it,' she replied with confidence. 'It will be presented to you at the same time as it is presented to the local authority. If they won't sue, we will.'

'Sue! Sue! What *right* have you to come to Bedmansworth . . .? God, you've only been here five minutes and start throwing your . . .' He hesitated, surveying her bulk, '. . . weight about like this.'

'I am concerned with the amenities and the environment,' she told him bluntly. She leaned towards him and her eyes narrowed. 'Amenities in every shape and form. We have to do everything we can.'

A plane making for Runway Two bellowed above the house. When it had gone and they could continue, she added emphatically: 'I am also proud to be a member of GROAN.'

'What's GROAN?' he asked helplessly.

'*You should know,*' she said regarding him with some scorn. 'Group Resistance Over Airport Noise.'

'Oh, you're dabbling in that as well are you?'

'Not dabbling, deeply concerned, as everyone should be.'

As if to emphasise her affirmation the shadow and roar of an outgoing plane passed the window. She waited until the sound had diminished. 'It's got to stop.'

'I doubt if it will stop,' he forecast easily. 'Not until somebody designs the silent aeroplane. And I should point out that the airport was in place some years before these houses. The price no doubt reflected their location.' The taunt went home. He rose. 'I must be off. I'm going to look at the stars.'

'Really,' she said firmly. 'I'm more concerned with earthly matters. I'm afraid, Mr Richardson, you will find that I don't give up. Never. We've always been battlers, my husband and I. We have battled at Leighton Buzzard, at Crawley and in Swindon. We have not always been the victors but we have fought.'

'And now it's my observatory,' he mused. 'I'm in impressive company.'

He made for the door. 'I don't intend to dismantle that observatory,' he told her doggedly. 'Other people also have

82

their ideas of freedom, you know. I can fight at barricades too. Goodnight, Mrs Kitchen.'

She remained at the door as he strode down the garden path. 'I like you,' she called after him. 'I'd like to be friends.'

Puzzled, he turned sharply. 'Let us hope that might not become too difficult,' he said.

Five

There was a hold-up in the northern tunnel and the staff bus was wedged in the stalled conveyor belt of traffic. The anxiety of people about to travel in the sky but finding themselves trapped below ground, was apparent in agitated drivers revving their engines, clouding the tunnel with fumes. Bramwell Broad, from his elevated seat in the bus, could see the faces of car drivers and passengers, pallid and set as masks with hollow eyes. The traffic began to edge forward; a horn sounded, a woman, her mouth moving silently behind glass, complained, a child banged its fist on a car window.

Outside the tunnel it was a warm, dim day, the air damp and thick; half the morning it had been drizzling and Bramwell was glad he was going away. Lettie had been moody at breakfast, her pink robe carelessly wound about her childish body, her face dark and pouting. He always thought she looked much browner when she was sulking. She had said she wanted her mother to visit her. She missed her mother. He had heard it before. By the time he had returned from a trip she had usually forgotten about it or could be assuaged with general promises. She would smile gratefully and suggest: 'Also my brother and our Pauline.' He would say: 'No brother and no our Pauline.' There would be further sulks, then she would easily brighten once he had paid attention to her, flattering her, telling her that no man in Bedwell Park Mansions had a wife like her, which was true. He would pour a glass of Tesco red for himself and a Ribena for her, they would raise the glasses romantically to each other and everything would be right. Lettie would sing appallingly as she took his soiled shirts and underwear into the utility room below and put them in the machine. He would put his feet on a footstool she herself had constructed from a kit he had bought to keep her occupied when he was absent and he would lean back rolling his shoulders into the armchair and read the newspaper.

For Bramwell striding into the terminal in his uniform was like entering into a different season, making a long journey in a couple of paces. Drizzle was cloaking the outside, soaking parking wardens, porters and policemen but to walk through the sliding doors was to step magically into light, warmth and animation. He enjoyed airports, especially Heathrow; they were full of excitement and promises.

As the glass partition opened he felt the warmth of the air within the terminal. It was like a fairground, the lights, the movement; the coloured check-in counters and the lit shops were sideshows, signs flashed, there were loud announcements and music played.

People criss-crossed the floors hauling bits of baggage on wheels. There was an emergency call for a lost bishop from Stockholm. At the check-in desks, trustful travellers were handing themselves over to authority, lock, stock and baggage; facing hours of regimentation. Girls on stools in smart flying uniforms went through the static routine of ticketing and weighing. A child, bound for Majorca, had wet herself in the queue and the mother was taking short quick steps to pass the responsibility onto the next in the line, an elderly man who stared at the puddle, uncertain of its origin.

Unruly children were dodging and shrieking among the legs of shuffling adults. A man deftly extended his foot to send one of the dashing infants headlong into a group of men wearing kilts and carrying golf clubs. Here was the world compressed into the area of a football pitch. There were girls with mini-skirts and knock knees; women hung with anxieties and coats and executives in earnest suits. Two threadbare Irish priests, chins stubbled, argued about the Departures indicator while two nuns stood trustingly. 'Father Brennan will know,' one told the other. 'You just see.'

Some passengers hurried, harrying those with them, others sat listlessly, as if they had already lost interest, others grouped to stare open-mouthed at directional signs. Bramwell had often thought it was a miracle that some of them ever left the earth at all and yet not one lacked faith that, despite all evidence to the contrary, they would sooner or later fly high and effortlessly away beyond the clouds to some far destination.

That morning Bramwell was on the flight to Bahrain, the first leg of the plane's eventual journey to Singapore and on to Sydney. The stage would take six hours and they would leave on time. It was an almost full flight. The captain, co-pilot and flight engineer were making pre-take-off checks on the flight deck, confined as astronauts in a space capsule. There would be one steward and two stewardesses for the eighteen passengers in the First Class section at the front of the plane; there would be four in the extended Cabin Class in the middle where there were sixty passengers, and nine to service the 278 Economy travellers at the rear. The Boeing 747–400 would be cruising at an altitude of 39,000 feet, far above clouds and weather but prey to occasional clear air turbulence, with a ground speed of 620 knots. The pilot might encounter difficulties as diverse as volcanic ash floating in the high atmosphere (which once stopped all four engines of a British Airways plane in flight), birds on the approach to a runway, and the mystery luminescence of St Elmo's Fire on the wingtips. Lunch and an afternoon snack would be served on this first stage; there was a movie, ten channels of stereo entertainment and an in-flight magazine.

Bramwell was the purser in charge of Cabin Class. He had seen Barbara Poppins at the crew assembly and briefing and she was now working with him. They busied themselves with their checks. Was the food lift working? Were the headsets on board? Was the *food* on board? There had been a flight which had turned back when well on its journey to Moscow because no lunch had been loaded.

'How's the Mercedes?' asked Barbara casually.

'Any more of that and I'll give you the washing-up,' said Bramwell. 'I've swapped it for a Vauxhall.'

Tarrant, the cabin service director, came into the galley. 'Bramwell,' he said in a low voice. 'Mr Richardson, the commercial manager, is joining this flight, so I've just heard. Look after him, will you. And I'm swapping Holloway around. He's coming in here instead of in Steerage.' He eyed Bramwell. 'You know Holloway's a Jehovah's Witness? He tends to pray during take-off and landing. Keep him out of sight of the customers. I wish I could do something to stop him, defrock him or something.'

'Holy Holloway? Well, once, under certain circumstances, you could have done,' suggested Bramwell. 'He used to be gay. Now he's a Jehovah's Witness, I don't know. Perhaps you can be both.'

'Well, on this service, *I'm* Jehovah,' said Tarrant. 'So no praying.'

Holloway, his pleasantly moonish face damp and beaming, wriggled along the aisle. 'Good morning, everyone,' he gently greeted each one in turn. The service director grunted and moved on. 'Bless him,' muttered Holloway. 'And us all.'

Barbara smiled. Bramwell said: 'No time for blessings now, Holy. Here they come.'

'Bless them,' said Holloway.

The first passengers were entering the cavernous Boeing; nervous-faced people, people clutching hand baggage and children, blinking as they came aboard, looking around them at the curved, enclosing walls. Another conga line was jolting slowly along the parallel aisle. Heads bobbed and moved from side to side trying to get a view ahead. People, separated, called reassurances to each other.

Once the front of the twin lines had reached the Economy section the progress was slowed and then spasmodically halted as people searched for their seats, their boarding cards held out like licences. Those struggling to heave baggage into the overhead lockers blocked the passage of others following. There were polite pushes, tight smiles and small concealed snarls. Two children began to wail, one at the extreme rear and one at the front of the Economy section. As if each recognised a rival the howls travelled the long length of the cabin.

There was a tight-lipped anxiety and a touch of ill will in the boarding of a large aeroplane. The strung-out line progressed roughly along the metal enclosure but by degrees the stumbling queue thinned. The last mother carrying a baby, its bottled nourishment, its linen and its transport, a folded pushchair, tottered her way into the aircraft and distractedly asked Bramwell: 'Sydney?' Bramwell confirmed it was the plane's eventual destination and made to relieve her of the pushchair and her hand baggage. Instead she dexterously transferred the baby to him. It had chocolate-matted fingers and, as though welcoming the opportunity, it caught hold of his white shirt collar. It began to snivel and its nappy was loaded. Bramwell rolled his eyes and, seeing Barbara hovering, passed the child gratefully to her. 'Have a nice baby,' he muttered.

Quickly he opened the toilet door; he had to get the chocolate off his collar. An old man was sitting on the lavatory, his trousers and woollen underpants piled around his ankles. Bramwell apologised. 'S'all right, lad,' replied the man. 'Couldn't wait. Forgot to lock the door.' He called out when Bramwell was outside again and the steward reopened a crack in the door and asked him what he wanted. 'It is all right, is it?' inquired the crouched figure. 'I mean, it's not like a train in the station?'

Bramwell reassured him, went into the adjoining cubicle and tried to get the chocolate smudges from his collar with a

88

wet tissue. He could hear the Club Class passengers coming aboard. Scowling at the brown stain in the mirror he said: 'Shit.'

He left the cubicle. Edward Richardson was settling into his seat. They wished each other good morning. Richardson's attention went straight to the marks on the collar. 'It's all right,' said Bramwell. 'It's Cadbury's.'

He turned to greet other passengers now, a handkerchief pressed to his collar. 'Good morning, sir. Which is your seat number? Yes, here it is.' A heavy, tired young man took the window seat next to Richardson. 'God, I'm shagged,' he said as if they had known each other for years. 'Glad to get back, I will be . . . to the good old Gulf. At least you don't have women after you. You can keep London. Bahrain for me any day, mate.' His leaden eyes closed and he dropped into an immediate sleep, his large chest heaving. Richardson nudged him and without opening his eyes he fastened his seat-belt. 'Women,' he muttered dreamingly. 'Keep them.'

No matter how far or how often he flew, no matter how difficult or delayed the journeys, Richardson had never ceased to enjoy the experience of aeroplanes. Twenty-five years before, when he had begun as a junior in the airline's public relations department, there had remained the last of a generation of wartime flying men who would not have settled into a peacetime life where their feet were on the ground. The boom in civil airlines was a boon to them and they were a boon to the infant industry for they could fly anything. They did, as their phrase had it, by the seat of their pants. Now pilots, generations on, sat up front in aircraft that, for much of the time, flew themselves, computers clicking them through the sky, each as much a passenger as a maiden aunt on a maiden flight.

The plane left on time, the company boasted that eighty-five per cent did. Richardson automatically checked his watch as they pulled softly away from the pier. Through the window he saw the ground engineer, his muffs like cartoon ears, give the thumbs-up sign. They had been been doing that since the infancy of flying; thumbs-up as the propellers whirled. Even the lifeboat crew who had attended, as a precautionary rescue team, the Wright Brothers' first flight in 1903 on the coast of North Carolina, had given the thumbs-up as the plane took off on its twelve-second flight. Now there were no propellers, only the humming silver pods below the wings. He remembered when a red-capped ground marshall would salute; in Japan the service crews lined up and bowed. But from Heathrow it was a cheery wave as the engineer marched away trailing his leadwires to his next check.

The plane turned with the studied grace of a curtsey and moved warily forward towards the open ground of the airport, between the glassy buildings, the piers and the other big, patiently waiting aircraft; great, dumb machines, asking nothing, not even respite, only that they should be fuelled and tended. As soon as this flight had reached Australia, after twenty-three hours in the air, it would untiringly turn its nose home again, cleaned, scrutinised, refurbished, and with a new human cargo, retracing its long, same and invisible path girdling the world. It often seemed to Richardson, especially in the night hours, that the plane sang to itself, romantic moonlight on its wide wings. The longer an aircraft flew, the better it flew and some had been airborne for years, the old Boeing 707, its engine pods like a grandmother's curlers traipsing around the globe still.

He had noted they were fourth in the queue for the runway, taxi-ing to the furthest extreme of the semicircle where the concrete became grass, where stone-deaf rabbits munched. A Cathay Pacific Boeing 747–400 was first to go off; it would not land until it came in from the mountains of Hong Kong, low over buildings, so low you could almost spy into windows, and touched down on the slender harbour runway of Kai Tek Airport. A British Airways Trident was next, fussily turning onto the runway at the three-quarter mark, bound for Glasgow, where, regular as a carrier pigeon, she had already been twice that morning. Immediately in front of Richardson's aircraft was a fat plane with the Cedar of Lebanon on its tailfin, Middle East Airlines, which had been trading in and out of Khaldeh Airport, Beirut, untouched through years of civil war.

On this good summer morning, there were three-minute intervals between take-offs, one airliner transformed into a smudge of farewell smoke in the sky before the next began to boost its engines. The Boeing gave a brief nudge as if to rouse itself, yawned, increased its speed between the bright lights along the runway and with a lazy curve lifted its nose from the ground, confident as a goose. The patterned airport, the motorway, other roads with their Monopoly houses, fanned out below the wings. Up among the ice-cream clouds the airliner droned. The horizon expanded; wide reservoirs flashed meaningless messages in the sun, the shadows of clouds smudged the flattened countryside.

Gaining height, its homely snout tilted, as if smelling out the route, the plane passed over Staines and Windsor, the castle set among clouds, the Thames like silver wire. On a clear day, at this point, Richardson could see his own village and, tracing the street to the church, pick out his house. Sometimes he thought he detected a farewell wink of sunlight from his rooftop observatory.

'We're now flying over Haslemere, having left Staines and Windsor on the right-hand side of the aircraft.' The reassuring voice came over the address system. 'Our route today will take us south-east across the channel. We pass over Belgium and then make our way down over Germany, Austria, Yugoslavia and to the Mediterranean . . .'

The everyday gazetteer, places ticked off one by one, far away and yet only hours distant, that not long ago had meant weeks of voyage. Now, leaving Windsor, Staines and

Haslemere increasingly behind, the big and glittering plane set course for the lands of deserts.

Richardson settled back feeling the hours spaced out before him. He often needed to work on the plane, but today he postponed opening his briefcase. It could wait. Sometimes he felt ashamed of his relief at getting away, escaping from Adele and their life. He held the stem of his champagne glass and began to read *Astronomy Now* which he had bought at the airport. The constellation Lyra, the Harp, with its blue leading star Vega, was overhead that month with Cygnus the Swan, Aquila, Scorpius, Sagittarius and company performing their unending dance on the stage of the sky; a fandango of stars, comets, spheres, meteors, mobile specks of brightness, joined far below, he liked to think, by the moving lights of aeroplanes. In the Gulf the stars would appear different, brighter, some incandescent, eavesdropping close to the earth.

The heavy young man, snoring mildly in the window seat, was one of a generation of workers in what had once been an unimagined region; shuttled now to the Persian Gulf and back, journeys which still took less time than a train from the South West to the North of England. What had once been merely a map on a classroom wall they familiarly called 'Saudi' or 'The Gulf'. They returned to Britain and their families only within the time allowance of their tax avoidance, then flew back to their monk-like lives of making money. Their fathers would scarcely have travelled beyond the next town, the next building site.

Club Class was ten short of full. Some favoured travellers had been up-graded from Economy. There were several women, one with a sleeping child, and businessmen, brief-cases ajar grafting like scribes at their tablets. There was a group of taciturn Arabs and the inevitable industrious Japanese, like earnest schoolboys, their only sparkle coming from their spectacles, two tapping silently on laptop keyboards while two more squinted neatly at minute notebooks. Each of them in turn would smooth his black hair.

Immediately in front of the movie screen the seats were vacant and four men, whom Richardson guessed to be military, wearing uniform civilian suits, sat further back, the line of squared shoulders like a parade. The other seats were occupied by tourists going to Singapore on the second leg of the journey, or to Australia on the final stage. A whittled Australian, parrot nosed and cracked faced, sat across the aisle from Richardson crushing a worn brown hat in both hands, his bright eyes fixed ahead. His sharp little wife muttered: 'We're still up here, Ted. We're still up.'

When Bramwell brought the lunch trays the man in the window seat stirred but decided he preferred to sleep. The meal was attentively laid out, no plastic in Club Class, and the menu read well, but despite the blandishments Richardson was aware that something happened to food the moment it left the ground.

The sense of anticipation was present; the improbable situation of lunching high above the clouds, the relaxed leaning back, the names of the wines, the French menu. Despite all this he could never recall eating his way through an airline meal. Now he picked at the shrimps and salad clotted with dressing, a dish which had visibly aged as it reached 35,000 feet, ate only half the Chicken Kiev and left the chocolate slice to glisten untouched. He drank two glasses of French white wine. They were trying a new importer. There was always a temptation to drink more in that elevated vacuum; the belief that, fastened into your seat, going far but going nowhere, a passenger could safely imbibe as much as he pleased. It was not true; flying hangovers were the worst, and Edward Richardson would never have allowed the staff to see him drinking more than two glasses of wine.

He refused coffee, slid the magazine into his case, and dozed, thinking of Mrs Kitchen and his observatory now

93

far behind. An hour later something roused him sharply and he saw that the film was being shown in the darkened cabin. He concluded that the projected picture had woken him but then, with a lurch, he saw that a man was standing before the screen holding his hand up into the beam of the projector. Silhouetted against the face of a laughing Shirley MacLaine was the shape of a hand grenade. 'Oh God,' he muttered.

Barbara Poppins, the stewardess, walked briskly into the cabin from the forward galley. The man reached out with his free hand and caught her around the throat. Her eyes bulged in the dimness, she tried to scream but the clasp under her chin prevented her. Richardson, looking swiftly around, said loudly: 'Remain in your seats please, everyone.' The youth next to him awoke and was staring in disbelief at the posed figure. 'Shit and corruption,' he muttered.

The Australian wife was reassuring her husband: 'It's just a practice, Ted. It's not real.'

'Grenade,' said the man in front of the screen, oddly like the demonstration of a safety routine. He held it high so that the silhouette could be recognised in the beam of the movie. Then, pulling the terrified Barbara in front of him, he slotted the little finger of the crooked hand that held her, into the clearly outlined circular pin of the bomb. Richardson saw the service director, Tarrant, and Bramwell appear at the port-side rear of the cabin and the steward Holloway from the opposite side.

'Lights,' ordered the man with the grenade. He had lowered the weapon so that it was next to Barbara's ear. Her eyes were closed in a sort of calm terror, her lips clenched, her face drained and rigid. Tarrant nodded and Bramwell turned up the lights and stopped the film. One drama was enough.

The man was an Arab, narrow faced, hair cropped, with black, fierce and unblinking eyes. He was wearing a light brown woollen jerkin zipped to his thin throat. His mouth

94

was as tight as that of the girl he held. He had a small butt of a moustache and a hooked nose.

Richardson felt no doubt that he would use the grenade. Desperately he visualised the rehearsed procedures for the situation. Tarrant was doing the same. But rehearsals were one thing, this was another. The passengers, including the military men, sat like wooden figures. People rarely panicked. The hijacker would make the moves. There would be accomplices, remaining concealed until they knew they were fully in control, revealing themselves only if they needed to. He prayed that the crew remembered the rules. He glanced at the quartet of Arabs. They sat as rigid as everyone else. To his relief he saw that the man had relaxed his armgrip on Barbara's throat. She had opened her eyes and was staring, beyond belief, at the passengers in the seats before her.

'I could deal with that bastard,' offered the youth in the seat next to Richardson in a whisper.

'You won't,' warned Richardson quietly. 'You'll not move, son. That girl's life is at risk.'

'If she goes, he goes,' grunted the young man.

'He doesn't care.'

'Mad,' said the youth. 'Fucking mad.'

'Baghdad,' said the hijacker to Tarrant like someone paying a busfare. 'We go to Baghdad. Tell the captain now. You tell him.'

'Just a moment, old fellow.' The steward Holloway began to move forward, slowly, arms outstretched. 'God loves you. Whoever is your God, he loves *you*.' Richardson almost fainted.

'Stop him,' he wanted to say but the words would not come. Tarrant had already moved forward but now, all at once, there was something which prevented them stopping him. There was a quick, new expression in the hijacker's face. Could he be afraid? 'I die, you die,' he said, but his voice was shaking. Holloway moved on, irrevocably, down the aisle, step after step, arms before him. Everyone else

95

was frozen. Barbara stared at Holloway, her mouth sagging. She clenched her eyes again, her face white with sweat.

'*None* of us are going to die, *you* know that, old son,' said Holloway softly. He was confronting the Arab now. My God, thought Richardson marvelling, he is going to do it. *He is going to do it.*

'Give me that,' said Holloway lightly but firmly. 'Let me take that silly thing.'

Abruptly the Arab crumpled. His body arched forward, he released his hold on Barbara. Half rising in his seat, Richardson thrust out his trembling hand and pulled the girl towards him. Her clasp was wet. Calmly Holloway took the grenade from the man's grip. The Arab began sobbing like a boy, leaning over the empty seat in front of him. Holloway put his arm around him and turned smiling to the dumbstruck passengers like a cabaret artist almost at his finale. But not quite. He leaned over to one of the seat trays and picked up a table knife. With this he cut into the grenade, slicing it halfway across and then upwards revealing a bright yellow interior.

'Always been partial to a nice little pineapple,' he announced with a radiant smile.

'I told you it was only a practice, Ted,' said the old Australian woman to her husband. 'See, it was only a pineapple.'

Bramwell sat on the arm of a seat at the back of the cabin and buried his eyes in his hands.

'A pineapple,' he echoed faintly. He looked up at Holloway. 'It takes one to know one.'

The captain of the flight had taken the decision to fly on to Bahrain. The weeping Arab had been taken off by the security authorities. The crew, Holloway apart, had been instructed to go to their hotel. 'I wonder what it's like in a mental hospital in the Gulf?' said Bramwell thoughtfully. Barbara remained silent and pale.

Ninety per cent of the passengers had been unaware of the drama, although the rumour soon filtered back. The failed hijacker was at first confined in a forward lavatory where he had sat with his black hair wet with sweat, his thin fingers held like a mask over his face.

Holloway took him a cup of coffee. Then he was left there with Holloway, his keeper, outside the door and a sign 'Toilet Out of Use' hung on the doorhandle. They were only an hour from Bahrain. It was as near as any alternative. It was midnight before the security man brought Holloway to the hotel. The Boeing's crew were all awaiting him among the debris of food and coffee.

He blushed. 'God was with me,' he told them simply. His finger pointed religiously up. 'I received advance warning.'

'From God?' asked Tarrant. Richardson glanced quickly at him.

'Of course. Who else?' replied Holloway. 'God doesn't appear in a shining cloud, you know. He works in a mysterious way. You must know the hymn, Mr Tarrant. "His wonders to perform".'

'And this was a mysterious way,' prompted Richardson.

'Most mysterious.' Holloway glanced around enjoying the moment. His smile spread blissfully. He sat down and minutely arranged the creases in his trousers. He savoured another pause, then said: 'I spotted our would-be hijacker acting in a peculiar way at Heathrow this morning. I was in the departure lounge and he was coming out of the gents toilet. I recognised him because of his brown pullover, his hair and his mad expression. There was no mistaking it was the same chap. He charged out, looking wild, as I say, and I went in and there was the toilet attendant going berserk. He was an Indian lad and he was upset because this chap had left one of the cubicles in a right mess – boot blacking on the loo seat, toilet rolls all covered in boot blacking, and a bag full of fruit.'

'Which he had brought through security,' said Richardson thoughtfully.

'No law against that, Mr Richardson,' pointed out Holloway primly. 'Nothing to stop anyone carrying a few apples and pears and a couple of baby pineapples through.'

'I've known people bring their own sandwiches,' nodded Bramwell.

'Who can blame them?' said Holloway seriously. 'I'd bring mine.'

'Go on, Holloway,' prompted Richardson.

'Well, in the plastic bag in the loo, a bag from a greengrocer's in Notting Hill, were bits of fruit, including one baby pineapple, plus the tin of Cherry Blossom black boot polish and a kid's penknife. On the floor there were shavings from another pineapple. He'd fashioned a grenade from the pineapple and blackened it with boot polish. I've seen some funny things left behind in lavs, believe me, but this is different.'

'And the pin was just the ring-pull from a beer can,' said Richardson.

He turned to Holloway. 'Well, you were terrific,' he said shaking his hand. 'I've already told them at Heathrow.' He looked around. 'Naturally they want this kept quiet. It wasn't real. It was more of a . . . hoax.'

'A hoax? We could have ended up in Baghdad, Mr Richardson,' pointed out Tarrant.

'The company view is that it was a hoax,' repeated Richardson solidly. 'And must be treated as confidential.' He looked around the faces. 'That's not me saying that – it's the company.'

'Poor chap,' regretted Holloway. He looked hopefully at them. 'Perhaps we should pray for him.'

Georgina Hayles drove from Heathrow into the morning rush-hour traffic on the Bath Road. Her car slotted between a red bus and a tanker towing a trailer. She felt grateful

98

she did not need to go towards London for more than a mile before diverting through secondary roads stirring themselves for another suburban day.

She had worked on the flight from Los Angeles, ten hours over the Pole. Now she looked forward to sleeping. She was pleased she had answered Barbara Poppins's advertisement in *Skyport*. The barge was quaint and quiet, it would be well suited for her purpose. Turning the car away from the interlocking streets, along one of the littered lanes that hemmed the airport area, she drove over a humped bridge above the canal, built in brick in Victorian times, and took a cinder track down to a half-field where there was a corrugated iron shed, some cannibalised cars and rusting farm machinery. The sheets of corrugated iron hung out like tongues, but as if some of the ancient agricultural vehicles lent a feeling to it, the place, for all its decay and rust, had a sweetish air of rural seclusion. Weeds, grown high all around, sprouted up the shed and curled around the wheels and frames of the old carts and cars. There were wild flowers and working bees, there were birds sounding and from somewhere came the comforting rasp of a cow.

'Cow,' repeated Georgina to herself. She grimaced at her self-criticism, but she had made a choice. After locking the car she walked around the shed, alarming a field mouse. In the hawthorn hedge was a sagging gate. There was a knack to opening it and she let herself out of the overgrown enclosure and onto the canal tow-path. The barge was lying with other elderly boats nudging the bank. There was a thick smell of water, elderberries and dandelions. In the flat sky above the random trees on the opposite bank she could see an airliner in the regular procession taking off from Heathrow. Had she turned a half-circle, she would have seen the spaced lights of flights coming in. She did not bother. It no longer struck her as a novelty that less than two hours before she had been suspended up there in the sky and now she was in this watery place, so quiet and so hidden.

There were two barges among the craft along the fringe of the disused canal. The water was so still the boats did not creak. The other barge had been long unoccupied and was gradually dropping to pieces. One day it would slide with a sigh below the thick surface. People arrived at weekends and sometimes on light evenings to work on their boats or to take them out for brief voyages through the overhanging suburbs, the streets and industrial estates by the airport and below the motorway bridge and the railway viaduct.

She was glad of the seclusion because, these days, she needed it. Barbara had ordered a new gangplank when Georgina had moved in and it looked solid and safe. She knew the trick now of hauling it by its chain from the deck to the bank. She put down her stewardess's bag and manoeuvred it into position, then walked aboard, opened the hatch door with the two keys Barbara had given her, and went into the long, low and homely main cabin of the barge. She put down her bag, closed the door and picked up the telephone. She dialled the Indian's number.

'Hello,' she said carefully when he answered. 'It's Candy here. My messages?'

'Ah yes, Miss Candy, you have many messages. I have made the times for you. I am looking forward to my next payment.'

'End of the month,' she said firmly. 'Like I told you. Aren't you satisfied?'

'Oh, dear, most satisfied,' he said. 'Most satisfactory. The money is more than I make from the sale of newspapers. Maybe I will stop the selling of bloody newspapers.'

'I wouldn't. This could stop tomorrow.'

'And I will not ever tell the police.'

She took a deep breath. She needed him because it worked so well. 'Don't you ever say that again,' she threatened quietly. 'The police would not be interested. There is nothing illegal, you understand that. Mention it again and I'll get somebody else to take the messages.'

He sounded panicky. 'I never will,' he promised. 'Never, ever. My wife Marika will not either.'

'Your wife knows?'

'She does not *know*. Only about the messages. Sometimes she has to answer the telephone. If I am not here. But she does not know why the messages are necessary, only that I get money for them. She likes money and she is obedient.'

'Good, well, remember just take the calls and forget them. You made a note of the right room this time?'

'The very room,' he said. 'Room 246, Flightline Hotel. I apologise for previous mistake. Most embarrassing for me.'

Not as embarrassing, she thought, as it was for that wrong room's occupant. 'All right,' she said quietly brisk. 'Appointments after five o'clock today . . .'

At five o'clock Georgina was in what the hotel called one of its small business suites, a confined sitting-room in pastel shades, a bedroom with one double bed and a bathroom. There was a television set with a video, a radio which was playing softly, a tea- and coffee-making tray and a drinks refrigerator. On the walls were two prints, eighteenth-century Thames scenes, and there was a bowl of polished fruit on the coffee table. For her it was convenient and, in its functional name, appropriate; she was there on business. She sat in one of the two compact chairs in the sitting-room, legs crossed, smoking and sipping tentatively from a glass of white wine, enjoying being alone before she got busy.

Georgina, Candy for a few hours, was wearing her air stewardess's uniform, the slick blue shirt and the buttoned jacket with the wings above the left breast, a white silk blouse showing at the neck. Her stockings were seamless and dark blue and her shoes had slender heels that would never have been permitted on an aeroplane.

Her visitors were rarely late. She charged from the time of the appointment. At precisely five thirty the bell rang modestly and she took a deep breath, touched her hair into place, extinguished her cigarette, and went to answer it. As she opened the door she adjusted her smile. 'Miss Candy?' said the man.

'Who else?' she murmured.

'Oh, indeed, I can see,' he said taking her in. His smile trembled. He was an American; forties, embarrassed, round faced and round bellied, but clean and uncomplicated looking, although, she knew by now, you could never tell.

She opened the door and invited him in. His eyes moved from one side then the other, as their eyes always did. He took a second step into the room once he was sure there was no one else there. She knew what to do; she walked into the bedroom, casually, calling him to follow so that he could see it was also empty. They frequently feared a trap.

From the beginning Georgina had decided that she would make it as civilised as it could be. Leading him by his pudgy hand, she returned to the sitting-room and turned the music dial of the radio down a little. 'I like that song,' he said smiling awkwardly. 'Reminds me of all sorts of things.'

'It's nice,' she agreed, listening to it for him. 'What's your name?'

'Phil . . . no, Ron. It's Ron.' His face turned blotchy. 'Some people call me Phil, that's all.'

'Whichever you prefer,' she assured him easily. 'It's your hour. Would you like a glass of wine?'

'That would be just right,' he said. 'Yes, please . . . Candy.'

'Do you smoke, Ron?' There were a lot of time-consuming questions she could ask. An hour was an hour and a surprising number did not claim the full time. Sometimes they went on to tell you about the wives and children they were missing, fumbling in their bedside clothes for photographs to show her.

Ron did not smoke. 'But I really don't mind if you do,'

he offered. 'I have no environmental objection.' He glanced at the dying stub in the ashtray.

'No, perhaps later,' she decided. She kept her voice very English. 'I'd really like to do what you want to do.' She smiled at him teasingly. 'Within reason.'

Ron became flustered. 'Oh, it will be,' he assured her. 'Within reason.' He ventured to touch her arm; as if it were now time. She permitted his fingers to rest on her skin and smiled at him, watching the hue of his face gradually deepen. Turning, she walked carefully to the side table and poured him a glass of wine. 'I *love* the uniform,' he said surveying it gravely. 'That's why I came, because of the uniform. Are you a . . . real stewardess?'

Georgina's slim fingers handed the slender glass to him. 'I was but I left,' she told him. She smiled directly at his nose, inches away, and he reddened further. She added: 'I prefer to deal with people one at a time.' She had almost said 'strangers'.

'Do you mind if we play a kinda game?' he inquired lowering both the glass and his eyes before raising the eyes, now lit with a different light, to regard her earnestly.

'Depends,' she said. 'No heavy stuff.' She leaned forward confidingly. 'I have security arrangements.'

He became concerned. 'No, nothing like that. I guess you have to protect yourself. I'd just like to play at being on a plane and you're the stewardess and I'm the guy who's a passenger. That's all it is. Nothing crazy.'

'That might be fun.' She said it as though it had never occurred to her before.

'I hope so. For you as well.'

'I'm sure it will be. But first I need two hundred pounds.' She flattened her hand and held it out.

'It's that much,' he sighed. 'Well, I might have known. You're a classy-looking girl and it's an hour. Okay.' He had the notes ready. He counted them out, in twenties, and handed them to her. Excusing herself she took them into the bedroom and, glancing in a mirror which showed him securely waiting in the other room, his fingers drumming on the glass table, slipped them into a safe in the wardrobe, playing quickly over the buttons. 'Ding,' she said to herself like the sound of a till. Standing before the mirror and avoiding looking into her own eyes, she smoothed her skirt, tunic and her smile again before returning to the sitting-room. He was upright in one of the chairs, his eyes fixed on her.

'Right,' she told him firmly looking down at him in the armchair. 'I'm the stewardess and I am in charge. Is that how you like it?'

'No,' he said a trifle uncomfortably. 'You're only in charge for *so long*, Candy. Then, when I begin to undress you . . . if that's okay . . . then *I* take charge. You don't . . . you don't, by any chance, have a life-vest here do you?' Anxiously he checked her expression. 'Like on the plane.'

'A life-jacket? No, I don't,' she confessed making a mental note to obtain one. 'You'd like to see me put it on?'

'Yes, I would have enjoyed that.' He shrugged. 'But it's okay. If I sit down here and imagine that I'm in my seat and you're showing the passengers the emergency drill, the exits and that kind of stuff. . . .'

'I could *pretend* I have a life-jacket,' she offered. 'I could go through the motions.' She looked at him as though taking him into her confidence. 'If this all goes well, and I mean "well" and only "if", would you like to pay me another fifty pounds?'

His face was becoming set and the conversation had given him an erection. 'Another fifty . . . ?' he muttered as if he wished she had not mentioned it. 'Well, yes, okay. If it works out right.'

'It will,' she promised. 'So you want to pay me now?'

'Later,' he suggested cautiously. 'I'll pay you then. When it's all over.'

She leaned towards him and tapped the head of his penis

with her little finger, the same small, sharp movement she had used on the safe. He jumped as if it were an electric shock. 'Do it *now*,' she suggested. 'Give me the fifty pounds now and then it's done. It needn't get in our way.' She moved even nearer to him, the breasts swelling her tunic almost touching his chin as he sat breathing heavily in the chair. 'It's no contest,' he agreed. 'Fifty. Okay. Here. But I don't have any more, after this, Candy. I need to get a taxi back to the city.'

'That's fine, Len,' she answered swiftly taking the money. This time she slid the notes in a pocket inside her tunic. His eyes followed them as they disappeared like the eyes of a boy trying to fathom a conjuring trick.

'It's Ron,' he said. 'By the way. Or Phil.' He regarded her unhappily.

'Whatever did I say?'

'Len. You said Len.'

'Silly me. That's being confused by Phil and Ron.'

Her proximity and her perfume were overpowering him. It occurred to her that one day, one of these men was going to have a heart attack. That would need some explaining. She flicked on her smile once again and with more power than she required, pushed him further back into the seat. 'I just need to go to the bathroom,' he said pleadingly. 'I have to pass water, if you'll excuse me.'

'Perhaps I won't excuse you,' she smiled wickedly. 'After all the aircraft is about to take off. We've fastened our seat-belts. You can't go to the bathroom now.'

The personal excitement caused by her words made him vibrate. 'I have to,' he pleaded. 'I just *have* to.' He jumped from the chair and followed her imperiously pointed finger towards the bedroom and the bathroom beyond. He went out at a crouch, like a rounded Groucho Marx. She glanced at her watch. Sixteen minutes, thirty seconds. She sighed and sipped the wine.

'You're back,' she said huskily as he reappeared, giving

the impression of relief, as if she feared he might have left her forever. In his haste he had forgotten to zip his fly and once he was seated again she leaned over, coolly and professionally, poked the end of his shirt in with her red-nailed finger and tugged up the zip. The action stiffened him again. His face was damp as though he had washed but not towelled it. 'You're back in your seat,' she repeated firmly.

'I am. I'm back,' he groaned then muttered. 'Let's . . . let's take off, Candy.'

The young woman stood before him, four feet distant, blue stockinged ankles close together, calves and thighs abutting beneath her slim skirt. 'So you want me to do the commentary, Ron?' she inquired conscientiously. She made a further mental note to get the tape of the take-off safety routine and play it while this was going on. There were always ways to improve the act.

'Please,' he answered. 'And go through the actions. Emergency exits, inflating the life-vest and the oxygen masks, all that stuff. Just go through it like you would. Please.'

Posed before him, she could have sworn his eyes were going pink as a pig's. 'First,' she recited huskily. 'The fastening of the seat-belt. For those of you not familiar with this type of belt, it fastens like this and opens like this.' She went through the actions. The man closed his eyes as if he could not bear it but immediately reopened them not wanting to miss anything.

'There are eight emergency exits on this aircraft,' she recited. Professionally po-faced, she held out her slim uniformed arms and with her palms flattened, indicated the door to the suite, the two Thames scenes on the wall and the door to the bedroom.

'In the unlikely event of the aircraft having to set down on water . . .' Who the hell had thought up that phrase, she had often wondered; 'Set down on water' as though they were flying a duck. '. . . The life-jacket, which is under your seat, should be put on like this . . .'

Ron was groaning. Again he briefly shut his eyes as though to exclude the anguish. Georgina deliberately paused until he had opened them again. '. . . The jacket fastens like this, around the waist . . .' She elegantly went through the motions with the invisible vest. 'And is tied at the front. . . .'

'Tied at the front,' Ron repeated desperately. 'Oh my God . . .'

'If you pull the toggle . . .'

'Pull the toggle,' he repeated like a litany. 'Jesus . . . yes . . . you pull it.'

'The life-jacket will inflate. But this must *not* – repeat *not* – be done inside the cabin.'

'No,' agreed her client earnestly. 'No . . . not inside . . .'

'On no account,' she added sternly. 'There is a light . . . and a whistle for attracting attention . . . and if you blow into this mouthpiece . . .' She blew provocatively into an imaginary tube.

'Please,' begged Ron. 'The whistle. Do with the whistle again . . . and then make the mouthpiece bit slower, will you.'

She did as he asked. She saw that it was the signal for him. He stood and held out both hands. 'Now, I want to undress you,' he mumbled.

'You want to undress the stewardess?' Her voice was husky and mildly surprised.

'Yes, I'd like to do that,' he said as if bordering on a trance. His eyes were trenches. She stood acquiescently, counting the glistening grapes in the fruit bowl over his shoulder. His fingers, with a sort of urgent slowness, began to undo the buttons on her tunic. He started from the bottom and when he had unbuttoned them he said: 'Would you please take it off. The coat, take it off.' She slipped out of it; the more time and trouble she took now the less she would need to work later. 'Shall I take my blouse off?' she suggested. 'It has small buttons.'

'You do that,' he agreed. He stood, almost stumbled, half a pace back while she slid the white silk blouse from her shoulders and without asking him, she unhooked her bra and let her breasts loll forward. His eyes almost fell out with them. 'May I touch these?' he asked like a man in a greengrocer's. He decided to make an offer. 'I have some more money and I need this to be real good. I don't need to get a taxi. Maybe there's a bus.'

'Another fifty?' she suggested. 'Pounds.'

'Sure,' he nodded. 'But not right now. Later.'

'Of course not now,' she agreed as though money were the last thing on her mind. His fingers went to the underside of her breasts and he played with them like a child. 'You're so beautiful,' he mumbled. 'Stewardess.'

'I've been specially chosen,' she told him. The line pleased her. She must remember to use it again. His hands trembled down her ribs and held onto her buttocks under the confining skirt. She undid the zip at the back and let it descend around her knees, then, with a wriggle, her ankles. She stepped out of it, bending gracefully straight backed, picking it up and putting it with care over the arm of the chair.

'White,' he confided to himself in a whisper. 'I *knew* she'd have white panties. I just *knew*.'

'White panties are regulation,' she informed him mischievously. 'Would you like to remove them for me?'

'Would I?' he answered, almost toppling against her as he dropped to his knees. He pulled the garment down the long length of her stockinged legs. He seemed incapable of getting up and pushed his nose into her pubis. Sternly she straightened him up. 'Not there,' she warned primly. 'Not like that, Phil . . . Ron. Let's get your clothes off.'

Her stockings swishing against each other, Georgina led him into the bedroom where he sat dreamily on the edge of the bed while, like a busy mother with a small son, she tugged away his trousers and underpants. In the same deft movement as she touched his penis she slipped a condom on it. Easing herself onto the bed, she opened her blue nylon legs and he climbed on top of her, sportingly taking his weight on his hands. She closed her eyes with a sudden weariness and disdain. She felt him ejaculate almost as soon as he entered her, as she was confident he would. They lay there for only a moment longer. He withdrew from her and in a sudden and surprisingly businesslike tone said he would have to leave. It gave her an excuse to check her watch. Thirty-one minutes, twenty seconds. The next client was not due for almost an hour.

'There's fifty pounds owing,' she pointed out. 'As agreed.'

'Okay,' he said offhandedly. He counted out five tens and put them on the bedside table. 'I had a good time. But I've got to go. I need to call home. I call home every single day.'

> *'Homelea',*
> *Anglia Road,*
> *Hounslow,*
> *Middlesex,*
> *England,*
> *Great Britain*
>
> *14th July*

My Dear Father and My Dear Mother,

I was worried with waiting but your welcome letter popped through the letter box today. Please affix the correct postage stamps. If you do not the letter takes longer and I have to pay more this end.

However it was excellent to hear from you and with all the added news. I am noting that you are well and that Benji is well and misses me. One day I will come back and take Benji for a walk.

So at last the men cleaned the well and put some concrete around it. I was worried about the tiger. When I tell the Brits that we have tigers near our village they think I am pulling their plonkas. One of the porters at London Airport (Heathrow) said he had seen on the telly that there are no tigers left. They have all been killed and eaten by the poor people, he says. All I can say is that it was not our part of India.

Here things are going first class. Uncle Sammi and Marika never seem to talk of the old days now, they are so long here. He is well pleased because as well as the emporium, which is soon to be open all night as well as all day, he keeps a social club. People telephone at all times to make appointments and I think it is making him good money. He is also considering starting a minicab. He is very clever.

It is summer and I am still waiting to be warm but I am getting used to it. In the winter, so the porters say, it is for brass monkeys. My position at Heathrow goes well and I hope for promotion before too many weeks.

My friend Jeremy Banarjee has a girlfriend who is a bar tenderess. She comes from Outer Wales. But I do not drink alcohol.

Soon I will write to you again. Tell the postmaster that he must put more stamps on your letters.

Your loving son,

Nazar

When the crew were leaving Heathrow, Barbara Poppins privately touched Bramwell Broad's sleeve. 'Come and take a look at the barge, if you like,' she said. He detected her motive. 'Just drive back there with me, will you,' she confirmed looking straight at him. 'I'm still shaky.'

'A pleasure,' he said. 'You don't want to go there alone.'

'Mr Richardson offered to send somebody with me, but I said it wasn't necessary. But it is. I'm not all right. I think I'll be looking around corners for some time yet.'

Together they went towards the glass exit to the terminal.

A summer's day was framed in the doors like a happy picture; a cut-out sky, the green heads of regular trees, the bricks of the central control tower red in the sun. 'It's hard to think it really happened,' mused Bramwell when they were sitting together on the bus. 'Nobody would believe you.' He shook his head. 'A pineapple.'

'It's supposed to be hushed up,' she reminded him. 'Anything *but* the real thing is secret. It's strange, isn't it. A genuine hijack, they tell the newspapers, an imitation and it's under wraps.'

'Mustn't do anything to frighten away the customers,' pointed out Bramwell. 'But they can hardly keep mum about the real thing. Holy Holloway would love to give a few interviews.'

The staff bus was almost vacant. At the front two stewards talked, heads close, then there were ranks of empty seats. With their uniformed shoulders against each other, Bramwell and Barbara said nothing more until they reached the car park.

'Pity about the Mercedes,' she tried a smile.

'Vauxhalls are so reliable,' he shrugged. She smiled genuinely. 'You are a fool, Bram,' she said.

'I know,' he replied looking into her white face. 'I always have been.'

She went towards her car and he climbed into his, waiting until he saw her go by in his mirror and then following. All around the day was beaming. As they drove in a long curve around the perimeter road, past the sewage farm, Concorde howled along its runway and threw itself with a shout into the fresh morning sky. Bramwell ducked and tooted his horn at its disappearing tail. To the east planes were coming in to land like cows coming home, one, two, three in the approach line and more behind them. He kept fifty yards to the rear of Barbara's car. He could see her orb of fair hair through the rear window.

He followed her from the Bath Road roundabout to the

minor road and then bent through a lane where dusty brambles brushed the sides of the car. There was dried mud in the lane but blackberry blossom on the thorns.

Barbara turned into an opening with a fallen iron gate and he followed. She was almost out of the car by the time he had pulled up and she came around to the open window. 'Where's this?' he asked looking around. 'A time warp?'

'A junkyard more like it,' she said. 'Come and have a look at the barge.'

She beckoned and he followed through the gap leading to the tow-path. Birds sang more loudly than he had heard for a long time. It was like being in some summer idyll. The whine of the motorway came faintly over the hedged fields and the chimneys of an industrial plant, straight and bleak, stood like a warning hand against the sky. He could hear the planes. But here there was a warm, confined peace, a concealed place, thick with the smell of old water and vegetation. 'It's like *Wind in the Willows*,' he called to Barbara who was already opposite the closed hatchway of the broad barge.

'We have to get the gangway across,' she told him. 'It's easier with two.'

He put his foot across to the deck and heaved himself over before shifting the neat gangway forward and then swivelling it so that it bridged the short gap to the shore. 'Just like the old days,' he laughed to Barbara on the bank. 'Manhandling the steps for Imperial Airways.'

'You're not as old as that,' she said, laughing at him in return. For the first time they looked firmly into each other's faces. She looked quickly away then mounted the gangway and, taking the keys from her satchel, unlocked the hatch. 'Welcome aboard.'

Following her down he found himself in the commodious room. He looked around admiringly.

'It's plenty for two.' She opened the curtains and the window and looked out onto the canal. 'And Georgina and

I are hardly ever here at the same time. She must be on a trip. Her car wasn't there.'

Two polished wooden doors with brass fittings stood against each other at the end of the room, and now one of them opened and Georgina in a silk robe came tiredly out. 'I'm here,' she mumbled leaning against the door frame. 'What time is it?'

'Oh God, sorry,' said Barbara. 'We didn't see your car.'

'I'm buying a new one,' she said. Her hair straggled over her forehead and her eyes and she threw it back with some irritation. It seemed damp as if she had been perspiring. Bramwell looked at her curiously. 'I left the Ford with them and they're bringing the new car around as soon as they get the documents sorted out.' Her face became alive. 'Barbara, it's a Porsche.'

'A Porsche! Have you met somebody rich?'

'Sort of. Well, I've known him a long time. It's my father.'

'Lucky you.' Barbara turned to Bramwell. 'Oh, sorry. This is Bramwell Broad. You may have met.'

They did not think so. The airline had several thousand cabin staff.

Walking to the galley kitchen Barbara put the kettle on. Georgina invited Bramwell to sit down. 'We had a terrible experience,' Barbara called calmly over her shoulder. 'We were hijacked.'

Shocked, the other woman half revolved. Quickly she returned to face Bramwell. 'You're kidding.'

'No,' insisted Barbara. She walked back into the room. 'We were hijacked, well, joke hijacked. Except it didn't seem like a joke.' Her voice trembled and she began to cry softly. Bramwell moved towards her but Georgina put her arm out to her. 'Don't,' she said. 'Don't cry. It must have been awful.' She offered to take the kettle but Barbara sniffled her away.

'He had his arm around my neck,' sniffed Barbara

pouring the water. 'God, it was terrible. I can't tell you what it was like. A strange man hanging around your neck.'

Georgina thought she knew.

Six

By now it was August and the evenings became a few
minutes shorter each day, sunsets were deep and the twilight
air warm and gritty. The countryside, that years before had
given a breath of sweet rural air to travellers leaving the
smell and the fogs of London, was now itself clouded with
the haze of machines and oil. At dusk Heathrow often lay
below a baleful halo of suspended smoke, the twin motor-
ways, the M4 and the M25, roared at each other like distant
lions.

Fifty years before, the Greater London Plan of 1944 had
spoken of a region here of isolated, purely rural villages,
away from roads and railways, agricultural land and
smallholdings that under no circumstances should be urban-
ised.

Rivers and streams had been ducted during the successive
constructions of the airport, and now they were penned in
set concrete confines although before dark they sometimes
had a little cloth of mist on them, a signal perhaps from
Nature that somewhere she was still lurking. The reservoirs
just beyond the Heathrow runways, which mirrored the
airliners as they took off, often pulled a private fog over
themselves like a sheet at bedtime. There, hidden from the
roads and runways, lived tribes of waterbirds. Sheep grazed
on the banks of the reservoir indifferent to and undisturbed
by the noise all about them.

At that time of the day Bedmansworth might easily have
been recognised by its inhabitants of generations before who

now lay side by side in the churchyard; the quiet street, the two inns, the church, the cottages and 'Vinards', the Georgian house which had remained unchanged for over two centuries and where Edward and Adele Richardson now lived in such unease.

'They've got the fire going,' called Richardson to Adele. At the bottom of the lawn he putted Pluto into place in the outer ring of his solar system of golf balls. She was inside the French windows, arranging flowers she had taken from her cutting area of the garden. She looked out. There was a low glow and smoke lying casually over the rising field where the Burridges lived in their tent.

She called to him: 'Are those Americans going? The mother and daughter?'

'I don't know. Probably.'

'They seem to have made themselves at home,' commented Adele. She was good at arranging flowers and now she looked at what she had done with a solitary satisfaction for Richardson never said he noticed them.

'What's Toby doing?' Richardson called. He felt glad and oddly guilty that he would see Rona again. He surveyed the small white planets against the green, giving Pluto and Uranus a touch with his foot to put them into position. Then he picked them up, dropping them into a canvas bag, and strolled up the garden towards the house.

'It's amazing that we're both at home,' she said. 'Both at the same time. Toby wants to come to the barbecue, so he says. I think he and Liz have been trying to make it up.' She laughed distantly and said: 'Young love.'

'That's what it's like,' he said coming through the French windows.

'I remember,' she said a little quietly.

He went to the sideboard and poured drinks for both of them. 'I had yet another letter from Gohm, Brent and Byas,' he said over his shoulder. 'They want me to go and have lunch. People always think they can buy you with lunch.'

'I saw it on your desk.'

'Did you read it?'

'Yes,' she said bluntly. 'It had their name on the outside of the envelope. What do you think?'

He walked towards her at the door and handed her the drink. 'I'm not interested,' he said with finality. 'I don't know why they keep trying.'

'They *want* you,' she answered as she walked out and sat on the bench on the terrace. He followed and stood looking over the fields, the drabness softened by the final sun of the day. Smoke, like a signal, rose from the barbecue fire two fields away. 'We ought to get going,' he suggested.

'You should be pleased you're wanted,' she persisted. 'There doesn't seem a lot of future for you otherwise.' He looked towards her sharply. 'I think I'm the best judge of that,' he said. 'I happen to like what I do.'

She took her gin and tonic almost to her mouth, then held it there and said: 'Gohm, Brent and Byas don't fly aeroplanes, do they.'

'That's exactly it. They don't.'

'What's so wonderful about flying aeroplanes?'

'I've been in that business all my life,' he said deliberately. 'I don't *want* to change. Whatever they offer. You really should have married your tycoon.'

'He wasn't a tycoon, as you call it, then,' she reminded him. 'Just someone with positive ideas, with a bit of courage, someone going places.'

'Through three marriages at the last count.'

She stood up and went into the shadow of the room. She felt miserable. He did too, and ashamed of his spite. 'I'm sorry,' he said.

'Let's go,' she answered. 'I'll get my coat.'

Liz was frowning, something she did well, when Toby got to the lych-gate. 'It's like being one of those brides who gets left outside the church,' she grumbled.

'I got kept at work.'

'Dusting off the Egyptian mummies?' she mocked. They began to walk but without touching.

'Egyptian mummies are worth thousands,' he said defensively.

'Horrible old things. How you can work among all that junk I can't think. You could get diseases. And that man who owns it. I've seen him and *he* doesn't look like he's made a fortune.'

'Plenty, he's made,' argued Toby stubbornly. 'He just dresses like that to make people *think* he's not rotten rich. It's no good standing in an antique shop looking like a millionaire.'

Liz sniffed lifting both her nose and her blunt breasts. 'You ought to get into a proper business,' she advised. 'Computers or something. That's where the money is. It's in the future, computers.'

Toby said: 'Everybody's doing it. Computers. I'd be no good at it anyway. I hate that stuff.'

'You'll end up wheeling a barrow round the streets, you will.' She laughed mockingly as they walked and gave a taunting skip. They were passing the Straw Man and Mrs Mangold called 'Hello, who's that?' through the open door from the dimness of the bar.

'Come and have a drink,' Toby challenged. 'Gin or something.'

'She won't serve you. Only coke,' said Liz. 'She knows how old you are.'

He knew she was right. He said: 'There's beer and wine at this barbecue.'

'That's something I suppose,' shrugged Liz. They continued walking separately. 'And *sausages*. God, how sophisticated!' She glanced at him sideways. 'I had two gins and some wine last week,' she said cagily. 'I went out to dinner with a chap in business.'

'How sophisticated,' he repeated.

Moodily they continued. '*I* don't intend to wheel a barrow around the streets, take it from me,' he told her eventually. 'And I'm not sitting in any dusty old shop. I'm only in the shop so I can *learn*. One day, when I'm ready, I'll go into the top range of the market, fine art and antiques. And that's money. Big money.'

'You reckon?' she said at once impressed.

'Millions. You only have to know what you're about, that's all. Be able to spot things. Ever heard of Hester Bateman?'

'No, I haven't. Who is it?'

'She's dead. Been dead years, yonks. One of the great English silversmiths. Brilliant she was.'

'A woman?'

'Exactly. And I'll tell you something, Liz, I can recognise her work just like that.' He snapped his fingers. A thrush flew hurriedly from the hedge.

'You've learned that much then.' She regarded him studiously.

'Masses. I can tell a genuine netsuke from a fake.'

'He's a painter is he?'

'Netsuke, pronounced net-ski, like that but spelt N-e-t-s-u-k-e, is the Japanese art of making little figures,' he said importantly. 'They used to thread the ropes of their robes through them like a toggle, and they carved them with heads and whatnot. The heads can even revolve. I bought a beautiful Meissen figure the other day. Or you might know it as Dresden.'

Now she was impressed. 'I've heard of Dresden,' she said. 'So you say there *is* money in it?'

'Thousands if you know what you're doing. Once I've got a good grounding I'm going straight to Sotheby's or Christie's and get myself right in there with the top experts. Then – when I'm ready – I'll break away and start out on my own. I wouldn't mind specialising in marine artists.'

Briskly Liz hooked her arm in his. 'How much do you

think you'll make, Toby?' she asked. They went into the field and began to walk up the slight slope to where figures were already gathering around the Burridges's fire. They could see the white tent like a pointed ghost in the background.

'Plenty. Enough to take you out to better places than your business friend did last week,' he forecast.

'He's creepy,' she confessed. 'He had glasses and they got all steamed up over the coffee. Like a bloody goldfish.'

Toby felt his cheeks warm. He put his arm about her thin waist. She pulled it closer. 'God, look,' she said. 'They've got the bloody wrinklies coming.' A minibus had stopped on the path leading up to the fire and the tent and four elderly forms were tentatively clambering out. An old lady reached for the ground with her thick-stockinged leg outstretched as if convinced it was a sheer drop.

'Talk about one foot in the grave,' said Liz. 'They give me the creeps.'

'They'll probably eat all the sausages,' he said trying to sound funny.

'They can have them,' she returned. 'As long as there's plenty of wine.' She looked beyond the old people and saw Lettie. 'Ah, I know her. That foreign woman over there. I've seen her in the shop. She's beautiful.'

Lettie was moving with Bramwell towards the glowing fire against which the guests were already outlined like heavy shadows. 'That's Bramwell Broad's wife,' said Toby. 'He's an air steward. They reckon he bought her, with money you know, like you'd buy a car or a house. She's from the Philippines. He just bought her and brought her back with him.'

'She's beautiful,' repeated Liz. 'I'd love to grow beautiful like that. Not so dark.'

'You wouldn't want to be bought though, would you. Just paid for like something from a shop.'

She screwed up her petty, pretty face. 'Oh, I don't know,' she shrugged. 'Depends who it was who bought me.'

'She's got her whole wretched family over,' Bramwell confided dolefully in Richardson. 'Well, not exactly *all* of them, thank God. They'd have needed a plane to themselves. It's bad enough as it is. Her crone of a mother, her vicious-looking brother and his wife – our Pauline as she's known – who looks like she's dying, and may be for all I know.'

They were drinking beer near the edge of the iron range which Anthony had built, stones topped with a farm grating. Sausages, brown and hissing, were laid out. At one end were onions and there were potatoes in silver foil. Toby was operating the tap on the beer barrel and Liz was pouring wine, gulping from her own glass. There were fifty people standing under the fading August sky and before the tent. Candles in painted jamjars were stood in a wide circle.

'That must have been a shock,' said Richardson. 'Finding them when you got home.'

Bramwell blew out his cheeks. 'Shock? I'll say it was. A damned nightmare. God knows when, or how, I'm going to get rid of them.'

Adele, a wine glass in her hand, moved across the grass to them. It was becoming damp with dew. Richardson said: 'Bramwell's been telling me that his wife's family have turned up from the Philippines.' Cautiously he glanced around. So did Bramwell. One man looked left, the other right. Lettie, holding her bottle of Ribena, was laughing with some of the young people from the village. She seemed happily at home with them, even the school children. Someone had a tape recorder and they began to dance.

Adele said to Bramwell: 'I saw your relatives in the shop. They were buying magazines.'

'Yes, *Film Fun*, I expect,' sighed Bramwell. 'They're crazy about the cinema. That's all they do at home, go to the pictures. They've got sunshine, sea, palm trees and they'd still queue up for *South Pacific*. I keep sending them to Slough, and Uxbridge, even Twickenham, to the pictures, just to get them out of the way. That's where they are now, Slough. The difficulty is finding epics they haven't seen. They're clamouring to go to the Indian films in Southall. It's costing me a fortune in minicab fares.'

'Send them on a coach trip to London,' suggested Adele. 'See the sights.'

Bramwell miserably shook his head. 'They're not interested in Buckingham Palace or Big Ben or Madame Tussaud's. None of that. It's Harrison Ford and Jodie Foster they want to see.' He drank deeply and took Richardson's tankard silently to Toby for refilling. Lettie picked her way across the slippery grass to them and Richardson carried Adele's glass to Liz who was giggling behind a stack of wine bottles. Randy Turner, his pigtail greased for the night, was showing her how to pour the wine into glasses without pausing. Lettie poured herself another Ribena from her bottle.

'Liz seems to enjoy pouring the wine,' Richardson observed when he returned.

'Suits her,' said Adele looking into her glass. Lettie was trying to find something to say. 'All the buzz,' she said eventually. 'All the buzz, wasn't it?' She looked anxiously at their puzzled expressions.

'The hijacking, Lettie means,' said Bramwell.

'A bomb like a pineapple,' whispered Lettie with enthusiasm. 'What a showdown!'

Adele said: 'Which hijack?'

'On the flight to Bahrain,' said Bramwell off his guard. 'The Arab nut with the . . .' He caught Richardson's eye but too late. '. . . pineapple.'

Avoiding Adele's gaze, Richardson said: 'Oh, it was just a joke. I forgot to mention it.' Bramwell put his face in his beer tankard.

Adele had paled. 'You were on the Bahrain flight . . . last week?' she began. 'And there was a hijack?'

'It was nothing,' grunted Richardson. Emerging from his glass, Bramwell agreed. 'No, it was over the top really.'

'Over the top,' nodded Lettie.

Adele had composed herself. 'Why doesn't someone tell *me* about it,' she suggested. 'Tell me about it, Edward.'

Richardson sighed. 'It was some poor demented Arab who had a baby pineapple of all things. It was sort of trimmed down and black, boot polish apparently, and he tried to fool us it was a grenade. But it was soon defused . . . the situation I mean. The security people took him in at Bahrain.' He looked into his wife's face, spread his hands and said again: 'It was nothing. Really.'

He saw Rona and her mother walking up the gentle slope towards them. Rona held the old lady's hand. She smiled towards them. Pearl laughed at the young people dancing. 'It's so noisy. How can they hear to dance?' she asked.

'Adele,' said Edward Richardson as they approached. 'This is Mrs Collingwood and her daughter, Mrs Train.'

Adele held out her hand. 'I wish you'd call me Pearl,' said the older American woman. 'I feel like I belong here.' She glanced at her daughter. 'And so does Rona.'

With a faint smile Adele shook their hands. 'I'm sorry if I look a little out of sorts,' she added. She studied both women carefully. 'I've just had a shock,' she said with mock amusement. 'My husband forgot to tell me he had been hijacked on an airliner.'

Richardson could see how angry she was. 'An attempted hijack,' he corrected holding out his hands. 'It was harmless really. A demented man with a pineapple.'

They laughed uncertainly but Adele half turned away as if trying to see an excuse and said: 'Ah, there are the people from St Sepulchre's. Forgive me for a moment. I'll just see they're all right.'

'What is St Sepulchre's?' inquired Rona watching her go. She could see the anger in her very walking away.

'It's an old folks' home,' explained Richardson. 'Not very well named.'

'They might have called it Resurrection, or something,' suggested the old lady. She peered across the flickering light towards the elderly folk moving studiedly up the easy incline. 'Maybe they need some help,' she muttered and moved off after Adele. 'Old people often do.'

Richardson and Rona were standing alone. He looked away, almost guiltily, following the old lady's progress towards the agedly moving group mounting the slope like some defeated patrol. Rona was watching her also. Her voice carried back to them: 'Welcome! Welcome!' Richardson laughed and Rona shook her head. 'Some of those people are probably younger than my mother,' she said.

Her smile was thoughtful. 'She won't own up to being elderly,' she said. 'She's just incredible. Hear her. It's like she's in charge here.'

While she was looking away Richardson took her in, the good profile, the half smile, her dark hair curling over her forehead. She turned and caught his examination. He said hurriedly: 'Would you like some more wine?' Holding the stem of her glass in two fingers and saying only 'Thanks' she handed it to him. The trestle table behind which Liz was pouring from the bottles was within reaching distance. The girl drained a glass and in one movement refilled it. Edward leaned over and picked up a bottle.

'I'll do it,' insisted Liz putting out her hand to take it from him. 'I'm the pourer.' Her hair was sticking across her forehead and her eyes were confused and bright. 'I won't always be poorer,' she said. She giggled at her joke. He handed the bottle and the glass to her. She spilled it and then slopped it over the rim.

'You'd never make a barmaid, Liz,' said Richardson taking the glass from her.

124

She screwed up her small face and said: 'Not that I'd want to.'

Handing the wine to Rona, he said: 'The story is that you arrived here almost by accident.'

'It was certainly strange,' she said. 'We came into Heathrow, six weeks ago now, for goodness' sake, and my mother became sick as we were being driven to London. We had hotel reservations, everything. She saw the church tower and insisted that the driver turned off.' She shrugged. 'And here we've been ever since.'

'She seems better now,' he commented looking over his shoulder. Mrs Collingwood was briskly shaking hands around the semicircle of people. Rona eyed her mother. 'She was recovered from the moment she got here. I really don't understand it. But in Bedmansworth she wants to be and here we are.'

'Have you done any touring?' he asked. He saw Adele observing them from the door of the tent where she stood with Annabelle Burridge.

Rona did not follow his glance. 'We've been to Windsor, because it's so near, and Bath and Stonehenge.' She counted them off. 'And we're visiting Stratford next week. And we went to London with the darts team.'

She put up her hand to stay his laughter. 'I know, I know.' She shook her dark hair. 'Mother wants to become part of the scene. We went to a show in the afternoon and did some sightseeing from the bus. They made a special detour so we could see Parliament and Buckingham Palace.' She leaned confidingly towards him. He was conscious of how near she was. 'The driver couldn't find them. We had a great run around trying to locate Big Ben. I really don't think he knew where it was.'

'That sounds like it,' he grinned. 'You'd be amazed how *local* people are. They're quite an insular community, you see, despite the airport on the doorstep and it's only fifteen miles from Marble Arch.'

It was dark now. The guests gathered nearer the fire and the griddle. Freebie, the horse, was being fed by the children. It sneezed heavily on them. The trees were dark but there were early signs of a moon.

'Mrs Mangold who keeps the Straw Man,' Richardson went on, 'told me that the last time she went to London was to buy a hat for her husband's funeral. And that was twelve years ago. In a funny way this place is almost as isolated, insular, as it ever was. People don't *think* much beyond it.'

'You travel a great deal?' Rona asked. 'You're in the airline business, aren't you?'

'I am and I have to,' he said. 'Really, to be honest, I choose to. I seem to be going somewhere or coming back most of the time.'

Adele approached almost stealthily and heard him. 'He doesn't have to,' she said firmly. 'He likes to fly away.' She waved her hands like wings.

'I don't,' Richardson said uncomfortably. 'But that's where the job is.' He pointed to the sky. 'Up there.'

There was a little silence then Rona said to Adele: 'You have the oldest house in the village. I've been admiring it.'

'Some of the smaller cottages are older,' said Adele. 'But it's seventeen sixty-nine – Georgian. It's been in my family for four generations. You must come and see it.'

Rona said: 'What, if I may ask, is that glass dome on the roof? I see it from the street.'

'It's my observatory,' put in Richardson. 'My hobby is astronomy. My telescope is up there.'

'One way and another he spends most of his time in the sky,' said Adele sweetly.

Rona was glad to see her mother approaching, shuffling enthusiastically at the head of a straggle of elderly people. 'The leader of the pack,' she said. The group was ushered on by a fussy fat woman swathed in a woollen headscarf. Pearl Collingwood was only a little breathless when she arrived: 'My new friends!' she exclaimed. 'United against the future!' Enthusiastically she introduced each by name. Sergeant Morris was regarding a foil-clad potato on his paper plate. 'Howitzer shell that is,' he said moodily. 'I'd leave my teeth embedded in that lot.' He indicated a thin, continually nodding woman at his side. 'So would she, if she could keep her head still long enough to get one in her mouth!' He confronted the old woman. 'Wouldn't you Minnie?' He shouted it a second time, close to her ear. Her nodding quickened.

He accepted two sausages, counted them, and helped himself to another. He bawled at Minnie: 'The bangers smell all right though! Have a banger!'

'Sergeant Morris, dearie me,' chided the woman with the headscarf. 'I'm the matron,' she explained a trifle helplessly to the others. 'I'm Mrs Bollom.' She indicated Adele. 'Mrs Richardson knows me.' Adele smiled in a strained way and said: 'Of course, Mrs Bollom.'

'Do you like being old?' inquired Mrs Collingwood forthrightly, surveying Sergeant Morris who choked on his food. Minnie, her nodding beginning to speed, patted him on the back. '*Me*? Like it?' he retorted when he had eventually dislodged the sausage. 'No I don't, madam. I can think of better ways of spending the rest of my life than being old, believe me.' He bit at his sausage again and swallowed it heavily. 'It's God's joke, old age. And He's got a few jokes, I can tell you.' He glared towards the vicar who had approached diffidently. 'Ask him.'

'Dearie me, Sergeant Morris, I believe you have a pretty good life,' said the matron unhappily.

'Hobson's choice,' he grumbled. He glared challengingly at her and then the others. 'Old?' he said. 'There's only one thing. Old is when you can say what you mean. Do what you like.'

'He put a sausage in my hand when I wasn't looking,' said Minnie.

127

'Oh dearie me,' said Mrs Bollom. 'Oh dearie, dearie me.'

'That's all she ever says,' complained Sergeant Morris loudly. 'Dearie me. Double dearie me.' He went away grumbling as he sloped off. Minnie followed him.

'I'm sorry,' said the matron helplessly. 'He's like that. They get annoyed, you know. Think that they've been cheated.' She looked at the faces. 'You ought to hear some of them complaining when they die,' she said. 'Oh, dearie, dearie me . . .'

Pearl and Mrs Durie were deep in discussion of the Abdication crisis when Pearl asked: 'Have you always lived here?' She leaned forwards as if it might be confidential.

'In Bedmansworth? I'll say I have, worse luck. Hardly been anywhere else. I've never been to the airport even, I've never been in a plane. That darts outing we went on was the first time I've been in London since Princess Diana's wedding. We lined up and waved.'

Pearl said: 'You must know everybody in Bedmansworth.'

'Oh, I suppose I do,' said Mrs Durie, casting her glance around. 'Just about. I grew up with the older people.'

'I'm getting to know people's names,' claimed Pearl. 'That's the Richardsons who live in the old house, I know the Reverend, and that's the air steward. Bramwell?'

'Bramwell, so he says,' sniffed Mrs Durie. 'You never know with him. Bramwell Broad. His wife, that Filipino girl, is called Lettie, poor thing.'

'And Anthony and Annabelle Burridge, of course,' continued Pearl. 'And Mr Dobson at the post office.'

'Dobbie,' supplemented Mrs Durie. 'He runs the band too.'

'Tell me some of the others.'

'Well now, let me see. That tall gentleman there, talking to Reg Latimer, who runs the paper shop and has got twin boys, that's Mr Broughton-Smith. He's got a medal from the war. Retired now, of course. He rings the church bell.' She moved her scrutiny a few degrees. 'Over there, that's

Thora Fickens, funny old package she is and she's with Miss MacNamara, I never know her first name, who teaches at the Sunday School.'

'Are the village schoolteachers here?'

'They come from outside. Maidenhead way. That's Mr Best, who's got the market garden, smallholding place. This is his field and Bertie Browning runs the garage on the Slough Road.'

'What about the children?' Pearl asked.

'I don't know all their names. There's our Randy, of course, useless kid, showing off to those little ones. The Richardsons's boy is called Toby, bit quiet, bit of a loner. That young girl is Liz something. Her mum and dad come from London. And the thin girl is Mary Powell. Her father died last Christmas, poor little soul.'

'What was school like in your day?'

'The old school used to be where the village hall is now. That man over there, Percy Gordon, I used to sit next to him in class. When I go in there now I can see it all again. Before the war.' She frowned like someone who has carelessly spilled a secret. 'Just before.'

Pearl looked towards her daughter who was talking with Edward Richardson and Adele. Most of the food had gone, the fire was glowering below the grill. Toby was still coaxing beer from the barrel. Liz, attempting to be delicate in lifting a glass of wine, tipped it on her dress and cried out. Toby glanced at her and then continued the glance around to see that they were concealed. He went to her with his handkerchief ready and began to rub down the front of her dress. At first she tried to push him away, but he rubbed the handkerchief slowly against her, his eyes becoming bright, and she lowered her hand to the front of his trousers and felt him there. An astonished smile broke across his face.

'So you were in Bedmansworth through the war?' Mrs Collingwood asked Dilys's mother on the far side of the tent.

'I'll say I was. Night-time we used to watch London burning. You could see it clear. We used to come up here, right up on this spot, where we are now and watch the guns and the searchlights and the fires. Just seeing it going on and thinking how those poor souls was suffering. I never could understand why they didn't all come out here with us. When they ought to have done. I said to my husband, long after, when he was alive, I said that Churchill should have ordered everybody to get out of London at nights and into the country and let the Germans bomb nothing, just buildings.'

She pulled up breathless. 'I like talking to you, Mrs Collingwood,' she said. 'You seem to bring me out.'

Pearl saw that Rona was still with the Richardsons. She asked Mrs Durie: 'Do you remember the Americans being here?'

'The Yanks,' her face lit at the thought. 'Oh, I'll say I do. I was just the right age then, and single, of course. Like film stars, we thought, talking like Clark Gable and giving us gum and jam. My old mum used to look forward to me coming home with a tin of jam or luncheon meat. They had lovely luncheon meat.'

Mrs Collingwood asked: 'Were they billeted in the village?'

The other woman tried to remember. 'Some but not many. They had some sort of place, like an office, where St Sepulchre's is now. But most came from further, and there was the Poles as well. They were buggers, those Poles. Oh, I'm sorry, Mrs Collingwood, it's not like me to swear. But they was. Buggers.'

'Maybe one afternoon, when you're not too busy,' suggested the American, 'we could go over to Windsor and take a look at the Castle. Rona doesn't want to keep me company all the time. And she's started painting again. We could have some tea.'

By the time people began to drift down from the field to the village it was fully dark. The single street lamp was supplemented by the dim light in the church and the shreds

130

of a moon, and the windows of the cottages and houses in the street were lit and open because it remained a warm evening. Some of the people who had been at the barbecue went into the Swan and others into the Straw Man. Above them, attracting no attention, planes came into Heathrow, their landing lights like candles in the purple sky stretching far back over distant London.

'Did you like it when I put my hand on your things?' whispered Liz slyly as they walked, clutched against each other.

Toby glanced behind them. The nearest walkers were fifty yards to the rear; he could hear the vicar laughing. 'Loved it,' he said, leaning and kissing her on her pale, damp neck.

Liz giggled with the wine. 'I just wanted to make sure you had some,' she said.

'Did you like me rubbing you down the top bit of that dress?' he asked.

'It was all right,' she said blandly. She squinted down at the dim front of her dress. 'Didn't get the stain out though.'

With another glance behind he pulled her more tightly against him. 'Let's go somewhere,' he whispered. 'If we go back there'll only be the television.'

'Clive James is on,' she told him. She appeared to weigh the conflicting attractions. 'All right, we'll go for a walk, if you like,' she decided casually. 'Let's go down the Slough Road. Didn't think much of that wine. I like my wine stronger than that.'

'I'd rather have scotch to that beer,' he boasted. 'A few pints and I've had enough of that stuff.' With a further backward look, he guided her from the village street to the Slough Road. In the anonymous distance appeared a yellow flashing light and the drone of a waspy engine.

Toby groaned. 'God, it's that nutter Bernard Threadle.'

'My mum reckons he's a peeping Tom,' sniffed Liz. 'She heard something in the front garden once and my dad went out and there he was, that Threadle, on his hands and knees in the bushes. Reckoned that he'd seen somebody climbing our wall. Trying to look into our windows more like it. Dad told him to bugger off and vigilante in somebody else's garden.' The bouncing light ahead began to slow. 'Oh sod it, he's stopping,' she sighed.

Bernard halted. The machine almost fell onto its side but he saved it desperately. ' 'Evening, youngsters,' he said raising his visor. He shone a torch in their faces. 'Ah, it's you two. Just checking. Off somewhere?' He lowered his torch.

'Just an acid party,' Liz told him wanly.

'Where?' asked Bernard swiftly. His eyes blinked. 'Where is it? You shouldn't be going to acid parties. Come on, where is it?'

'Reading,' said Toby.

'Reading? But that's miles.' He returned the torch to their faces. 'Are you having me on?' he said.

'No,' said Liz emphatically. 'Would we do that? We're getting a lift from the main road.'

Bernard turned the torch on his own round face. 'You can see I'm being dead serious,' he said into his own glare. 'If you go to this acid party I'll go straight to your fathers. I know where you both live.'

'I know you do,' answered Liz. 'My dad caught you crawling in our front garden, remember?' Bernard had lowered the torch from his face but they saw him react in the darkness. 'That . . .' he stumbled. 'That was a mistake . . .'

'It's not what my dad reckoned. Anyway don't worry yourself. We'll be all right.'

They turned from him and walked on. Bernard's snort was answered by the snort of his motor cycle. He revved it feverishly and started off towards the village. 'Watch this,' laughed Liz. She emitted an echoing scream. Cupping her hands she shouted: 'Help! Help!'

They heard the motor cycle coming back through the dark. They hurried on, laughing wildly.

Bernard skidded to a halt abreast of them. 'What was that?' he demanded, balancing dangerously.

'What was what?' asked Toby. Liz pretended to search the hedge.

'Screams,' Bernard said heavily. He sniffed around as though he might detect something. 'Somebody calling for help.'

'We didn't hear it,' said Liz blatantly. She looked at Toby. 'Did we?'

'Probably a cow,' suggested Toby. 'When they moo it sounds like somebody calling for help.'

Bernard put his torch to his face and glared at them again. He transferred it to them once more. They were regarding him innocently. 'Wasting my time,' he mumbled helplessly. He pulled down his visor, turned the thin vehicle and crackled down the road towards the village. Toby and Liz clutched at each other in their laughter. They hung and held onto each other. 'There's the bus shelter down there,' she said resourcefully. 'Let's go in there.'

Hugged together they stumbled to the bus shelter.

'Does it pong?' she inquired sniffing close to the door. 'People come and pee in here.'

'Want to go around the back?' asked Toby. He was desperate not to lose her now.

'No,' she whispered. 'Inside it'll be safer.'

It was going to *happen* at last. He *knew* it. Toby could feel his breath constricting and his heart bumping against his chest. They guided each other into the pungent darkness. He leaned her against the lapped wooden wall and kissed her feverishly on the mouth and all over her neck. 'I'll get splinters in my bum,' she mumbled. But her lips sucked his chin and he began to rub her scarcely detectable breasts. 'Not too hard,' she whispered. 'They might fall off.'

'I'm bursting out of my flies,' he groaned.

'Don't do that,' she choked. 'Don't burst, darling.'

It was the first time anyone but his mother had called

him darling. 'I can't stand it any longer,' he moaned. 'Can I take it out?'

'No, I'll do that for us. I know where to find it.'

Feverishly they kissed again and both wiped their chins. Her eyes were brazen in the dark. She dropped both hands to his fly and unzipped it with a tug of triumph. 'I can feel it,' she whispered. Her fingers plunged inside. 'There!'

'Christ, so can I,' he responded, gritting his teeth. 'Hold it, Liz. But not too tight.'

She manoeuvred his penis over the elastic on his underpants. 'It's quite a size,' she said in a low voice. 'As they go.'

'Let me,' he groaned. He lifted the hem of her dress and grappled with her knickers. Somehow he got them down around her straight thighs before cramming his eager fingers inside them. 'Lovely soft hair,' he murmured.

'What did you expect, bristles?' she whispered. They sniggered against each other's faces.

'Let's do it, Liz. I can't stand it like this. I'm going to go bang.'

'Don't go bang. They'll think it's at the airport.' She had become composed, enjoying watching him in his excitement. 'Have you got something to wear?'

'To wear?'

'Not like an overcoat. A condom,' she said. 'Like they tell you on television.'

'No. I haven't.' Panic made his voice tremble. Oh God, he could not let himself lose her now. He must not fail this time.

'Why haven't you?'

'Well . . . because I haven't. I don't just carry condoms around. This . . . doesn't always happen . . .' He withdrew his hand from her and put it against her face. 'But, there's no need,' he pleaded. 'I'll be really careful and I'm not HIV positive either, I'm positive. Come on, Liz.' Casually she rubbed his penis tip with her fingers again and he put his hand back inside her elastic waistband. 'All right,' she decided. 'But don't blame me.'

His desperation was washed away with relief. 'I love you Liz,' he groaned. 'I wouldn't let you come to any harm.'

They clutched passionately at each other. As they did so a rough male voice outside the bus shelter said: 'Want to go in or out?'

'Stay out here,' said a woman. 'People go and do their business in there, dirty pigs.'

The boy and girl gripped each other in fright. *'We'll* do our business out here,' laughed the man outside.

'You're crude sometimes, Curly, you're really crude,' the woman said.

'You love it,' he told her. 'Go on, deny you love it.'

'I love it,' she confirmed, her voice low. 'I'd love it now, Curly.'

Liz tried to pull Toby's zip up and caught his skin. His face creased in the dark and his mouth opened in a silent scream. She tugged it down again. He took his hand out. They remained holding each other and afraid. Regular thuds came from the outside of the bus shelter. They could feel the wooden wall vibrating.

'I don't reckon that pub gets any better,' said the man's voice conversationally. The thumping continued.

'They ought to have some music,' she agreed breathlessly. The wood was sounding like a drum.

'Have one of them karaoke bars,' he said. There was a pause. 'There.' The thumping and vibrations ceased. Toby and Liz remained locked and motionless.

'That was all right,' said the man in the tone of someone finishing fish and chips. 'Enjoy it?'

'Lovely, Curly,' she whispered. 'You know I always do.'

'Better get you home. Harold will be wondering where you are.'

'He'll be gone up to bed. He always goes straight after Clive James,' she said.

They moved away and the two young people saw their shadows shuffle by the open door of the bus shelter. 'I've got to go,' said Liz after a full minute. 'I feel sick.'

'Me too,' whispered Toby. 'That was horrible.'

Unspeaking, Edward and Adele Richardson walked down the dewy field leaving the knot of people still outlined against the red flush of the barbecue fire. The tent, with its lantern inside, glowed like a lantern itself. At the gate Bernard Threadle was fussily preparing to push his motor cycle up the slope.

'Why don't you leave it here, Bernard?' suggested Richardson. 'You'll only have to wheel it down again.'

The vigilante's expression suggested that Richardson had found some flaw in an otherwise perfect plan. 'Can't, sir,' he answered solidly after consideration. 'Mustn't be parted from the vehicle.' He began to manhandle it up the slope. 'I might ride down,' he called back at them.

'He probably thinks somebody will steal the thing,' said Adele.

'It's his persona,' Edward said. 'Away from the bike he's not himself.'

'That's an official sort of word,' she observed. She walked slightly ahead and did not look at him. Her earlier irritation remained. 'Persona.' He did not respond. Sometimes he felt it was better to say nothing. Adele pursued it spitefully. 'Is that the sort of word you use in your reports?'

'It can be useful,' he said without emphasis. They walked silently through the village, below the church wall, by the lych-gate, skirting the green. Both inns were now closed but they could see Mrs Mangold's shadow as she cleared up. The sound of muted television programmes murmured from some houses, the windows still open on the warm night. 'What did you think of Mrs Collingwood?' asked Richardson eventually.

'Mrs Collingwood and her daughter,' said Adele as if

correcting his oversight. 'I simply cannot think what they came here for. A very odd business.'

'It is,' he said. 'One day they may tell.'

The coughing of Bernard's motor cycle now trailed them along the street. 'Oh, damn,' breathed Adele. 'The Lone Ranger again.' Her expression dropped further as the sounds decelerated. The armoured figure wobbled alongside them.

'I meant to tell you, Mr and Mrs Richardson,' said Bernard. 'There's a big acid party, so watch the youngsters.'

'An acid party? Where?' asked Richardson.

'Reading, according to my informants.'

'Thanks,' said Adele almost snapping at him. 'We might go over there.' Then, with finality: 'Goodnight, Bernard.'

'Yes. Goodnight then,' said Bernard touching his helmet in a hurt way. 'I'll be on my way.'

'On your bike,' muttered Adele as she walked to the front door. They were inside by the time he had gone back up the village road.

'He's harmless,' said Richardson. 'He only thinks he's doing some public good.'

'I deal with them all the time,' she said with weary irritation. 'So does everybody working in the social services.'

They stood in the close dimness of their hall. He switched on the lights. They looked at each other immediately as if to make a check then both looked away. 'The damn world,' she said, 'is full of potty people who mean well.'

'Do you want a drink?' he asked, knowing they were going to quarrel.

'No thanks. I'm going to bed.' She remained at the foot of the stairs. 'I want to know one thing,' she said firmly.

'What's that?'

'Why didn't you tell me about this hijack business?'

He shrugged but turned towards the French window. The curtains were open and he could still see the glow of the Burridges' tent. He felt a touch of envy for them. 'It was nothing. Some mentally deranged Arab.'

'Why didn't you tell *me*? Everyone else damned well seems to know. Even that Lettie. Bramwell Broad was telling everyone in sight.'

Richardson said: 'He can't keep his mouth shut. We prefer it if these things don't get about. It frightens the passengers.'

'Oh shit,' she said bitterly. 'You and your bloody passengers.' She mimicked him: 'It frightens the passengers. I felt a bimbo, believe me, when I didn't know a damned thing about it.'

'You'll never be a bimbo,' he said quietly. He was tempted to add: 'Not now.' She stared at him, then turned and walked sadly and angrily up the stairs. 'You've got an odd set of priorities,' she said from the landing. He suddenly thought how they had both aged. 'Any other man would have come home and told his wife,' she said her voice low. 'To hell with it being a secret. What's it a secret for anyway? It's bloody ridiculous. We *are* married, you know.'

'And have been for some years,' he replied. He felt sorry he had said it. She was looking hard at him as if trying to remember him from a previous time. 'I did not want to worry you,' he said shrugging.

'It worries me more, you not mentioning it,' she said with finality.

He began to mount the stairs. 'I'll go and spend an hour in the observatory,' he told her.

'Go on,' she responded. 'Stare at the damned stars. Tell *them* your secrets.' As he went towards the study she had her last word. 'Give my love to Venus.'

'Venus is . . .' He halted. He had meant to retaliate but in the end he could not bring himself to do so. He almost said instead: '. . . the evening star.' It was a moment when, facing each other in their hopelessness and anger, they might have tried to save themselves; either one by just reaching out. But neither did and the moment passed.

Heavily he climbed the steps to the observatory. He heard

their bedroom door shut fiercely. A few minutes later he heard the front door open and shut almost as strongly and for an alarming moment he thought that Adele had gone out again. Then he realised that it was Toby coming in. His son trod heavily on the stairs and he heard the door of his room close.

He moved into the articulated seat, adjusted it and settled back in silence and relief. Years away the stars were as unworried as ever. He sometimes liked to imagine he could hear them calling softly to each other. He turned the switch and the music began, the long, eerie, aching music of Walton. It filtered to his ears and he swung the telescope across the breadth of the sky.

Now, despite his growing unhappiness and doubt, he sat back in the chair and swivelled the telescope to the southern horizon. It was his most fruitful hunting ground because to the north the ever-luminous airport diffused even the gleam of the stars.

He knew what he would find to the south. The heroic Hercules, Ophiuchus, the Bearer of the Serpent, and the Serpent itself, Serpens. The Pleiades, with its million stars seen tonight as it was shining 22,000 years ago. He could not believe that they were only beautiful chemicals, somewhere there must be a cool, calm star, or several, or many, where beings peered through their telescopes at the earth and wondered if they would find any sign of life.

He felt himself dozing as he watched. He looked at his watch. It was quarter past two. He disentangled his long body from the telescope with his usual difficulty, turned off the stereo, extinguished the lights in the glass dome, and went with care down the steps to the warm landing. He went into the spare bedroom and only taking off his shoes, stretched himself on the bed and went to fitful sleep.

Seven

Autumn was less than glorious in the threadbare countryside around the airport. Fallen leaves cloaked mud, unkempt trees rattled while the wind shrieked through the strident pylons and their long, looped wires. Skies grew colder. Grey planes arrived and took off from Heathrow with a computerised monotony unaltered by the seasons.

Edward Richardson left Bedmansworth at eight thirty on a September morning while the Reverend Henry Prentice was already sweeping leaves from below the lych-gate of the church. He slowed the car. 'I'm more of a recumbent than an incumbent,' said the vicar straightening up. Uncertain sun lay in patches across the old sides of the church and gave the golden ball with its arrow a rich hue. 'It's a fixed feast this one. Where are you off to, Edward?'

'Mombasa, East Africa,' Richardson called back from the car. 'All our people there have gone down with beriberi.'

The vicar leaned on his broom. 'You'll be there before I've finished this lot, I expect,' he forecast. 'Then tomorrow there'll be some more to sweep. God timed the seasons rather inconveniently. The leaves drop when the children, who might be persuaded to sweep them up, are back at school.' He regarded the wet pile mournfully. 'And the Scouts don't want to know. Bob-a-job is history.'

He laughed resignedly and Richardson moved the car on. They all lived in a small world. He thought, not for the first time, how odd, yet how ordinary, it was that on this Monday morning, the villagers, Jim and Dilys Turner and

Mrs Durie at the Swan, Mrs Mangold polishing the brass in the Straw Man, the vicar grousing at his leaves, Adele driving to her social services desk, Toby on the bus to Windsor, Bernard Threadle trapped behind his chemist's shop counter, Anthony Burridge under his bowler, heading for London, and all the others were occupied with their unremarkable concerns, while he was going to a distant continent.

He passed the school, its playground filling, and had rounded the bend onto the old rural road before the motorway, when he saw Rona Train at the bus stop. He slowed and stopped the car.

'Am I going your way, Rona?' he asked leaning towards her. 'I'm going to Heathrow.'

'Just the place,' she smiled.

'You're not leaving us?' he asked. 'I hope not.'

She laughed. 'No. And especially not by bus.'

She got into the car beside him making him at once aware of her nearness, the brush of her skirt, her arm. 'I didn't know whether I was early for the bus or too late,' she said.

He moved the vehicle forward again and glanced sideways at her. Her deep eyes came around to face him. 'You can never tell with the bus,' he said hurriedly.

'I'd rent a car,' she said. 'But it really doesn't seem justified. We don't travel far. Mother doesn't seem to want to move, to go anywhere. She spends her time rummaging around the church. She's been locked up in the vestry with the parish records. She's thinking of writing a history of Bedmansworth, so she says. I'm going to try some sketching at Heathrow.'

'How long have you been drawing?'

'A few years. Five or six. I only try,' she said. 'I don't think anybody really *believes* they can draw or paint. I guess even Monet and Matisse were only trying. It's a comforting thought.'

'Sketches at the airport,' he mused. 'Well, there's plenty of movement.'

'I was worried if it would be okay. How do I get by about the security? I'll only be in one of the terminals and I'll sit there quietly and rough things out as the basis for a series of paintings.'

He thought about it. 'I don't think there could be any problem,' he told her. 'It's hardly loitering with intent. If you do have any difficulty, just give my office a call. I'll give you my card.'

'That's kind of you, Edward.' Rona glanced slightly at him.

'I'm off on a trip,' he said. 'But I'll tell my secretary to get somebody to help you if you have any problems. Her name's Harriet. She enjoys skirmishing with the security people. They've tried stopping her when she's riding her bicycle. They think she looks suspicious.'

Rona laughed. 'She rides a bike at the airport?'

'You should see her. Six feet tall and wears short shorts.'

They were on the main road going west. He stopped at the lights. 'My office is just about in the middle of the three terminals on this side,' he told her. 'Come up and have a coffee and I'll introduce you to Harri. Then if you have to call her you'll know each other. Will you be coming here to sketch on other days?'

'I'd certainly like to.'

He parked the car and they walked towards his office. 'It's like a city, isn't it,' she observed as they went along the pavement. 'A moving city.'

'Fifty thousand people work here,' he said. 'Not counting those trying to get in and get out.' A United Airlines Boeing appeared, apparently from the middle of the building before them and steeply climbed an invisible hill.

'You love it, don't you,' she said watching with him as it vanished, leaving a paw-mark of smoke low on the horizon. 'I can tell.'

'It fascinates me,' he admitted. 'I can never get used to it.' He touched her elbow and they went into the lobby of the office where he checked her through security, then through a further set of doors where Richardson had to play out the numbers on a dial.

'Where are you flying today? Or maybe I shouldn't ask?' she said.

'East Africa. Mombasa. All our station staff are in hospital, struck down by some bug. We're flying replacement people there but I've got to sort it out, which is not going to be easy, knowing Mombasa.' They had reached his office. Harriet was in the storeroom adjoining. He could hear the cups. 'Morning, Harri,' he called. 'We have a visitor for coffee.'

Harriet came from the back room, pole like, bespectacled, and wearing cycling shorts. She had once been described by a radio officer as thin as a morse message. She apologised as Richardson introduced them.

'I don't always look like this, honestly,' she said. 'Do I, Mr Richardson? I get changed when I get here. I was just about to put my dress on. I'm decent by nine o'clock.'

'Harriet is one of the pioneers of cycling at Heathrow,' smiled Richardson.

'Reviving it,' corrected the secretary. She indicated the fading airport photographs on the wall. 'See, there's a delivery man on a bicycle in this one, another just dismounting outside the tent here and here, look, two air hostesses on bikes, and wearing white gloves.'

Rona stepped towards the photographs. 'That's amazing,' she said reading the inscription below the main picture. 'Heathrow nineteen forty-seven,' she repeated. 'Well, well. Tents and bicycles.'

'Even the bookshop is in a tent,' said the secretary pointing.

Richardson said to Harriet: 'Mrs Train is going to do some sketching in one of the terminals.' Harriet smiled in a knowing way he did not recall seeing before. Her nose

143

wrinkled as she glanced sideways. The slim American woman was still studying the photographs. Rona turned. 'I hope I won't be in the way.'

'Everyone gets in everyone's way at Heathrow,' observed Harriet. Richardson said to her: 'If there are any problems with security or anyone, I've asked Mrs Train to give us as a reference. So she may telephone for help.'

Rona said: 'I hope it won't be necessary. I'll sit quietly in a corner.'

'That way they're bound to think you're suspicious,' laughed Harriet. 'Everyone else is in a frenzy, even when they're sitting.' She went outside and brought in the coffee on a tray. The telephone rang and Richardson picked it up. He laughed. 'Hello, Doctor. Well, you'll be going a bit further than Fulham today. You've got the faxes and all that stuff. Hope you've got your passport. Right. I'll pick you up on the way.' He checked his watch. 'The flight's at eleven fifty. There's room in First Class today, I hope.'

Rona finished her coffee and picked up her case. 'Terminal Three is in front of you as you go out of the door,' said Harriet. 'The others are not far, One and Two that is. Terminal Four is miles, practically at Gatwick. I'll have to come down with you to check you out. They won't let you into these buildings, and then they won't let you out.'

When Rona had gone down with her Richardson sat behind the desk staring ahead, then stood and went to the window. She was walking on the opposite pavement towards the terminal. Harriet returned. 'A nice American lady,' she said carefully.

Richardson did not look up. 'She is,' he agreed. 'Have you got a complete list of the personnel at Mombasa?'

'I'll get it,' said the secretary disappearing into the store. She emerged immediately. 'When Americans are nice, they're *nice*,' she persisted.

'Yes. She and her mother are staying in the pub down in Bedmansworth.'

'Here we are,' she said bringing over a file. 'Odd place to stay.'

His eyes came up. He took the file from her. 'This is dated August twenty-first.'

'There have been no changes,' she said. 'I checked when they asked yesterday. You'd think Americans would go into London, wouldn't you.'

He sighed at her assiduity. 'The old lady,' he said patiently, 'Mrs Train's mother, was taken ill on the way and they ended up in the village.' He was looking through the papers in the file. 'Bill Allsop was finishing next month,' he said. 'Due to come home.'

'End of tour,' she agreed. 'Back home on November thirtieth. What's wrong with them? Are they *all* sick?'

'Some dreaded African lurgi,' he said. 'That's why Dr Snow is coming.'

'He was married to an opera singer, you know,' said Harriet.

'A violinist, I believe,' he corrected. 'Poor old Allsop.'

'She went off with somebody,' said Harriet smugly.

'You seem to know a lot about Dr Snow.'

'His nurse cycles to work,' she explained. 'She's one of our movement. PEDAL it's called.'

'I presume that stands for something,' he observed. 'GROAN stands for Group Reaction Over Airport Noise, you know.'

Harriet said she did. She sat at her desk and stared into the screen of her word processor as if seeking a message or reassurance. 'We're trying to find some appropriate words to fit PEDAL,' she admitted. 'And they're still there then?'

'Who?'

'The American ladies, Rona and her mother.'

'Harri, I have to go to Africa.'

'I know. Your tickets are here.' She produced them. 'I was only interested.'

'I'll keep you posted,' he promised.

He signed a sheaf of letters. 'The rest of it will have to wait.'

He picked up his travelling bag and his briefcase. 'I'll call when I get there,' he said moving towards the door. 'Anything otherwise, put it on the fax.'

When he had gone Harriet went and changed into her office dress. She returned to the room and, imitating Rona Train, walked precisely to the photographs on the wall. 'I'll sit quietly in one corner,' she said mimicking the American's voice. She turned towards the door from which Richardson had exited and poked out her tongue.

Dr Snow, unsuitably tweed suited, was standing anxious faced with his two cases. As Richardson arrived, his surgery nurse followed with a newly-purchased toilet bag. 'There's toothpaste, razor, shaving cream, everything you'll need,' she told him pointing each one out. She said to Richardson. 'He's like a boy going on an outing. Next he'll be wanting a bucket and spade.'

'What's the latest on the patients?' asked Richardson. 'God only knows what it's like in the office down there. It's always chaotic and with all of them smitten at once it must be murder. We've sent out a couple of chaps as stopgaps. They went yesterday.'

The Scot peered over his glasses at a fax lying on top of the machine. 'Well, they're all still pretty poorly by the sound of it. They're in an American missionary clinic.' He looked up quizzically. 'Rather better than the local hospital, I would guess.'

Richardson glanced at the clock on the wall behind the desk. 'We should be going,' he suggested. 'I have a couple of things to check at the terminal first but I won't be long.'

'I'm ready,' said the doctor picking up his bags. His nurse patted him on the arm and then kissed him on the cheek. To Richardson's surprise she said: 'Don't be nervous.' Snow looked a little peeved but then grinned unsurely at Richardson. 'Nurse Robinson seems to have got some notion that I'm worried about flying. And me, an airline doctor.'

The nurse studied his tweed suit. 'Are you not going to be a little warm in that?'

'I'll take my coat off,' said Snow.

Richardson regarded him curiously. 'You don't fly a great deal, do you,' he said.

'Not really. Every year for the Tchai Festival, that's all.'

'He *could* go anywhere,' sniffed the nurse disapprovingly. 'Staff concessions and the like. But he doesn't.'

'It's like Harriet, my secretary,' said Richardson. 'She could travel all over the place for ten per cent and she prefers cycling.'

'I go to Suffolk, it's very level,' said the nurse. She looked at Snow unconvincingly. 'It's quite safe, flying,' she said.

'I'd rather it be *safe*, than *quite* safe,' the doctor said. He turned to Richardson. 'I'll be all right as long as I don't look down.' The nurse kissed him on the cheek again and like a mother ushered him to the door.

The two men went from the building. 'Was it you suggested I came?' inquired Snow screwing his face to study an aircraft rising into the sun.

'We needed a medical man from here,' said Richardson. 'And I thought you'd like the change. I hope you won't miss too much Tchaikovsky?'

'Nothing outstanding this week,' Snow assured him. He was a deliberate walker and Richardson had to reduce his normal brisk pace. 'Su Yung played the violin concerto on Saturday at the Barbican. She's very good.' He looked reflective. 'Those wee Orientals are marvellously dedicated,' he said.

'There won't be much Tchaikovsky where we're going,' said Richardson.

'I shall listen to him in my head.'

They went to the airline crew room and then towards Departures. At once Richardson saw Rona sitting against the window watching passengers go through the first gate check. 'I see a friend,' he said to Snow. 'She's doing some sketches.' They went over to her. She was drawing quickly on a block. She looked up and Snow blushed as Richardson introduced them.

Richardson asked: 'Are we allowed to see?'

'It's just skeletons,' she said exposing the pad. 'Outlines.'

'A good place to sketch,' approved Snow. 'A lot of dramas at Departures.'

'It certainly is,' agreed Rona. 'Already I've seen more tears, more rending apart, more brave faces, more vanishing smiles, than you'd see anywhere. Look there.'

They watched a young woman tightly embracing a man who was telling her not to cry, making her smile with some joke. Abruptly, as though wanting to be done with it, her arms remaining spread but now empty, he strode towards the gate showing his ticket and his boarding pass. He rolled his hips as he waved goodbye. She was still trying to laugh and not to weep as he vanished through the door, going into another room leading to another country, perhaps another life, another woman.

As he went she turned and her ordinary face collapsed into sobs which she carried in her hands towards the exit stairs where she paused and looked back hollow faced as if he might reappear.

'He's not coming back,' said Rona softly.

'He may never,' agreed Snow shaking his head.

'Or he may,' said Rona. 'And maybe she'll not be here to meet him.'

'At Departures you see it all,' said Richardson. He glanced at the doctor. 'I think we'd better go on to our particular drama,' he said. He laughed quietly. 'I can't imagine what it would be like for someone to cry when I was going away,' he said. He glanced at Rona. 'It becomes so ordinary.'

He and Snow said goodbye and walked through Departures. After they had gone beyond passports and put their hand luggage through the security X-rays, Snow said: 'What a beautiful woman. And gentle.'

'Yes,' said Richardson. 'She is.'

As they made their way to the plane Snow dropped to silence. Richardson knew that there were people afraid to fly although they earned their livelihood at Heathrow; perhaps that was why. Harriet had once looked from the office window at yet another airliner hanging unsupported in the sky and said: 'The most I want my feet to rise above the ground is on the pedals of my bike.' There was a Heathrow air traffic controller who could not be levered into an aeroplane. To him, aeroplanes were all-too-adjacent dots on a tight screen, far out in the long drop of the sky.

'Years ago,' remembered Snow when they were sitting at the gate, 'in the fifties, I was in Turkey and I hitched a lift to Paris in an American Air Force freighter.' It was almost as if he needed to get it off his chest, talking to fill the clean, dismal and vacuous room where they waited with two hundred others for the flight to be called. 'There were no seats and I spent all night on the deck jammed against a fellow who was coughing his life away. First it was cold, then it was hot. When I couldn't stand it any further, I went up to the flight deck. And my God! They were all *asleep*! It was on automatic and the pilot, co-pilot, flight engineer, were all snoring.'

Richardson regarded him wryly. 'You might have gone on forever like the Flying Dutchman.'

'Until the fuel ran out,' corrected the doctor.

'How did they wake to change course?'

'An alarm clock,' Snow said glumly. 'They had a tin alarm clock.'

The ground stewardess at the head of the long room switched on her microphone. 'Flight AB430 to Mombasa and Harare is now ready for boarding. Passengers with seat

149

allocations numbering fifteen to thirty-three please board now. Have your boarding cards ready.'

Snow rose, stretching his tweed legs resignedly. Richardson said: 'Let them all get aboard first.'

'The longer I can keep my feet on God's earth, the better,' said the Scot. 'What's Mombasa like?'

'Mid-Africa,' shrugged Richardson. 'Urban mid-Africa, I should say. High-rises, a triumphal arch or two and the rest slums.' He grimaced at the tweed suit. 'You won't need a jacket,' he said.

'I can take it off,' said Snow. 'It's not an encumbrance.'

'Most airline crews don't go out of the hotel in Mombasa,' continued Richardson. 'Aircraft to hotel, hotel to aircraft and that's it. A surprising number are not very adventurous.'

Snow surveyed the African passengers lining with their bundles and bangles. One man carried a pair of bicycle wheels as hand baggage and another a wrapped car exhaust. Many of the people were glistening ebony, the women in bright shawls and furled native headdresses, the men in uncomfortable western suits.

'We've kept Mombasa going, a bit of leftover from the days of the Empire,' said Richardson. 'One day, I suppose the company thought, it was going to prove useful again as a staging post to South Africa. And that's how it's turning out.' Most of the passengers had boarded now. The two men moved forward and the man and the girl at the gate recognised Richardson. 'Couldn't you find somewhere else to go, Mr Richardson?' grinned the man glancing at the computer screen.

'I could, but the firm couldn't,' shrugged Richardson. They walked through the inclined, carpeted tunnel. 'This is my first wee nasty bit,' suggested Snow in a Scots whisper. 'Like walking through the Fallopian tube.'

At the door of the aircraft the cabin service director

greeted them. 'Room in First today, Mr Richardson, Doctor,' he said a little under his breath.

'So I heard,' said Richardson as the man went before them into the cabin. He smiled encouragingly at Snow. 'Champagne and canapés.' They sat in the two front seats, Snow next to the window. As soon as he was seated he scrutinised the ground and then, like a man making a final decision, pulled the shutter down. 'We're right in the nose,' he muttered leaning towards Richardson. 'There's nobody out there.' His finger pointed dolefully. 'Not a soul.'

'Not even the pilot,' said Richardson. 'He's upstairs.'

Snow ran his teeth together. 'So if we should . . . er . . . say tip forward this position will hit the ground first.'

'Roughly, yes. But I don't believe they're planning that for today.' The steward appeared with a tray of champagne and Snow brightened. He and Richardson briefly toasted each other. Richardson said sympathetically: 'I understand, believe me. For myself, I have never worked out how they keep a train on the railway track. And there are times when they don't. Travelling at over a hundred miles an hour when you're still in contact with the earth doesn't fill me with confidence. The air is a good deal softer. And the way trains wobble and the way they skim past each other, inches between them . . .'

Snow was slow to convince. The engines of the Boeing began to hum. 'It doesn't seem natural, that's all,' he said. 'Every time I see a plane take off from Heathrow, and I'm there almost every day, I feel uncomfortably sure it's not going to make it.' He sipped his champagne furtively. 'And need they fly so *high*?'

Richardson grinned. They both accepted another glass from the steward. 'It must be difficult for you when you make your annual trip to Tchaikovsky,' he suggested.

'Sheer and utter terror,' admitted Snow. 'My love of Tchaikovsky fighting my fear of flying.' He brightened again briefly. 'But now it's easier, now the Iron Curtain is no more,' he said. 'I'll go by train.'

They passed over the broad, deep green snake of the Nile Valley, curling between fawn deserts. In a couple of hours the great heads of the mountains of Africa were reduced to an exhibition: peaks embroidered by clouds, smudges of ice smitten by the sun. The stupendous Rift Valley, stretching in a swathe, had shrunk to a tyre track. Edward Richardson looked at the doctor who was still asleep, his lips palpitating with a snore. They had changed seats and Snow was now on the aisle. Edward thought he might wake him and show him how things were diminished; so he could realise how wonderfully arrogant the aeroplane was, crooning above it all, high and mighty, beyond everything. But another snore rippled from his companion. Richardson left him to sleep.

An hour later they had tacked away from the mountains and were cruising over a serpentine river. From their initial altitude it appeared as a thread but towards the conclusion of the journey as the plane lost height, it thickened to a brook, then a stream, and then became a great waterway, spreading itself across half the visible land, its sinews brown and glossy. At a touch from the steward Snow awoke and adjusted his seat. As the plane descended further, villages came into view along the river banks, boats and logs floating on the flow; then the cobwebs of more habitations until they were low and roaring above thatched huts and yards. Snow sat up as a herd of goats scampered under the plane's shadow. People waved from the ground. The lights of the runway appeared, streaming alongside. The aircraft flattened and bumped down as though onto a cushion. 'Welcome to Africa,' said Richardson.

'We made it,' said Snow fully waking. 'Amazing isn't it.' He stretched towards the window, beyond Richardson's shoulder, and grinned 'Well, well,' as though he had never believed it was really there.

Mombasa Airport was renowned for chaos; pyramids of luggage confronting puzzled officials running with dockets. An Indian customs officer shrugged at the delay: 'One of the conveyor belts out of action,' he sighed. 'For past two years.'

They carried only hand baggage but it took almost an hour before they were clear of complex immigration. The passport officer studied Snow's photograph intently and then transferred his examination to the doctor's face. 'Not a good likeness,' he commented handing it back. 'Not for a doctor.'

They emerged eventually into the airport's fetid forecourt where a man in a red singlet and shorts was struggling to start a bus with a cranking handle; two buffalo grazed on the verge; balancing women passed them with suitcases and bundles, their hands gesticulating, conversing as they padded by, showing no awareness of the burdens on their heads. A spare young girl followed with a bundle hovering above her straight face. Her opal eyes shyly, fearfully, turned on the two men.

They went first to the company's airport office. It was brown and hot inside the room, a single fan, turning tiredly, like a fighter weary of taking on all-comers. Flies droned across the ceiling. There was only a nervous clerk there. He knew nothing.

Richardson was unsurprised. He asked Snow: 'Do you want to check into the hotel or go straight to the patients?'

'Go and see them,' said Snow decisively. 'The sooner the better.' He had taken off his heavy jacket and was sweating in his flannel shirt and tweed trousers. Richardson directed the driver of the dusty car to the American Mission Clinic. The man did not know where it was. Getting out he went to other drivers and the Englishmen watched them arguing. He came back cheerfully and said: 'These men know nothing. I find it.' He restarted the engine.

'I suppose in a place like this a hospital is a luxury,' observed Snow viewing the passing town. He wiped his sweating face with a red handkerchief. There were huts and shanties and ranks of black-mouthed workshops with cannibalised cars piled outside and half-naked men who swung blow torches. Chickens, goats and dogs scavenged through debris. Men sat cross-legged beside dilapidated walls and clogged waterways. One was kicking a donkey which wearily tried to kick him back. There were stalls and cooking fires upon which lumps of flesh smoked and massive pots boiled. Scarcely clothed children sat scraping the dust. A dignified man occupied a stool below a tattered sunshade engrossed in a ledger, a counting frame beside him. A youthful woman, handsomely black, stared arrogantly at them as the limousine passed her. The windows were shut so that the air-conditioning could function and few sounds penetrated, so the exterior drama was in dumbshow. A clutch of ragged men toothlessly shouted and waved arms like bones in a greeting or a threat.

'It's like Hogarth,' said Snow wonderingly. 'Like Rowlandson.'

'These are the people who can't get any bribes,' Richardson told him. 'They have no money, no power, nothing to give. Everyone else is on the make. From the politicians to the police, with doctors, teachers, and a whole ladder of people in between, each one taking and giving backhanders. And the ones at the top of the ladder. They just take. What you see out there are the *unnecessary* people, bottom of the heap.'

The car went over a flimsy bridge spanning a creek of muddy mauve water.

'They can't get out of it,' Richardson continued. 'They buy candles to read books if they can get the books, and if they can read, just in the hope of getting some job an inch above the rest. Any village shop here sells pathetic pencils and bits of paper and candles and copies of *The Power of Positive Thinking*.'

The driver called back. 'Bwana, I think I find the place.'

They turned off the dust-clouded road into a gateway between glaring white walls. Two black boys were painting the stones that led up to the door of a low building with shuttered windows. The driver pulled up and opened the door. At once the buzzing heat of the day closed like a trap around them. Snow's handkerchief was wet. 'God, but my legs are hot,' he muttered. The boys painting the stones looked up with large, dumb eyes. A black woman in a bright white nurse's uniform came to the open lobby.

'The three men we have here are much improved,' she said rubbing her hands like someone satisfied with a job accomplished. Richardson sighed his relief.

'There were four patients,' said Snow. He had now, naturally, taken charge, a suburban man in a strange, heated country.

'One man, Mr Allsop, would not come.' The woman rolled her heavy shoulders in a shrug. 'Wanted to stay at home. Maybe he'll die there.'

At her invitation Snow followed her into the clinic leaving Richardson outside. 'They may have something that you haven't had a jab for,' he suggested. 'If you get it, that will be big trouble.'

'What about you?' asked Richardson.

'My blood is like kerosene, laced with Famous Grouse,' said Snow solemnly. 'Nothing will touch it.'

Richardson walked into the forceful sun of the garden. Flame trees bordered the road. The sky hung hard blue over shrubs lolling in the heat. Brilliant flowers lay across the stone path. It must have been a private garden at one time, some colonial nabob making it his home from home, with penny labourers, and twopenny gardeners. There he would sit on African evenings dreaming of Sussex.

There was a teak seat below a brilliant jacaranda and he sat and looked down a lawn of tufted grass, dense as a rug, to the overwhelming colours of the flame trees and the native shrubs. His flying fatigue, which in years he had never conquered, lay on him. He felt his eyes droop.

He remained there for half an hour, almost asleep, before Snow reappeared, and came along the path. 'They're on the mend,' he said gratefully. 'Some sort of amoebic infection. Very nasty indeed, but the clinic people did a good job.' He looked at Richardson quizzically. 'But Allsop wouldn't be admitted. Flatly refused. I don't like the sound of that. We should go and see what his situation is.'

'He's a funny chap,' said Richardson. 'A bit lonely. He's an Aussie but he's lived in England for years.' They drove out of the town, below two triumphal arches erected over hopelessness.

'Is he married?'

'Yes, but his wife stays home.'

They were abruptly engulfed in traffic, trucks, buses, rickety cars and shoals of cyclists. African life eddied about them. Along the roadside were oily workshops, open cooking places. A man cut through a metal drum. Another was lying under his bicycle with three engrossed children standing over him. 'He's been knocked down by the look of it,' said Snow. He glanced at the driver in front. 'I'd better take a look.'

'Only drunk,' the driver called casually over his shoulder. 'Drunk so he fall off bike. See, they take him.'

Two men were carrying the man to the side of the road. One of the children, a boy, had mounted the fallen bicycle and was joyfully riding away.

Over his shoulder the driver continued: 'No special time for drunk in Mombasa,' he said. 'He eat when he can get, he drink when he can get. Sometimes he get, sometimes not.'

Allsop's house stood back from a wild beach where palms lay prostrate, there were miles of empty sand and waves came in blue and white and fierce from the Indian Ocean. It was a wooden bungalow, its paint peeling in the salt wind. There was no garden, only a track running from the beach. A dog was tied below a tree and it barked hysterically at them. The driver had been there before. 'He had a boy,' he said as he pulled up. He searched about him. 'But not now.'

'I'll go in first,' cautioned Snow again.

'But I know Bill Allsop well,' said Richardson.

'You don't know what he's got though, do you?' returned Snow getting out of the car. He walked along the path to the shabby door. The dog, choking on its rope, tried to reach him.

Richardson left the car by the other door and walked down towards the sea. The breakers came in like empty grins. The driver followed him and loped at his side. 'This man good and sick,' he confided. 'He go crazy when they want him go to hospital. I saw. Won't go. Tell everybody fuck off.'

A shout came from behind and they turned and saw Snow at the door in the distance. He beckoned and Richardson hurried up the beach and through the legs of the palms. The driver stayed and began to throw pebbles at the breakers. Snow looked suddenly haggard. 'He's not up to much,' he reported. 'He's very poorly indeed.'

'I must see him,' said Richardson. Turning his eyes sharply at Snow, he said: 'What do you think it is?'

'He's told me what it is,' said the doctor. 'According to him he's got Aids.'

Shocked, Richardson said: 'How . . . how the hell did he get that . . . them?'

'In this part of the world there is a selection of ways,' said Snow sombrely. 'He found one. I'd say he's dying.'

The doctor closed the latticed shutters and Allsop thanked him. He had been a big man, now sprawled, shadowed and helpless, in the unkempt bed. Richardson tried to fix his expression for he had known Allsop a long time. 'The birds

Australia

kept flying in and crapping everywhere,' said Allsop apologetically about the shutters. 'I just couldn't get out to do it. The houseboys have buggered off. They have a sixth sense. Even at night the bastard birds got in and there was a monkey too. Came under the shutters. I chucked a bottle at him.'

The discourse exhausted him. 'Haven't said that much for God knows how long,' he muttered lying back on the stained pillow. 'Haven't had any sod to talk to.' Richardson realised he was talking quickly only to cover his embarrassment. He casually touched the narrow hand.

'You should have had some proper attention, Bill,' he said. Allsop's great gaunt eyes looked at him. Even the effort of lifting the lids seemed almost too much. 'We'll get you fixed up, don't worry.'

'Too late, Edward, old mate,' muttered Allsop. He glanced at Snow. 'Ask the doctor. He knows.'

Snow regarded him gravely. 'It's never too late.' It was inadequate and he knew it.

'It is with this lot,' said Allsop. 'A lot too bloody late.'

'You should have come home right away,' said Richardson. He sat on the cane chair at the side of the bed. He remembered how Allsop's face used to be, broad, big nosed, and a zig-zag grin.

The Australian assembled part of the zig-zag. 'What would my missus have said? "I've just come home, darling, because I've got a sexually transmitted disease." That would go down a treat. She thinks STD has something to do with telephones.' He moved with difficulty in the greasy bed. Together Snow and Richardson helped him. Snow said: 'We'll get some clean linen here. You should really be in hospital.'

'What about our other blokes?' asked Allsop. 'I wouldn't want to be with them in that clinic. There's enough on their plates with whatever they've got without having a bloke who's pegging out from Aids in the next bed.' He glanced at Snow. 'They're on the mend, then.' It was wistful.

'They should be all right,' said Snow. 'A wee local virus. It's you I'm concerned about.'

'Ah, what's a life? It's over sooner or later anyway.' He regarded Snow solemnly. 'You'll sweat your balls off in those trousers, Doctor.'

'I am,' said Snow. 'I thought it would be like Bournemouth.'

They all laughed and Allsop looked at each of them, one each side of the bed. 'I didn't know I had it until I got taken with this other thing, the lurgi the rest of them have. One of the local quacks, who's not a bad bloke, gave me a blood test and he told me. Then, with this new infection, it started to gallop. And it's galloping all the way home now. Straight for the line.' He lifted his sparse arms. 'As you can see.'

Resignedly he collapsed back on his pillows. Through the shutters came the drone of the ocean. 'That's all I hear all day,' he grumbled half shutting his eyes, as if the action would block the sound. His thick eyebrows and the rings below his eyes formed complete black ovals. 'Been driving me mad, those waves, breakers. I'm Robinson Crusoe but with complications.'

'We'll make arrangements to get you back as soon as possible,' said Richardson realising the hollowness of the promise.

'In a long box, you mean,' said Allsop. He closed his eyes completely then a quarter opened them. 'That will be simpler.' His purple tongue licked around his lips. 'The whole bloody thing's a bit futile, isn't it, anyway. All the whole show. I used to play golf once, you remember, Edward.'

Richardson nodded. 'We had some good times,' he said.

Allsop said quietly: 'I played on the edge of the Sahara once. Fourball. Right on the side of the desert. And there was I trying to tap in an eighteen-inch putt, for a win and a tenner. You know, concentrating. Then I realised I had an audience. Some Bedouins on their camels. They'd stopped and were watching me putting. I can see them now, looking at me with a sort of pity. Disdain. Fancy spending your life knocking a ball into a hole.'

Richardson said: 'You were a good putter, Bill.'

'I suppose you want to know how I got it,' said Allsop. He laughed in a cackle. 'Not the putt, the Aids,' he said.

'There's no need,' said Richardson.

'It happens,' muttered Snow. 'As we know.'

'I've got to tell you,' persisted Allsop. 'I wouldn't like you to think I'd picked it up from another bloke. I wouldn't want Brenda to think that either. We've been apart most of our marriage, but that's our business. Because one of us had to live in some of these awful holes it doesn't mean that both of us needed to. Have you got a cigarette?'

Neither Richardson nor Snow had. 'There might be some in the kitchen,' Allsop pointed. 'I can't remember. In the knife drawer.' He laughed sourly. 'I used to keep them there like a warning. By the carving knife. That represented death, you see, and I could see it if I was ever tempted to smoke again. But it looks like we've got around that little problem. I could do with one now.'

Snow went into the kitchen. Once he had gone Allsop began to cry quietly. 'Oh, Ted, what a fucking state I'm in.' Richardson leaned forward in a clumsy embrace.

'It'll be all right, Bill,' he said helplessly. 'We've just got to get you out of here.'

Allsop dried his eyes like a child and suddenly asked: 'How's the company?'

It took Richardson by surprise. He said: 'All right, I suppose, considering the general situation,' he said. 'They keep threatening us with economies and redundancies, rationalisation they call it. Cuts for this and that. A lot of the time I'm out of the way.'

160

'Watch them, mate,' said Allsop as if he knew something. 'That Grainger, he'd piss in paradise.'

Snow came back. 'Found them,' he said holding out a packet of cigarettes. Shakily Allsop took them. 'And a lighter,' added Snow. He lit a cigarette for Allsop.

'Nobody else?' asked Allsop. Neither of them smoked but they each took a cigarette and lit it, Richardson awkwardly. 'It's been a long time,' he said.

'Getting you into bad habits,' said Allsop with his cackle again. 'There's a bottle of scotch in there too, Doctor. Let's have a snort, shall we. Make it a party. Get a few willing women in.'

Snow had seen the scotch. He brought the bottle in and three glasses. 'They're new, never used,' said Allsop nodding at the glasses. 'So don't worry.'

Richardson, muttering that he should not think like that, poured the scotch. 'Don't be so sure,' said Allsop. 'You can get Aids from any bloody thing in Africa. From the air even. This lot was from a nice girl in Dar Es Salaam.' He glanced at them through the smoke of his cigarette. Snow began coughing over his. 'Takes a while to get used to it again,' he apologised.

'Knew her for years,' said Allsop thoughtfully. He sighed. 'It's better than biting your knuckles. She was fun. Knew the missionary position upside down and inside out.'

They laughed and he cackled. A pall of smoke was now lying across the bed. The three men puffed on arduously. 'I'll be gone this time next week,' said Allsop. 'Probably sooner. I won't keep you long.'

Snow half tilted the whisky bottle over the bed in an invitation and they each had another glassful. It was clammy in the room and it was now adrift with smoke. Coughing, Allsop handed around the cigarettes once more. 'Might as well use them up,' he said. 'And the scotch.'

They continued drinking and smoking. They drank toasts, proposed in turn. To the airline and its employees. To that bastard Grainger, the only man to piss in paradise, to themselves and their loved ones, to Tchaikovsky, to Jupiter and Mars, to people with Aids, particularly those in Dar Es Salaam. They began to laugh heavily, especially Allsop. Snow went into the kitchen and found a bottle of gin.

'No' as good as scotch,' he said philosophically. 'But then nothing is. But it will do.'

He poured the gin neat. Richardson began to feel the room going around slowly with the smoke. Allsop asked: 'It's an old medical tradition, isn't it, Doc, helping a man to die, easing his way . . . ?'

'The doctor and the priest,' agreed Snow. 'And it's the doctors who drink. But I don't think you've got to worry, Bill. There's life in you yet.'

They fell to silence, three sad and drunken men surrounded by smoke.

'Let's have a bit of a sing-song,' suggested Allsop. With abrupt extravagance he flung his arms wide and his gin splashed from the glass onto his face. 'I've had a belly full of silence.' Snow leaned over and tenderly wiped the gin away with the sheet. He replenished Allsop's glass. 'A sing-song,' the Scot agreed, his head wagging. 'Cheer us up.'

'You start,' encouraged Richardson. He slipped from the chair to the floor and had difficulty in regaining his seat while they laughed hideously. 'Go on, Doc, start,' he encouraged. 'You like music.' Snow thought only for a moment. Then he sang:

> 'Speed bonnie boat,
> Like a bird on the wing . . .'

All three men howled: 'Onward the sailors cry!'
  His voice wavered:

> 'Carry the lad,
> That's born to be king . . .'

They chorused: 'Over the sea to Skye!'

When he had finished the others madly applauded.

Richardson felt his whole body was spinning. The smoke whirled like clouds around a high aeroplane. They said it was his turn so he sang:

> 'Where have you been all the day,
> Billy boy, Billy boy . . .
> Where have you been all the day,
> My Billy boy . . .'

Allsop was rocking to and fro in the bed. 'My old dad used to call me that,' he interrupted. 'My Billy boy.' He began to cry. 'If he could only see me now. His Billy boy.'

He sniffed back his tears. 'He used to like a song, my dad. He was a Londoner, you know, went out to Aussie after the first war. But he never forgot where he was born.'

He gathered his wasted frame together in the bed. The bones at the top of his chest stood out like rafters. Clutching his pillow with one hand and his gin with the other, he sang as loud as he was able:

> 'I'm Burlington Bertie,
> I rise at ten thirty,
> And stroll down the Strand
> Like a toff . . .'

Haphazardly the others joined the song, getting the words and the tune drunkenly wrong, but eventually joining together for the chorus:

> 'I'm Burlington Bertie from Bow . . . ow . . . ow,
> I'm Burlington Bertie from Bow!'

Out from the solitary bungalow flew the song, the London

words mixing with the sea, the sound of the palms, and the wind from the foreign ocean.

The airline office in Mombasa was a shop in a row of shops, the only one with a proper window. In the window there were posters and display cards showing Big Ben and the Beefeaters at the Tower of London, the green sweep of the Thames through Runnymead, the Malvern Hills, and a lighthouse. A scrawled notice said: 'Apply Inside!'

It was next to a doctor's surgery where sick Africans squatted dull eyed on the pavement. A child lay between its mother's legs as though dead, buzzed by huge flies, a man tried to hit a youth with his crutch. On the other side of the road was a fetid eating house where sizzling chickens were hung in the open; flies darted at the hot chicken skins like daredevil pilots, and the exposed fire paled under the sun's flare.

Agitated, Snow walked into the office. 'Have you seen what's out there?' he said to Richardson. Richardson lifted his head from the desk where he was trying to organise some flight services with a nervous, nodding junior, white faced from England and a big-hipped native girl who hummed pop songs.

'The Savoy Grill,' suggested Richardson. 'Local style.'

'No, I mean the surgery. Those patients look as though they've been sitting in the gutter for days. There's a lad there with open sores and insects scampering all over him. There's another who's got flies instead of eyes. And a torpid child.' He thrust his head forward angrily. 'I really feel I should do something about it.'

'Don't,' said Richardson. It was a half-warning, half-plea. 'Please don't. If the local quack finds you're queering his pitch he'll call up the devils in no time, the ho-ho devil and the eeby-jeebies and all the rest of them. And that will stir things up, believe me. We don't want to have an office here with no windows. Or a window with no office. How is Bill?'

Snow regarded him bereftly. 'He wants to go home.'

'Christ,' breathed Richardson. He put down his pencil. 'That's a humdinger. What can we do?'

The doctor shrugged. The English junior and the African girl, who had stopped humming, were watching him. 'Can we have a few words?' he suggested.

Richardson rose and went into the inner office. It was almost dark in there, the window shuttered, a single electric fan toiling its poor best in the dense heat. Richardson switched on the light.

'I think we ought to take him home,' said Snow simply.

'With Aids?'

'He's unlikely to have sexual intercourse on the plane.'

Richardson thought about it, then said: 'Grainger would go mad. And he wouldn't be the only one. Jesus, if it got out.' He took in Snow's expression. 'All right,' he decided. 'Stuff Grainger. Let's take him.'

Snow smiled as though with relief and supported himself on the edge of the low dusty desk, with a lopsided chair and a battered cabinet the room's only furniture. Richardson sat on the other end and as he did so the desk, as though it could take no more, broke complainingly along a join at its middle, tipping the ends down and depositing both men on the floor. Richardson quickly regained his feet, brushing himself down. He helped Snow. 'The ho-ho devil?' suggested the doctor.

They further dusted themselves. Dirty clouds came from their trousers. Richardson looked at the cracked desk. 'It's like a big open mouth,' said Snow almost dreamily. 'A scream.' He became businesslike. 'So you think we can get him out?'

'I don't see why not. If we keep it quiet. He can just be another disabled passenger. We pride ourselves on disabled passengers.'

'He's babbling of green fields,' said Snow. Richardson said: 'Poor Bill. All right, I'll make the arrangements. I've just been checking on tonight's flight. It's fullish from Harare but I imagine we can get three quiet seats somewhere.'

'Good,' said Snow. 'I'll go and tell him. It should cheer the man up. The bungalow's all been cleaned up and the new boys you sent are there. It's surprising what double wages does. There's another lot hanging about outside the gate. But he hardly wants to eat and I think our piss-up put him off the booze for life, what he's got left.'

Richardson looked sombre. He checked his watch. 'We'll get him to the airport early, push him through all their red tape. They make it up as they go along here. It sometimes takes three bloody hours to check in.'

They draped a blanket around him in the plane, his thin head poking from the top so that he looked an ancient, wild-eyed monk. 'Great,' he whispered to Snow. 'I'm going home.' He half bent towards Richardson on the other side. His neck was so narrow Snow thought it looked as though it would snap. 'To see the wife.' Few of the other Club Class seats were occupied. He smiled a terrible smile. 'I could do with a glass of champagne.'

'It's coming right up,' said Richardson. He could see the steward in the galley balancing the tray. The man brought it to them. He looked at Allsop and then looked at him again carefully. 'Hello sir, Mr Allsop, isn't it?'

Allsop seemed unwilling to admit it. He nodded over the rim of his blanket.

'And what's happened to you, sir?' said the steward as he distributed the glasses.

'Fell off an elephant,' answered Allsop.

'He has no' been too well,' put in Snow primly enough to make the steward move on. Snow raised his glass and Allsop raised his without taking his hand from below the blanket. Snow could see the edges of his fingers like a pair of scissors. The three men touched glasses. 'I'll drop this one afterwards,' whispered Allsop. 'Break it.'

He drank his champagne quickly, as if it were a medicine and then fiercely broke the glass on the bulkhead in front. Richardson beckoned the steward and he came and took away the pieces in Allsop's napkin. He brought back another napkin and another glass of champagne. Allsop cackled when he had gone away down the aisle. 'Some customers cause a lot of trouble, don't they,' he said.

The local airport authorities had kept the plane on the ground for an hour after its scheduled leaving time, an everyday trick enhancing, as Richardson well knew, their penalty fees for late departures. It had been necessary to bribe the baggage loaders.

Eventually, as the flight took off, Allsop peered over Richardson's shoulder at the receding lights below. 'Goodbye Africa,' he muttered sadly. 'Good riddance. And good riddance to me.'

At once he became apologetic. 'Sorry Ted,' he murmured. He turned to Snow. 'Sorry, Doc.' He head dropped below the grey airline blanket. 'I appreciate what you're doing,' his muffled voice emerged. 'Against the rules.'

Quietly, Richardson said to him: 'I don't know of any rules, like that. Disabled people have as much right on flights as anybody else.'

'Thanks, anyway. Both. I won't inconvenience you by snuffing it during the flight. I know how complicated that can be.'

He fell asleep. They took it in turns to stay awake. They went out to the crew's galley in turn and ate from a tray there. At three forty in the morning Allsop died. Richardson, who was awake, felt him stir and heard him say: 'Fuck it.' He leaned over and pulled at Snow's sleeve. The doctor blinked and turned immediately to Allsop. He looked up after a minute. 'He's gone,' he said. 'He won't see England now.'

Eight

Furtive as a spy, Bramwell stepped delicately into the hotel
lobby. Barbara spotted him at once and watched with
amusement while he scrutinised the surroundings through
thick, dark glasses. She sidled behind one of the rubber
plants in the lounge. Eventually he all but tiptoed into the
extensive room and, while making a show of being casual,
checked on the occupants. She emerged from behind the
screen of leaves and with a final swift glance left and right,
Bramwell briefly smiled and came guiltily towards her.

'You really enjoy the secrecy, don't you,' she told him.
'I've never seen anyone look so suspicious.'

The waiter came for their drinks order. After he had gone
Bramwell again turned his eyes around the lounge. She
laughed. 'Stop it. You don't think Lettie is going to turn up
here?'

'Her brother may have followed me,' he said half seriously. 'He was a jungle tracker. I swear he's got a machete
hidden down his trouserleg.' His expression changed: 'Are
you looking forward to this? I am.'

She smiled and said: 'I've always enjoyed going to Nice.'
As she leaned towards him, she was interrupted by the
waiter with their drinks. When the man had left, she said:
'Listen, if it doesn't sound too cold-blooded – as long as we
both know the rules, Bram, then it's all right. But I want
you to stay faithful – only *me* and your *wife*. No playing
around elsewhere.'

Bramwell blinked. 'I think this will be as much as I can

manage,' he smiled back uncertainly. He checked his watch. 'We should go soon.'

As Barbara was finishing her drink she glanced over the room and out into the foyer. 'Georgina,' she said almost to herself. 'That's funny. I thought she was working. She was going to Los Angeles.'

He peered in the same direction. 'She's gone,' said Barbara. 'I'd swear it was her.' They rose and picked up their weekend cases. As they went towards the foyer she asked quietly: 'Where are you supposed to be, by the way? As far as Lettie is concerned?'

He grimaced. 'Away,' he said.

'Just away?'

'To Lettie away is away,' he said. 'She never asks where I'm going or where I've been. I'm like a one-man football team – home or away.'

They had reached the animated lobby. Briefly they looked around. 'It certainly looked like Georgina,' repeated Barbara. 'She was in uniform.'

Outside they got into their separate cars. Parked four places from Bramwell's Vauxhall, although he failed to see it, was a red Porsche. He drove out and at the exit waited until he saw Barbara's car in his mirror. They turned onto the dual carriageway, doubled around the roundabout and went back towards the airport entrance.

By that time Georgina had taken off her uniform and was in her silver slip. She lounged into the chair, slipping into her part like an actress, in her fingers a long-stemmed glass of wine, its sheen reflected by the table lamp onto the silk undergarment. Her client was late. Ten minutes after the appointment time the doorbell rang and he was there, pink faced and perspiring, frustrated in a winterweight suit and a starched shirt. Over his arm he carried a macintosh and in the other hand was a corpulent briefcase.

'You've been held up,' she said in the tone of a fond and anxious wife.

'Bloody Hammersmith,' he replied in a relative voice. 'Flyover jammed to hell. *And* I came by taxi and the fares have gone up again.'

Sympathetically she guided him in and smoothed him down with a drink. The art was making familiars of strangers. She was relieved to hear he had travelled by taxi. That was why he was carrying his raincoat. If he had arrived in a car he would have surely left it in the vehicle. She was nervous of unnecessary macintoshes.

Once she had him settled he calmed. The colour reduced in his face. 'Love the slip,' he said toothily. 'Exactly right. Almost silver.'

'It was what you wanted,' she answered gently. 'I had to buy it specially.'

'Well, I expect you'll use it again,' he told her like a man practised in doing deals.

'You didn't require the uniform,' she said making conversation to use up the time. Already his ten-minute delay had been counted into his hour.

'The stewardess get-up?' he said scathingly. 'No damn fear. See enough of those when they fling the plastic trays around. No, no,' his voice deepened. 'The silver slip is fine.'

Five minutes later he was pedantically hitching it up to her hips. 'Fantastic,' he approved. 'Love this stuff. Silver silk. Always liked airships and Zeppelins and things. During the war, when I was a kid, I used to masturbate looking at the barrage balloons.'

Georgina, wearing Candy's face, lay near to him and gave herself up to a few minutes of his more-or-less innocent madness.

It was evening, darkness gaining, by the time they reached Nice, the lamps of random villages studding the sides of the Alpes Maritimes. West, across the Bay of Angels, the last of the daylight was pared. The plane banked above the inky sea bordered by the lights of the city.

'I've never done this before,' said Barbara quietly but suddenly. Her face was away from him; almost as if she were telling herself. 'Going off with someone.'

'I'm flattered,' said Bramwell uncomfortably.

'With a married man,' she explained turning to him. 'I've had serious boyfriends but nobody married. There was Charlie who used to take me away and I'd hardly see him again. Played golf all the time. He'd come back to the hotel exhausted and not be able to move his legs.' Her eyes met Bramwell's. 'You're not a golfer are you.'

'I would never take you away and then not be able to move my legs,' he promised.

'Another was a steward, Patrick.' She seemed to need to tell him. 'He was just trying me out. Well, trying *himself* out. I was his final attempt at being straight. But I failed him. He went off with another steward. Then along came Marcel who was killed in a crash. The aircraft went into the Mediterranean and he was never found.' She looked briefly through the window. 'He could be down there now.'

Bramwell held her hand and kept holding it as the aircraft lost height and dropped into Nice-Côte d'Azur Airport at the sea's edge. 'I've never done that either,' she said easily squeezing his fingers. 'When I've seen people holding hands, taking off and landing, I've often wished I had somebody to hold mine.'

The night air was close and calm as they left the plane. French Immigration and Customs were preoccupied with a televised football match. Even the men on check duty kept looking over their shoulders. Formalities were swift.

The hotel was off the Rue Smollett. They had a bottle of champagne. Barbara stood at the long window of their room watching the mountain lights.

'Those people live up in the sky,' she said.

'Same as us,' he pointed out. He stood behind her and,

setting down his glass, moved his arm around her neat waist. He could feel the brief mound of her stomach. She turned from the window and pushed her fingertips up the sides of his face. 'We mustn't expect too much from this,' she said frankly, looking into his eyes. She dropped her forehead against his chin. 'Just a bit of pleasure.'

They kissed and a breeze filtered through the open casement pushing the lace curtain against her hair. He moved a little way. 'You look like a bride,' he grinned.

'Not me,' she said. 'And *not* in a veil. A nun, maybe.'

They fell onto the bending bed and lay there against each other. She wriggled her shoes off and said: 'Where are we going to have dinner?'

'Do I have to feed you first?'

'You certainly do. I want this to be romantic.'

She eased herself from him and padded into the bathroom. He watched her thinking how it was that a woman became a girl when she walked without shoes. The bathwater began to run. He stretched back on the coverlet and listened to her sounds. She began to sing in a small voice. A finger of steam beckoned from the door.

'Would you like another glass?' he called.

'When I'm in the bath,' she answered.

He lay back again, a tranquil smile moving across his face. Someone began to play a piano in a room quite near.

He poured the champagne and asked her if she were ready.

'Ready, when you are,' she called.

Holding the two glasses he went in. She was in the bath sitting up, froth piled around her. Her nipples were covered but the tops of her wet breasts glistened. He kissed her on her damp lips and handed her the glass. His hand touched the slope at the side of her bosom.

Barbara quietly took his hand away but kissed his fingers. 'This is going to be very good isn't it,' she said. 'I know it is. I want it to last.'

He stood away from the edge of the bath. 'I'll find out from the concierge where we should eat,' he said.

He went into the bedroom and she started to sing again, a trite, incorrect song. While he was speaking on the phone, she appeared at the bathroom door wearing a cotton Victorian robe that went to her feet. He said 'Merci' to the concierge and, taking her in, put down the telephone.

Bramwell regarded her gravely and she walked, like someone who had made up her mind, towards him. He had remained sitting on the side of the bed and she pushed him firmly backwards onto the quilt, and climbed on top of him. 'I'm too young,' he whispered.

'Stop it,' she smirked. 'I've come for you.'

His hands went around her buttocks, warm from the bath, sliding over the cotton robe. Then he brought them to her waist and to her breasts. They kissed each other's faces. 'Show me how,' he mumbled.

'Stop fooling, Bram,' she warned. 'This is lovely.'

'I have to take my clothes off.'

'I'm not shifting.'

'I'll have to manage.'

'I'll help,' she promised.

While she still lay lightly above him they manoeuvred his shirt off. She assisted with his trousers, tugging at one side while he levered the other. 'I must escape,' he moaned.

'You sound like Bulldog Drummond.'

'Bulldog Drummond?'

'My father liked him. You must meet my father.'

'Some other time.'

When he was naked, she remained prone above him, her body taut beneath the plain robe. He helped her to ease the front of it up a little and felt her damp and friendly legs against his. 'Are you staying up there long?' he inquired.

Barbara had become dreamy. She mumbled: 'I was just playing' and languidly rolled away from him. He turned on all fours. Her hands fondled him. Warmth filled him. He

173

pushed away the gown at the front, exposing her stomach and he kissed the cushion. 'Let's take our time the *next* time,' she suggested half opening her eyes directly in front of his face. 'I'd like you now, if you don't mind.'

'As I am?'

'As you are,' she confirmed quietly.

He shuffled towards her, a movement at a time. They touched and joined and he advanced further, his face concerned, hers verging on a smile, her nice nose uplifted, her eyes tightly closed. They moved, tentatively at the beginning, but then firmly and finally with fierce passion. When it was finished they lay languid and relieved, heads together, hands holding. He kissed her nipples with his tongue. 'I wondered if you'd noticed them,' she whispered.

'I was keeping them for later,' Bramwell said.

'What happens when you've loved me all over?'

'We go back to the beginning.'

'You'll go back to Lettie,' she teased sadly.

'But then I'll come back to you.' He uncoiled from her. She tugged the bedcover across them. 'Now you've really done it,' he complained. 'Mentioning Lettie.'

They lay thoughtfully, scarcely in contact, cooling. She said: 'What are you going to do about Lettie?'

'Run away and never come back,' he said. 'The trouble with her family is you can't just throw them out of the house.' He recited the roll call. 'Her mother and her brother and our Pauline. They won't go. Every time they're off to the pictures I hope against hope they'll keep going and somehow arrive back in Manila. But they come back. They're always there when I go home.'

'What about Lettie?' she asked.

'I should never have brought her over,' he said.

'Where you live can't be anything like the Philippines.'

'Bedwell Park Mansions isn't a lot,' he agreed. 'But . . . I feel . . . well, I'm responsible for her.'

'I'll say you are. Do you love her?'

'If I did I suppose I wouldn't be here with you now.'

'Or with anyone else,' she said. She kissed him abruptly. 'It was lovely, wasn't it? For a first time.'

Tenderly he traced with his finger from her right nipple, drawing it across her breasts and laying it against the left. They kissed and Barbara said: 'It's terrible when two people get together and they do what we've just done and then they've got nothing else to say. We must find out all about each other.'

'We could discuss what we've just done,' he suggested. She eased her legs together and in one movement slid from the bed and trailing her robe behind her walked towards the bathroom door. 'You're lovely, you are,' he said lying back against the pillows. 'I could fall for you.'

She waggled her bottom at him and kicked her leg back around the door.

She bathed and dressed and he followed her. They felt surprisingly comfortable in their friendship. He poured the rest of the champagne and sat on the bed and watched her putting up her hair. 'There are few better things in life than observing a good-looking woman messing about with her barnet,' he said watching her over the top of his glass.

'Could you really fall for me?'

'I could give it my best try,' he said. He got up and stood behind her, kissing her on the small of her neck and placing his hands on the skin of her shoulders.

'Fix my clasp, will you Bram?' she asked, holding up a gold chain. It was slender and the light of the room caught it like a strand of hair. Carefully he looped it around her neck.

'The little ring opens and fits into the other little ring,' she instructed watching him in the mirror.

He did it and said: 'I'm going to be very useful to you.'

'I need somebody useful.'

When they left the room they both sensed it was as though they had long been familiar. She had put out all the lamps but one, had tidied the bed and laid her gown across the foot of it. Bramwell opened the door and when they were in the corridor locked it. It was like a known routine.

'Who looks after the key?' he said.

'I'll put it in my bag,' she said holding out her hand.

They walked along the carpeted corridor. Briefly he stooped to examine a used tray left outside a door. 'Room service looks all right,' he said.

'We must try it sometime,' she said. Their fingers locked.

'Isn't this surprising?' she said.

'You mean, us getting on like this.' He nodded. They were at the lift.

'Yes. I feel we've been with each other for years.'

There was a cobbled street outside, the stones dimpled in the glow of old heavy lamps and the windows of the shops. 'The concierge knows our secret,' said Bramwell. 'Did you see him roll his eyes?'

She had her arm lightly in his and they strolled comfortably. Barbara said: 'This is the first time we've ever walked like this together. We seem to be doing things in the wrong order.'

'Our romantic concierge has asked the restaurant for a special table,' Bramwell told her doubtfully. 'I don't like the sound of that. You don't want an order of gipsy violins, do you?'

'If you promise not to sing,' she said.

The evening was still genial, the shadows of passers-by were wrinkled on the worn cobbles. People ate at white-clothed tables on the pavement and a youth played an electronic keyboard making a sound like an old hurdy-gurdy. The restaurant was not far. There were diners sitting in the open air but they were led inside and into a separate room. 'What do you think we'll talk about?' asked Barbara.

'I could tell you some lies,' he suggested as they surveyed the room.

There was a table set in an alcove and the rest of the area was occupied by two substantial oval tables, each laid for eight. The waiter detected Bramwell's doubtful expression.

'*Monsieur*, it is very good,' he assured them. '*Très discret*. And we have no more places.'

They sat down and Bramwell ordered drinks. He grinned at Barbara across the table and she reached her fingers towards him. Then she picked up her menu and said, while she read it, and without looking over its top: 'This *is* just for fun, isn't it?'

'Like a hobby?' he asked. He peered over his menu.

'Yes.'

'You can become engrossed in a hobby.'

'Obsessed,' she agreed.

Their serious eyes met and as they did so a party, a family, was led into the room by the head waiter who was patently pleased to see them. They were conversing in cultured but resounding English. 'Oh God,' muttered Bramwell. 'Pretend we're French.'

The party was arranged around their table by a tall, but slightly stooping, man who had once, it was apparent, been stiffly upright. He had thick hair and gleaming cheeks. 'Dodo, you sit there,' he pointed, his voice military. Dodo, a fluffy girl, obeyed, smiling in a docile way. A woman, her hands clasped before her and wearing a black dress and a distraught expression as if she would have rather been elsewhere, placed herself next to the host.

'And Reggie.' The man indicated the seat next to Dodo. 'That looks made for you.' There were four seats and four young people left. He studied them, first the seats and then the expectant faces and then the seats again, as though deploying forces to the most appropriate positions. 'Yes . . . well, Hugh and Prunella, you go next to each other. I'm sure you have lots to discuss. And Tertius here and you jostle in there Bonzo.'

They took their seats and the elder man sat in his and studied the arrangement with satisfaction. 'There,' he sighed. 'How grand that we're all here reunited again.'

'And at *our* table,' ventured Dodo.

'Our special table,' he intoned. She blushed.

'At *our* restaurant,' put in Bonzo dutifully. 'Anton's.'

'In the Rue Smollett,' added Tertius. He regarded the others smugly.

'Indeed,' summed up the father. 'Here we all are.'

'In *Nice*,' put in his mild and worried-looking wife, having the last word, perhaps uniquely.

They all laughed at their small performance. The elder man caught the eye of the hovering waiter. 'And I think, since we are here, pastis is called for.' Without awaiting their approval, he said: *'Huit pastis, s'il vous plaît.'*

'Would Smollett have approved of Nice now?' wondered Hugh. He had not contributed to the original exchange and he apparently now considered it his duty to lay the foundation of a discussion.

Bramwell touched Barbara's hand. 'I'm afraid this is going to be a performance,' he said. The waiter appeared and served the *moules* they had ordered. He poured the wine. None of the party had looked towards them.

'Doubt if Smollet would approve,' said the father. 'A bit of a moaning traveller, you know. Nothing ever really suited him.'

'He and his wife brought several weeks' supply of food with them in seventeen whatever it was,' put in Bonzo.

'Seventeen something,' agreed Tertius.

'Including larks' tongues,' said Bonzo doggedly. 'In aspic. And he just hated garlic.'

'You've been swotting up on Smollett,' accused Dodo.

They all laughed. 'On the contrary,' said Bonzo. The pastis was brought and distributed. They began to explore the menu and as they did so a second party was shown into the room. They piled against each other at the door with shrieks and ribald remarks. The man at the head was younger than the big father at the other table, but he had a stomach. He wore an expensive light suit bent around his middle. His wife, who followed him, sniffed short nervous sniffs and scanned the room as though the whole thing might be a trap. While the pair paused on the short flight of steps the rest, pushing untidily behind, peered around their shoulders. 'It's a bit dark, Mum,' said a perky girl.

'It's supposed to be,' answered one of the males. 'It's so you can't see what you're eating.'

'Would you mind,' demanded the father over his shoulder. He smiled and gave a smooth bow to the diners occupying the first large table. He led his entourage around the room.

'I'm not sitting next to Dean,' squeaked the girl. 'You know what he does.'

'Don't want you to,' said Dean, his hair thick and black as a bucket. The girl was mouse faced and wearing a pink and turquoise dress. ''Orrible,' she said. 'You are.'

'Sit down and stop nattering,' ordered the father. He directed a shrugging smile towards the other table.

'Yes, sit down, the lot of you,' put in his wife. Her head was sweating as it projected from a small fur jacket. She had a rose in her gingery hair. Her husband continued: 'You Josie sit next to Dean. I don't care what he does. And Mandy pipe down and sit the other side.' He reached out and contacted a nervous and hovering old lady, not looking at her but feeling for her as someone lost in the dark. 'And you Mum, you're there.'

'I hope I'm going to like it, Bernie,' she told him.

'Don't start moaning already,' Bernie replied still avoiding looking at her. 'There'll be *something* you can eat.'

'Didn't want to come in the first place,' she grumbled. She sat down and scraped her chair under her. 'From the start.'

'Let's pack up moaning and order some drinks,' said the father firmly.

179

'Not before time,' said Dean. 'I could do with a lager.'

'Pastis, we're having,' pronounced Bernie. 'Like the locals 'ave.' He peered blatantly over the heads of his own family to the adjoining table. 'Like those people next door.' His group, some revolving in their places, peered at the shocked diners at the next table. 'Eight pastis please squire,' he ordered loudly. 'On the rocks.'

'I only like sticky drinks,' whined Josie. 'Is it sticky?'

'Let your father be the best judge of that,' put in Bernie's wife. 'French drinks usually are sticky.'

Entranced, Bramwell and Barbara watched. Bramwell moved the shells of his mussels around his plate. Barbara avoided his eyes. Silently he poured wine.

Mandy, who had sat so far with vapid resignation, looked up at the fan revolving on the ceiling. 'Wouldn't like to get my 'ead caught in that,' she observed.

'The fan would come off worse,' nudged Dean.

Mandy scowled at the menu. 'Rue Smollett,' she recited. 'It's called the Rue Smollett.'

'Rue Smell-It more likely,' giggled Josie pleased with herself.

'Garlic, that's what it is,' said her mother informatively. Bernie darted looks around the family. 'Do you *mind*,' he said. The pastis arrived and was placed under suspicious noses. Bernie, with a paternal smile, raised his glass. 'Cheers,' he said. 'Happy holidays.'

'I'm not drinking *that*,' said Josie emphatically having tried it and banging her glass down with equal force.

'It tastes like 'orrible cough mixture,' put in Mandy. 'Like when we used to 'ave coughs, Gran.'

'That Dean used to be 'acking all night,' remembered the oldest woman philosophically. 'Coughing 'is lungs up.'

Bernie said: 'Well, we've come a long way since then.'

'Paganini died in Nice.' The father's intonation from the next table was deep and deliberate. Conversation among his company had been, at first, stilled by the advent of the second party and later exchanged in whispers, but now the original family began to gather its forces. From their alcove table Bramwell and Barbara watched riveted, their entrée almost untouched. Bramwell, pouring the wine, blindly missed the glass. The occupants of the second table, some turning in their chairs, gazed at the occupants of the first and hung on the father's next words.

'Playing his violin to the moon,' continued the senior voice. He, and his family, ignored the attention from the next table. No eye looked in that direction.

'Mad, I take it, quite mad,' put in Tertius. 'Poor Paganini.'

Bernie's family remained dumbly observing until Josie scraped her chair. 'English are you?' she asked cheerily. 'Like us. Where are you from?'

A frown worked its way around the other table. 'All over the shop actually,' offered Tertius at last. 'Herefordshire, Wiltshire, and . . . well, of course, London.'

'Leytonstone we are,' put in Bernie sonorously, assuming control. 'Just off Epping Forest.'

'Near London,' added his wife. She wagged her hand across the gap between the parties. 'You 'aving a good time?'

She was answered with mumbles. Two waiters arrived.

'Ah, here's our entrée,' said the first father with hearty relief. He turned half left. 'So nice meeting you.'

'Mutual, I'm sure,' said Bernie's wife. 'It's time we got ours. Where *are* they?'

Bramwell and Barbara watched as the two parties settled, like rival camps settling for the night having posted sentries.

The main course had been eaten by the first family and they were settling into their fourth bottle of wine. Abruptly and chummily, Bernie, his napkin at his neck splashed with sauce, called over the heads: 'What's the vino like then?'

The other father choked. Eyes glowered. 'Not all that nice then?' chortled Josie.

Tertius responded: 'It's something they reserve especially for us.'

'Ooooo, just listen to that,' demanded Mandy. 'Reserved *special*. In't that nice?'

Bramwell leaned towards Barbara. 'Now we should see some fun.'

'It is actually,' Dodo confirmed. It was as though it was her duty to take on the other girl. 'Extremely palatable.' She turned deliberately away and towards her father. 'Wasn't there some controversy over Paganini's death in Nice?' she intoned.

'So I believe,' replied the man ponderously. 'The body . . . ,' he could not resist a backward glance to the other group, '. . . was not properly interred for many years.'

'Poor bloke wa'n't even dead,' put in Josie loudly over her shoulder. 'Saw it on the box. Buried alive, they reckoned,' she looked doubtful. 'According to the telly anyway.'

'I reckon what I'm eating is what's-'is-name's leg,' said the grandmother. 'Paganini's leg.'

To Bramwell and Barbara it was unclear at which point the physical hostilities broke out or what critically ignited them. By the time the two families had reached the dessert stage they were both drinking copiously as if in defiance or competition. Josie said that she, anyway, was getting out of the rotten place, but her father ordered her back to her seat.

Then Bernie's wife bawled: 'What you 'aving for pudding over there?'

Shocked looks flew around the table before Tertius responded heavily: '*Petites fraises et chocolat* . . .'

'Fucking hell,' said Dean, looking into his spoonful of fruit salad.

'I beg your pardon,' said Tertius rising.

'You 'eard,' said Dean rising also.

They had been waiting for the moment and had weighed each other up. Both families sat transfixed. Bernie had his second brandy halfway to his mouth. He swallowed it at a gulp and choked violently, his wife banging him on the back. Josie picked up a salad bowl set beside the cheeses and threw it with abandon into the blades of the revolving fan above their heads. It was a wooden bowl and it struck with a splintering impact, flying around with the fan and then rocketing across the room sending pieces of tomato, lettuce, cucumber and peppers, plummeting onto the heads of both families.

It was the signal. At one moment everyone but the oldest lady, who bawled and waved her fists, was on their feet, shouting and threatening and at the next they closed for combat. Josie joyfully continued throwing dishes of food at the fan. Bramwell, like a Red Cross volunteer under fire, attempting to guide Barbara to safety, left the alcove table and then went at a crouch around the fringe of the mêlée, but a heavy metal bowl spinning from the fan struck him on the forehead and he fell spectacularly under the stumbling heavy forms of Bernie and the other father who were grappling like puffing leviathans. Bramwell lay at the base of a mound. The battle increased. The French staff tried to intervene but were thrust aside by both sets of protagonists as if this were no matter for them. Barbara frantically tried to extricate Bramwell from beneath both cursing fathers but he was the last to be released, and that was only after the police had arrived with dogs and tear gas. Bramwell was groaning bitterly: 'My leg, my leg.' The officer who examined him rose and made a puffing motion with his cheeks followed by an expressive fracturing mime with both hands.

Barbara surveyed Bramwell unhappily, from his foot which projected from the swollen trouserleg up to his pain-drawn face. 'What are we going to tell your wife?' she asked.

'That,' he responded heavily, 'has been worrying me.'

They had returned from the hospital and it was now almost daylight. The lanterns of the Port Olympe fishing boats were homing across the leaden bay towards their harbour. The lights of Nice had grown pale and the dark shoulder of Château Hill leaned heavily against the eastern sky.

'It could have been romantic,' she sighed. 'But it wasn't meant.' They were outside the hotel when the taxi had gone. Bramwell awkwardly stumped his crutches and said: 'I'm sorry about the romance.'

She kissed him on the cheek and began clumsily to assist him up the steps into the lobby. The night porter looked as if he might have been sleeping in a cupboard. He rose wan eyed and black chinned from behind his desk and wished them a puzzled good morning. He regarded Bramwell's disability with only semi-sympathy, not knowing whether it was an old condition or a recent injury. He came from behind his desk, one hand holding up his trousers, and opened the lift gates for them.

'I'm going to have to lie in my teeth even more than usual,' said Bramwell when Barbara had him propped against the wall of the lift. He sighed. 'Be sure your sin will find you out.'

Her face puckered. She needed to steady him with both hands as the lift jolted to a stop. 'Don't let me go,' he pleaded. 'Don't let me slide down this wall.'

She began to laugh and he jerkily joined her. 'Christ, what a mess,' he said emerging strut legged from the lift. 'And it's so bloody sore.' She supported him as they staggered and rolled towards the room and propped him against the door as she opened it with her key. 'Come on,' she said encouragingly. 'Let's get you on the bed.'

'If I remember rightly, that was the original idea,' he moaned as she guided him over the room. He looked through the curtains at the mountains tinted by the morning. 'We've been up all night.' He dropped one crutch.

'Perhaps you should have stayed in the hospital,' she

suggested taking the second crutch and easing him onto the bed. 'Mind the leg,' he kept muttering. 'Mind the leg.'

Closing his eyes he said: 'Stayed there? At their prices? It's going to cost enough as it is.' He groaned 'An arm and a leg' then opened his lids in alarm. 'Barbara, it's not the money – it's *explaining* it. I didn't think to take insurance.' He added wistfully: 'Somehow it didn't seem right, insurance on a dirty weekend.'

She shook off her shoes and stretched out next to him on the bed. 'It's *explaining* things,' he repeated. 'That's the trouble when you're married. How in God's name do you explain a hospital bill in Nice? Lettie's very hot on money.'

'You were supposed to be on duty,' she pointed out wearily. 'She'll think it's down to the company.'

'And the company won't pay. Knowing Lettie the first thing she'll ask about is compensation.' A further truth struck him. 'And, God, I'm going to be stuck indoors with our bloody Pauline.'

'Stop it,' Barbara said. 'You're making me laugh.'

She rolled towards him and kissed him. 'Watch the leg,' he muttered. He squinted at it down the length of his body. 'I couldn't help wondering if that doctor knew what he was doing,' he pouted. 'Probably a moonlighting taxi driver. I was afraid he'd set it the wrong way around, back to front or something.'

Her body rolled against him, and she laughed against his shirt. 'Oh what a tangled web we weave,' he said. She put her face to his and they kissed. 'Let's try and get some sleep,' she suggested. 'You must be exhausted. I am.'

She moved a cautious distance from the stiffened limb and slept almost as soon as her eyes had closed. Bramwell moaned as he moved but weariness engulfed him and he slept too, waking in pain, swallowing aspirin and drifting to unhappy sleep again. They awoke just before noon.

'Time to get to the airport, Bram,' she said. 'Can you manage?'

Screwing up his face as he shifted, Bramwell said: 'I'm going to *have* to manage. Now we'll see how good our famous flight service for the afflicted is.'

They got a taxi to the airport. It took the efforts of the driver and two others to get Bramwell from the back seat into a wheelchair. Barbara self-consciously propelled him to a corner at the terminal. While she was checking-in a child approached Bramwell, a boy with a stick with a windmill at its end, and staring from a sweet-stained face with a kind of unblinking challenge, began to tap him tentatively on his projected leg. Bramwell picked up a crutch like a weapon. 'Sod off,' he muttered darkly. 'Go on, sod off.'

The tormentor went away backwards, still eyeing him and his leg. Bramwell followed the child with his eyes and saw it pointing him out to his mother. He grimaced towards them. Barbara returned and the flight was called. She wheeled him towards the gate, down the ramp and to the steps of the plane.

'Watch the leg,' he whispered. 'Please be careful with the leg.'

'You could sue those English idiots,' she said when they were at last in their seats. The aircraft began sauntering towards the runway. 'It was their fault, stupid lot. Both lots.'

He looked pained. 'I think the less said about the history of this the better,' he said to her.

'What are you going to tell Lettie?'

'I fell down the steps on the aircraft. After that I'll just have to keep on telling lies regardless.'

'I'm coming with you.'

His head jerked back with fright and astonishment. 'Where?'

'Home. To Lettie. You'll have to have somebody with you. She's not going to believe that the company sent you home in this state in a taxi unaccompanied. I'll go home, change into uniform and come with you. At least it will *look* genuine.'

He nodded dubiously. 'I see the point, but it's risking it a bit,' he said. The plane ran down the runway, eased itself from the ground and took a curling path over the Bay of Angels. 'But Lettie might just swallow it. God, what a mess.'

As they ventured up to Bedwell Park Mansions, Barbara eyed the toast rack of houses, each scarcely distinguishable from its neighbour. It was Monday morning. Unable to face the ordeal the previous night, Bramwell had stayed propped in an armchair on her canal boat.

Barbara drove sedately. The houses stood dumb and bright. They gained the summit of a mild hill and came upon two red-clad infants, propelling tin tricycles along the pavement, the only apparent inhabitants. Bramwell directed her around a bend, its fringes planted with gaunt saplings, and then up a further and steeper slope. The two red children were now below them moving like earnest lady-birds.

Barbara's eyes went along the ranks of detached houses. She was aware of the risk but she wanted to stay with him; the compulsion of a woman wanting to see her lover's wife was strong. She remained calm. 'Which one is it?' she asked.

'Could be any of them,' he sighed. 'It's not far now.' He thought again of the coming moment. 'Perhaps you'd better drop me. I could walk from here,' he said.

'Like a wounded soldier coming home,' she said. 'Lettie won't swallow that.' She realised she now referred to his wife as someone she knew well, as if they were partners. He stiffened and groaned. 'We're here,' he said in a low voice.

'Which one?'

'The red door.'

Barbara followed his unsteady finger and drove brazenly up the sloping drive to the block-shaped house. A dark head appeared briefly at a picture window and a moment later the door was opened by Lettie. Her amazed expression at Bramwell on crutches was quickly followed by another, a swift mix, interest and suspicion, directed at Barbara. The women sized each other up. Bramwell was miserably trying to get out of the car. 'Help me somebody,' he said pathetically.

'I'm afraid your husband has broken his leg,' Barbara announced.

'My darling!' howled Lettie almost leaping from the front door.

'Steady! Steady!' Bramwell's face lit with alarm. Tentatively he prodded the front step with his right-hand crutch. Barbara realised how she had moved forward protectively and discreetly withdrew. Lettie hovered like a panicked butterfly. 'My darling!' she repeated and, looking at Barbara, reiterated: 'My *poor* darling.'

'Lettie,' said Bramwell eventually mounting the step and just balancing on his crutches, 'this is Barbara Poppins.' He waved towards Barbara. The women smiled the sort of smile that they smile at such times, but this action caused him to overbalance and he was only saved from falling by the hands of both. Together they restored him to the upright and, clamping his crutches to his arms, he stumbled towards the door.

'How? How you do this?' questioned Lettie as the trio sidestepped through the small entrance hall.

'Fell down the steps of the bloody plane,' said Bramwell.

'This way,' guided Barbara edging him towards their sitting-room in a manner which suggested that she had lived there for years. 'Let's get you sat down.' She regarded Lettie earnestly. 'He must sit down as much as possible,' she advised.

'We have chairs,' said Lettie a touch huffily. 'Plenty of chairs.'

Reasserting her right, she led the way into the sitting-room. Quickly Barbara took it in. 'This nice modern one should do,' she said guiding Bramwell that way. 'It looks the right shape.'

'His favourite,' said Lettie abruptly subdued. She stepped back blinking unsurely as Barbara confidently helped Bramwell to sit. The crutches fell to the floor and each woman bent to pick up one. 'Put the kettle on, darling,' Bramwell said to his wife. 'Lettie makes a nice cup of tea,' he said haplessly.

Lettie, still trying to fix the situation in her mind, went towards the kitchen but Barbara said: 'No tea for me, thank you, Lettie.' Lettie turned looking relieved. She went into the kitchen anyway.

'I must fly,' insisted Barbara when she had returned. 'I mean, *not* fly. We've just come back. But I must be off.'

'You must fly,' agreed Lettie. She held out her hand, the nails long and sharp and bright red. 'Thank you for bringing back my husband.'

'It was nothing,' said Barbara, her eyes still on the nails. She knew her composure was dissolving. 'Anyone would have done it.'

'But it was *you*,' insisted Lettie. Limply they shook hands. 'Goodbye, Mrs Bobbins.'

Bramwell said 'Poppins' and Barbara said 'Miss'.

'Goodbye Bramwell,' Barbara said with a quick, tight wave. 'Hope it gets better soon.' It was a good touch, the insinuation that they were unlikely to meet until some indeterminate future.

'I will take care of him,' said Lettie like someone with the gift of healing. 'Soon he will be better.'

Barbara left. Bramwell winced as he heard their further insincere goodbyes. Lettie, returning from the door said: 'She is a pretty lady.'

'Yes, quite nice,' he observed as if he had scarcely noticed. 'Very decent of her to bring me back.'

'There is no ambulance?' she asked succinctly.

'The kettle's boiling,' said Bramwell. A continuing whine sounded from the kitchen.

'The company must have ambulance,' she said as she made towards the noise.

'I didn't *want* to come home in an ambulance,' he called to her. 'I didn't want to upset *you*, darling. It's only a compound fracture. Barbara was good enough to give me a lift.'

The cups were clattering in the kitchen. 'There will be some money?' she called back. 'From the company?' Almost as an afterthought, and when she was appearing carrying the tea tray, she said: 'How do you fall down the steps?'

'Top to bottom,' he said sorrowfully.

'That is *big* money,' she insisted. 'A long way, top to bottom.'

'Is that all you care about?' he grumbled, giving her a disappointed stare. 'The compensation. What about my leg?'

'That poor broke thing,' she said leaning and peering at it. Her full Pacific island eyes turned on him. 'Must be careful making love.' She continued the remaining inches to his face and kissed him luxuriously. 'How long will it be?' she asked.

'What?'

'When the leg will be mended.'

He looked around her neck to his outstretched limb. 'Weeks I imagine,' he said.

'I will see that you get number one compensation,' she assured him. 'I will talk to Mr Edward Richardson. He is some boss in your company. I tell him how broke it is.'

'Don't go bothering Mr Richardson,' he said desperately. 'It's not his department. Everything will be settled, Lettie. We'll get the compensation.'

Lettie became excited. 'Will I have my own car?'

'Perhaps,' he sighed. 'Where are your relatives?' He glanced around as though he thought they might be hiding.

'Our family,' she corrected. 'Gone to the movies.'

He moved his leg and groaned. 'Tell me everything,' she said kneeling down and stroking the cast.

'Everything?'

'About your leg. Falling down the steps. Everything until Mrs Bobbins brought you home.'

'Poppins,' he said.

She returned to the kitchen. 'I was going to fix the vegetables,' she said. 'I was going to make you special dinner, darling. Now it must be even more special.'

She came back with a bowl and a chopping board. The chopping board had a crevice into which a knife fitted. She sat beside him on a stool, balancing the wooden board on her lap. She took out the knife.

'It was very friendly to bring you home,' she said. She selected an already peeled carrot from the bowl and laid it on the board. His eyes were drawn to the carrot. She did not look up. 'She is very kind lady.'

With one fierce chop of the knife she sliced the end off the carrot. Bramwell felt himself pale. 'I think I need to rest,' he said.

Nine

The two ladies walked down the stone slope from Windsor Castle, picking careful progress over the humps of the cobbles and between other straggling tourists. Mrs Durie surveyed the ramparts with a searching eye. 'I wonder where her kitchen is,' she said. Before crossing the main road she helpfully held Mrs Collingwood's elbow but, by performing an adroit twist of arms and responsibility, the American ended by guiding the Englishwoman across the street.

'What a job,' sighed Mrs Durie as she sank into the cushioned chair at the Castle Hotel. It had been a warm afternoon. 'No wonder the Queen looks weary sometimes.'

Professionally she scanned the lounge and people sitting at tea. 'This place could do with a dust,' she confided. Before them the low table was already set out and she picked up the cups and examined each one minutely at both the rim and the base. Then, like a ceramics expert, she subjected the plates to a similar scrutiny and finally turned her squeezed eyes on the bowls of the teaspoons and the prongs of the forks. 'Seems to be all right,' she announced grudgingly. 'But you can never tell. They don't wash up like they used to.'

The waitress came and, after diplomatically consulting with Mrs Durie, Pearl Collingwood ordered tea, sandwiches and cakes.

'It *was* nice,' said the Englishwoman genuinely. 'Thank you ever so much. I'd probably never have gone in the

192

Castle if it wasn't for you.' She prepared to whisper as though worried about the consequences of what she was about to say. 'It was a bit dusty in there too, didn't you think, Mrs Collingwood? And draughty. I couldn't feel at home with all those windy corridors.'

'There's Buckingham Palace as well,' pointed out the American woman. 'And that looked quite solid, quite draught proof, Mrs Durie.'

They had staked out their relationship well, each knowing where she stood and was comfortable. The waitress brought the tea. 'Do you really like it here?' Mrs Durie asked seriously. 'Not in this hotel, I mean, in England?'

Pearl Collingwood appeared astonished. 'But of course I do,' she enthused. The other woman had taken charge of the teapot as if her companion could not be expected to know how to deal with it, and was now busy with the strainer, which, for a moment, she briefly peered through like a magnifying glass. The American went on: 'I just love it here. It is everything I would have imagined.' She accepted the cup of tea and placed it carefully in front of her. 'Otherwise,' she added firmly, 'I would never have stayed.'

Mrs Durie was eyeing the sandwiches. Stealthily she opened one, as though raising a lid. She squinted at the salad contents. 'Quite well filled,' she murmured grudgingly, 'in the circumstances.'

She returned her attention to Mrs Collingwood, handing the sandwich plate across and saying: 'There's ham as well.' With her free hand she made another snap check of the ham contents. Her head bent forward and her nose twitched. 'Quite fresh,' she decided. She looked about her with less suspicion. 'Quite a good hotel.'

They went through the commonplace ritual of sugar and milk. 'Bedmansworth, I mean, not just England,' pursued Mrs Durie. 'Staying.'

'I just love it,' Mrs Collingwood assured her. 'And so

193

does Rona. If we'd checked in to some London hotel we would have just gone along with the usual treadmill of sightseeing and returning home, not too much the wiser. But now we feel we know so much more.'

'People thought it was very odd,' divulged Mrs Durie. 'There was some that reckoned you might be spies.' She giggled, holding her hand over her sandwich-filled mouth. 'Spying on the airport.'

'And who might we be spying for?' Mrs Collingwood inquired, amused. Mrs Durie smirked: 'It was only silly old Bernard Threadle, him with the motor bike. Spies. He looks under his bed at night.' She pressed forward as if to get something off her chest. 'But nobody could understand why *Bedmansworth*. I mean, it's not pretty. And it's not near anything much, except Heathrow, all those noisy old planes and the smell of them, the fumes.'

'We were pleased we came,' reiterated the American as though to close the subject. She patted the other woman's hand. 'And we feel we've made a whole lot of friends.'

'Oh, you're very popular, both of you,' said Mrs Durie hurriedly. 'Everybody likes you. You're novelties. We're all quite proud of you.'

They ate another small sandwich each. Mrs Durie had poured hot water into the teapot and now she lifted the lid tentatively like someone monitoring an experiment. 'Which cakes would you like?' she inquired. 'You choose. I've got a weakness for cakes.'

Mrs Collingwood selected one. 'There are two of these,' she said. 'We can have one each.'

'Maids of Honour, they're called,' said the Englishwoman. 'Historical. I think it's something to do with Henry the Eighth.' She looked at the pastry closely and flicked away a non-existent speck of dust. 'My information on royalty doesn't go back that far,' she said. 'Queen Victoria and onwards, that's my field. I like the name Victoria. I wish they'd have another one.'

'You seem to know so much,' said Mrs Collingwood admiringly.

'I read it up,' said Mrs Durie stoutly. 'My daughter and Jim, they have a laugh at me, but I like it. That Randy, with his pigtail, he's so ignorant. He thinks I'm mad. One day he'll grow up.'

'What's his real name?' asked the American.

'Randolph. I said to them if they'd given him a proper name, even Jim like his father, he wouldn't still be trying to be something he's not. He's feckless. Not an ounce of feck.' She drank her tea fiercely.

'Does he work or is he still at college? I've never worked it out.'

'College? He couldn't go to college, not as brainless as he is. And he works when he feels like it, which is not often. On the dole otherwise. I'd make sure he worked or I'd show him the door.'

They continued their tea in silence, Mrs Durie merely re-muttering 'feckless'. Eventually Mrs Collingwood said: 'Every small place in England has a remnant of history. Not just Windsor with a big castle.' She glanced momentarily at the guide book she had brought. 'But villages like Bedmansworth. That was on the map more than three centuries ago.'

Mrs Durie garnered the crumbs on her plate into a tiny pile and then genteelly pushed them to the rim. 'You don't have many old things in America, I suppose,' she said.

'A few. But in this country you have so many, a cottage, and people still living there, and it goes back into the mists.' She finished her tea and waited until Mrs Durie had poured them both a second cup. 'Tell me about the War,' she suggested. 'When the Americans came.'

A modest flush seemed to come to the other woman's face. Mrs Durie looked up and said: 'Oh yes, you said you had an interest in that. Well, let me see.

'It was quite a time for us, of course, just growing up,

195

girls never been anywhere. We'd only seen Americans on the pictures. We never even knew they called them Yanks until they came over here.' She became suddenly sad as if recalling the best time of her life. 'They just swept us off our feet, like they used to say. Their voices like cowboys and laughing like they used to and those lovely smooth greeny uniforms. And it wasn't just us young girls. The local blokes didn't like them much naturally, but most of that lot was away in the forces anyway, but the older people, especially our mums, thought they was marvellous. I told you they used to bring us that jam and luncheon meat. Stuff you couldn't get.'

'You had a special . . . Yank?'

'All us girls did.' She paused as though trying to picture him. 'We was all *engaged*. At seventeen and eighteen! Funny to think of it now. Mine was called Zachary, Zac. He wanted to take me home with him to America. I could have been over there living next door to you. And then, one day, overnight, they was all gone . . . vanished. Everywhere seemed empty. Up at the camp gate there was just a couple of military police, snowdrops they were called, chaps with white helmets on. We all went up there to find out. In a bunch standing outside. But they'd gone. "Gone with the wind," I remember one of the girls, Gracie Dorkings, saying. She went to see that film eighteen times. She's dead now.'

Mrs Collingwood said: 'So the camp was nearby?'

'It was a bit of a distance. Over towards Slough. It's part of the airport now, where they repair them. We had to get on the bus and sometimes, being wartime, the bus didn't turn up and we'd walk or get a lift with some other Yanks.'

'They helped to rebuild the wall of the churchyard after it was bombed,' said Pearl. 'The vicar told me about that.'

Mrs Durie looked surprised. 'You're right,' she affirmed. 'Absolutely right, Mrs Collingwood. I'd forgotten all about that. I think some of those Poles helped too, but they were devils, the Poles. And some of the Yanks from what's now St Sepulchre's helped.'

'The old folks' residence.'

'That's it. As it is now. Then it was some sort of office they had, or an officers' mess or whatever. We never went there because they were officers.' She smiled a little coyly. 'Being young we just went after the soldiers.'

A clock chimed deeply in the hall of the hotel. 'If we want to catch the bus we must be off,' advised Mrs Durie. 'It goes at twenty past.' She pinched up the tiny pile of crumbs and with an absent-minded gesture put them into her mouth. She asked if she could go half with the bill but the American woman shook her head.

'I've had a lovely time,' said Mrs Durie. 'I've really enjoyed myself.'

'It has been nice,' agreed the American lady. 'And so enlightening.'

Richardson heard Adele come home at five o'clock in the afternoon, her arrival lifting him from a day's sleep loaded with dreams of guilt and unhappiness. She began moving about in the house; he put on his dressing-gown and went downstairs.

She was in the kitchen making tea. He had not telephoned her from Mombasa. 'How was it?' she asked. They kissed incompletely as they always did now. 'How was Bill Allsop?' She had known Allsop from their early days.

'He died,' Richardson said hopelessly. He lightly punched the kitchen table. 'Died on the plane coming back.'

'Oh, Edward.' Her voice dropped with a sadness that caused her to reach out to him and, though accidentally, their hands touched. 'What was it?'

'Aids,' he said flatly. 'He got it out there.'

She was so shocked she had to lean against the refrigerator. 'Aids? Bill Allsop? But that's ridiculous.'

'You can get it in a variety of ways,' he said. 'In Africa.'

She sat down on a kitchen chair. 'Poor Bill,' she said. 'What was his wife's name?' Then, all at once realising, she stared up and whispered: 'You brought him back on the *plane?*'

Richardson picked up his cup of tea and stirred it aimlessly. 'He wanted to come home,' he told her simply. 'So we got him on the flight. He just didn't make it, that's all.'

'They'll realise of course. Grainger will.'

'There'll be a hell of a row, I expect. Snow and I, that's the doctor who came with me, could say we didn't know what Bill had – but it would come out anyway. Snow wouldn't tell them he didn't know anyway. There's a doctor in Mombasa who had already given Bill a test. He was HIV positive and then he got this local illness that they all contracted out there and when we arrived we found him alone in his bungalow and dying. So we brought him back.' He shrugged: 'He wanted to die in England but we were somewhere over Greece when he went.'

'My God, you get yourself in some amazing situations,' she said.

'Don't start being bitter about it, Adele.'

She regarded him starkly. 'One day you'll realise that you can't take the world's problems on your shoulders all the time.'

'It wasn't the world, it was Bill Allsop,' he pointed out.

'For God's sake, you know what I mean.'

'I don't want a fight about it.'

'Neither do I. I'm amazed you told me. You don't confide in me often.'

'I have just confided in you and you still don't like it. I have to go back to Heathrow this evening. Grainger has called me in. Snow as well. Grainger's upset.'

Adele grimaced. 'That unpleasant man frequently is. He's in the job you should have had – and he knows it. Perhaps he'll fire you.' She said it with a touch of hope.

He put his cup down and walked to the window. 'I've

told you I don't *want* to go to Gohm, Brent and Byas. I don't want to go there so much I wrote to them and told them to forget it. Forever. I instructed them to stop bothering me.'

The telephone rang. Richardson went to answer it. 'Grainger's brought forward the meeting,' he said when he returned. 'He's got another appointment.'

'Rush, rush, rush for Mr Grainger,' recited Adele.

'He's the boss,' he said quietly. They both realised that Toby was standing in the hall listening to them. 'I'd better get a move on.'

He went upstairs towards the bathroom and, glancing from habit through the half-open door of his study, he saw a single letter on his desk. He had opened his mail as soon as he had returned that morning but he saw this had the large inscription 'By Hand'. He opened and read it with receding patience and walked back into the kitchen. 'That damned woman,' he said to Adele. Toby had gone out into the garden again and was walking, hands in pockets, towards the bottom fence. He saw him kick one of the golf balls. 'That Mrs Kitchen.'

Adele was putting the cups in the dishwasher. She looked up sharply. 'What now?'

'She wants me to go and meet her committee. What she describes as a "last opportunity to discuss the problem of your observatory".'

'What are you going to do?' she asked in a dull voice.

'Go,' he told her. 'If this Mrs Kitchen and her bloody committee want a fight, they can have it.'

She was not very interested. She went out of the room saying: 'Mind you don't take it out on poor Mr Grainger.'

Heathrow, at night, shone like a circus; floodlights, coloured lights, moving, flashing, blinking and rotating lights; the beams of aircraft in the dark sky like the trapeze performers, the luminescent elephant shapes of the planes on the ground.

Richardson drove below the tunnel and parked in the reserved area outside Snow's office and surgery. Snow was inside. He could see him through the window conducting an imaginary orchestra. 'Ah, Barbirolli did have one big advantage over me,' the doctor smiled quietly when Richardson interrupted him. 'He had the Halle.'

They walked through the traffic to Hardy Grainger's office. 'He's a pedantic little dictator,' said Snow genially. 'He reminds me of a doctor I once knew who corrected the grammar of patients on the point of death. He'd put them right on their last words.'

Grainger's secretary Moira, with her perpetual expression of someone expecting the worst, and still worse to follow, asked them to wait. 'He should not keep you too long,' she said as though that might be the best they could hope for. 'He has a dinner appointment.' Grainger was suspected of keeping people waiting for the sake of keeping them waiting. 'He's had a day,' Moira said. 'And he didn't want to stay this evening.'

They sat in silence. 'Tchaikovsky,' said Snow quietly after a few minutes, 'had a terrible time coming to terms with his homosexuality.'

Moira glanced up in a sort of maiden fear. Everyone knew she had not married because she was afraid of leaving Grainger. 'Did he?' Richardson said glancing at the secretary at her desk. She lowered her face to her work.

'It's said that he committed suicide because he had made advances to a young man whose father found out. There is certainly serious doubt on the theory that he died of cholera after drinking iffy water.'

The telephone rang on Moira's desk. She did not pick it up but smoothing her skirt down she went smartly, head down, through to the inner office. She returned, like someone perpetually grateful to survive.

'Mr Grainger will see you now,' she half whispered. Pulling the door completely behind her but softly, she said, like a warning: 'He's gone very quiet.'

'Perhaps he's merely calm,' Snow pointed out pleasantly.

They went in, Snow first. The room was panelled with photographs of ceremonies, many involving Grainger, which marked milestones in the company's history. Sitting on a couch against the wall was a fattish man with splayed feet whom Richardson recognised as one of the company's lawyers. Grainger was at the desk making a performance of signing documents. He waited until he had finished and went over the papers again before looking up. 'Oh,' he said as if he were surprised they had mustered their courage.

He invited both to sit down on two chairs already arranged. 'You may not know Mr Chandler,' he said waving towards the other man. They exchanged nods, Chandler's scarcely a nod at all. He widened the angle between his shoes. It was not a time for handshakes.

Grainger pretended he did not know how to start, opening and shutting his limp mouth, staring at and fidgeting with his pen. 'I've asked Henry Phillipson from the press office to come in,' he said eventually. 'He ought to be in on this. He's gone home but he's coming back. I'd prefer him to be here at the outset.'

He surveyed each of them. 'If there's anything else you would like to discuss while we're waiting, then perhaps we could do so. First, I have to make a phone call.' He rose from his desk and went to the third room in the suite.

'No, you'd never think he was a homosexual,' said Snow conversationally to Richardson. Chandler sat abruptly upright on the couch.

'Who? Who is that?' whispered Chandler urgently. He glanced at the door through which Grainger had gone to make his call. Snow turned carefully towards the couch as though he had forgotten Chandler was there. 'Sorry, old chap,' he said. 'Who was what?'

'A homosexual,' hissed Chandler his heavy middle rolling

forward. His feet had moved to a quarter past nine. 'Who . . . you were just saying.'

'Ah, Tchaikovsky,' replied Snow sweetly. 'You're interested in Tchaikovsky?'

Chandler coloured and sat back with a grunt. There was a knock and Moira entered with Henry Phillipson wearing a Scout-master's uniform. 'Where's he gone?' he demanded, striding in. 'I was just on my way to the lads.' He had a broken tooth at the front.

Grainger re-entered the room. 'If you mean me, I'm here,' he announced. He surveyed Phillipson's costume with embarrassed surprise. 'Oh, I didn't know,' he muttered.

Phillipson said: 'I got here as soon as I could.' He was not in awe of Grainger. He straightened his neckerchief and dragged a chair from the wall as though about to start an indoor activity. He sat down and leaned forward, his fractured tooth exposed like a fang, then produced a grubby notepad and wiped his spectacles on his shorts.

'I don't think you'll need the notebook, Henry,' said Grainger impatiently. 'The less of this that is taken down in writing, the less will be given in evidence.'

'I'd forgotten you were once in the police force,' commented Phillipson putting his notebook and pencil in his back pocket.

Grainger reddened and said: 'I was a special constable. Purely voluntary.' Richardson and Snow began to enjoy it.

Grainger placed his hands flat on the blotter. There were pale fibres on their backs which quivered in the low rays of the desk lamp. He peered over and then through his severe glasses. 'I assume we all know the situation,' he said. 'I gave Henry a résumé on the telephone. In a nutshell, Bill Allsop being brought back to this country from Africa – and dying on the plane. And we all know what from.'

'Acquired Immune Deficiency Syndrome,' Snow told him.

'Quite. Aids,' muttered Grainger. He glanced at each in turn leaving out Chandler, still sitting like a forgotten safeguard behind them. 'And let's not be too prissy about this. To have one of our senior employees die on one of our services is bad enough, but to have him die in this way is disastrous.'

'It certainly was for him,' said Snow.

'May I finish, Doctor?'

'Please do.'

'Look, let's not beat about the bush. I have to think what the *customers* are going to think.' His eyes paled as if he needed help. 'This business, and this job, are difficult enough without . . .' He left the sentence unfinished. Assertive again he thrust his head towards Richardson. 'You went out, Edward, to sort out the situation.' It was an accusation.

'I did,' said Richardson. 'I found that the entire establishment was laid low with a tropical infection, although when Dr Snow and I arrived they were over the worst of it. They were being looked after at the American clinic in Mombasa, but Bill Allsop had refused to go there. He was dying privately at home.'

'How did you know he had Aids?' asked Grainger. He said it as though with difficulty and added: 'For Christ's sake.'

'For Christ's sake, indeed,' put in Snow. 'Allsop told me. He said that he had known for some time that he was HIV positive, as the popular phrase has it. His system just could not combat this infection.'

'And you brought him home,' said Grainger, his eyes sliding slightly left to Richardson. 'Why?'

'He wanted to come home,' said Richardson simply. 'He asked to see England and his wife.'

'Very nice,' muttered Grainger. He turned his attention to Snow again. 'Was he a homosexual?'

Snow leaned sideways and called to Chandler. 'Not Tchaikovsky this time, Mr Chandler.'

Grainger, amazed and hurt, almost snarled. 'For God's

sake, Doctor, let's get this done. How did he get Aids in the beginning?'

'There's a selection of ways in Africa,' Snow told him as though recommending a visit. 'But he was not a homosexual. Not that I would have thought *that* would have mattered, not in the airline business.'

Grainger's teeth clamped. He looked bitterly at Richardson and then to Snow again. He spoke slowly. 'Didn't it occur to either of you that this was, to say the least, an inadvisable action? It's the image of the thing. . . .' He glanced severely at Phillipson who had produced a piece of string and was tying knots in it. '. . . What if the press get onto this?'

'It's a very good story,' admitted Phillipson with what sounded like a touch of relish. 'Aids . . . dying man . . . Africa . . . wants to see England and wife . . . brought home . . . expires . . . upsets airline's passengers.'

'Let's hope to God nobody sniffs it out,' sniffed Grainger. 'If anybody does then you are going to have to deny it point blank, Phillipson.'

'Let's hope it does not arise,' replied Phillipson as though apprehensive for his Scout's honour.

'I'm going to have to take this to the board anyway,' said Grainger. 'Something like this has to be. Let's hope the press *don't* get hold of it. It's difficult enough these days to get passengers, without them suspecting that they're sitting next to somebody . . . who is likely to die. Thank you.'

His thanks was a dismissal. They got up and went towards the door. 'Incidentally,' said Richardson almost over his shoulder. 'Bill Allsop's funeral is on Monday.'

'I have to be in Paris,' said Grainger trying to sound regretful. 'You are going?'

'Of course. And Dr Snow will be.'

'He's our baby,' said Snow.

Edward slept brokenly, a sleep riven with dreams; Allsop bawling 'Burlington Bertie' and haunting the Strand with

204

his gloves on his hand; Tony and Annabelle begging him to run to refuge in their tent. And in between the frenzy a dream of Rona, sketching, talking to him: 'I want to draw you.'

It was late that evening when he had returned from Allsop's funeral in Cambridgeshire in a wind-cleft church-yard in the fens. Allsop's widow had remained expressionless throughout the service and the burial. The only words she had spoken to Richardson and Snow were: 'I'm glad he wanted to come home.'

They had stopped at an inn on the return journey and had dinner. 'It's difficult to tell with the bereaved,' Snow had mused. 'You could not make out whether she was grieving or what. There's no occasion when people hide their feelings so well.'

Strangely exhausted, Edward had returned to the dark-ened house. Adele did not stir but eventually his fitful turns roused her and they lay awake but unspeaking, side by side, staring at their ceiling, powerless to stop what they had – they *owned* – slipping away from them. Their past was moving out of their sight.

'Am I keeping you awake?' he asked eventually.

'You woke me up,' she said without complaint. 'You were rolling about.'

At one time, earlier in their lives when they slept together, they would have turned and embraced until they were settled and able to sleep again. He half wanted to face to her in the present darkness. He almost did so but she said: 'Why don't you go into the other room. We'll both sleep then.'

'All right,' he responded quietly, wearily. He put his feet on the carpet and stared at them; two white fish lying in dim water. Then he picked up one of his pillows and went out onto the landing and into the smaller room.

In the room was a rocking horse that Toby had ridden in childhood and which they had always meant to give to someone else. He watched the pale-faced horse and fell into a light, brief sleep. Then he awoke, got up and, putting on a sweater, his grey flannels and tennis shoes, deftly let himself out of the house. It was early, empty daylight. Adele's patterned front garden was embroidered with dew. An elaborate spider's web was glistening across the front gate like a miniature suspension bridge. Rather than break it he climbed over the gate into the silent street.

It was a clear morning although the forecast promised cloud and showers later. Sunrise shadows stretched becalmed across the street, the spire of the church furthest, projecting over the road, the shadow of its gilded arrow weathervane resting against the shut door of the Swan.

Jim Turner was in the yard at the side glaring at a pyramid of barrels and crates as if trying to move them by sheer willpower. 'You're out early,' he said to Richardson. He sighed: 'I look at this pile and I wonder if it's all worthwhile. Don't you feel like that sometimes?'

'I wish it were only beer barrels,' laughed Richardson. He hesitated then asked: 'How are your American guests?'

'Just fine,' said Jim doing an imitation of Pearl Collingwood's accent. He stepped two paces closer, confidingly. 'They pay up on the nail, they're nice and friendly, they never complain about the food or the service, such as it is. But all the time I wonder what they're *doing* here. I mean, *here*. Bedmansworth. Can you believe it, I can't.'

'Just . . . being here,' suggested Richardson. Jim shook his head. 'Getting free from their usual life,' Richardson went on. 'Opting out, I suppose you could say.'

'Running away,' said Jim.

'Yes, you could call it that.'

The publican looked thoughtfully at the crates and barrels. 'Suit me, that would, running away. That kid of mine drives me mad. That bloody pigtail. Can't get a job. I told him it could be *because* of the pigtail. I certainly wouldn't employ a freak like that.' He regarded the other man with almost comic appeal. 'Did you know that if Queen Victoria had lived she would be a hundred and seventy-three years old by now.'

'Ah, your mother-in-law.'

'That's another one,' said Jim thinking of his worries. He shrugged. 'But you *can't*, can you. Run away. At least I can't.' He looked wistful. 'There's never any time.'

Richardson continued along the village street. He had decided on collecting the newspapers almost as an excuse for getting up early. The shop was open with a spectral yellow electric glow issuing from its open door. He went in. Mrs Latimer, the newsagent's wispy wife, finished counting through a pile of magazines before looking up from the counter. 'Richardsons' papers are gone,' she said as if concluding there was nothing else he could possibly want. 'They'll be through the letterbox by now. They're gone with the twins.' She threw her arm wide and he smiled, grateful for her cheeriness.

'How are the twins?' he asked.

'Still the same,' she replied enigmatically. 'Some people still can't tell them apart and they're eleven now.'

'They have to start work early,' said Richardson.

'Oh they love it. Like lightning they are. Run, run, run all the time. They want to be footballers, you see. Their father wants them to play for Fulham. He says they've got to aim for the top.'

Richardson walked from the shop and passed the twins as they cloned their way up parallel garden paths, each with his sacking bag large around his neck. 'Come on Fulham!' he called to them. Both stopped and stared at him. 'Stuff Fulham,' they responded as one.

Anthony Burridge came into undulating view around the edge of the churchyard wall. He was in a blazoned tracksuit, jogging thoughtfully, mildly sweating. He continued to prance slightly, on the spot. 'Half an hour and then shower

207

in the bucket and change and off to work. I'm knackered,'
he confessed to Richardson.

He breathed heavily. 'It's keeping it up is the trouble.'
Still jogging on the spot he suddenly said: 'We're having a
baby. We're scared stiff.'

Richardson shook the perspiring hand. 'But it's the tent,'
said Burridge. 'You can't bring up a baby in a tent. Not
unless you're an Arab. We've got to find somewhere for the
winter.' Then he said: 'I'm cooling. I must go.'

Richardson watched him jog away and then returned to
his house. Adele was in her dressing-gown in the kitchen. 'I
thought you'd run away,' she said.

'I was going to but I got frightened,' he responded. They
both laughed. It was like a door opening and for a moment
their hands reached out and touched. 'There's tea in the
pot,' she said. 'I've got to rush. It's the county committee
this morning.'

'The Burridges are having a baby,' he said.

'What? In that bivouac?' She frowned. 'They must be
mad.'

He poured tea from the pot. 'How was Brenda at the
funeral?' she asked.

'Just . . . blank,' he said. 'She had no expression at all.'

'To lose your husband is bad enough,' she said looking
into her cup. 'But to lose him like that must be hard.'

Toby sat beside him in the car as they drove towards Windsor. The trees were swiftly losing their leaves now, one night
of high winds would strip them. But the sun flecked through
the branches as they drove. Richardson was aware that it
had been a long time since he had been alone with his son.

'Mr Old's got a flat above the shop,' said Toby. 'Well,
it's really only a bedsitter but he says I can have it if I
like.'

Richardson was almost shocked. 'I think your mother

might have something to say about that,' he said. 'Have you mentioned it?'

'Not yet,' said Toby. 'I haven't had the chance. She's been dashing around all the week.'

'She's busy.'

'Yes, she is. You're pretty busy too, aren't you, Dad?'

Richardson sighed. 'It's not often we get the chance of a chat,' he confessed. 'Is that what you'd like to do, go in the bedsitter?'

'I think it's a good idea,' said Toby realising that at least one parent might be persuaded. 'Mr Old doesn't want to have to come in to open the shop in the morning. But he didn't mean right now. Perhaps next year. He only mentioned it.' He paused, keeping his eyes ahead. They were running into Windsor, the autumn morning shadows deep across the High Street, the Castle large and grey, casting a big shade. There were not many people since it was before nine o'clock. 'I would have a place to myself then,' added Toby thoughtfully. 'I'd be out of your way.'

As Richardson pulled up outside the antique shop, the proprietor was opening the door, sniffing the cool air as if seeking the scent of buyers. He waved as Toby got out of the car.

'He's a good lad,' he called to Edward. 'Very good. Learning all the time.' He came across to the car and Richardson pressed the button to lower the window. Mr Old looked surprised. 'What will they think of next?' he said.

Edward grinned at him. 'He says he wants to come and live over the shop.'

Mr Old looked mildly surprised. 'Well, I did mention it,' he agreed. 'But I didn't mean yet.'

'No, he said it would be next year,' said Richardson.

'Yes, when he's got a bit of age,' said the antique dealer. He leaned forward confidingly. 'I think he's feeling his . . . feelings,' he smiled. 'He wants a bit of freedom.'

209

When Richardson thanked him, waved to Toby who was standing in the doorway looking importantly at an embroidered sampler, and driven away, the antique dealer added quietly: 'And he's lonely.'

Richardson had intended to drive straight to his office at Heathrow, but it was an imperturbable day, the walls of the Windsor houses peaceful in their shades and colours, the sun floating in misty bands through the gaps between the streets and along the Thames. Aware of his own lack of peace, he parked the car and walked through a tapered alley emerging at its narrowest onto the river bank. At once, as if he had known she would be there, he saw Rona.

She was sketching, sat intently on a folding stool by the tow-path. He looked at the scene she was taking in; skiffs and other small boats gathered for the winter, nudging each other near the bank, suburban swans picking through floating plastic containers, nudging the flotsam with their beaks, their necks like white ropes. Ducks loitered hopefully. A solitary fisherman, his shoulders drooping with lack of luck, stared at the river as if hoping for an answer. The water was like suede. On the far bank the buildings were still romantically misty.

Rona was so attentive to her task that she was not aware of his approach. 'Am I allowed to look?' he asked. She turned her head and smiled. Their hands touched in recognition.

'There's not much to look at right now,' she said. He studied the started sketch and then the scene. 'I'm trying to get it before the mist goes.'

'Before you can see what the distant vision really is, a petrol station and the roof of a supermarket,' he suggested.

'You're right,' she laughed. 'If it's romance you want sometimes you need to compromise.' They looked at each other steadily but she then, swiftly, turned away to her sketch.

'I drove my son Toby to work,' Edward said as if he had to explain what he was doing in Windsor. 'He's in the antique shop in the High Street. How did the airport sketching go?'

'Just fine,' she replied. 'But claustrophobic. I guess you can only spend so long in an airport.'

'Don't I know it.'

'You don't sound very happy, Edward.' Her eyes were still away from him. 'How was the trip to Africa?'

'That's one of my problems. Bill Allsop, our manager out there, he died.'

'That's sad. You had known him a long time?'

'He was an old friend, although we didn't see each other often. Despite aeroplanes, distances are often still distances.'

Rona began to draw again. 'The thought of distance, the idea of it, is still there. It's not measured in hours,' she agreed. 'That was one of the factors I tried to work into my airport sketches. You get a whole lot of emotion in a very few yards. People arriving, people departing.'

'Greeters and weepers, they're called at Heathrow,' he nodded with a brief smile. 'It's as much about emotions as flight times. The airport is like a theatre, nothing's quite real.' He sat on the wall beside her and asked if he was disturbing her.

Rona said: 'Not at all. Sometimes it helps to have someone to talk.' She continued drawing using swift and decisive lines. Then she said: 'Watching those planets of yours must be very silent.'

'Those planets of *mine*,' he said smiling at the emphasis. 'Oh, I listen to music.'

'What's your favourite?' she asked.

Edward was surprised. 'Oh, there's a few pieces. "Nimrod" for one, from the *Enigma Variations*, of course. "The Planets Suite", Gustav Holst. Then there's the music that William Walton wrote for that old film about Captain Scott, the *Antarctic Symphony*. It's eerie, it's all about cold, open, remote places.' Then he said: 'It's just about all I've got.' The ducks began squabbling over some passing debris. One of the swans cruised by and casually removed the tit-bit.

'It must be some experience.'

'If some people have their way then I won't have an observatory for much longer. They want to dismantle it.'

'But . . . why would that be?'

'They say it contravenes a covenant. But I'm fighting them.'

Richardson stood and brushed the back of his trousers. 'I must be on my way, Rona,' he said. 'I have a meeting at ten thirty.'

'Good luck with your observatory.'

'I'll need that.' They touched hands again. 'I'm glad I didn't disturb you.'

'Not at all,' said Rona. He *had* disturbed her and she knew that she had disturbed him also.

Loaded with his thoughts he drove to Heathrow. He had to go to Terminal Four to a brief meeting with the catering contractors. He drove along the perimeter road, the long curving back route, about the circumference of the airport, passing on its way the fire station, the catering block, the long line of taxis waiting to be called to the terminals, the veterinary hospital, the police car compound and the Thames Water sewage works, its existence threatened by the demands for a new super-terminal on the site of its filters and ponds. Today, in the quiet season for the airport, the peripheral route was as uncrowded as a secondary high-way. Richardson could see fields and cattle from there, the distinct tower of Bedmansworth church with its arrow and its golden ball glistening like the sun itself.

The Longford River imprisoned in its culvert flowed slow and grey; there was an old farm and a row of low cottages, dwellings of agricultural labourers built before there were airports, when Heath Row was a hamlet between the

Magpie Inn and the few houses at Perry Oaks. The road followed the way of an ancient carting track.

On the left was a higher perimeter wall with the tails of Boeing 747s standing above it like banners. The homely jumbo had changed the world; the gentle, indomitable aeroplane, both cumbersome and graceful, had travelled the world's skies in its thousands.

Richardson left his car in the staff section of the car park and walked over to the newest of the airport's terminals. Alongside was a hotel, hat shaped, like a late twentieth-century Victorian railway station. He watched a small jet from Air Malta, which used Terminal Four among the major airlines, fussing out to the runway. There were two KLM aircraft in their pale blue and white colours standing at the piers and then a long run of British Airways tails like a huge hand of cards stretched to the infinity of the buildings.

He walked into the terminal building, roomier, higher than the other three, built years before, but with its concourse crowded with all types and nations, colours, costumes, languages, all moving and preparing to be scattered throughout the world; to New York, to Toronto, Buenos Aires and to Katmandu, Timbuktu and Trengganu. He stood for a moment, in isolation, watching it all but thinking of a woman standing at an easel by the autumn River Thames.

The sub-postmaster of Bedmansworth, Dobbie Dobson, was manoeuvring his tuba through the door into the long porch of the village hall as Richardson walked up the paved path. The other players of the Bedmansworth Band stood on the ragged grass waiting for the bulky bandmaster to get in; a big, scowling girl with a drum, a youth clutching a flute like a weapon, another giving his trumpet a tentative kiss, and a girl with a white face and a violin. Among the others was a middle-aged woman who carried a pair of exposed cymbals and brought them together quietly, but with a touch of impatience.

'There's an art in this, Mr Richardson,' said Dobson. 'Getting through this door or tunnel if you like.' He demonstrated twisting and rolling the bulbous instrument and his own rotund body. 'A turn this way then a wriggle that.' He performed the movements as he spoke. 'There.' He went into the doorway. The girl with the violin case stood aside with a mumble and, thanking her, Richardson followed Dobson into the porch.

'Is it band practice?' he asked. 'I thought the Residents' Association were here tonight.'

'Tuesdays, band practice,' Dobbie informed him solidly. 'There *was* some people going in a bit earlier, I saw them, but I expect they'll be in one of those pokey rooms off. We have to have the main bit, because we do our marching up and down as well, see.'

He had worked his way along the confined porch and he shifted himself and the tuba to make room for Richardson to pass through. The shabby hall with its melancholy flags, hanging from the ceiling, was empty and glowering with indifferent light. Velvet curtains sagged like an old skirt across the stage. A complaining voice echoed from a door half open at one side of the stage. The pink-and-white face of Mrs Kitchen appeared. She saw Richardson. 'Ah, there you are! We're in here! We've been waiting!'

Taking his time, Richardson crossed the scuffed floor and crouched into the low-ceilinged room where Mrs Kitchen and four others squatted in self-conscious discomfort on kindergarten chairs. In one corner was propped the head of the giant from *Jack and the Beanstalk*, the last pantomime, the plaster nose fractured and horribly hanging. 'Good evening,' said Richardson.

'This,' said Mrs Kitchen briskly, 'is the Central Action Committee.' She waved a lumpy hand.

'Of what?' inquired Richardson looking casually for some-

214

where to sit. There was a spare infant chair but he ignored it.

'The Bedmansworth Residents' Association,' returned Mrs Kitchen with accentuated surprise. 'Naturally. Please sit down.'

Richardson sat on the edge of a table wedged among the chairs, so that he was head and shoulders above the committee, a manoeuvre not lost on Mrs Kitchen. She grunted her annoyance and after regarding the tiny chair sniffed: 'It might have been better if the hall had provided some proper seats. Apparently they've been taken elsewhere on hire. They allege that these fitted better into this silly room.'

Outside the door, in the main hall, the band began assembling. There came a mild fumf-fumf from Dobbie Dobson's tuba. 'Band practice,' Richardson smiled to the Central Action Committee.

'Drat it,' said Mrs Kitchen. She stood, opened the door, and shut it again fiercely, her cheeks pouting. 'The Residents' Association is required to watch its expenditure,' she said confronting Richardson. 'We are not like an airline.'

'No,' agreed Richardson surveying the room's occupants. 'There is a difference.'

She rolled her lips. 'So we had to take the room at its lowest rent.' There was a further fumf-fumf and one explosive bang on the drum. 'But I did not realise the hall was being used for band practice.' She regarded Richardson with something akin to a plea for sportsmanship. 'I think the quicker we get into our business the better, before they start.'

Suddenly Edward realised he was going to enjoy himself. He said: 'Let's be quick by all means but I feel I should have the names of the . . . Central Action Committee, Mrs Kitchen. I recognise only one person. . . .' He nodded across to a twitching woman in a thick green coat and a hat with a fractured feather. 'Fumf,' sounded the tuba from beyond the door. Cymbals clashed. Mrs Kitchen winced.

215

'One person. . . .' proceeded Richardson. 'And I'm afraid I don't know her name.'

'Not familiar with your fellow residents,' said Mrs Kitchen swiftly. She glanced towards the door.

'Not *these* fellow residents I'm afraid,' admitted Richardson. He smiled at each in turn. The woman in the green coat said with a twitch: 'Mrs Fickens, I am, Thora.' She bridled away from her chairman's glare. Dobson's voice came from outside the door, calling the band to order.

Not surrendering his initiative, Richardson nodded genially at a pipe-shaped man with wispy hair scraped without hope across his forehead. 'Mr Gordon,' the man said answering the nod, adding 'Percy', with a sign of shyness. The squat man next to him put together a scowl. 'Bert Kitchen,' he muttered.

'Ah, the better half,' acknowledged Richardson pleasantly. Notes of discord and random clashes of cymbals and drums came from the outside room as the band pulled itself together. Mrs Kitchen was becoming angry.

'And that's Miss MacNamara,' she jabbed her finger at the woman who appeared startled in a meagre way. She gave Mrs Kitchen a look of hurt and hatred. 'That's me,' she confirmed.

'And I am Edward Richardson,' said Richardson with exaggerated kindness. The band began to play 'Colonel Bogey'. They played it loudly and badly. A shout from Dobbie Dobson and the noise clattered and collapsed. 'This is *hideous*,' muttered Mrs Kitchen. 'They should have told me. It's that half-witted caretaker, whatever he's called. Smith.'

'Mr Henry Broughton-Smith . . . MC . . . Military Cross,' Richardson informed her. 'Been in the village for years. Retired solicitor. He does the hall voluntarily.' The band started up again, the massive music shuddering against the walls and ceiling. Mrs Kitchen sprang up angrily and strode the three paces to fling open the dividing door.

'Stop!' she bawled. 'Will you stop this racket!'

Edward sat, leaning forward to see, on the edge of the table, and happier than he had been for some time. The committee on their infant chairs stared towards the door with collective apprehension. Undeterred the music blasted on. Through the open door, around Mrs Kitchen's big shoulder, he could see Dobbie Dobson. The band wavered to a halt.

'Did you shout?' inquired Dobson peering towards the open door.

'I said *stop*. We're having a meeting.'

'Are you now,' blinked Dobson. 'And we're having a practice. Tuesday's – band practice.'

'I didn't know that.'

'Well, you do now.' He revolved and raised his baton. 'Ready. One, two, three!' Mrs Kitchen bellowed something further, drowned in the din of the music. She returned to her miniature chair and sat down, looking as if she were going to cry.

'Madness,' she moaned. 'Absolute madness.' She lifted her head with a half challenge, half plea, to Richardson. 'We will have to shout,' she said.

'That shouldn't be too difficult,' he said looking directly at her. He raised his voice. 'In any event I'm sure that we can get through this matter very quickly. You want me to take down my observatory and I'm not going to take it down.'

While he was speaking the band had subsided into a fortissimo and then stopped altogether, apart from Dobson's pleadingly instructive voice. But, as Mrs Kitchen opened her mouth and as though they had only been waiting the opportunity, they struck up again.

Mrs Kitchen's face tightened. The pink spots on her cheeks deepened. 'I will not be beaten,' she squeaked. 'They will not defeat me.' Attempting to raise herself from the small chair, she caused it to tumble backwards. For a

217

moment she trembled, knees bent, like a circus elephant dismounting from its coloured tub, but then, her weight proving too much for her knees, she began to collapse. For a split moment she had a choice; to fall backwards or forwards. She was confronting Richardson who had instinctively slid from the table to help. Mrs Kitchen chose; she projected herself forward. With an impassioned moan she fell at Richardson's feet, the moan pitching up to a howl of pain as her plump knees struck the floor. The committee remained rooted.

'Now look what's happened!' howled her husband. He tried to lift his wife like a tug trying to right a freighter.

'Get away,' she said through grinding teeth. Apart from Mr Kitchen none of the committee had moved. 'I'm all right. I am not injured.'

Mr Kitchen clenched his fists. Before his wife had even regained the chair, placed upright at last by Thora Fickens, he was at the door, had flung it open and howled at Dobson and the village band: 'Do you know what you've done? Do you know?'

' "Colonel Bogey",' Dobbie told him appearing glad at the interest. 'Now we're doing "Blaze Away".'

'Bastard band!' bellowed Mr Kitchen. Mrs Fickens tutted, and looked at Miss MacNamara as if they should not have been there. Mrs Kitchen was squatting on the child's chair rubbing her knees. 'We must reconvene this meeting,' she demanded.

'I think,' said Richardson steadying his expression, 'we *have had* the meeting.'

Mrs Kitchen's cheeks expanded. The band was striking up again. They were marching up and down the hall and Dobson could be heard shouting: 'Left, right, left, right, about turn!'

'This,' said Mrs Kitchen like someone making a final foray, producing an envelope, 'is a letter from our solicitor. A summons will follow unless you comply with its instructions.' She thrust the envelope towards him. He hesitated but then accepted it.

'Meeting adjourned!' bawled Mrs Kitchen.

The Central Action Committee stood and, in disarray, stumbled after their chairman from the room. Mrs Fickens offered Richardson a shy wave. He heard Mrs Kitchen berating the band.

When they had all gone, leaving the three-quarter semi-circle of chairs like a wooden model of a Druid temple, Richardson remained on the edge of the table, laughing to himself. He opened the letter. Legal proceedings would commence unless he forthwith complied with Covenant 874/2 of September 21st 1937. The Residents' Association it said, had an unanswerable case. With a grimace he folded it up and put it into his pocket and went out of the confined room. The band were resting, odd shapes, faces, sizes and ages, grouped bent backed, holding their instruments or wedging them against the floor, while Dobson mopped his forehead with a custard-coloured handkerchief. 'Hope we didn't interrupt *you* too much, Mr Richardson,' he said.

Richardson laughed. 'Well, you *did*, Dobbie, but it was just the thing, in fact. The Residents' Association Action Committee could do with a little music.'

'Sour-faced old lump,' muttered Dobson.

'Mrs Kitchen,' supplemented Richardson. He glanced towards the village musicians. 'I've never seen a violin in a marching band before.'

'Mary Powell,' said Dobson. He nodded at the spare and pale girl and seemed about to add something about her but then changed his mind. 'Would you like us to play something for you?' he suggested.

'Thank you,' responded Richardson with surprise. He hesitated while Dobson beamed appreciatively but then his expression clouded. 'Within reason, of course,' warned the bandmaster. 'We can't get to grips with Sibelius yet. There's not much we can do, to tell the truth, try as they do.' He took on the look of someone who has decided to come clean. 'In fact, they only know three marches and "God Save the Queen". Unless it's your birthday. They know . . .'

'Anything will do,' Richardson assured him. 'How about "Colonel Bogey"? They played that well.'

Dobson was patently pleased and relieved. 'Just the number,' he said. 'They're getting quite decent at that. Would you like them marching? They get more into the swing of it when they are marching.'

'Of course,' said Richardson backing to the wall.

Dobson tapped his baton on his knee briskly, like a chorus girl. 'Right, musicians,' he said. The faces of the band looked up. 'Mr Richardson,' announced the bandmaster, 'has requested "Colonel Bogey". Marching.' The band remained impassive although the housewife with the cymbals clashed them briefly.

'Right, form up,' ordered Mr Dobson. 'And try and keep straighter this time. No wriggling, Sarah Browning.'

'That Bertie Bent was poking me with his instrument,' complained the girl half turning and glaring at the freckled boy next to her. He held his trumpet guiltily as if it were stolen. 'Didn't touch her,' he disclaimed. '*Wouldn't* touch her.'

'All right, all right,' chided the bandmaster. 'Form up and no poking.' They shuffled into three ragged lines. Not one musician seemed to be the height or shape of any of the others; some of the largest instruments were carried by the smallest players; the woman with the cymbals had a plaster on her nose. Dobson picked up his golden tuba. Every instrument shone, a polish accentuated by the shabbiness of the room. When the bandmaster lifted the tuba its surface was reflected on the dim ceiling.

'One, two, three!' he timed. There was a false start. An old man had dropped his music and was attempting to pick it up with uncoordinated fingers. The cornet player next to him tried to help but in doing so struck the ashen girl with the violin who cried out in protest.

'It's like getting race horses into the starting stalls,' apologised Mr Dobson inaccurately. He rallied them once more and at his signal they blared an initial note and set off marching down the hall. It was scarcely long enough for the musicians at the front to take more than half a dozen paces before they had to about turn for the march back, Dobson fumfing at the side while his players swivelled and, swerving like footballers, attempted to avoid those coming towards them. But the march blazed bravely, resounding against the roof. Richardson imagined he saw the dusty flags flutter as though from old memory. All the players played their utmost, stepping out, the white knees of the girls with the baggy trousers of the old man, and the boys in their stained tracksuits and creased jeans, the cymbal-clashing housewife and the heavy girl in wellington boots belabouring the drum.

Eventually they finished and stood puffed and perspiring, each one almost glaring in hope, in anticipation at Edward Richardson. Dobson gave a final fumf on his tuba and remained sweatily beaming. 'There,' he said happily. 'That's the best they've ever played it.'

Richardson clapped them and shook the bandmaster's hand. 'That was terrific,' he said as they went to the door into the porch. He lowered his voice. 'They try tremendously hard,' he said.

'Aye, they try,' said Dobson a trifle sadly. 'But it doesn't come easy to them. You said about Mary Powell with the fiddle. Really and truly she can't play anything. She just marches along and scrapes. The fiddle was her dad's who died just before last Christmas.'

Richardson said: 'So she just goes through the motions.'

'That's it.'

'Like a lot of people do,' said Richardson.

Ten

It was dark by the time he returned to his house, the garden laden with shadows and the night drift of Adele's autumn flowers. The gate scraped familiarly and there was a subdued light glowing in the hallway, but he knew she would not be home, and doubted if Toby would be. He often returned to the house when it was empty.

At one time there had been a dog, a homely terrier which had always been there with a greeting. Two years before Richardson had gone on an overseas trip; Adele had decided to take a holiday, and Toby was then at boarding school. The dog, Teddy, had been sent to a kennels where it had died on the first night of an intestinal blockage. He had never been replaced. It was almost as though, even then, they were preparing for some change in their lives, shedding some of their assets, some of their ties.

Moodily he wandered into the sitting-room, took off his jacket, lifted a glass from the cabinet and picked up the whisky decanter. From the window he could see the evening dark and empty in the village street but, a few hundred yards away, the light over the sign of the Swan, like a near and friendly star. He considered it for a moment, and then set the decanter down and replaced the glass. He put on his jacket again and went out of the front door.

Although it was autumn the late air was mild and still. A plane lumbered towards Heathrow, its landing lights blazing like guns. Ducking his head Richardson went into the closeness of the Swan. There were a handful of drinkers: Dobson, the bandmaster, and the woman with the plastered nose who had been playing the cymbals, were sitting intimately at one end of the small dark tables. He acknowledged them with a brief wave and Dobson guiltily raised his glass. The couple finished their drinks and went out into the dark.

Jim Turner was reading the newspaper from Reading propped behind the bar. Richardson ordered a scotch and bought Jim a beer. 'I hear your lad's working in an antique shop,' said Jim. 'I wish I could get that kid of mine to do something like that. He's useless.'

On cue the door at the back of the bar opened and his son emerged and, without a word, went out at the rear of the room. 'He *looks* like an antique with that pigtail,' grumbled Jim. 'Like a Toby jug.'

The publican's mother-in-law was conversing with Rona and her mother who, having finished their dinner, were sitting at what had become their customary distant alcove table. Richardson excused himself and went towards them as Mrs Durie rose. 'I must be getting on,' she said and, as if she believed she owed Richardson an explanation, she added: 'I was just saying about the unexpected passing of King George the Sixth when poor young Princess Elizabeth, Queen as she is now, was abroad and had to come back.'

When she had gone, wiping her hands on her pinafore, Richardson said to Rona: 'You'll know more about royalty than the Royal Family does if you stay much longer.'

'Oh, we'll be staying awhile yet,' put in Mrs Collingwood with uncompromising haste. 'We're in no hurry at all.' Rona shook her head. 'Some time, Mother, we'll have to go.'

'I don't see *why* we have to,' argued the old lady. 'It's just getting interesting.' She rolled her elderly eyes. 'We've had the low-down on Princess Margaret Rose,' she said, 'but we haven't seen Mr Richardson's house yet.' She looked up bluntly. 'And I'd certainly like to.'

Rona laughed and tapped her mother's forearm admonishingly. Richardson asked: 'Would you like to come and see it now, Mrs Collingwood?' The old lady was agreeing before he had completed the invitation. 'We won't see anything of the garden but you're welcome,' he warned. 'Adele won't be back until later but I'd like you to come.' He glanced at Rona. 'You can see my infamous observatory while the stars are available.'

'I'd love that,' said Rona. 'We'll walk over now, shall we?'

'Sure, sure,' said the old lady at her daughter's glance. She stood up carefully and called to the landlord. 'Jim, we're going to the Richardsons' house.'

'Not for good, I hope.' Jim's face ascended from his newspaper. 'This place wouldn't be the same without you.'

'Don't worry yourself about that,' returned the old lady. 'We'll be home before drinking-up time. If not leave the back door on the latch.'

Rona touched Richardson's sleeve. 'She's practising the local phrases,' she laughed quietly. 'She's even attempting the accent.'

'See you then,' called Pearl waving as they went out the door. 'We won't be late,' promised Rona.

Richardson took the elder woman's arm as they walked along the hollow street. A distant dog barked and there was an owl in the churchyard. Rona walked on her other side. Their steps echoed.

'We *do* have a local accent here,' said Richardson. 'Even though we're only down the road from London.'

'Handed down over generations,' asserted Pearl with an odd pride. 'And, take a look at it.' She wafted her hand about. 'It's as quiet tonight as it was a hundred years ago.'

A droning Boeing, climbing an invisible hill, crossed the sky. 'Well, almost,' said Richardson.

'My mother likes the planes as well,' said Rona. He looked at her and her eyes turned towards him.

'I most certainly do,' confirmed the old lady. 'If they

stopped it would all be *too* silent. They're like theme music in the movies.'

'We have a lady called Mrs Kitchen in Bedmansworth who belongs to something called GROAN,' Richardson told her. 'Group Reaction Over Aircraft Noise. I must tell her that to some people it's theme music. She's the lady who's also trying to make me take down my observatory.'

All three stopped their walk. 'It's crazy,' said Rona. 'I don't understand.'

'She's hijacked the local residents' association,' said Richardson. 'According to her I'm desecrating the place.'

'I've seen that woman,' decided Pearl as they continued to walk. 'And I didn't care for the face of her. She was in the Swan with some others. Talks loud and drinks lemonade.'

'You were going to a meeting,' said Rona.

'It was this evening – a meeting of the "Central Action Committee", would you believe, but it coincided with the Bedmansworth band's practice night and it was chaotic. Nobody heard a thing.'

As they walked the final few yards along the street to his gate, he acted out for them the farce at the village hall and they were still laughing when he opened the front door and led them into the subdued light of the house.

'I can just feel the oldness,' said Pearl standing in the hall as he put the lights on in the sitting-room. 'It's coming out of the walls.'

'It's the woodlice,' he smiled returning to them.

'It's a house that closes around you,' said Rona quietly.

'It's relieved when someone comes back,' said Richardson. He glanced at her. Her mother had wandered into the sitting-room and was pressed close to the French windows scrutinising the indistinct garden. 'Would you like a glass of wine?' he asked.

'Thank you,' said Rona. 'White if you have it. I'm trying to wean Mother off the two half pints of beer she insists on having in the evenings.'

225

'You'll never do that,' warned the old lady over her shoulder. 'Nobody's going to stop my ale.'

Richardson poured three glasses of wine. Pearl left the darkened window. 'It's by no means an uncommon house,' he said as they looked around. 'In the villages around here, there are some really impressive Georgian houses, almost on top of the airport. They haven't quite fallen down under the weight of the twentieth century.'

'The proportions are very careful,' said Rona looking at the ceiling. 'Everything is at home with everything else.'

Richardson said: 'It's been in my wife's family for generations. Those are her parents.'

Two portraits in oils occupied one alcove. 'Your wife looks just like her mother,' said Pearl. She moved close to the painting as she had the window. 'Same eyes and hair. Same shape of the face.'

'There's quite a startling likeness,' he agreed. 'Everyone comments on it.'

'Don't you feel the ghosts?' asked Rona. They moved away from the portraits.

He smiled. 'They may be here but we've never heard them. They lived here and they're content to let us do the same.'

'It doesn't *smell* haunted,' agreed Pearl almost sniffing around. 'It's been well lived in.'

They sat in the long, comfortable room, occupying the two settees. Richardson was so aware of Rona that he hardly dared to look at her. It was almost with relief that he heard the front door open and Toby's voice call up the hall. His son came into the room and reacted with surprise at the visitors. Edward introduced them.

'An antique dealer?' said Mrs Collingwood. 'You're a young antique dealer.'

'Just learning,' said Toby. He felt uncomfortable with these sudden women in his home. The younger woman was beautiful. 'But I know quite a bit already. I aim to have my own business. Tobias Richardson Antiques.'

'Sounds irresistible,' said Rona. Toby felt his face warm at her voice.

'Tobias,' sighed her mother. 'Don't some people have some fine adornments.' She repeated it: 'Tobias.'

'Tobias, Matthew, Ar . . .' recited Richardson.

'*Don't* please, Dad,' protested the boy seriously. 'All those ancient names.'

'Blame your grandmother,' smiled Edward.

'People liked a lot of names once,' said Pearl. 'In America too. Something to do with confusing the Devil.' She pulled a face. 'I have a string of names I wouldn't tell anybody. One of them is Posy.'

'It's a lovely name,' protested Rona gently. She turned to Edward. 'I'd love to spy through the telescope.'

'The sky is fine tonight,' agreed Richardson. He led the way up the staircase. Toby went to the kitchen. 'Your mother will be in soon,' Richardson called.

'It's okay, I can do it myself,' his son responded. 'I only want a sandwich.'

Mrs Collingwood mounted the stairs carefully, not in any difficulty but to savour each old tread and each rolling touch of the carved bannister. 'Just think of the folks in the past who have trodden this staircase, who have put their hands on this rail,' she mused as though to herself. 'See how worn and dark the wood is.'

He preceded them along the galleried landing and opened the heavy door to his study, turning on the lights as he did so. Both women stopped; the furniture, the desk, the illustrations of ancient celestial skies on the walls, the brass, curved bands of his astrolabe glowing in one corner. 'What a fine room,' breathed Rona.

Richardson switched on the desk lamp and then turned up the other lights. Each of the planetary prints was illuminated by an overhanging picture light.

Pearl Collingwood sat in his chair. 'I want to be here,' she announced in her decisive way. 'I want to rest in this room.' She pointed to the short, brass-railed stairway to the observatory. 'And up there, I guess, are the Heavens.'

Richardson laughed. 'A little more distant than *up there*,' he said. 'It's in the right direction,' she insisted.

Rona was looking at the coloured astronomical maps, with their extravagant designs. 'These are so beautiful,' she said lightly touching one of the dark frames. 'Stars and gods and animals. And what colours.' She pointed to the print in front of her. 'It's exquisite, Edward.'

'Andreas Cellarius,' he told her. He bent to see the small wording of the inscription, saying: 'Seventeenth century in Amsterdam. Ah, there's the date, sixteen sixty-one.'

'A Ptolemaic View,' she read. Her slow finger traced the encompassing global circle. 'Of the Universe.'

'That's Mars charging on his war chariot,' Richardson pointed. 'And the lady lying on the swansdown couch is Venus, naturally. When this was drawn Cellarius believed that apart from the earth, the sun and the moon, there were only five planets, Mercury, Venus, Mars, Jupiter and Saturn.'

Together they moved to the next frame. 'This is earlier. Giovanni Cinico who worked in Naples in the mid-fourteen hundreds. His map of the Northern hemisphere. See, he has Ursa Major and Ursa Minor, the two bears, lying back to back at the centre.'

Rona pointed. 'And here we have the Ram, Aries, right?' Richardson nodded. He was at her shoulder. He felt he had never been so close to anyone.

He said: 'And the Twins, Gemini, arguing over the owner-ship of a harp.'

Rona smiled with pleasure. Her mother sat still and watched them from the chair behind. Rona pointed at the chart. 'This twin looks as if he is saying – "I can play it

228

better than you." And there's Aquarius with his jug, and the Lion, very lively.'

'All the astronomers enjoyed drawing Leo,' Richardson said. 'Look at this.' He indicated a squared illustration, rich in colour and lettering. 'Oh, he's grinning,' she said putting her fingers against her cheek. 'What a great smirk.' She looked further along the gallery. 'And these two bears. . . Their eyes! The big one is so cheerful and the little one very doleful,' she said. 'But they're both well fed. Almost portly.'

Richardson said quietly: 'This is one of my favourite maps. It's by an Indian astronomer called Pathak. . . .' He leaned closer to the frame. 'Durgansankawa Pathak, I think he used to pronounce it. This is a bit later than the others. Eighteen forty. It's full of animals. Like a zoo. Lots of snakes.'

'They're all exquisite,' she sighed. 'What fun they must have had spying them out in the sky, giving them names and then drawing them.'

'The father of all the astronomers was not so happy, nor so lucky,' Edward said. 'Copernicus wrote a sensational book on the universe and the day the book was finished by the printer and delivered to his house, poor Copernicus died.'

Rona said: 'Some things just come too late, don't they.'

'Yes, it seems like it.'

They moved away from the wall towards the steps leading to the observatory. Pearl was already on her feet. 'Let's go see the real thing,' she exclaimed. 'Stairway to the stars!'

Richardson led the way. He eased open the door at the top of the steps and, feeling a happiness he always felt at this moment and, added to it now, something more, gazed up to the bowed roof with its panes displaying the covering cloth of the night. The telescope rested in its cradle, waiting for him. He switched on the low light. He heard Rona's

229

intake of breath as she climbed the steps behind her mother and came into the chamber.

The three stood beneath the exposed dome. Rona's chin was tilted as she surveyed the lid of purple above. But her mother suddenly exclaimed: 'Lordy, look at Bedmansworth! Just look at it. You can see every little thing from here. There's the Swan and there's the Straw Man, and the corner of the church and the road. . . .'

They laughed. 'Oh, Mother,' said Rona. 'You climb up here to see the stars and you're looking at the village.'

'I'm more familiar with the village,' replied her mother with a small drop in her voice. She looked at them with a strange embarrassment as if she had said something they were not meant to hear. 'But I've never seen it all at once before.'

There was a moment of hesitation between each of them. Then Richardson swung himself into the tubular seat below the telescope. 'Let's see who's up there tonight.' He pressed a button and the circular path for the telescope opened in the dome. The night air drifted in. He swivelled the instrument and peered into the viewfinder. 'There they are,' he said almost to himself. 'Our friend the Great Bear, Ursa Major, Andromeda showing off, Aries and Aquarius.'

He vacated the chair. 'I'm first,' insisted Pearl. Indulgently, they helped her into the chair and he adjusted the lens. She touched the telescope on its swivel. 'It doesn't feel heavy,' she assured herself. She pressed her eye to the viewfinder. 'Oh wow,' she breathed. 'They're so *near*.' Her tone softened. 'So near . . .'

'I feel they are,' Richardson told her. 'Up here, late at night, you can feel you are floating among them.'

Pearl remained for several minutes scanning the sky before she relinquished her place. 'Okay, you have a turn,' she invited Rona. 'You're a romantic. You'll really enjoy it.'

Richardson turned the chair and Rona slipped easily into

it. Her fingers felt for the stem of the telescope. His touched hers as he guided them to the controls. She folded herself forward, looked into the lens, and gasped quietly. 'Oh how astounding,' she breathed. She held out her hand. 'I feel I could touch them.'

They stayed for another twenty minutes and then went down the steps to his study again. Pearl said in her uncompromising way that she was tired. 'I have a whole lot to do tomorrow.'

Rona glanced smiling at Richardson. 'That sounds important,' she said. 'Thank you so much Edward. It was really amazing. Don't ever let that woman, whatever she's called, or the residents, or *anyone*, make you take your observatory down.'

They walked down to the hallway. Toby was watching television and came from the room to wish them goodnight. Adele was still not home. Richardson said she would have been sorry to have missed them. He went out of the door with them and walked along the street, moist and empty towards the Swan. As before they strolled each side of the old lady and she linked her arms in theirs. 'They ought to be left alone,' she ruminated, talking about the planets. 'We don't have any business. It's their country up there.'

Along the street came the waspy whine of Bernard Threadle's motor cycle. He turned the corner and waved to them importantly as they passed. '*Our* wandering star,' commented Richardson. 'Although maybe not wandering, because he keeps to the same path every night, certain roads at certain times. More like a fixed planet.'

'But noisier,' commented Pearl Collingwood. 'I hear him in the early hours.'

They reached the Swan. They could see Jim clearing the bar through the window. The door was still open. Pearl thanked Edward again, they shook hands and she went in. They heard her tell Jim she had seen God's heaven.

'Thank you, Edward,' said Rona. 'For letting us

eavesdrop.' She was standing very close, almost facing him. She leaned slightly and he felt the swelling of her breast against him as she kissed him on the cheek. He kissed her cheek and said goodnight.

'What a shame about Copernicus,' she said.

'Homelea',
Anglia Road,
Hounslow,
Middlesex,
England,
Great Britain

3rd October

My Dear Father and My Dear Mother,

Your news although welcome was very upsetting for me. Poor Benji being drowned in the floods. Will you get another dog? There was nothing in the UK papers about the floods but these papers do not seem to know that India is a place in the world. India we see on the films, on the telly, and we laugh but are sometimes angry because it is damn nonsense. Sometimes there is a small paragraph in a newspaper about Pakistan or Bangladesh. But Uncle Sammi says, and he is right, it is only about a bus full of people falling from a mountain into a river or some such thing.

My position at the airport is first class. Soon I may be risen to another posting. There was a strange happening since my last letter. An Arab left a pineapple and some boot polish in the conveniences and there was much trouble about this. It was treated most seriously by the authorities. Many investigations were made. At first it was believed they were only the sanitary authorities, but then I saw the representatives had guns so the matter was seen in a different light altogether. But it was only a hoax, that is what they call a trick.

One thing you could do with in India is an underground. It is one of the great things in London. For sixty pence I can travel anywhere in London and far afield. It is not possible to leave the train until I

return to the next station, to Uncle Sammi's, which is Hounslow
East, which is where I commenced, but the trip can take all of a
day.

Some of the time there is nothing to view because it is below
ground (except for the interesting people who get on and off) but it is
also above. There is a map in each tube so I change trains and
change again. It is most interesting and cheap. Today, my rest day, I
am going to Ongar.

I am,
Your respectful loving son,

Nazar

Hobbling to his front picture window Bramwell did his
best to crouch before spying out, checking the landscape of
Bedwell Park Mansions as if it were a hostile frontier. It
was mid-afternoon and the colourless scene was unmoving.
He stumped back into the house and telephoned her.

When she answered he almost dropped the handset. He
looked guiltily around once more.

'Hello, Barbara. It *is* you?'

'Bramwell! I've been so worried about you, darling. How
is the leg?'

'Terrible. I can't move. It's like being in irons. I'm only
ringing now because I've managed to get rid of Lettie and
her tribe. I *must* see you.'

'I've wanted to call. I tried once but it sounded like
Lettie's mother answering.'

He groaned. 'She answers the phone all the bloody time.
According to Lettie she's only being useful, silly old cow.
She watches the television squatting by the phone. The only
time she's not there is when she's at the pictures. That's
where I've just got rid of the lot of them, Lettie as well.
I've sent them to see *Fantasia*. I told them it was funny.

I'm fed up to the teeth with all of them. Oh, Barbara, I want to see you.'

'Could you come over now?' she said readily. 'I can't leave here, I'm on standby.'

'God, I *could*,' he breathed, realising. 'They're gone for the afternoon. I can get there and back easily. I'll get a minicab.'

'Do it,' she urged. 'Don't waste any time. How long have they been gone?'

'Only ten minutes. I rang as soon as they were out of sight. They're walking to the bus stop. I'll be there as soon as I can.'

'I'll be waiting.'

Bramwell put the receiver down and strutted on his encased leg to the cabinet where the telephone directories were kept. He stumped back to the phone and called a taxi, then sat down to wait, his stomach quivering, his leg stiff.

The minicab was there promptly. Bramwell left the front door unlocked and swung his leg and his single crutch along the garden path towards the vehicle. The driver, seeing his disability, left his seat and opened the rear door. 'To the hospital, is it?' he asked.

'Not likely,' replied Bramwell. 'Down by the canal. I'll show you the way. Go towards the Bath Road and I'll direct you from there.'

'The canal,' repeated the driver doubtfully as he moved the car forward. He studied his passenger in the mirror. 'Not thinking of ending it all are we, sir?'

'No, I'm going for a nice swim,' Bramwell said testily. 'To exercise my broken leg.'

They had reached the bottom of the hill and, to his sudden alarm, Bramwell saw Lettie and her relatives still standing in a line at the bus stop. With a brief, choked, cry, he somehow pulled himself down, his head jammed against the back of the seat in front, his leg and the crutch thrust into the seat well. His exclamation caused the driver to check in the mirror again. For a moment he thought that his passenger had gone. The car swerved. Then he saw the quarter moon of Bramwell's balding head. 'All right are we, sir?' he called wide eyed.

'Fine, fine,' gritted Bramwell. He remained hidden. 'Mislaid something, that's all.' They were well past the bus stop before he inched his way into a sitting position again and attempted to look backwards. Then turning, he saw the Slough bus coming towards them. He muttered in relief.

The driver asked: 'Did you find it?'

'What? Oh, yes, thanks. Just a penknife I dropped.'

'People are always dropping penknives,' said the man. 'We're coming up to the main road now. Which way?' He sounded anxious.

'Left, then the second on the right. Towards Datchet,' instructed Bramwell. 'It isn't that far.'

'Good,' said the driver.

He followed the directions. 'Down this lane on the left,' pointed Bramwell. The driver hummed his surprise. 'Into the jungle,' he said.

'The canal is along here,' Bramwell assured him. 'Turn at the end of the lane. Into that gate on the right.'

Mystified, the driver turned into the gate and found himself in the overgrown yard with its rusty vehicles and ancient engines. 'If you didn't have a buggered leg I would have thought you'd brought me here to rob me, or worse,' he said pleasantly. 'Seven quid.'

'No chance of me doing that, mate,' Bramwell told him as he grumblingly paid, adding a twenty-pence tip. The man backed the car as his passenger stumped towards the gap in the hawthorns that led to the towpath. Turning the car into the lane the driver put down the window and called: 'Try jumping!'

Bramwell lifted two ill-natured fingers in his direction and almost toppled over in doing so. He limped onto the canal side and his heart lifted as he saw the curtains move in the

235

window of the barge. Barbara came to the hatch, her face glad. The gangway was already in place and he swung his straightened leg up it. 'Got a spare parrot?' he groaned.

Laughing she helped him through the hatch and down the awkward steps inside. They embraced tightly, kissing and holding each other. 'Are we alone?' he asked glancing towards Georgina's door.

'Georgina's away,' Barbara said. She frowned. 'But you, surely . . . we . . . can't. Not with your leg like that . . . can we?'

He kissed her again fervently. 'I can't tell you how I've missed you. I've tried ringing.'

'And I've missed you,' she answered sincerely. They were still holding each other. She led him to a chair. 'Come and sit down.'

'I want to lie down,' he told her honestly. 'I've been having dreams about you.'

'Darling, stop it. How can you, you poor thing?'

'Let's try. Please let's try.'

She regarded him solemnly. 'Let's have a glass of wine. I'm not allowed, I'm on standby, but one won't hurt.' She went to the galley kitchen and filled two glasses from a cardboard cask on the shelf. 'It's hardly the Côte d'Azur,' she said handing him one.

'What a nightmare,' he remembered. They smiled wistfully together. 'Not all of it, of course. But breaking this leg, those idiots fighting and all that.'

'What about Lettie?' she asked.

'I've stuck to my story,' sighed Bramwell. 'But she nags on about the compensation from the company for falling down their steps. I have to keep putting her off, telling her it will be a long time, there may be a court case. You know what they're like about money.'

'And her family?'

'Mother and brother and our Pauline just sit stunned around the television. I stay in my room as much as possible. I have my own room now because of my leg. Or I stumble down the garden and stare at the privet hedge. I can't even get to the pub.'

'You poor old thing,' said Barbara. She held him against her breasts. Letting the crutch take his weight, he kissed her enjoyably. 'Let's try, darling,' he pleaded. 'We've only done it once.'

She looked at him quizzically and then, making up her mind, she helped him into her bedroom. 'Give me a hand with the trousers, will you?' He was sitting on the side of the bed. 'It's not very romantic, I know.'

'Lettie does the trousers for you, does she?'

'Well, yes. There *is* nobody else.'

She began to laugh. She knelt in front of him and tugged at the trousers. 'That poor leg,' she said looking at the cast. He stroked her hair and she dropped her face into his lap. The crutch clattered to the floor when she lifted her head. His erection was standing inside his underpants like a snow-covered hill. She slipped down her jeans and pulled her sweater away. He watched her. When she had taken off the rest of her clothes she levered him onto the bed and pulled of his pants.

She smirked. 'This,' she said crawling beside him, 'is going to be interesting.'

'And difficult,' he added. 'Watch the leg.'

'Can you move it over a bit? Just a couple of inches. Here, let me do it.'

Her professional sense of initiative took over. She lifted the heavy leg and with care swung it aside like a derrick, then moved it fractionally more. 'That's it,' she said patting the cast. There was a full expression in her eyes as she climbed onto him. She had a fawn suntan, white skin where her bikini had been. His arms went up to her sides and his hands to the pale breasts. Carefully, then confidently, they coupled. She eased herself down tightly to him, so her face

237

was against his and her hair lay scattered around his neck. 'It's still not right,' she whispered. 'That leg is so hard.'

'I can't unscrew it,' he said unhappily. They were still locked into each other. She giggled and he felt it.

'I know,' she suggested. 'Let's drape something over it. Like my dressing-gown.' She arched to her knees and had almost left him when she said: 'No, I've got a better idea – darling, put the leg *inside* the bed. Tuck it under the duvet.'

Barbara heaved herself upright. She made a face as he took himself from her. 'I'll get withdrawal symptoms,' he warned.

'It won't take a moment. Don't let it get cold.' She opened the duvet and like someone lagging a water pipe, she swung his rigid leg and replaced the covering over it. 'Very erotic,' she murmured regarding him stretched naked, one limb missing. 'Is it comfortable?'

'*It* is. *I'm* not,' he complained. 'Come back to me, poor one-legged man that I am.'

Her expression becoming earnest, she bent her body like a bow. Bramwell reached out again to hold her ribs, to support her while she placed herself above him. 'Jesus, God, you are wonderful,' he breathed feeling her.

She whispered. 'Oh Bram.'

The telephone rang. 'Oh shit,' said Bramwell.

They paused, poised. 'Please leave it,' he pleaded.

'I can't,' she said. 'Darling, you know I can't. I'm on standby.'

'So am I.'

'I must.' She could not reach the bedside receiver from their tight situation. With a brief kiss she abandoned him once more and slithered over the bump in the duvet. 'Watch the leg,' he muttered.

Just as she reached the telephone, it ceased ringing. She picked it up anyway but heard only the regular tone.

'Can't be the company,' Bramwell said. He lay comically

on the bed. 'They wouldn't have rung off. Can we start again?'

'Let's move nearer the phone,' she suggested diffidently.

'I'll have to transport the leg over there.'

'So you will.' She looked as if she might laugh or weep. 'Bram, what a mess we're making of it all.'

'It's the others, not us,' he said stoutly. 'Every time we get together.'

'Let's try again,' she said softly.

'Please,' he asked.

Her light hair had dropped all around her face; she crawled over the bed towards him with her eyes shut and biting her lip. 'Remember the leg,' he whispered. She eased herself across the protuberance below the duvet, then inched up his body. 'You still want me?' she said.

'Didn't you notice?'

'I can feel.' Once again they coupled and began to rock together. Again the phone rang. 'Shit almighty!' Barbara sobbed. 'Please,' Bramwell said. 'Stay. Just now . . . for one moment.'

'I will,' she whispered. 'Here it is, Bram. I can feel you.'

The telephone kept ringing. She collapsed against him. Then, mumbling, she slid herself away and once more crawled across the bed. 'The leg,' he mumbled.

Barbara picked up the phone. 'Hello.'

From where he lay Bramwell heard the voice at the other end. 'Hello, Missus Bobbins. This is Lettie. Have you seen my Bramwell?'

'Drop me here,' he instructed the minicab driver. 'This will do.'

It was a different man. He seemed concerned. 'Got far to go on that leg?' he asked. 'It won't cost any more to take you right to where you want to go.'

'No. No. that's perfectly all right,' mumbled Bramwell

239

searching for his money. 'I need to take a bit of exercise. It's not far.'

He scanned the immediate area to reassure himself. They were at the foot of the brief hill. His house was out of sight around the climbing bend. He paid the man who came around to assist him from the back. 'Did my leg once,' the driver said. 'Fishing.'

Once the car had driven away, Bramwell adjusted his crutch and began with genuine difficulty to mount the easy hill. Lettie saw him as soon as he had rounded the slope and came from the house. He could see her frown below her blowing hair. His stomach began to bubble like a stew. 'Hello darling,' he called weakly. 'Just went for a stroll.'

She stepped out towards him and for a moment he expected the worse. But he realised that the eyes were uncertain. 'How was *Fantasia*?' he smiled.

'No good,' she said in a low voice. 'Walt Disney but not funny. Why did you go for this troll?'

'It's *stroll* not troll. Help me, will you, sweetie.' He gave her the arm on the other side from the one occupied with the crutch. He had seized the initiative and he intended to keep it. 'I just couldn't stand being penned in any longer,' he told her breathlessly as she helped him up the last stretch of incline. 'Especially as you weren't home. I missed you. I thought I'd try and reach the pub. Have a cup of tea. Look in the church. Anything.'

Her Filipino eyes had narrowed but she was wavering. 'You didn't go to see Missus Bobbins?' she asked.

The negative encouraged him. 'Missus Bobb . . . who is? Oh, that woman Poppins. Good God, no. Why would I want to see her? She doesn't even live around here . . . I don't think.'

They had reached the front door. He knew she wanted to believe him. 'I shouldn't have tried it,' he moaned. Lettie's mother and Pauline had come into the hall to witness his arrival. '*Fantasia* no good, eh?' he said smiling wanly at them.

'Not much Donald Duck,' said Lettie's mother grimly.

'Only a bit Mickey Mouse,' grumbled Pauline.

'That's bad luck.' Already Lettie was guiding him to a chair. 'I rested by the church gate,' he said piously. 'I shouldn't have gone that distance. Foolhardy. And getting back up the hill . . .'

'Why you don't telephone?' asked Lettie, her suspicions lingering. Her brother now appeared and said: 'Fillum not good.'

'Too bad,' Bramwell sympathised. He knew he was home and dry now. He turned to Lettie. 'I didn't realise you'd be back, love,' he said. 'Or I would have phoned. You could have carried me up the hill.'

Lettie bent near him. 'I thought . . . I thought you sneak away to Missus Bobbins,' she confessed. 'Our Pauline found her telephone number under your bed.'

'What was our Pauline doing under my bed?'

'Just looking,' said Pauline.

Bramwell scowled and growled: 'I don't need this sort of treatment. I only took her number to thank her for helping me.' He tapped his plaster cast forcefully. 'Which I forgot to do, incidentally.'

'So sorry,' said Pauline. 'Big mistake.'

'Big mistake indeed,' added Bramwell. Lettie was near to weeping, the edges of her dark eyes red. 'I get you a drink or a cup of tea,' she offered.

'I'd like a cup of tea, if you please,' he asked putting his fingertips together primly.

As she went from the room Lettie was sniffing. She turned to Pauline at the door to the kitchen. 'Our Pauline just bloody fool,' she said.

Bramwell sat back and smiled.

A loaded October moon, the sort of moon the one-time inhabitants called the parish lantern, hung hugely above the roofs and moulting trees, giving to the golden ball and arrow that topped Bedmansworth church tower an almost ethereal glow. A pilot or passenger in an incoming aircraft could, on such a lucid night, have easily traced the course of the village street by its window lights.

There was an added illumination on this evening because the monthly youth disco was taking place in the hall, and the thrum-thrum of the Ark Raiders of Slough pulsated through the open windows. The Reverend Henry Prentice always made a precautionary call at the hall at ten thirty, and liked to join in the dancing, if only to encourage the youthful that both the Church of England and the Bedmansworth vicar were lively bodies; that, below the clerical garb, his heart was with them. On a sultry night the previous summer while dancing with a flushed teenager, he had become oddly frenzied, his clerical collar had burst and the girl had rushed weeping from the hall. Outside she had snivelled that she was going to tell her father although the priest had heard nothing further.

The vicar's stated object for his ten-thirty visit was to ensure that all was proper for there had been disturbances and once a drum was thrown through the window, followed by its drummer, although this had been done by interlopers from Maidenhead.

Henry Prentice made his pastoral way to the hall now, pausing for a sly smoke beneath his own lych-gate, and enjoying the secrecy and the solitude of the street. There was a football match on television and the ululation of crowd and commentary coming through the cottage windows followed him as he walked. The Ark Raiders of Slough seemed exceptionally loud, he thought anxiously. An aeroplane, passing above, was reduced to silence. Inside the steamed windows he could see the shapes of young people jumping up and down like pistons; outside, tucked into the shadow of the long porch, were two entwined forms which parted as he approached. 'Just getting a bit of air, Vicar,' said the girl pulling down her sweater.

In the short tunnelled entrance the atmosphere was fetid, the hammering of the musicians accentuated. He grimaced but walked in beaming. There were about fifty youngsters casting about on the dance floor. The volunteer caretaker, Mr Broughton-Smith, the retired solicitor, always insisted on scattering chalk on the boards as he did for village dances, lending the surface a sliding quality advantageous in the tango and the foxtrot. With the dancing of the young this was unnecessary, although he had not realised it, and the chalk rose in knee-high clouds. Some of the young people fantasised that they were dancing amid dry ice in a pop video. The disco was popular, not only because it was held on a Tuesday but also because it was free, the group or the disco jockey being paid for by the adaptation of a clause in the will of Mrs Henrietta Garbold who, in the 1920s, had left a sum for financing parish entertainments. She had been a popular local contralto.

Swishing the contents of his plastic glass, Randy Turner noted the vicar's arrival: 'Here comes Creeping Jesus,' he muttered, his new ragged moustache resting on the rim as he drank.

Toby Richardson swished his Coca-Cola also. 'The vicar?' he said. 'Oh, he's all right. Somebody's got to do the job.'

'Why?' argued Randy. He tugged at his pigtail. On these nights he wore his flowered coat. 'Religion, worst bloody thing in this world or the next, I reckon.'

He regarded Toby aggressively. 'That's what I reckon,' he repeated having run out of words. He glanced at Toby's plastic glass. 'How old are you now, then?'

'Sixteen,' said Toby. 'Last August.'

'And you're drinking that piss?'

'What else is there?' demanded Toby examining his drink. 'You tell me. Except Orangina and lemon and soda.'

Mrs Mangold from the Straw Man, the disco's voluntary

bartender, waddled across the floor towards the vicar. Slough's Ark Raiders banged tirelessly. 'Get some of this down your neck,' invited Randy glancing briefly to either side. He fumbled under his flowered jacket and produced a half bottle of Navy rum. Toby's eyes widened. Randy unscrewed the top and slopped some into his Coca-Cola. 'Thanks . . . thanks,' Toby said. 'That's great.'

'My private supply,' bragged Randy. 'Fell off a lorry outside my old man's pub.' He poured some into his own glass, whirling it grandiosely, and flinging it down his throat. He choked spectacularly. His face reddened, his cheeks bulged. 'Shit,' he spluttered. 'Went down the wrong way.'

The music staggered to a halt, the dancing stopped, and the chalk clouds subsided. 'No decent women,' sniffed Randy surveying the company. 'Me, I go to Reading. Great chicks there. And they *do*. Ecstasy, everything.' He winked hugely at Toby, his rough face creasing. Some of the dancers had come towards the bar, Mrs Mangold had returned to serve them and the Reverend Prentice had called 'Goodnight all!' and left through the porch followed by a scattering of response. The Ark Raiders of Slough restarted as though someone had exploded a device behind them, the drummer laying into the drums, the guitars swinging like doors, the keyboard legs collapsing.

'Get the talent here,' complained Randy. 'There ain't any.' He moved closer to Toby and indicated a sparse-looking girl. 'If you screwed her she'd fall apart.'

Toby nodded unsteadily. The fumes of the rum were lifting to his nose. He eyed Mrs Mangold and felt glad her attention was elsewhere and that the vicar had gone. 'You had a cool bird, didn't you,' continued Randy craftily. 'Fancied that myself. She give you the rush?'

Toby twisted the rum and coke. 'Want more?' offered Randy. He produced the half bottle and poured a portion

244

into each of their glasses under the concealment of his jacket. 'Plenty where this came from,' he promised.

The aroma of the rum filled Toby's head. 'You finished with 'er?' pursued Randy. 'That Liz what's-'er-name.'

'I got fed up,' answered Toby unsteadily but truthfully. 'You know how it is. Scared of getting fixed up permanently.'

'Like me,' agreed Randy. He became intent again. 'But if you've finished with 'er, I wouldn't mind giving her one.'

'She's expensive,' warned Toby. The rum was making him feel giddy. 'Dinner and drinks, the lot. And she wants somebody with wheels. I haven't had lessons yet.'

Randy grimaced. 'That's the trouble with good lookers,' he acknowledged. 'You've got to have dosh. I'm on the rock and roll.'

'She wouldn't go out with anybody on the dole,' said Toby. 'Unless it was Richard Branson.' He felt the rum washing around thickly in his stomach. 'I'm going out for a pee,' he said hurriedly.

He skirted the dancers, reached the porch gratefully and plunged through the door into the sharp air. He hurried around the corner of the hall and was sick among the weeds. As the nausea rolled over him he leaned against the building, feeling the vibrations of the Ark Raiders coming from the other side. He breathed deeply, leaning his sweating forehead against the wall. The Ark Raiders throbbed against his skull. He felt terrible. Why could he never do anything right?

When the first onslaught had passed *Toby* decided miserably to go home. The swollen moon looked as if it were balancing on the point of the church's golden arrow. He regarded it caustically. A girl's voice said: 'What's the matter with you?'

He had seen her on the dance floor, like a stick, bone-thin arms and legs, taller than him, but with long brushed hair and a small face. 'Just thinking I might kill myself,' he sighed.

'That's dangerous. What for?'

'Women trouble,' he said.

'Can't you get any?' she asked. To his astonishment she then coolly reached out with both hands and placed them on his cheeks before pulling his face towards her and kissing him on the lips. 'You've been drinking,' she said. 'I can niff it.'

'A couple of rums,' he said. His hands went to her skinny waist. She had no breasts that he could see; thin all the way down. 'I can't drink those kid's drinks all night.'

'Is that your sick over there?' she inquired pointing at it.

'Sick?' he turned. 'No . . . not me. Nothing to do with me.'

'Oh,' she said sounding surprised. 'I bet it was. It's still steaming.'

'It's not me,' he argued. 'I don't throw up.'

'I do,' she said honestly. 'Ever such a lot.' She put her arms about his shoulders. She seemed three inches taller. 'I followed you out here. Do you know my name? I know yours. I found out.'

'What's yours?' he asked. God, but she was thin. He could feel her ribs through her dress.

'Dee,' she said.

'Dee?'

'Just Dee, that's all,' she repeated impatiently. 'I've got a bearskin.'

'You've got your clothes on,' he said weakly.

'And I've heard that plenty of times too. No, I've got this bearskin in my bedroom and sometimes I lie on it, with nothing on.'

'A bare skin against a bearskin.' He persisted.

She sighed. 'Old jokes.' She summed him up in the moonlight. 'Fancy coming home? I've had this place. I've got that chalk up to my knees. It's all on my black stockings.' Without coyness she lifted her skirt to her thighs.

'Home?' he asked staring at her legs. He looked up into her plain, expectant face. 'Where's that?'

'Only a bus ride,' she said leaning and kissing his nose.

'All right then,' he nodded slowly, hardly able to believe her. He regarded her suspiciously. 'Did Randy Turner send you to set me up?'

'Him with the greasy pigtail. Yuk.'

She put an arm like string around him and encouraged him towards the road. 'I don't mind you being littler than me,' she said. 'I like it in fact.' She bent and kissed him at random. 'Wait till you see my bearskin.'

Toby was thinking that nothing, surely, could be as easy as this. 'Don't let's miss the bus,' he said.

When they turned the bend in the street the bus, cheerily lit, was waiting, a standing invitation, the conductor and the driver sitting in the passenger seats, one reading a book, the other a newspaper. As they approached the latter checked his watch. 'Five more minutes,' he said as though to reassure them. 'Then we'll have lift-off.'

'Upstairs,' said Dee decisively. She began to climb at once. Toby glanced up guiltily as she turned the bend in the stairs. There was a flash of skin at the top of her black stockings. He had a vision of her lying naked except for those stockings on her bear rug. God, this was going to be *it*! It was actually going to be *it*! And it was all so easy.

She was occupying the seat at the back by the time he reached the upper deck. Before he could sit down she had lounged across the whole seat and pulled up her rod-like legs, her skirt slipping up. 'Do I look like one of those women?' she invited.

'Which women?' He had difficulty in keeping up with her.

'Them what show all they've got. Legs and boobs and suchlike.' She thrust out her flat chest. 'Like in the papers?'

'You look better than that,' he told her. He had remained standing, torn between hoping she would continue with her display and wanting to insert himself into the seat next to her.

'You're quite nice,' she said smoothing her stockings and wrinkling her face. 'This bloody chalk, look at it.'

The engine of the bus quivered and the lights dipped momentarily. 'Lift-off,' she said mimicking the driver. 'Looks like we'll have it all to ourselves.'

'The disco doesn't finish until eleven,' he said consulting his watch importantly. It had been brought into the shop with a box of miscellaneous effects. Mr Old said he could have it for a pound.

'That's posh,' she pointed. 'That watch.'

'It's very old,' he told her solemnly. 'I'm in antiques. I pick up the odd treasure.'

'Antiques!' She appeared thrilled and entangled her legs like a film star. He sat in the seat in front of her and gazed over the back. 'I'll be going into business on my own before long,' he said.

'It's my lucky night,' she breathed.

He was about to say 'Mine too' when the conductor mounted the stairs. The bus was beginning to drag forward. The man was stooped as though pulled forward with the weight of his ticket machine. He had ringed eyes above a moist moustache.

'Legs off the seat,' he said at once to Dee. 'One seat per passenger.'

She scowled but obeyed. Toby sat next to her. The conductor said: 'Where will it be tonight? The Hilton?'

'Hilarious,' she said. 'Stanwell Plain. Two.'

Stanwell Plain sounded remote. 'What time is the last bus back?' asked Toby.

'This is it,' replied the conductor with a mean satisfaction. 'This bus turns about face and goes straight back to Slough, calling at Bedmansworth. This is the ultimate bus.'

He produced a small book from beneath his tunic. 'Have

you read this, either of you?' he asked. 'Bertrand Russell. *Problems of Philosophy.*'

'Read it last week,' said Dee cheekily. Toby laughed.

'Don't laugh,' said the conductor. 'Do you the world of good. It's changed my life.'

Toby paid the fares and he whirled his machine. He replaced the book beneath his tunic and with almost a balletic revolve on one foot turned and went down the stairs.

Dee giggled. 'I can still put my legs up,' she said. To his joy she did so, this time stretching the thick black stockings across his thighs as he sat in the next seat. Pretending to dust the chalk away he began rubbing them with both hands. 'That's nice,' she said looking at what he was doing and then bringing her eyes up to his. 'That's warming me up.'

They kissed, her contribution so savage that he thought she had drawn blood. He wiped his mouth and looked quickly at the back of his hand. It was unstained. He kissed her more gently and felt her curl. 'Wait until we're on my bearskin,' she whispered.

'How can I get back?' He cursed himself for worrying.

'You don't,' she promised. 'You stay all night.'

'Is it a real bear? Was it?'

'Don't know. I haven't asked it. Probably. It's furry like it's real.'

'It might be worth something,' he told her seriously. 'We get them in the shop sometimes.'

His hands had gone to her chest but it was so devoid of undulations that he ended by giving it a general rub and transferring his exploration back to her legs. He buffed gently on the heavy stockings to the knee, then higher.

'Only to the top,' she warned. And as though there were demarcations: 'Not on public transport.'

'The top's quite a good way up,' he said moving his hands higher. He contacted where the stockings ended and the chilly skin began. He hooked his fingers into the top. 'What about your parents?'

Dee seemed surprised. 'Parents? I don't have parents,' she said. 'I've got a mum and dad.'

'Sorry. I meant them.'

'They won't be any bother,' she forecast. 'Mum goes to bed early because it's the old man's night for boozing. He goes to the institute and comes back blind. Every Tuesday . . . It's some sort of cheap night for drunks they have.' She extended herself to him. 'It will be all right for us, pet.'

As they grappled pleasurably again the worry over the consequences of not going home that night nor getting up for work the following day briefly nagged him but he buried the thought. He had accidentally discovered someone who wanted him.

The bus swayed through the black countryside with the halo of Heathrow glistening on the near horizon. An incoming plane bellowed above the bus and they saw its lights flatten out as it homed onto the blazing flight path. 'Noisy old things,' she grumbled. 'My dad reckons they ought to get people back on the railways.' She gave him another kiss and he slid his hand up her skirt, stopping when he arrived at her skin. 'My father works at Heathrow,' he said.

'Oh, so does mine. In one of the kitchens.'

'Mine's just in an office,' said Toby diffidently. 'He goes abroad quite a bit.'

'That must be nice,' she said patting his face as though trying to replace something. 'I like the idea of abroad. My dad and mum went to Spain but he fell down some steps when he was blindo and they had to come back. She's fed up with him.'

She squirmed around and began looking into the darkness beyond the window. 'We're here,' she announced suddenly. 'That's chatting for you.' His heart jumped. She laughed as

250

they hurried down the stairs. 'Don't push,' she called back. 'There's not that much of a hurry.'

The conductor viewed them morosely. 'Don't forget what I told you, you two. Bertrand Russell.' He took the book from his coat and waved it at them. 'It'll change your life.'

'I'll buy it tomorrow!' Toby called back. Dee laughed wildly as they trotted from the bus, their arms about each other's waists. Then, abruptly, sensing something, she held her finger to his lips. 'Better be quiet from now on,' she said. 'Don't want to wake them up.' They walked a few paces. The moon had gone and the night was autumn cold. 'Mind, it would take a lot to wake the old man.'

They had to walk from the road along a nettle-hedged footpath. It was very dark and she led the way holding her hand out behind her to guide him. 'I never get scared going along here,' she whispered. 'I reckon God looks after me.' A few more paces. The path was muddy below his shoes. He began to wonder where this was. A dog barked in one of the cottages and disturbed birds rustled in the rough hedges.

'There it is,' she said like someone making a discovery. Before them, barely outlined against the sky, was a black oblong, a cottage standing alone. 'Don't make any row,' she warned again.

He followed her at an ape-like crouch, his confidence draining. They reached a porch leaning shabbily to one side. Dee opened her purse. 'I've got my own key,' she said. 'I 'aven't,' came a deep voice from the shadows. Toby felt himself jump. A massive shape materialised.

' 'Ello, Dad,' said Dee dismally. 'Won't she let you in?'

'No, she bleedin' well won't,' said the man. 'Like usual.' He wore a flat cap and a bulging sweater. 'Bolted it.' He apparently noticed his daughter's companion for the first time. 'Who's that?' he asked pointing at Toby three feet away.

'Tony, I mean Toby,' she said. 'He's my friend. He's . . .
missed the bus.'

'I have,' said Toby truthfully and glumly.

'Now we're all stuck out here,' said the father sombrely.
'That's a bastard and no mistake.'

He scratched his head and the action seemed to summon
an idea. Although he was swaying his mind and speech
seemed clear. 'I know,' he said. 'What we'll do is to tell her
that *you're* here.' He nodded at Toby who said: '*Me*? But
she doesn't know *me*.'

'That's just the point,' said the man craftily. 'We'll say
we found you stranded and you want a bed for the night.'

'That's right,' said Dee vigorously nodding her head.
'Appeal to the better side of her.'

'If she's got one,' said her father doubtfully.

Toby was trapped. It was turning into a nightmare.
'But . . . I'll have to go home,' he said.

'How?' challenged Dee folding her thin arms.

'Somehow,' he repeated miserably. 'I have to go to work
in the morning.'

'You think of that *now*,' she said with brusque meaning.

'Once we're inside you can be on your way,' her father
told Toby helpfully. He turned to his daughter. 'But you'll
have to phone. She won't answer to stones chucked at the
window. She never does.'

Dee sulked in the shadows. 'Oh, all right,' she sighed.
'I'll phone.' She turned to Toby. 'You stay here with him.'
She nodded to her father as though there might be some
doubt who she meant.

Confusion and depression filled Toby. His anticipation
squelched, his body cold, he nodded. 'Won't be a minute,'
she said brightly. 'It's only down the road to the box.' She
strode away on her stem legs.

Toby found himself standing below the saggy porch with
her father. 'Play dominoes do you?' inquired the man as
though he wanted a game.

'Dominoes? No . . .'

'Good game,' said Dee's father solemnly. 'Brings out the best in you.'

'Yes, I expect so,' muttered Toby meekly.

'I work at the airport,' continued the man. 'Kitchen porter. Most important place at Heathrow, that is. More than Air Traffic Control. It would all stop, just like that, without us.'

They lapsed to moody silence. The telephone began to ring eerily in the cottage. Dee's father stiffened. 'Wake up, wake up,' he muttered as it continued. Then it stopped. 'She's got out of bed,' he said. 'She won't be pleased.'

From within the house came a woman's angry voice. A window was opened above. The father left the porch and Toby followed him. 'Watch out for yourself,' the man warned.

They stood looking up at a face in the cottage window. 'This lad,' called out the man pleadingly. 'He's lost. Can't get home. Let him in, Rose.'

The face vanished although the window remained open. They remained staring up hopefully. What, for a moment, Toby thought was the face then reappeared, round and pale, but the man let out a hollow half cry: 'She's got the pot!'

Gallantly he pulled Toby back, taking the full force of the contents himself. There was some left and the woman projected this from the window, hitting Toby on the chest. He cried out and sat backwards into the mud of the garden. 'She's done that trick before,' mentioned the man.

'I'm going,' said Toby staggering away. 'God . . . ugh . . .'

'Don't blame you,' said the man philosophically. 'It's not a nice smell.' He added: 'Goodnight, son.'

'Goodnight,' sobbed Toby. He took off his coat and trailed it frantically through the grass. Dee appeared along the path. 'Did it work?' she asked in her bright way.

Toby stared at her and said deliberately: 'She threw the chamber-pot over us.'

'I wish she wouldn't do that,' sighed Dee. 'Was it a lot?'

'Plenty.'

'I reckon she saves it up,' said her father.

'Yes,' said Dee sombrely. 'Hoards it.' She turned to Toby. 'Can't you wear your coat?'

'No, it stinks.'

'You'll be cold without it,' she said. 'Wait a bit. I'll get you a blanket. It's the dog's, or was, he's gone and died, but it will keep the chill off.'

She darted around the side of the house. Toby could not believe this was happening. He was tempted to run away, fast and far, but he still waited for her.

As though reading his thoughts when she reappeared, she kissed him, holding her nose at the smell of his coat, and said sadly. 'It's not as good as the bearskin. Sorry.'

'Don't mention it,' muttered Toby. He put the blanket around his shoulders. It smelled only marginally less offensive than his coat, but it was dry. He turned and tramped away down the muddy path towards the road. 'Goodbye,' she called through the dark. Then romantically: 'I suppose it *is* goodbye.'

'I'll say it bloody is,' he muttered to himself. He had a faint hope that the bus might still be there but it was not. How far was Bedmansworth? Three or four miles at least.

Through the bare and ragged night he tramped. Not a vehicle passed him on the road. There were only rattling trees and moody cows in fields. The moon came out again, as though to get a clear view of him, but having done so hid itself in clouds. More than an hour later he was nearing Bedmansworth. He heard a clock chiming a distant three and groaned.

He decided to take a short cut over the hill where the Burridges had their tent. They kept a lantern outside set on a stone and he could see it flickering like a small lighthouse in a dark sea. He climbed a stile and puffed up the gentle hill and then down the other side. He was afraid he might disturb them and he wanted no one to witness his plight. Quietly he passed by. He could hear a snore and he felt a pang of envy, a man snoring peacefully alongside a warm woman. On the down slope, when he was halfway to the gate into the village, he heard a whinny from the raised ground behind and saw the outline of the old horse, Freebie, that hung around the Burridges' tent. It stood challengingly against the sky. As though to give him a better view, the moon showed itself once more. The horse gave another whinny and began to trot towards him.

'Oh God, oh no,' he cried to himself. He turned: 'Go on! Sod off! Get away!' He waved his hands and Freebie swerved and trotted gamely up the slope. Toby began to run. The horse came cantering down the hill after him. He shouted as he ran and turned and waved his coat and the blanket. The animal pulled up short, snorted, and veered away. 'Oh Jesus,' said Toby like an exhausted prayer. He reached the gate and somehow got over it. The horse was just behind him and stood snorting at the barrier. 'Sodding thing,' sobbed Toby.

By now he was almost staggering but it was only ten minutes to home. He had almost reached there when the insect sound of Bernard Threadle's patrol bike caught his ear. He had sworn more in the last two hours than he had in his entire life and now he swore again. He hid in a gateway while Bernard trundled by, did the circle at the head of the village, and went past the other way.

Toby reached his house. It was tranquilly dark. God, what a night. He left his coat and the blanket and his mud-caked shoes in the garage and, letting himself in silently and wearily, climbed to his room.

He washed his face and hands and cleaned his teeth, put on his pyjamas and fell aching into bed. He was still awake though and he lay thinking how disastrous his life had become. He took the bolster from beneath his pillow and tucked it between his legs. He stared at its blank white linen face in the darkness and kissed it. 'I'm home, darling,' he said hopelessly.

Eleven

Before the harvest festival service on the middle Sunday in October the Reverend Henry Prentice was standing in the church porch, his vestments blowing like banners, greeting each of the morning worshippers and wondering where he was going to dispose of the surplus fruit and vegetables before they went rotten.

The line was long, reaching down to the churchyard gate, for it was a popular service with always the same rousing hymns. He saw Pearl and Rona halfway along the queue and smiled to them. Pearl lingered while Rona walked into the church conversing with Mrs Mangold from the Straw Man. 'I want to read the lesson today,' Pearl firmly told the vicar.

'Today?' The priest looked bewildered. 'But we've already got two . . .'

'Today,' repeated Pearl. Her voice descended to a whisper. 'If you don't I'll tell your wife about . . .' She made the motion of puffing a cigarette. 'You know what.'

'First or second lesson?' asked the vicar.

'The first.'

'Mr Dobson was going to read it. He can do it another day. I'll have to tell him. He was looking forward to it too.' A glance showed that she would not be shifted. 'It's marked in the Bible on the lectern,' he said.

'I know. I came in yesterday and practised it. The Book of Ruth. . . . Thank you, Henry.'

She moved on to join Rona inside the church. 'The Reverend's asked me to read the lesson,' she said to her daughter.

'That was short notice,' said Rona.

'An emergency,' replied her mother. They sat in their pew.

Dobbie Dobson was coming along the aisle. 'You can read it Mrs Collingwood,' he said. ' 'Course you can.' He looked doleful. 'Except I've been rehearsing and I've had my suit cleaned. The vicar says I can do it Christmas.'

Produce was piled around the chancel steps; apples, pears, potatoes, kiwi fruit, and other goods in tins and packs, gone past their supermarket sell-by dates. The display was continued along the choir stalls and the pulpit was decorated with a sheaf of plastic corn used in the Christmas crib.

Rona, when she remembered it as she did many times over the ensuing years, could hear the choir singing down the aisle: 'Fair waved the golden corn in Canaan's pleasant land.' As they reached the steps one of the footballing Latimer twins suddenly had a melon at his feet. It was passed to his brother and then back along the line, shoes poking from beneath white cassocks to touch it on.

The vicar preached a rousing sermon. 'What plenty!' he exclaimed throwing his hands wide over the unwanted fruit and vegetables. 'What munificence! What plenty!'

But the moment Rona would never forget was when her mother, at a nod from the Reverend Prentice, stepped upright to the lectern and read the first lesson in her strong American voice. 'The Book of Ruth,' she announced.

Rona sat with tears scarcely held back and her mother recited. ' "And she said, I pray you, let me glean and gather after the reapers among the sheaves; so she came, and hath continued even from the morning until now, that she tarried a little in the house . . ." '

Pearl's voice was fine and clear. No one stirred in the church. It became stronger: ' ". . . whither thou goest, I will go; and where thou lodgest, I will lodge; and thy people *shall be* my people . . .

' "Where thou diest, will I die, and there will I be buried . . ." '

Pearl Collingwood had borrowed a red, white and blue golf umbrella from Jim at the Swan and, feeling quietly grand beneath its striped shelter, she walked through Monday morning rain to the church.

It was raining only gently, scarcely weeping, but the Middlesex clouds were low, crouching as they came over the flattish land. The lights of the airport shimmered on the misty sky.

She whirled the umbrella below the dark lych-gate, striking the spokes on its wood as she did so, showering herself with drops of water. Then she manoeuvred it out into the churchyard and held it in front of her, for the rain had changed direction there. She made for the church door like a yacht with a coloured spinnaker pushing through heavy weather. In the porch she efficiently collapsed it and left it leaning against a bulky bicycle.

The vicar and his helpers were already there, three ladies already sizing up the piles of fruit and vegetables left from the harvest festival service. 'It goes rotten quite quickly,' said Henry Prentice when he had greeted her. 'It's often more than ripe when it gets here. Then all the wretched flies come in.'

'I'm here to help,' offered Pearl in her determined manner. 'What do I do?'

He introduced her to the three other women. They all knew her by sight, or had heard about her, for she was now a figure in the local landscape. 'Mrs Phillips, Mrs Batrick and Mrs Johns,' he recited. Pearl shook hands with each one. 'If you could sit in the front pew, dear,' said Mrs Phillips, 'and wrap the kiwi fruits and put them in the boxes.'

'I can bend,' Pearl told her stoutly. 'I can touch my toes. I do every day. I don't need to sit.'

'No, no,' insisted Mrs Phillips whose face was red from picking up the fruit. 'You'll be doing a useful job if you sit there.'

'Imagine, kiwi fruits,' sighed the vicar sitting beside her. He began to help her with the tissue-paper wrapping. 'And Cape gooseberries . . . lychees. Harvest festivals aren't what they were. We plough the fields but we don't scatter. We have some difficulty in giving the produce away now. Soon, I imagine, we will be forbidden to do so unless it's all hermetically sealed and stamped.'

'Regulations,' she nodded. 'I heard.'

'Lots of them. European regulations.'

Pearl looked reflective. 'We needed a civil war before all the states joined together. Some still don't consider they've joined.' She continued wrapping the fruit. 'Times change and change again. Maybe in San Francisco they put grass in the church at Thanksgiving.'

'Grass?'

'Like they smoke.'

He gave a short grimace. 'Times, as you say, change. My father, who was a vicar of a parish in Hertfordshire, used to give the identical harvest festival sermon every year. It's the same one as I used yesterday. "What plenty!" he used to bellow, waving his arms over the marrows. "What plenty!" The congregation would wait eagerly for it. And he never disappointed them. He also had the same sermon every year for Easter, Whitsuntide and Christmas. He never varied them. Mind you, these days you can buy a cassette and it not only tells you *what* to say, but *how* to say it.'

At the end of an hour the fruit and vegetables were packed into boxes and crates and Mrs Phillips and Mrs Johns began to sweep the chancel and the aisle. 'At least it don't make as much mess as the Christmas tree,' philosophised Mrs Johns. Mrs Batrick, a farmer's wife, was carrying boxes,

Vicar

one under each hammy arm, to the door. 'Some of the produce goes to St Sepulchre's,' the vicar told Pearl. 'But the old folks are very picky, I'm afraid. Few have any real teeth for a start.'

Pearl said: 'I have the same teeth as when I was married. All mine.'

'How long have you been a widow?'

'Five years,' she said without sadness. 'Time goes by. I married during the War. Mike was a good man, a regular guy as they say.' She looked up as though uncertain whether to tell him something, then said: 'He was in the US Air Force in the war. We had only been wed for a year before he was sent over here to England.'

Vic 'I remember you asking about the Americans when you had just arrived, when we first met in the churchyard.'

'Still dragging?' she asked slyly.

'I'm afraid so.' He glanced furtively at the women with their brooms. 'On the quiet. Are you?'

'You started me over again,' accused Pearl.

He grinned. 'Feel like one now?'

'Sure thing. But it's raining outside. Do we get behind the organ?'

'No need. We'll stroll over to the vicarage. Hilda has gone to Salisbury. Her sister runs an ecclesiastical tea room there. If we open the study window the smoke will waft away.' He glanced at her artfully. 'It usually does.'

Pearl agreed. 'Monday is the vicar's day off,' he said as they walked along the dripping churchyard path. 'If I'm lucky.'

Pearl had collected the golf umbrella and she twirled it in the grey-green churchyard, its colours like a whirligig. They went into the vicarage. A spaniel, asleep in the hall, woke and barked once, then returned to slumber. The vicar took the umbrella from her and stood it in the compartment in the hallstand. He sat her in his study and went to make the coffee. She looked from the French window out onto the dripping green garden and to the tower of the church beyond with its jaunty arrow and golden ball. 'I love that,' she said pointing it out when he returned. 'It looks so . . . so optimistic. When everything is grey like today, it still shines.'

He smiled agreement. 'It's only a weather vane, but it looks like the very panoply of God, doesn't it. When it was brought to the church, just under a hundred years ago, to celebrate Queen Victoria's Jubilee, it was carried through the village street in a procession. Carriages, farm carts, bicycles, people on horseback.' His smile broadened. 'It was the very thing that made me want to come here in the first place. It seemed to be pointing the way.'

She accepted the cup of coffee and they each had a cigarette and puffed enjoyably. Then she said carefully: 'Henry, are you familiar with a line of poetry that goes:

And we forget because we must,
And not because we will.'

He shook his head. 'It's not something I recognise,' he said. 'But it may be in the *Oxford Dictionary of Quotations.*' He stood up and went to the bookcase, took down the heavy book and found the index. 'Let's see . . .'

'And we forget because we must,' the American woman prompted quietly.

'Yes, let's look under "forget". That's the key word.' He riffled the pages. 'Easy,' he said. '. . . forget because we must. Here it is. ARN page . . .' He turned the pages. She watched sharply.

'Yes. Oh, it's Matthew Arnold,' said Henry. 'He was from these parts. Buried in the church at Laleham. It just quotes those same two lines. They're from a poem called "Absence".'

'I thought it might be something like that,' she said thoughtfully. He was still studying the book. 'And here's something appropriate in another Matthew Arnold quotation: "the bolt is shot back . . ." ' He laughed. 'We're back to the church arrow.'

'He was a famous English poet?' she asked. He raised his head from the book.

'Yes, I suppose so,' he said. 'I only know his poem . . . some of it. . . . "On Dover Beach".' He looked at the book once more. 'I learned this years ago:

> . . . Ah, love, let us be true
> To one another! For the world, which seems,
> To lie before us like a land of dreams,
> So various, so beautiful, so new,
> Hath really neither joy, nor love, nor light . . .'

He looked up at her again, her cigarette had burned an inch of ash. Realising from his look she searched in alarm for an ashtray. He produced one from a drawer in his desk. 'Thank you,' he said in a relieved tone. 'My wife has the nose of a bloodhound.'

She stood and said she must be going. 'So Matthew Arnold is buried near here,' she said.

'Yes. At Laleham. Only five or six miles. On the Thames. I know because I stood in for the vicar there when he was away and Arnold is the church's claim to fame.'

She thanked him and they shook hands affectionately. 'Don't forget to open the window,' she said conspiratorially. She collected the umbrella at the door. The dog roused itself and barked just once again. 'He counts you in and counts you out,' said the vicar. 'Thanks for helping with the fruit. The vegetables we sell to the Swan, so you may be having harvest festival potatoes tonight.'

Halfway down the vicarage path she turned and waved slightly. It had stopped raining though the trees were dripping. There was no one in the street although there were two people coming out of the lit village shop further down.

Pearl turned and walked steadily back to the Swan, carrying the furled umbrella on her shoulder. But then her pace slowed and her eyes were wet. 'Well, well, well,' she said to herself. 'Like a land of dreams.'

Edward Richardson, on his way to see Grainger, walked along the ranks of taxis and cars discharging passengers and their luggage; people cheerfully or fearfully flying away, others going, perhaps wondering if they were doing the right thing, back home; earnest businessmen carrying undistinguished overnight bags. A pushchair collapsed, almost devouring its baby passenger; the mother cried out in chorus with the child and righted it. A crew were going on duty, the braided captain, firm-jawed, striding out purposefully like a drum major at the forefront of a band with unflinching eyes on the horizon, steady ahead as if he were already flying the plane. Stride for stride, but one pace to the rear, were his fellow officers carrying their oblong black cases like morticians, the stewardesses in unsuitably tight uniforms tugging dainty wire trolleys each bearing a single piece of luggage. Soon they would be on the distant side of the earth.

A pair of armed police-dog handlers passed like conscientious men exercising their pets. They paused and one spoke into his radio phone while the other held both dogs. Firemen, bright in toylike yellow, were checking a hydrant just outside the airport church. That day they had been rushed out from their base on the north perimeter of the airport to standby as an incoming flight reported a hydraulic emergency, although it was only a faulty flight-deck light; to a blazing chip pan in a Terminal Four kitchen; to a collision between a courier's motor cycle and a Nigerian in tribal dress; and another between two out-of-control baggage trolleys careering on the downward slope of Arrivals at Terminal Two during which an elderly man's leg was bruised and a youth received a blackened eye. There had also been three well-intended and two malicious false alarms and a

call to free an engineer, cursing with pain and embarrassment, who had put his hand deep into the trap of an airliner's toilet and could not withdraw it. But nothing serious
or dramatic.

Much of airport life was trivial. That morning Edward
had dealt with little more than trite matters. Public
Relations had a complaint from a journalist, well known for
his self-esteem, that he had not been upgraded to First Class
apparently because he was not wearing a tie; a child had
concealed a white mouse in her hand baggage on a flight to
Majorca; the arrangements for a dinner for three colleagues
who were departing under the voluntary redundancy
scheme; a passenger disgruntled because it had rained too
much in Australia; a party of folk-singing nuns who wished
to rehearse in Economy Class to Rome.

It seemed that Moira, Grainger's secretary, hovered at
the door as though to make sure that Richardson actually
entered the room and stayed there. Grainger was in the
ante-room acting out his ploy of keeping underling visitors
waiting, and Richardson half turned to see Moira's anxious
face still projecting around the door. She blushed stupidly
when she realised she had been found out and said 'Just
wanted to make sure,' before going out. Richardson briefly
wondered what her life was like.

Grainger appeared ominously wiping his hands as if he
had garrotted someone in the next room. 'Sit down,' he said
omitting Richardson's name, an indication the interview
would not be pleasant. Richardson sat.

Grainger studied a sheet of paper on his desk as if he did
not understand it. 'Why they worry me with summer schedules now I can't think,' he muttered.

'They're provisional,' said Richardson pointlessly. 'You
sent for me?'

'Yes,' confirmed Grainger as though he was glad Richardson had brought it up. 'The Board.' His eyebrows rose

slowly. 'You have the opportunity to appear before them if you like. . . .'

'What's it about?' asked Richardson although he knew.

Grainger looked hurt. 'About the Allsop business, of course, Edward. What else could it be about? As I say, you can go and see them if you like and put your side of the story as you did to me. They have seen your written report, however, and while not unsympathetic with your humanitarian motives in bringing Allsop back, they feel that the risks involved were such that you should not have attempted it.'

'The risks to the company, you mean,' said Richardson.

'Yes, of course,' said Grainger in a surprised tone.

'He was dying and he wanted to come home.'

Grainger spread his clean hands. 'But there were ways of doing it.'

'Letting him die in that hole and then bringing him home in a box?'

Grainger sighed. 'Let's not discuss what might have been. Only what was. The Board have decided to reprimand you, Edward. There it is.'

He handed an envelope to Richardson who glanced at it and put it in his pocket. Grainger seemed disappointed that he had not opened and read it.

'What about Dr Snow?' asked Richardson.

'That's another matter. I'm not at liberty to discuss his case.'

'I merely want to ensure that because he's the medical man he doesn't get the rough end of things. I can stand up for myself and I was the one to make the decision.'

'That was your responsibility,' agreed Grainger. 'That was taken into account.'

He put on a transparent fatherly air, his face creasing, his hands held tightly in front of him. 'You've got an excellent record with this company, Edward. The Board, of course, took that into consideration. But things appear to have been getting on top of you a bit lately.' He glanced up. 'We all feel the pressures at times. I do, God knows. But you can surely realise what a mess we would have been in if it had got into the press about Allsop. Dying of Aids on one of our scheduled services.'

Richardson clenched his teeth. Grainger held up a warning hand. 'And everyone knows that your decision was prompted by the right human responses. But in this case they were the wrong ones. Fortunately it did not get into the press.'

'I'm happy I did the right thing by Bill Allsop,' said Richardson simply. 'I wasn't going to leave him there.'

Grainger regarded him painfully. 'Why don't you take a couple of weeks' leave before Christmas,' he said. 'Tack it onto your Christmas break.'

'I don't need it,' said Richardson. 'I thrive on this stuff.'

'Perhaps your wife . . . Adele . . . might like to see a bit more of you,' said Grainger.

For a moment Richardson thought he might know something. 'Adele is very busy at the moment too. In any case I'm due to go down to Australia tonight. Ray Francis is going to take over in Sydney, as you know.'

'Francis, yes, I know. I've had my grave doubts about that. Let's hope he doesn't go off with an Aborigine woman.'

'His wife is going too. They've got a daughter there. He's the right man for it.'

'Do *you* have to go?' asked Grainger.

'It's what I do,' said Richardson, surprised. 'It's not just Ray Francis, there's a dozen things to be sorted out down there, the Brisbane office has been under six feet of floodwater for a start and there . . .'

'Someone else could do it,' suggested Grainger carefully. 'We could get someone out tomorrow.'

'It's my function and I have to go,' said Richardson firmly. He was not going to let them pull that trick.

'All right, all right,' said Grainger putting his hands in

front of him as if to ward off the consequences. He stood up and so did Richardson. 'I'm on the flight tonight,' Edward said. He went towards the door.

'Before you go,' said Grainger, 'think about the reprimand. Let me know if you want to appear personally. Otherwise you must accept it.'

'You mean lump it,' thought Richardson.

Snow was in his office adjoining the surgery. He was sitting at his desk looking at what appeared to be a garden slug in a small tin box.

'A leech,' he said to Richardson. 'You don't see many of them these days. At one time they were in such demand by medical practitioners that they were sold secondhand.' He looked up and smiled in his gentle manner. 'This was a box containing snuff. I hope I don't start him sneezing. He seems to be all right.'

Richardson sat down and studied the leech. 'Reminds me of someone we know,' he observed.

Snow grinned pleasurably. 'Ah, you've been to see him. No, actually they're still used, these little fellows, you know. When I worked in Glasgow they were useful. Brides beaten up the night before the wedding, and so forth.'

'In what way?' asked Richardson cautiously.

'The application of a leech is wonderful for making bruises disappear,' said Snow. 'Not a trace. Bride radiant as she walks down the aisle to meet her assailant at the altar steps.'

Richardson said: 'What happened to you? Do you mind me asking? I have had an official reprimand from the Board.'

'Oh, that. Well, it wasn't so bad. Early retirement it's called. But I'm ready for it, Edward.'

'We could both appear before the Board if you like. We could fight it.'

'Ah, no. I don't want that. We did the right thing, I'm satisfied. I'm ready to go. I've only got a couple of years anyway and they'll have to shell out. We did our best by that poor soul, even if it wasn't the proper best. I shall devote the rest of my life to Tchaikovsky.' He picked up the leech on his pencil. 'Won't I, Grainger?'

He returned to his office through the terminal, past the general Departures gate, the goodbye groups with their tears, their awkward farewells; faces in relief, solidified smiles. He glanced towards the window corner where Rona had set up for sketching and with a disconcerting start of pleasure he saw she was there. Skirting the crowd in front of the barrier he went to her.

'Still finding it a good subject?' he asked.

'It's ever changing,' she said. She had not seen him approaching but she looked up unhurriedly with her fine eyes. 'No brushes with officialdom?' he asked.

'Not officialdom,' she answered smiling. 'But I've had plenty of painters and people who draw and others just being interested, all coming over to see what I'm doing. Everyone's giving me tips. Artists are always very clever with the work of others. They all know a better way. One man just stood and tutted. And there was a girl who asked me not to put her in the sketch because she had been crying. Her boyfriend was leaving and she didn't think he was coming back.'

'She told you that?'

'Right then she needed to tell someone.'

'May I see?' She nodded and he looked over her shoulder; the sketch was hardly started, just shadows. 'How many have you done?' he asked.

'This is number three,' Rona said. 'I want to do six. Arrivals and Departures, I'm going to call them. I had thought of maybe drawing other aspects of the airport but somehow the check-in and the snack bar didn't grab me.'

'Are you going home . . . back to Bedmansworth on the bus?'

'That was my plan. Now I know the times and the

idiosyncracies of the drivers it works out fine. It's funny though, bumping along here on those country lanes is like coming to some futuristic city by stage coach.'

'I'm leaving here at mid-afternoon,' he told her. 'I'm off to Australia tonight. If you're ready to leave about then I could give you a lift.'

'Thanks. That would be useful,' she said. 'Usually I quit about three.'

'I'll come and pick you up,' he said. 'Unless you'd like to come to the office.'

'Sure, I'll drop over. I know where it is.'

'Call from Reception. I'll come down.'

She watched him walk back through the scattering of people and disappear down the stairs and returned to her sketching with a troubled heart. She should have made an excuse. She had not wanted this to happen to her.

Rona remained for another hour before going to the snack bar for coffee and a sandwich, sitting among moody passengers holding plastic cups, blinking untrustingly at the flickering departures screen. Those who had come to bid them farewell sat lost for words; children fidgeted, spilled coloured drinks and made demands. On the screens, like some list of available bargains, the destinations clattered: 'Cairo, Dubai, Sydney, Singapore, Jakarta, Cape Town, boarding Gate 14, boarding Gate 23, boarding . . . delayed . . . delayed . . . boarding . . . ,' a changing poem in blank verse. Travellers, weary even before they had travelled, stood as the destinations altered, gathered their hand baggage and children, and moved towards the final doorway.

She returned to her position by the window. A pink man with a full white moustache came to her side and observed what she was doing. 'All the joys and sorrows there,' he said realising her theme. 'In the old days it was different.'

'How was that?' she inquired politely, still sketching.

'Going by ship,' he explained. 'Farewells then, the final embarrassment, was at a decent distance. You know, just hundreds waving from the dockside, streamers and bands. It was not so . . . so claustrophobic . . . you were safe. Beyond them.'

She stopped sketching. He wore a well-cut grey suit with a waistcoat and a striped tie. There was a carnation in his lapel. 'Are you travelling?' she asked. Her fingers had become tired. She flexed them. 'Or seeing someone off?'

'I was,' he sighed. 'They've gone now. The agony is over. My daughter. We see each other only at long intervals, and there's a mutual sneaking feeling that this could be the last time, not that we'd ever admit it. It's a moment for musing over opportunities lost, paths not taken.'

When he had gone she continued sketching. But her swift, decisive hand had slowed. She watched the leaving people file through the outgoing gate, showing their boarding cards, and knew that she and Pearl too must soon be departing. They could not remain in the village, in this country, for much longer. They must go home. Even if it were running away.

Just before three o'clock she walked out of the terminal and across the airport road to Richardson's office. The receptionist telephoned Harriet. 'Oh, is she?' remarked Harriet. 'Wait a minute, will you.'

In her certain tone she called across the office. 'Mr Richardson . . .'

Edward looked up from his desk. 'Mrs Train is downstairs,' he finished for her. 'Say I'll be down right away.'

She looked miffed. 'Yes. As you didn't mention . . .'

'I know. Sorry, Harri. Slipped my mind.'

'I bet it did,' whispered Harriet to herself. She said into the phone: 'He'll be down in a few minutes. Would you ask the lady to wait.'

He was already gathering his papers and pushing them into his case. 'How about the new schedules?' Harriet reminded him. 'You were going to look at them.'

'Let's have them,' he said. 'I'll do it between here and Sydney.' He walked briskly across the office. Glum-eyed she handed a file to him. 'Back next week then,' she said. She opened her desk diary. 'Saturday or Sunday you thought, didn't you.'

'I thought,' he said grinning at her gruffness. 'But you never know. I might meet somebody interesting.'

'I suppose there's always that chance,' she sniffed. She peered up from behind her wide glasses. 'There's a new lot of tactical redundancies coming, so I hear.'

'I hear that too – all the time. Don't worry about it.'

'I'm not worried, not for me,' she said. 'I'll get a job. I might start a bike shop. It's you I worry about. They've got the axe out for senior staff.'

'I'll start a bike shop with you,' he said. 'I must be off.'

'Yes,' she said pointedly. 'Don't keep Mrs Train waiting.'

'Harri.'

'I'm sorry.'

He kissed her on the cheek.

'Have a good trip,' she said. She had a superstition about saying a 'safe' trip. When he had gone she took the teacups in the outer room and began moodily to wash them. She did not like changes. The telephone rang and she returned to the office. It was Adele Richardson. 'He's just left, Mrs Richardson. He's on his way home . . . I think he is anyway. He's on the flight to Sydney tonight you know.'

Adele sounded annoyed. 'I know, Harriet. The trouble is I have to go to an emergency welfare committee meeting and it's imperative. If he's not home in twenty minutes I'll miss him. I'll have to leave a note because I won't be back until late. All right, Harriet. Thank you.'

Harriet put the telephone down thoughtfully. She went back to washing up the cups. 'Emergency committee,' she muttered to herself. 'I'd stay at home with him. I wouldn't let him out of my sight.'

As they drove the late autumn afternoon brightened briefly, the clouds hemmed by the sun. Rona said: 'When I was

272

watching those people in Departures, I had a feeling that Mother and I must soon be on our way. We can't stay here forever.'

'You have a lot of things to do at home, I imagine,' he said. He felt abruptly sad.

Rona looked straight ahead. 'Not too many,' she said thoughtfully. 'Apart from getting my life straight, starting over. I left a vacuum in California.' She smiled slightly, still looking to the front. 'My mother is not going to like going. I swear she really believes she's here forever. But . . . we really have to go home.' She hesitated. 'Where we belong.'

'It's necessary to belong somewhere,' he said. 'In my case I sometimes wonder where.'

'You are not very happy, are you.'

'Adele and I? Oh, we're like a lot of married people, I suppose. We've drifted a bit away from each other.'

'How did it happen?'

'Without our noticing it. Our interests are opposites. She's always buzzing around on committees and suchlike and I'm frequently away. A few years ago she had a good job but it didn't fit with mine, so she quit but, looking back, it was probably a mistake. Now it's too late. It's what's called a quiet marriage.'

Rona gave a short laugh. 'Mine was so quiet I hardly noticed it – until he wasn't there. I was the one with the career. I was in a lawyer's office, I loved it, and I let it take up my life. Jeff was a steady sort of guy. He was an accountant with a computer company. He just wandered away with somebody else, older. That's what hurt.'

A silence fell between them but as they turned off the main road, her eye was taken by a cloud of seagulls, like white paper floating in cold sunlight, wheeling and dipping over the horizon of hedge and muddy bank. Richardson saw that they had caught her attention.

'It's a rubbish tip,' he said. 'When the lorries come to

273

dump the stuff the gulls are waiting for them. I wonder if they ever see the sea.'

'Edward, do you mind if we take a look?' she asked. 'I'd like to photograph them.'

Richardson pulled the car off the road. A gate, draped with pieces of torn cloth like the remnants of some long-ago celebration, was open. The entrance was paved with cinders and gravel, scored with wheel marks. A man, rough and walking with a crouch, came along the path, skirting a bank of weedy debris. He was carrying two full sacks on a pole balanced on his shoulders like a yoke. He was calling to them. Edward lowered the window. 'What was that?'

'I said you won't find much up there today,' shouted the man above the din of the gulls. 'Gypsies got here first.'

'Thanks,' responded Richardson uncertainly. He smiled at Rona. 'And I was hoping to find treasure.'

'Why don't we go see,' she suggested quietly. 'Maybe we will.'

He drove through the tip valley, the slopes rising thirty feet on either side. Much had grown over with tenacious greenery. The gulls were ahead, diving and screaming. The track became muddier, more savagely rutted. They turned another bend and came to an area piled with newer rubbish, jagged metal and broken crates, cascades of cans and cartons. A tip-up truck was discharging its load, its back canting. The gulls, unable to wait, grabbed at the trash as it slid to the slope. A man in orange overalls, luminous as a clown, stood observing the snatching birds. They whirled around him madly but he remained unmoving. In the cab of the lorry another orange man had a newspaper to his face. Both heard the car but having turned, went back to what they were doing.

There was room behind the truck and Richardson drove around it. The outside man took the trouble to wave, like a traveller meeting others unexpectedly in a strange and wasted land. There was a firm area, lined with cinders at one side. 'Will this do?' he asked.

'Just fine,' Rona said, keeping her eyes on the gulls. She took a camera with a long snout lens from her large holdall and climbed from the car. He got out and standing at a distance, watched her taking the photographs. She was wearing grey trousers and a blue tweed jacket. She stood, firmly, legs astride, her dark hair pushed by the rubbish dump wind. The gulls swooped and screamed. And now, now of all times, he reflected, she was talking of going home.

She completed the photographing quickly and climbed back into the car. 'That was terrific,' she smiled. 'Unusual situation, to say the least.'

'You'll use it in a painting or a sketch?'

'Sometime. I think they're great as just pictures.'

He started the engine and reversed the vehicle carefully against the opposite bank of debris. As they drove past the tip-up truck, its back portion now returned to the horizontal, the dungareed man who had been standing at the side called: 'Nice day for the seaside!' He and his companion in the cab laughed.

'There's a harbour called Bosham,' said Richardson as they left the gate and regained the road. He turned towards the motorway. 'In Sussex. It's famous for waterbirds, especially at this time of the year.'

'Winter feeders,' she said. 'How far is it?'

'Hour and a half's drive,' he calculated. 'Not much more. It's the place where, so they tell you at school, King Canute ordered the tide to go back and it wouldn't.'

'Now that's a story we didn't learn,' she smiled. 'So he got wet?'

'Very. It wasn't his fault. It was his hangers-on who convinced him he was all-powerful. It's a lovely place, a big, flat harbour, lots of mud at low tide.'

'How do I get there?'

He took a breath. 'I'll run you down, if you like.'

For a moment she did not reply. Then she said: 'Thank you, I'd like that.' She did not look at him. 'When can it be?'

'This trip to Australia is a there-and-back job, a few days. I'll be home by Sunday of next week. Perhaps we could fix it for Monday, say. If that suits you.' He glanced at her. 'You won't be heading for the States before then, will you?'

Rona laughed briefly. 'I'm not in that much of a hurry,' she said. 'It will take a while to break it to Mother. I'd like to come with you, Edward. Very much.'

'Toby,' Mr Old said, 'today is the day you take charge.' Toby straightened up from the cabinet he was polishing. Its base was peppered with worm holes. 'Done with a shotgun by the look of it,' said Mr Old. 'Worms go in slow.' He appeared to count the holes, then said: 'You've been here long enough now, haven't you. You know silver from brass, pottery from porcelain, a Klee from a Canaletto.'

'A Klee?' asked Toby.

'No matter. Nobody is likely to bring one in, nor a Canaletto for that matter. I'm going to see some stuff in Northampton, rush job. The chap was only cremated yesterday but his widow's in a hurry, and you know my Mrs Old, she doesn't enjoy coming to the shop, mixing with the general public, such as we get of them. And her dogs are having their nails clipped. So it's you, boy. It's your big chance.'

'All right, Mr Old,' smiled Toby. 'I'll be okay. I won't buy anything that I don't think is worth it.'

'Don't buy *anything*,' corrected Mr Old, louder than he had intended. 'Nothing at all. Not even the Crown Jewels, all right? Just *sell*. Make out it's a trade price you're giving them. Tell them a *story* about what they're buying, like it is *said* it belonged to Augustus John or Jack the Ripper. You know the sort of thing. Provoke a bit of interest.'

'I know,' said Toby. 'Don't worry.'

'Let me see though, yes, that knocker from Brighton might

be in. Percival Pope-Harvey, as he calls himself. You've seen him, the grubby one. He'll bring in some stuff he's bought for a song and he'll want paying, so I'll leave some cash. But nothing over twenty-five pounds and nothing chipped or damaged. He never has anything worth more anyway.'

'I remember him,' Toby said. 'I'll manage. I'll enjoy it.'

'Good lad. I'll leave a hundred and fifty quid. Twenty-five pound limit on each treasure, remember. Whatever he asks halve it and bargain from there. Good experience for you.'

He picked up a little brown suitcase and went out, blinking anxiously back from the other side of the door. Toby began polishing some brass candlesticks and he waved with the duster. He waited five minutes and then went out of the door. Mr Old had vanished. The street was chilly but busy. Toby, with a proprietorial puff, stood and looked up and down the autumn hill. Windsor Castle was draped in mist. He was wearing his paisley waistcoat that day, and he thrust his thumbs into the pockets and returned inside.

All day after his long return from Dee's house every part of him had ached, particularly his pride. The following evening, tempted, he had telephoned Liz but she informed him that she was considering a proposal from somebody more mature and might or might not be in touch with him at some later date. There was also the matter of his parents. Sadly he wondered how long they would be together; if they parted what would happen to him?

The door sounded and two wispy women stumbled into the shop and approached the counter holding each other up. 'We would like to see someone senior,' demanded one. Her feathery grey hat looked like the continuation of her hair. Her face was lined with veins and her eyes streaming. Her companion appeared to walk with closed eyes and he thought she might be blind until the lids lifted and she picked up an old chemist's bottle from the junk tray on the counter and sniffed it. Her lids dropped again. 'Quite revolting,' she muttered.

'I'm in charge,' said Toby firmly to the one who had wanted to speak to someone senior.

'Do you know about ancient things then,' she asked archly.

'Quite a bit,' he replied eyeing the pair. 'But I can't buy anything today.'

They regarded each other and then him with a sort of shock. 'We're not *selling*,' said the one with the closed eyes. 'We're too proud for that, aren't we, Clementina.'

'Far too proud,' confirmed Clementina wiping her cheeks. 'Far too proud, dear.'

'Oh, beg your pardon. What was it then?'

'The little Staffordshire dog in your window. We'd like to see it. It matches one we already have.'

'Of course,' said Toby. 'Beautiful little figure isn't it. Very early Staffordshire. It's in one of the books. I think it's possible, it may just have come from . . . ,' he nodded towards the door and up the hill, '. . . across the road.'

'Windsor Castle? Good gracious, why would HM want to sell a Staffordshire dog?' The eyes disconcertingly remained shut as if she did not want to see him.

'Perhaps the other one was broken,' said Clementina caustically.

The situation seemed to be moving away from him, so Toby went to the window. He took the Staffordshire dog from the display and brought it to them. They held it, turned it, looked at it upside down, and muttered over it. 'How much?' asked the first lady.

'Fifty,' announced Toby firmly. Then: 'I could make a small reduction. Trade, is it?'

'I think I could manage fifty,' intoned the second lady. 'We are *not* trade,' she added icily. Lifting her lids she stared at her companion's clutched purse. 'Half each.'

Toby watched with increasing horror as they each pain-

278

stakingly counted out twenty-five pence. 'There,' they said in unison. Clementina said: 'We'd like it wrapped up.'

'F-Fifty pounds,' stammered Toby. 'It's fifty *pounds*.'

Both regarded him as if he had gone mad. They began sliding their coins away. 'Good morning,' they said as they turned and left.

'Good morning,' whispered Toby. He put the dog back in the window and sat, still stunned, behind the counter. The door immediately opened and admitted a tiny and grimy man he recognised as Percival Pope-Harvey. 'Do I have some bargains for you,' he promised.

'Mr Old's away for the day,' said Toby diffidently. He steadied his voice: 'I'm in sole charge.'

'Then,' said Percy. 'Who *is* a lucky boy? It's your chance to earn a fortune.' He carried an eroded carpet bag, with chapped leather handles. This he opened, looking up with surprisingly fierce eyes. 'I'm a knocker,' he said as if it were a secret he was reluctant to share. 'Do you know what that is?'

Toby said carefully: 'You knock on doors and . . . see . . .'

'See what treasures they've hoarded inside,' agreed the visitor. 'Sometimes people have stuff they've had for years and they're short of money and they don't realise what their bits and pieces will fetch. I help them to realise.'

'Yes, I understand.'

Putting both hands into the carpet bag, Percy said: 'And today I've got something better than ever. One item only, but better than ever.' He kept his hands within the bag as though to sustain the suspense. 'Want a look at it?'

'Yes, yes of course,' stumbled Toby. 'But Mr Old said that . . .'

'It don't matter what Mr Old said, son. . . . What's your name?'

'Richardson,' said Toby assuming a businesslike tone. 'Tobias Richardson.'

'To-buy-us!' exclaimed Percy. 'What a good name for antiques!'

'Yes . . . I suppose it is. I've never thought of that.'

'In this trade you have to think of every single thing, every angle,' warned the visitor, wagging a grimy finger. He had taken one hand from the bag but had still not revealed what he was holding within but now, his eyes switching to right and left, like a spy, he withdrew a small framed picture.

'I can't buy any Klees,' said Toby.

'Klee! Klee! This is not a Klee, not any skinny thing like that. This, *look at it* will you, is a lovely little landscape.' He held up the frame. There was a fluffy sky, a river, meadows and cows. 'Look at that. Perfect. Signed too. Fred Sunderland. See there in the corner.' He dived into his pocket and produced an eyeglass. 'Here, use this. You'll see it proper.'

Confused, Toby took the small eyeglass and fitted it with difficulty into his eye. He leaned towards the corner of the painting.

'Other way,' suggested Percy not unkindly. 'You got the eyeglass in the wrong way round.'

Toby felt his face warm. 'Wondered what was wrong,' he mumbled.

'That's all right. We all got to learn. There, take a decko. In the corner. Frederick Sunderland. Clear as clear. And what a nice picture. A gem this is. Mr Old knows me. I'm straight as straight. He knows I've got to come here again. I wouldn't do you.'

'How much?' Toby faltered.

'Four hundred pounds,' said the knocker decisively. 'And that's a gift.' He tapped the frame: 'Fetch a thousand in the right place.'

Toby gazed at the little picture then transferred his eyes to the man. 'You'll . . . you'll have to leave it,' he said. 'He'll be back tomorrow. He's gone to Northampton.'

'Ah, Northampton, is it,' said the knocker thoughtfully. 'Wonder what treasure trove he's got there?' He quickly returned to the situation. 'I've *got* to sell it today,' he warned. 'If not here then to somebody else – and who'll be lucky then? I've come all the way from Hove, you know. Well, Brighton. And I'm not a big business. I can't *afford* to carry stock. I have to turn it over.' He regarded Toby solemnly. 'This could be the day you make your first killing,' he said. 'Only four hundred. For a Frederick Sunderland. And my guarantee that it's right.'

Toby heard himself saying: 'Three hundred.' His mouth remained agape. Percy appeared hurt. 'Not a chance,' he said. Then, kindly again, he leaned forward and confided. 'Never go down in hundreds when you're bargaining, son. Nor up. Fifties, yes. Twenties, tens, depending. But never hundreds. He cocked his head half sideways. 'Three fifty.'

'Three hundred,' said Toby, amazed at himself.

Encouragement flooded the knocker's eyes. 'Good boy,' he said. 'All right. Done. In cash.'

'I'll have to get some money from the bank,' said Toby. He had already made his decision. 'Mr Old only left a hundred and fifty. I'll get the rest from my deposit account. I'll go halves with him.'

'What enterprise!' enthused Percy rubbing his hands. 'Pure initiative. All right. Off you go. I'll mind the shop.' He saw Toby's concern and held up a hand to stay it. 'I've been coming in here for twenty years.'

'All right,' the youth said. 'It's only up the street. I'll be a few minutes.'

He put on his coat making sure his bank deposit book was in the pocket. 'I'll get myself a cup of coffee,' said Percy. He nodded towards the kettle and the instant coffee jar in the corner. 'I know where everything is. Off you go.'

Toby ran up the hill and arrived panting at the bank. It took him ten minutes to withdraw all but ten pounds of the money in his deposit account. Then he ran down to the shop again. Percy was sitting benignly behind the counter. 'Done some business for you,' he said.

'You have? What was it?'

'Little Staffordshire bow-wow in the window. Nice early one. Fifty to two old women.'

'Fifty? Fifty what?'

Percy spread the ten five pound notes on the glass counter. 'There. I reckon I ought to get a fiver commission.'

'Yes, of course!' exclaimed Toby full of relief. He took the forty-five pounds and put it in his pocket handing Percy a five pound note. He said: 'They came in and said they thought it was fifty *pence* this morning.'

The knocker laughed. 'Trying it on,' he said. 'That's what, crafty old cows. There's plenty of that sort. They knew what it was worth all right. Did you cop the rings they had on?'

'Well, thanks so much. I'm ever so grateful, really,' beamed Toby. 'I've got your cash.' He put the hundred and fifty on the glass and went to the safe and withdrew Mr Old's hundred and fifty.

'Share the risk, share the profits,' nodded the visitor sagely. 'Except there's no risk.' He held out his brown hand and Toby shook it, then he folded the notes in his pocket and went out with a dapper walk. He was back in a moment. 'If you want to move it quick,' he advised nodding towards the painting that Toby was studying anxiously. 'Get it in Pettifier's auctions in Richmond. It'll fetch its money.'

He was gone again. Toby studied the clouds, the meadows, the river and the cows and, minutely, the signature. He went to Mr Old's ragged shelf of reference books and took down an almost dismembered copy of *English Landscape Painters*. There was no mention of Frederick Sunderland.

He was there early and had already unlocked the shop when Mr Old arrived in the morning. 'How was it?' his employer inquired. 'I hope you had a better day than me. All the way to Northampton for a load of junk.'

'The Staffordshire dog from the window went,' said Toby cautiously. 'Actually Mr Pope-Harvey sold it. Fifty pounds and I gave him five commission.'

Mr Old's tangled eyebrows rose. 'What was Percy doing selling the goods?' he asked, a frown merging with the eyebrows.

Toby took a deep breath and said: 'I had to leave the shop. I had to go to the bank for some money.'

'The bank! Oh, my God what . . .'

'It was *my* money,' Toby assured him hurriedly. 'I bought half of it with my money. It's a bargain. . . .' he said.

'What?' asked Mr Old visibly forcing himself to calm. 'What is this bargain?'

Toby went to the side room. He returned with the painting. 'Landscape,' he announced. 'River scene with meadows and cows. Frederick Sunderland.'

'Never heard of him,' said Mr Old shaking his head violently. 'And you can't shift pretty pictures, not these days. . . .' He picked up the frame and at once softened. 'Not bad, though, is it. Nice puffy clouds. The name does ring a bell come to think of it. Sunderland. Not well known. He looked hard at Toby: 'How much?' he asked.

'He wanted four hundred,' swallowed the young man. 'But it had to be right there and then or he was going to have to sell it elsewhere.'

'How much?' repeated Mr Old with slight emphasis.

'Three hundred. I put a hundred and fifty and the other half was the money you left. I hope it's going to be all right.'

Mr Old again shook his head but more gently. 'Well, I don't know, I'm sure. But you gave it a try. Can't blame you for that. Do you want your money back now, if it's from your savings?'

'Oh no. I didn't mean that. No, I'll take the risk with you.'

The proprietor laughed. 'Good boy. Maybe you'll make a fortune one day.'

'I'd just like to make something on this.'

'We can always hope.' He jabbed an inquiring look at Toby. 'How are we going to shift it?'

'Pettifer's,' said Toby firmly. 'They've got a sale next Thursday. I rang them. They'll get it in the catalogue.'

'You *have* been on the go,' approved Mr Old. 'Well, why not? We'll put it in and wait and see. This business is all about waiting and seeing.'

Pettifer's auction rooms was on the brow of Richmond Hill overlooking the crowded old roofs of the once-royal town and the Thames.

'Christie's it is not,' said Mr Old as they trudged up the hill. 'General antiques and chattels.'

Mrs Old had been persuaded to sit in the shop. 'She won't sell anything,' forecast her husband phlegmatically. 'She might even *give* something away but she won't sell. Never gets it right. Once she sold a silver sauce-boat for eight seventy-five, our serial number on the label. Thought it was the price.'

Toby had slept badly the previous night. 'Will it fetch the money do you think?' he asked repeating the question insistent through his dreams. 'We've got a reserve,' shrugged Mr Old. 'Three hundred. What it cost. If it don't move we'll keep it in the shop. Every day it gets older, remember. And the artist might become popular. Andrew Lloyd Webber might buy him. Stranger things have happened.'

He did not appear convinced. They entered a room copious and dusty as a cavern. It was a gloomy day and the lights only served to cast shadows. There were stacks of furniture, prints, boxes of crockery, and ugly ornaments. A sad moose head stared from a wall. 'Not much here, by the look of it,' sniffed Mr Old. He picked up a clock and said: 'Early Fred Astaire.'

'Where's our Sunderland?' inquired Toby anxiously. His eyes travelled along the pictures hung askew on the wall. 'Down on the left,' said his employer. 'Right down. See it?'

'Hardly. Who's going to see it there?' The youth surveyed the motley people cruising the sale goods, shuffling, picking up, putting down, feeling, occasionally smelling, and shuffling on. Each clutched a curled catalogue and they went about their business all but silently.

'They'll spot it, those that want to,' remarked Mr Old. 'Don't fret, there's a few around here that could spot a Hogarth under a pile of rotten rugs. Mind you there's others who wouldn't know any better than to buy a ruddy rossignol.'

They sat down on a sofa from which the stuffing was oozing. Mr Old pushed the horsehair back into its split. 'Nice piece,' he approved. The arm moved under his touch. 'Soon fit back together again. Peep at the back, pretty curve. You don't see curves like that now.'

'Will you buy it?' asked Toby turning and looking.

'And carry it on my back? Or yours?' smiled the dealer. 'It's not *that* good. It's just a shame they let things go like that. Looks like a goat's been sleeping on it.'

'Who was Rossignol?' asked Toby. 'A painter?'

'A nightingale, a singing bird,' said Mr Old. 'That's a rossignol. It means a bit of junk. You buy something, some piece, some ornament, and it sticks in the shop for years and years, singing at you, taunting.'

'I see. I hope Frederick Sunderland doesn't turn out to be a rossignol.'

Two men in bulging overcoats, buttonholes torn, strolled towards their picture and stood sniggering at it. 'They're laughing,' whispered Toby horrified.

Mr Old was unimpressed. 'Charlie Parks and Tom Dingle, a right pair. Up to everything.'

The men remained pointing and smirking at the painting. Dingle took it from the wall and examined the back. Then held it at arm's length and curled their lips. They replaced it untidily on the hook and went away shaking their heads.

'A good sign,' whispered Mr Old. 'Trying to frighten others away. Laughing it down.'

'I've got my savings riding on that,' said Toby sombrely. He grimaced towards the men at the far side of the room.

'It's done now,' counselled the dealer. 'Forget it.' He glanced with mock ruefulness at the boy. 'You've put me in it too, remember. This could mean ruin.'

Toby glanced at him concernedly, then grinned as he saw his expression. 'It could be a killing,' he suggested.

'Yes,' nodded Mr Old. 'Ours.'

The saleroom was filling. People entered engulfed in coats and scarves and shawls although the dim room was warmed by two gas fires which were to be sold. Some sat in the rows of chairs and sofas, others lounged against furniture or stood at the back of the room reading their catalogues close to their eyes in the indifferent light. 'Lots of bidders,' suggested Toby looking around.

Mr Old half revolved. 'Come in out of the cold, most of them.'

'Nobody looks as though they've got much money,' whispered Toby.

'Them that has don't show it, not if they're wise,' remarked his companion. He checked his pocket watch, drawing it from his deep waistcoat pocket like an angler carefully landing a prize fish. Almost as if the action had prompted him, the auctioneer appeared, a short, brisk man wearing a green coat. 'Mr Mobley,' said Mr Old. 'Very knowledgeable – about chattels.'

Mr Mobley sat behind the raised desk and banged it with his gavel as if to test its sound or safeness, and bringing the room to order. He surveyed the prospective bidders.

'Good morning, ladies and gentlemen. We have an

interesting sale today. Three hundred and something lots. So I will begin without more ado. Lot one. A dressing-table case with costume jewellery. . . . What am I bid . . . ?'

Toby watched, his eyes moving around the room, and listened. After ten lots Mr Old bid for, and got, a box of miscellaneous cufflinks and an ebony hairbrush in a case. Three pounds.

They had to wait for almost a hundred lots before the painting came up. Toby, counting the numbers past, felt stifled. 'Calm, calm,' advised Mr Old as their moment neared. 'This, son, is the time for nerves of steel.'

'Lot ninety-eight,' intoned Mr Mobley. He checked around the room over his glasses as if to ascertain the people were still there. 'Nice little painting. Frederick Sunderland. Signed and dated, eighteen seventy-three. "The Thames at Chertsey".' He examined the audience again. 'What am I bid? Who will start me off at two hundred and fifty pounds?' There was a snort from the middle of the room.

Toby felt his heart quicken and then slow as no bid came. It was as though everyone had conspired to remain silent. He could hear the mass breathing. He glanced at Mr Old who, still dreamily studying the auctioneer, responded by tapping his wrist reassuringly.

'All right,' sighed the auctioneer. 'Two thirty.'

'Two thirty then,' said the man called Charlie Parks, raising a dirty-nailed finger from the sleeve of his overcoat. It was as if he were doing a favour. Toby looked aghast.

'Two forty anywhere?' inquired Mr Mobley apparently without much hope. Then with relief: 'Ah, I have two forty.' He pointed to the rear of the room and then peered at Charlie Parks. 'Two fifty?' he asked.

'Two fifty,' muttered Charlie wearily.

'Two sixty at the back,' pointed Mr Mobley. 'And two seventy to the left. Three hundred anywhere? It's worth it. Pleasant little painting. Chertsey and the Thames.'

He got three hundred. Toby's head was darting around.

Mr Old remained immobile. 'Three hundred and fifty,' signalled someone. They were in profit! 'Three seventy-five,' muttered Charlie Parks apparently disgusted. 'Three seventy-bloody-five,' he muttered to the man Dingle at his side. 'Must be mad.'

'Four hundred,' bid Dingle loudly. Parks glanced at him and went to four fifty. Dingle said four seventy-five. The bidder at the rear went to five hundred. Toby was crouched over with his eyes squeezed together. 'Go on, go on,' he whispered.

The bidding stalled. 'Five hundred I'm bid. At the back,' said Mr Mobley sounding surprised but pleased. 'Five twenty, new bidder.'

Charlie Parks turned in his encumbering coat, his face as heavy, trying to see the new bidder. 'Five fifty and that's it,' he grunted towards the rostrum.

'Five seventy-five,' nodded his companion Dingle.

'Christ,' swore Charlie. 'Six hundred and no more.'

He got it. 'Going going gone!' said Mr Mobley with a small sniff as if he were pleased to have scored over the dealers. 'Lot ninety-nine.'

With restrained joy Mr Old and Toby walked down Richmond Hill. 'I think we ought to treat ourselves to some lunch,' suggested the dealer. 'There's a pub just along here. Good steak and kidney. Do you drink?'

'I will today,' promised Toby. 'Six hundred pounds!'

'Five fifty when we've paid for Pettifer's percentage and our lunch. It was a decent little painting though. You've got a good eye.'

They went into the bar. Full of happiness Toby sat in a corner while his employer bought two pints of bitter and ordered the steak and kidney. Toby stared at the pint tankards being borne towards him. This was a new day for him, a new life. He took the tankard, studied the column of liquid amber and took a sip. It was bitter on the tongue. He made himself drink. 'I didn't realise it was called "The Thames at Chertsey",' he mentioned.

'It seemed like a nice title for it,' said Mr Old. 'Gave it a bit of local interest. People like local interest.'

Toby regarded him narrowly. 'Then it wasn't?'

'Suffolk by the look of it,' shrugged Mr Old. 'But it could have been anywhere, I mean, couldn't it? Sky, bank of river, fields, buttercups, cows. Anywhere.' He became pensive. 'But somehow it *looked* very much like Chertsey. Same sort of buttercups.'

Toby watched him with awe. 'Why did you buy the cufflinks?' he asked.

'Oh, out of boredom,' replied the dealer gently. He drank his beer. 'But it let the auctioneer know I was in the room. Might even get a pair to match up.' He took the worn box from his pocket. 'And it's a good hairbrush. Good back.'

A girl came with their food. Mr Old broke open the pie crust and observed the escaping steam with approval. Toby ate hungrily and sipped the beer gingerly. 'Good job the bidding started up again,' he said. 'I thought it had stuck. I wonder who began bidding again.'

'I wonder,' said Mr Old. He opened the box of cufflinks. 'Now look at that,' he observed happily. He took one of the pieces out. 'Bit of onyx if I'm not mistaken. That would make a lady's ring.'

> *'Homelea',*
> *Anglia Road,*
> *Hounslow,*
> *Middlesex,*
> *England,*
> *Great Britain*
>
> *2nd November*

My Dear Father and My Dear Mother,
   I was sorry to hear about the landslide and Uncle Sammi and

Marika and the family all hope that the Ritz cinema can be rebuilt as soon as possible. Also the fire in the tyre depot.

Here the fire engines, police and rescue crews are always dashing around making terrible noises with their sirens but nobody seems to take any notice of them. At London Airport (Heathrow) there are always small alarms but not big ones fortunately.

My work goes well but I have no news of promotion. My friends the porters are teaching me more English words that do not appear in the dictionary. Some I fear are not to be written down.

Uncle Sammi's business progresses well and when he starts the minicab service I am going to learn to drive. This is called moon-lighting.

If you cannot understand some of the words in my letters ask Asif at the Pavilion café as he lived here in Croydon, London, and he will tell you. Otherwise you will be up the creek.

Your loving son,

Nazar (Barry)

Twelve

This part of Airport country was a ragged land of cabbage fields, used car sites hung with washed-out flags, strips of pebble-dashed houses and small shops, garden centres lined with gnomes, gravel pits, industrial sites and musty yards. Pearl surveyed it from the taxi. Ancient inns had been provided with plastic beams and even battlements to make them appear quaint. Jolly giants with gaping mouths awaited children.

It was a country of motor fumes, litter trapped against railings, people beleaguered at bus stops, and over the snorting of the traffic the regular roaring of aircraft moving on the Heathrow conveyor belt.

But, as often happened in that region, the way quite abruptly turned into what must once have been a perfect English village. Laleham was noted in the Domesday Book and, although it was difficult now to isolate it from the late twentieth century, it remained doggedly beautiful, clinging to its curve in the River Thames, if only just.

There were some distinguished pale-faced Georgian and Regency houses, a row of rural cottages, a lane leading to the river, and two ancient inns. On this early winter's afternoon the red bricks of the church tower glowed.

Pearl got out of the taxi by the frowning gate and the driver turned across the road and parked by a sparse green triangle at the head of Blacksmith's Lane. Immediately outside the gate was a garage workshop with cars parked against the church wall. The gate creaked slowly as she opened it. This was going to be a difficult time for her. It was a confined churchyard, its gravestones lolling against each other and the branches of its yews entangled. She went into the porch and turned the door handle. It was locked.

'We have to, unfortunately,' said a cheerful voice behind her. 'Thieves today are neither religious nor particular.' He was young, had a bald front to his head like a badge, and wore a jazzy pullover. She liked him at once. 'I'm the vicar,' he said. 'Charles Grey. You'd like to see the church I take it?'

'That's why I came,' said Pearl. 'I'm Pearl Collingwood. From Bedmansworth.'

He unlocked the door. 'That doesn't sound like a Bedmansworth accent,' he suggested.

'It's not,' she agreed. 'It's more Los Angeles. But I live in Bedmansworth, and I have for a long time.'

The church, with its brick tower, had appeared massive from the outside but, she was glad to find, its interior was reduced, comfortable. Heavy stone columns and brick arches which lined the nave would have supported a much weightier building. 'Please look around,' invited Charles Grey. 'I'll be in the vestry if you would like to know anything.'

'I do,' she said in her firm way. 'But I need to find it myself.'

He was accustomed to hearing people's needs. He bowed to hers and went towards the vestry. Pearl was already searching, staring up to the ribs of the roof, along the small, worn pews. She was at once relieved and sorry that she had not gone in there alone. But now she was by herself; trying to imagine what it had been like. Even the altar was subdued, hardly noticeable in the dim daylight; the chancel was lined with memorial tablets like pictures on the walls of a gallery. Pearl began to read them, some with difficulty, for they were old, and the light was not good. There were rhymes to soldiers, dead in forgotten skirmishes; praise for a churchwarden and more for a Lord and Lady. The one she was seeking was not there.

She walked to the side aisle. The stone columns had been scoured deeply with initials and she wondered who could have done that. The vicar came briskly through the church and saw her. 'How are you progressing?' She was touching the cool stone of the columns and she said: 'Why would people carve their initials in a church?'

'Vandalism has been around a long time,' he shrugged. He peered at the incisions as though he had never noticed them. 'Visitors, I suppose. I hardly think that worshippers would have been able to do that. Not unless it was a very long sermon. Did you find what you were looking for?'

Pearl decided to enlist him, but at that moment, she thought she saw it. 'Ah, here it is,' she said.

'Ah, the famous Thomas Arnold, Headmaster of Rugby School. He was a parishioner here, although he's not buried at this church.' He checked the tablet as if to make sure. 'He died in the Isle of Wight.'

'Thomas Arnold? Not the poet?' asked Pearl. '*Not* Matthew Arnold?' Disappointment creased her face.

'Ah, no. That was his son. He *is* with us. His grave is in the churchyard.' He nodded to the porch entrance. 'Just outside the door.'

He could see how relieved she was. 'I'll show you if you wish,' he said.

Pearl thanked him. 'Just point the way. I'd be grateful,' she said.

He was also used to people's secrets and he smiled understandingly and led her out into the dim churchyard, made darker than the winter's day by the burdened yews. 'Here it is,' he said. 'Not a very impressive grave, you might think. It doesn't even mention he was a poet, only who his father was.'

He was standing in front of a modest stone with two smaller stones, one on either side. A curb was edged around

293

the grave. 'They have a backyard all of their own,' said Pearl. The small area was compacted mud. 'In the spring there are crocuses,' said the vicar as if to apologise. He knew when to leave. 'Goodbye then,' he said. 'My regards to Bedmansworth . . . and Los Angeles.'

'I'll tell them,' said Pearl.

When he had gone she stood before the commonplace grave reading the inscriptions. 'Matthew Arnold,' she recited to herself. 'Born December twenty-fourth eighteen twenty-two. Died April fifteenth eighteen eighty-eight.' The poet's wife who had lived to see the twentieth century and his sons who had died young, were also commemorated on the stone. But there was none of his poetry; only a verse from a Psalm.

She had seen enough. Carefully Pearl picked her way along the path, went out of the roofed gate and around the cars at the garage. Her driver was parked by the patch of green opposite but she told him to wait. In front of her was Blacksmith's Lane. She had the sensation that she already knew it well and she walked down it towards the River Thames. It was terraced with cottages with the intrusion of a few postwar houses. It was not far; it turned and led directly onto the river tow-path.

The hushed Thames moved around a broad curve. There were houses facing the water and others on the far bank, wooden bungalows with boats pulled up outside them. The water was thick, green and slightly gleaming in the pale November sun. Pearl began to walk along the tow-path, the grey wind chill on her face. Ducks and moorhens were busy on the bank but otherwise it was an empty scene. Just as she knew it had been on that day.

Jet lag was something to which no one seemed immune; east to west, west to east, only flying up and down the globe seemed to leave the flier unaffected. Pills, strategies for sleep and for keeping awake, ample alcohol on the flight, no alcohol on the flight, exercise, relaxation, mind games; in the end it all came down to one disturbed night for each hour of time difference. Air crew had learned to accommodate it but never defeat it.

Richardson came in on the morning flight from Sydney, twenty-three hours in the air even when to schedule, and went to bed as soon as he returned home. Adele and Toby had already left the house, although it was Sunday. He slept unsatisfactorily and awoke at five in the afternoon. He went down to the kitchen and made himself tea. He was sitting at the table, rustling through the *Sunday Times*. In the Business section a name caught his eye: Peter Rose Property Company in liquidation. As though in response, he heard Adele's car.

'Are you fit enough to go for drinks tonight?' she asked as soon as she came in. She said it briskly, as though to catch him off guard. For them his returning from Australia was as routine as another husband coming home on the commuter train from London. She seemed to realise her omission and asked how the trip had gone.

'It was all right,' he said. 'Got Ray Francis installed, and his wife.'

'That stupid man.'

'Francis is a good station manager,' he answered evenly. He drank his tea and continued to fidget with the newspaper.

'At least his wife's with him,' she said. She regarded Edward seriously. 'Grainger didn't want you to go, I gather.'

He looked up sharply. 'How did you gather that?'

'I spoke to his secretary,' she said a touch guiltily. 'Moira, is it? She chatters on the phone. I tried to get Harriet but she had a couple of days off apparently and the calls went to this Moira.'

'She,' said Richardson, 'should learn to hold her tongue. In that job.'

Adele had poured herself a gin and tonic. 'Well, she probably thought that as I *am* your wife, it would be all right. Most husbands and wives know each other's . . . what's happening in each other's lives.'

'Grainger got it into his head that I needed a rest, that's all, that somebody else could go down to Sydney,' sighed Edward. 'But it's my job and I don't need a rest. Where are these drinks tonight?'

'At my chief executive's house. It's not far from Maidenhead.'

'Right,' he said. 'Of course.'

'Don't sound so enthusiastic.'

'Look, I'm tired. I've had a long flight.'

'You didn't have to go.'

'It was apparent to me that I did. That's what matters. We'll go and have drinks with your chief executive at his house outside Maidenhead.'

Adele regarded him cagily. 'Then there's a lunch tomorrow. The Lord Lieutenant of Buckinghamshire . . .'

'I'm busy tomorrow, even to the Lord Lieutenant of Buckinghamshire. I already have a lunch.'

'There's nothing in your diary. I got Moira to . . .'

'Moira!' he exploded. 'Bloody Moira ought to be out on her ear. I have a *lunch*, I've told you. I fixed it from Australia. Harriet didn't know about it, so it *wouldn't* be in my diary.'

Adele gritted her teeth. 'This is important to me, Edward. My promotion may depend on it. *I want you to come.* Most people don't think I *have* a husband. . . .'

He remained seated. 'I'm already engaged,' he said flatly. 'And I'm not coming.' Because he was tired he said: 'Why don't you take old Peter Rose? He sounds like he's down on his luck. He'd like a lunch. . . .'

She picked up her gin and tonic and threw it over him as he sat in the kitchen chair. She screamed 'Bastard!' at him. He remained seated and she went from the kitchen. He wiped his face with his hand. When he looked up he saw Toby was standing, stricken faced, at the door.

The boy walked into the room and reached forward. 'You've got a lump of lemon on your head, Dad,' he said, taking it off.

They had planned that Rona would wait at the bus stop outside the village. How strange, she thought, that such a mundane arrangement had taken on aspects of a plan, a plot, an agreement that they were to become lovers. But it would not do for Edward Richardson to call for her at the Swan; Bedmansworth people, in their cul-de-sac village, watched, noted and talked.

He was on time. Wearing her long, dark coat she had waited only three minutes, under the grubby bus shelter, out of the rain which had been falling since early morning, below the shadows away from anyone who might recognise her with a passing glance. Her mother had stayed in bed late, with breakfast brought by Mrs Durie, carrying both the tray and news of the birth of Princess Maud, third daughter of King Edward the Seventh. The previous evening Pearl had said that she planned to look through the church registers that day.

'She must know more about local history than anyone who lives in Bedmansworth,' said Edward as they drove along.

'She's very secretive about it,' smiled Rona. She had taken off the long coat. She wore a grey sweater and grey trousers tucked into boots. They were driving through the eddying rain. 'She makes notes and mutters over them but I still can't quite grasp what she's going to do with it all. And she won't tell. As far as I know, she hasn't started writing the Definitive History of Bedmansworth.'

Being together felt entirely comfortable, their shoulders just touching; he was aware of the light scent of her face and neck. She said: 'A couple of days ago she went on an expedition. To . . . Laleham . . . ? Yes, Laleham. On the Thames.'

'Matthew Arnold is buried in the churchyard there,' said Edward. 'Adele's family have always been keen on Matthew Arnold. Her mother was almost obsessed. Apparently at some time he had stayed in our house.'

Rona shook her head. 'I'm not familiar with the name.'

'He was a Victorian poet. He wrote "Dover Beach" and his father was headmaster of the famous Rugby public school. Do you know *Tom Brown's Schooldays*?'

'Ah, now that strikes a chord. Even with an American.'

'Adele's family were fascinated by him and his work. Apparently, a hundred or so years back, one of their forebears was a friend of his, that's how he came to stay in the house. I remember Adele's mother on family outings to Laleham and Cobham where he also lived. We had to go at least once a year. Adele's mother used to put flowers on the grave on Christmas Eve, which was his birthday, and she knew his poems by heart. Toby's middle names are Matthew Arnold. That was to please her.'

The landscape was grey, lumpy as a stormy sea. 'This is new country for me,' Rona said peering from the window through the thick rain.

'Not much of a day for viewing it,' he said. 'Once we're off the motorway we go down through Surrey and into Sussex.'

'Surrey and Sussex sound wonderful, even if we can't see too much of them,' she smiled. 'How was Australia?'

'Just coming into summer. Not that I saw much of that. No more than we're seeing today come to think of it. On that sort of trip all I see is the interiors of airports, offices and hotel rooms. I could have been anywhere. Their summer was outside the window.'

'And you come back into winter,' she said.

'I'm used to changing seasons every week or so. In any

298

case . . . I was looking forward to today. Going down here will be a change from the rubbish tip.'

'The photographs were terrific,' she said laughing. 'Those gulls. You could almost see the wind around them. I'm glad you were looking forward to this.'

'My life has become very predictable,' Edward said quietly. 'Even though I take off every couple of weeks, even though I'm in exotic places, changing climates, it all falls into a pattern. I always come home.'

The rain eased as they drove over the hump of Surrey but there were piled clouds hurrying from the west and before they reached Sussex, it was back. They neared Chichester, the cathedral spire standing against dark and ragged skies.

Taking the main road west, they turned towards the sea. The flat coastal countryside cowered under the weather. The trees were bowed. 'It looks mysterious,' she said.

'Smugglers' territory,' he said. 'Imagine the barrels being carted up these lanes. The coast is full of creeks and inlets.'

They turned the last corner and the road ran through Bosham, an irregular village street, a long thatched hotel, and a maritime church standing square against the Channel weather.

'We've run out of England,' observed Rona as they reached the foreshore. The tide was running away quickly, gurgling through muddy channels, islands and peninsulars which formed as they watched. Gusty rain threw itself against the car windscreen. 'Not a good bird day,' said Rona. 'If they're wise they'll be hiding up somewhere.'

The road circuited the rim of the natural harbour, low and wide. There were high tide warnings displayed but the way was now wet and clear. He turned the car along the shoreway and drove slowly around the perimeter to the distant side. 'So your King Canute didn't have any luck,' she said.

'He ended up muddy,' he said. 'The tide did its usual thing.'

On the far bank he braked and stopped the engine. It still rained, obscuring the view from the windscreen. They were acutely aware of each other's presence. 'Maybe we should have some lunch and see if it clears later,' she suggested. 'I must buy you lunch for bringing me here, I insist.'

'How could I turn down an offer like that.' He restarted the engine, the wipers cleared the view and he backed the car, turning it towards the harbour bend again, into the village and to the thatched hotel.

It was old and comfortable, with chintzy curtains and cushions on window seats. They sat in the restaurant watching drenched ducks in the garden. A stream ran deeply between the lawn and the village road.

'I think it's clearing,' he suggested when they had almost finished. 'The weather comes from the west.'

'There's even some blue out there,' Rona pointed. 'Maybe it's the summer coming from Australia. I suppose the weather can lose its way.'

She insisted on paying the bill. They walked out into the reception lobby. A deep-faced young man was standing at the door. 'It's going over,' he said, studying the sky. He saw Rona's camera. 'You come for the birds?'

The man had a moustache almost as long as his face. He sniffed as if fighting a cold. 'I come for them too, I do. The birds. Love 'em. Broke up my marriage, bird-watching. I can go anywhere now. Gave up my job, well, got made redundant, which is better. I been up in Scotland, all over.'

They moved out of the door with him. 'Couldn't see a thing early,' said the stranger. 'But now it should be good. They'll be feeding close in. Brent geese, pochard, all sorts. Saw a lovely little golden-eye yesterday. It's good 'ere.'

They walked with him through the last of the village towards the shore. He had a huge pair of binoculars so weighty around his neck that they seemed to drag his head forward. The pockets of his anorak bulged. His face looked old; drawn and lined by weather. 'I'll show you where,' he offered. 'They come right close in. Brilliant some of them.'

Rona took her camera from its case. 'Nice,' said the young man. 'Good lens that. Can I 'ave a look?' She showed him the camera. '*I'm* going to America next,' he said to her. 'I can now, no worries, nothing. I've promised myself. She couldn't understand what I was doing for hours watching birds.' He faced them as though about to tell some awful truth. 'Thought I was out after the other sort of bird,' he said incredulously. 'Me!' He grimaced and pulled his long face longer. 'Who'd want me?' he said as if he hoped they might have some answer.

They progressed below the village walls butting onto the harbour where salted windows overlooked the tidal basin. They could see flocks of birds feeding on the mudflats and in the shoals. 'If I 'ad the money I'd buy a house 'ere,' said the man. 'Right along 'ere, watching the water. You could see 'undreds without getting out of bed.' He laughed, his mouth dropping into a long bag shape. He almost tiptoed to a slipway and led them down to where the tide had left mud shining and smooth as velvet. 'There's a diver,' he said looking through his binoculars. 'Red throat with 'is nose in the air.' He offered them to Rona. 'See. And just left there's some greylag and some little scaup. Lovely.' She peered at the feeding birds. 'And out there, just a bit to your right.' He guided her hand familiarly. 'See, white fronts, a whole load of them.'

They left him eventually and got into the car, driving to the far side of the harbour where they had been that morning. There was no colour in the day, a land and seascape, shades of grey. It was cold, clear, the rain gone.

Rona pulled on her coat and left the car to take photographs. He had resisted the conscientious temptation to call Harriet on the car phone, but now he did.

'Wherever are you?' Harriet asked. 'Mr Grainger was

asking. And your wife rang.' She paused. 'Can I hear sea-gulls?'

'I doubt it. I'm at Gatwick.'

There was a silence. Then she said: 'Oh, are you.'

She relayed the rest of the day's messages and he replaced the telephone and sat watching Rona's long coated silhouette balanced on the edge of the empty scene. She was gazing out into the blank afternoon, her hair moved by the small breeze. He left the car and walked to her.

'It's so empty,' she said. 'And I always thought England would be small and crowded.'

They were standing together. It was only a moment for them to turn face to face, to hold on to each other. Her skin felt chill. 'I want to stay here,' she whispered close to him. 'For just one more day. I want to stay here with you.'

From the room below came the deep, padded sound of a grandfather clock striking three. She stirred against him, their skins warm with sleep. He touched her. 'I would never have guessed that you would be so passionate,' she murmured.

'Nor me,' he answered.

'It's been such a long time for me,' she whispered.

'Me too, really.'

'That's how it is with Adele?'

'Yes. Except for quarrels, we're avoiding each other.'

'It's so hard like that.'

'Like playing a game, knowing the rules of pretence.'

'It's no way to live,' she said. 'With me, I thought everything was okay. We went away for the weekend, upstate. It came as a terrific shock when he just didn't come home from his job.'

'I think it would be some time before Adele really noticed. Yesterday we had a fight.'

'What about?'

'Today.' He saw her eyes react in the dimness of the

302

room. 'She wanted me to go to some official lunch with her. It had to be today.'

'Edward,' she said. 'I'm not going to break up your marriage.'

'It doesn't need you,' he said.

'This is just for now. I'm going home.'

He kissed her deeply. 'All this time you've been just out of reach,' he said. 'Just beyond my touch.'

'I'm not beyond it now.'

Gently he slid his hand below her. 'I can hear your heart beating when I do this,' he said.

'Let me hear yours like that,' she said. She held him. 'It's pounding.' Her hair flowed over his neck.

Their bodies close, limbs clutching, breast to breast, they loved each other again. The soft clock struck the quarter hour. Afterwards they lay letting themselves cool, not speaking, both staring full of thoughts and sadnesses into the shadows.

They kissed wearily and then she turned and sat her buttocks in his lap. He began to grow against her again. She laughed privately. 'You really are . . .' she said.

'I can't help it,' he said. 'It's you.'

She turned. The faint light was enough for him to see the sadness of her face. 'This may be the only time,' she said.

When Toby tried to replace the telephone his hand shook so much he dropped it and it swung on its cord like a hanged man. He looked guiltily around. He knew there was no one else in the house but he went once more into every room to make sure. These days they did not even have a dog. His stomach refused to stay still. Going into the kitchen he poured himself a large Pepsi-Cola, drinking it hunched on the stool, staring ahead, thinking about what he had done; what he was about to do.

He looked at his watch. Two hours. He would have to get ready for her. God, this was going to be something: the *real* thing. And no mistakes, no accidents, no disappointments; no lonely walks home and ending up with his unresponsive pillow.

He bathed and cleaned his teeth, then shaved, although he had only done so on the previous Sunday before taking Liz out. Yet another disappointment. Now he was not merely on a promise; he was on a *certainty*. As certain as the day – and night. At last he would *know*. What it was like, how it felt, what you had to *do*.

He put on his blazer and flannels, after rejecting his best suit. There was a tie he had been given at Christmas and now he put it around his neck and knotted it before taking it off and throwing it aside. *Casual*, that's how he should look, a man of the world. He opened his shirt collar. That looked as if he were opening the batting. 'No bloody good,' he said in anguish surveying himself in the mirror.

He tried his sports jacket; that was worse. Nobody went out to have sex wearing a check sports jacket, for Christ's sake. Why get all dressed up when the whole idea was to get your clothes off? He kept checking his watch. It was slow, it was fast, it was stopped. It ticked on solidly. Two buses had to be coordinated. He peered out at the early dark evening. There were splashes of rain on the window pane. 'Oh shit,' he muttered in despair. Now he would have to wear his anorak.

He left the house in the anorak and blazer with a roll-necked sweater which he had worn at school, a combination, he thought, of the formal and the relaxed. With the rain thickening there was no avoiding the anorak. After giving it a brushing he pulled it on, tugging up the hood before he went out of the door. It would do but he could not let her see him wearing it.

He hurried along the village street, crossing over to avoid the lights from the Swan, pulling the hood of the anorak closer. 'Good evening, Toby,' said the vicar coming out of the church gate like some white-collared warning. 'Not a nice one, wherever you're off.'

'J . . . just going somewhere,' muttered Toby. The vicar turned in the same direction and put up an umbrella. They walked together, the vicar asking questions about his job and how his parents were. To Toby's relief he went into the village hall but then Bernard Threadle chuggingly materialised along the street. He stopped. 'Off somewhere?' he demanded, like a man not to be denied an answer. 'Going to see somebody,' replied Toby miserably. 'In Maidenhead.'

'I've got friends in Maidenhead,' said Bernard as though he might ask them to keep an eye on him.

'Here's the bus,' said Toby as he saw the yellow lights splashing through the rain. Thank God for that.

'Be off with you then,' said Bernard in his guardian manner. And, as though he knew something: 'And behave.'

Gratefully Toby climbed on the bus. Already aboard were the odd group of Filipinos he had seen in Bedmansworth. They were talking volubly. 'Maybe we kill him,' said the only man without lowering his voice. 'Like in *Robocop*. Blow him away. Hah!'

To avoid them Toby went upstairs and, to his consternation, saw that the only other occupants were Randy Turner and Dee, the girl who claimed to have the bearskin rug. They both greeted him. 'Where you off then?' asked Randy. 'Boy Scouts?'

'Pack it, Randy,' smirked Dee pulling the youth's pigtail.

'I've got a date,' sniffed Toby. 'In Maidenhead.'

'Oh,' said Dee. She looked annoyed. 'Stretching our wings, are we then.'

'*We're* going to Dee's place,' said Randy. Smugly he put his thick arm about the thin girl. 'She's got a . . .'

'Bearskin rug,' finished Toby for him.

Randy glanced at Dee as though she were less than he had hoped. Dee said: 'But *you* never saw it.'

'Didn't get a chance,' said Toby defensively. He wondered how he could have gone through all he had for her.

'She's got a surprise for me, haven't you darling?' boasted Randy.

'Yes, it's her mother,' Toby said soberly. 'She throws the piss-pot over your head.'

He turned and went downstairs again. 'Thanks!' bawled Randy after him.

'My pleasure,' he called back.

The Filipinos were still plotting. 'Maybe,' suggested the old lady, 'maybe you break one more leg.'

Toby squinted at the conductor. The man sniffed. 'They're like that,' he said like someone with an extensive knowledge of the world. 'Where they come from life's cheap.' Toby sat at the back and peered out at the wet night. 'What I can't understand,' said the conductor as if it were the only thing, 'is why they let them in in the first place.' He bent to see if a bus stop was visible through the vacant rural darkness. 'It's getting to be like Hong Kong around here.'

Toby left the bus and waited, hunched under the metal shelter, until the next one came. It went west along the main road. He got off at the stop opposite the airport.

He was nearly there. He walked, his stomach churning with excitement and doubt, into the bright lobby of the hotel. There, away from the damp night, was light and warmth and softly broadcast music. Conversing people on leather couches lifted drinks that glistened in their hands. He almost turned and ran away.

But he steadied himself. He looked around. No one was watching him. He began to work to his plan. The first thing was to divest himself of his anorak and to fold it lining side out. He glanced about him cagily but still no one was paying any attention. He patted the inside pocket of the blazer.

There was a sign saying 'Elevators' straight ahead. He ambled towards it, his trembling held in iron restraint. A whole airline crew, pilot and co-pilot, stewards and stewardesses, all in pale blue uniforms like the chorus of a musical show, converged on the lifts and he stood, short, ordinary and conspicuous among their glitter and chatter. He let them get into the lift, intending to wait for the next one, but one of the stewardesses smiled with huge sweetness at him and said: 'Plenty of room for you.'

'Oh, yes. Thanks,' he replied unsteadily. She smiled again. He stepped in with them. He was facing her; she was tall and the buttons on her tunic were level with his nose. He was conscious of the perfume and the proximity of the tightly skirted thighs. His chest contracted. The elevator halted and they all left. The girl who had suggested he joined them smiled once more, her bright lips parting to reveal big white teeth. '*Merci, au revoir,*' she said. Her legs swished along the corridor.

He counted the numbers along the padded passage; the carpet was so thick, the walls so plush and enclosing, that he already felt he had passed into a different, dreamlike, place. There were pictures, London scenes on the walls, the air was warm and deftly perfumed, or it might have been that the stewardesses had passed along there so recently. It was as if he were following a scent. Then he came to the door: 'Room 608' it said in curled script. Oh God, he ought to run. He ought to run now.

He began to retreat up the corridor, picking his way in reverse, his hand against the wall for guidance. He halted, struck his fist silently into his open hand, and walked forward again, now with clenched teeth and slow determination. Room 608. Almost there, his step slowed and once again he retreated, this time almost colliding with a waiter balancing a tray like a tightrope act. 'Where you off then?' asked the waiter, waltzing around him.

Toby fearfully spun about, ducking under the large tray as he did so. He said: 'I'm lost.'

'What number was it? Odds are on the right, evens on the left.'

'Ah,' Toby raised a finger as though some deep revelation had been offered. 'Evens this side. Yes, I see.' He started forward again. 'I'm all right now, thanks.'

There was no turning back now because the waiter, posed at a door, was observing him. He nodded at each door along the silent corridor, like someone greeting a line of people; and when once more he arrived at 'Room 608' he raised his knuckles and, turning to grin stiffly at the still-loitering waiter, he knocked. When she opened the door he thought he was going to faint.

Georgina was wearing a pale blue nightdress with a lace-trimmed negligée draped beautifully across it, tied at the neck with a silken bow. Her face was fine, hair piled blonde and thick. Unbelievingly she stared at the boy. 'Yes?' she inquired.

'Candy?' It was half a whisper, half a groan. He heard the door down the corridor open and the waiter's diminishing voice.

Georgina felt herself pale under her make-up. 'You . . . ?' she inquired.

Relieved that she was as shocked as he was nervous, he ventured further. 'I made an appointment.' He swallowed violently. 'Mr Arbuthnot.'

Turning pink, she said: 'Please . . . come in . . . Mr Arbuthnot.' Her face relaxed and she began to giggle, putting her hand to her mouth. The boy stepped into the hotel room. He had never been in a room like that before. The excitement was overwhelming him. She was shaped and silken, her face lovely, her perfume made him catch his breath.

As he stood inside the door trying to still his nerves, she closed it without fuss and turned to scan him. 'Mr Arbuthnot,' she asked coolly, '. . . how old are you?'

'Old enough,' he replied amazing himself. He tried to smile patiently as if the mistake was common.

'Over sixteen?' she inquired.

'Well over.'

She whirled in a small circle, her hands to her face as though she did not know what to do. 'And . . . Mr Arbuthnot . . . Please, what is your first name?'

'Spike,' he said blatantly. 'Well, I wasn't christened Spike obviously, but everybody calls me Spike. All my friends.'

'Spike Arbuthnot,' she repeated. 'It certainly has something. Spike . . . please sit down.'

Toby went backwards, with small stuttering steps, towards the chair she indicated. He sat down and inclined so far backwards that it almost swallowed him. With a struggle he sat upright. 'Candy,' he said bravely, 'I know what I'm doing. Honestly I do.'

She sat on the edge of the coffee table like a shy angel. Her legs slid from her nightdress. He tore his eyes up to her face.

'You know what it's all about, then?' she asked.

'Well, not *everything*,' he admitted glancing away from those eyes. 'That's why I came. To find out.'

She shook her head and laughed. 'But the arrangements . . . how much it costs and that sort of thing.'

'The man on the telephone said it was from a hundred pounds up, depending . . .'

She nodded. She had instructed the Indian to underquote. 'So, you know that's what it costs?'

'For an hour,' he agreed like someone who had studied a contract. For a moment he feared she was going to send him away but as he gazed at her he saw that it was all right. 'Fine,' she said standing up. 'If you're quite sure.'

'Quite sure,' he said. 'You look great, you really do.' He fumbled in his back pocket. 'And here's the money. One hundred in twenties.'

Georgina had never accepted money so slowly. Her face flushed. 'I don't know what to say. I haven't had this situation before.'

'Neither have I,' he told her simply. There was a new certainty in his expression. 'That's why I'm here.'

She held out her fingers, her arm emerging from the silk garment. She asked him slowly: 'You haven't . . . done it? Ever?'

It was his turn to colour. 'No, never,' he said. His voice strengthened. 'I'm getting fed up waiting.'

She was pouring out two glasses of white wine. 'But . . . you're a nice-looking young man. Don't you have girl-friends?'

'On and off. But they mess you around. I want to know what it's *really* like. How it feels.'

'I can't believe this is happening,' she said looking at the ceiling as though hoping for help. She handed the glass to him. 'You . . . you do drink, I take it?'

'Like a fish,' he boasted. He drained the glass and choked. She patted his back in a motherly way. 'Well,' she said when he had apologised and recovered. 'Let's make a start, shall we.'

'Please,' he said.

'Let's go into the bedroom, if it's your first time . . .'

'It is. Honestly.'

'Then you should never forget it. In fact both of us should remember it.' She took his hand and led him through the door. He stared at the bed, its coverlet suggesting a reflection from the lamp at one side. The other lamp was unlit. 'How did you know?' she asked. 'About me. Did somebody tell you?'

'No,' he said stoutly. 'I haven't said a word to anyone.' He looked embarrassed. 'I wouldn't give you away, or any-thing.' She had sat on the side of the bed and patted the coverlet in invitation. He sat, as though on a garden seat, beside her. 'I work in a shop . . . an antique shop not an ordinary shop. I did a good deal, that's how I got the money.'

'I'm glad it's not your savings.'

'It's not. Don't worry about that. I made a lot on a picture in a sale.'

'That's very clever.' She regarded him anxiously, close to, and he saw for the first time the small lines under her eyes and the lines at the corners of her mouth. Her lipstick looked less smooth. She added professionally, checking her tiny watch, 'We won't count this towards your time. I'm just asking you because I'm interested. So how *did* you know about me?'

'Well, I was wrapping up some stuff in the shop, in newspaper, and I saw your name and your number in one of those small advertisements. That's when I made up my mind.' He looked at her hopefully. 'When can we start?'

'Now,' she promised firmly. 'We won't waste another moment.'

Sitting on the bed with her had been so normal, so natural, like his mother had once done, but now she leaned towards him, he felt the sheen of her cheek and her lips, firm, almost brutal, as she kissed him. She picked up his hand and laid its palm against her breast, half skin, half silk. He felt his penis rise as if it wanted to leave the room.

Next he placed his hand on her thigh. 'That's right,' she encouraged, then confidingly: 'Listen, why don't you take your clothes off and get into this bed. Get in that side. And wait for me.'

'Where are you going?' He looked anxious.

Georgina laughed again. 'Only to the bathroom.' She nodded: 'In there.'

'Oh right,' he said. 'Yes, that's all right.'

She leaned towards him again, overwhelming him, kissing him luxuriously. His hand found her breast again and he began to stroke her. 'Now you're turning *me* on,' she said. 'That's not supposed to happen. Haven't you ever kissed like that before?'

'Only girls,' he grimaced. 'And they struggle. You know, play hard to get. None of them have any . . .'

His hand went to her breast again.

She chastened him with a pat. 'I won't be a tick,' she said. She stood up and went into the bathroom. Left alone, Toby rolled in the ecstasy of anticipation against the smooth coverlet. Glancing towards the bathroom door, he hurried around the other side of the bed, tugging off his clothes as he went. He flung the garments on the floor, and almost leaped under the cover. Then after peeping out at his pile of disarranged clothes, he got out again, folded up his trousers and put them and his other things on a chair. She was moving in the bathroom. The flush gushed. Oh Christ, this was going to be magic. He held onto his penis.

Eventually the door opened and she extinguished the light. His head was eagerly projecting from the bed-cover like a boy hoping to see Father Christmas. He rolled his eyes towards her. He could barely breathe. Now, oh God, she was wearing only the nightdress, slim and rippling, showing the skin of her arms and shoulders and the shapes of her slightly lolling breasts. 'Would you like another drink, Spike?' she asked.

He had forgotten he was called Spike and for an awful moment he glanced around in case someone else had appeared. Then he realised: 'Oh no, no thanks, Candy. I'm not thirsty.'

She giggled openly as she came to the bedside. 'This *is* different,' she said as though to herself, looking at his head poking from the bed. 'Very different.'

Georgina eased below the sleek counterpane. He began to shake and she put her hand on his stomach to calm him. They were both lying on their backs but she turned onto her hip, towards him, and he followed. 'What would you like to do first?' she asked.

Tentatively Toby put his hands on her waist. 'I don't know,' he croaked. 'How do you usually start?'

Georgina grinned. 'You really *are* something,' she said.

Her fingers went to his hoping face. She sighed. 'Spike Arbuthnot. That's a lovely name.'

'It's not really my name,' he confessed uncomfortably. 'I thought I would have to lie to you.'

'Lots do,' she said. 'Don't worry, you're Spike Arbuthnot to me.'

'Can I . . . Can I . . . see you?'

'Why not? That's why we're here.' She guided him to the straps of her nightdress. 'You do it.'

His breath seemed to have congealed. His very fingers vibrated as he eased away the delicate straps over her shoulders and rolled down the silk. First one breast then the other bounced out; they seemed to return his gaze. 'Oh, they're . . . very good,' he said.

Scarcely restraining another smile she asked: 'Do you want to kiss them?'

'Not half,' he mumbled. She took his face and eased it towards her nipple, nuzzling him to it. 'There *is* one on the other side,' she suggested.

He came away from her damp, bright eyed, pink faced. 'I know,' he said with difficulty. She guided him again and she held his head, pretending to suckle him. Her hands went to his groin.

Suddenly she burrowed below the cover and enclosed him in her mouth. He squeaked like a mouse. His whole body stretched. 'Take it easy,' she cautioned, reappearing. She looked at the bedside clock. 'You still have half an hour. Let's have another glass of wine. She slithered from the bed pulling one strap of her nightdress over her shoulder, and walked into the other room. Staring at the ceiling he thought, God, even he had never imagined it would be like this. The feckless Liz, the disappointing Dee and even his faithful pillow were all in the past now.

Georgina returned with two glasses of white wine. She put them on the dressing table and slipping away the single

313

strap allowed her nightdress to roll to the floor. 'This is all of me,' she said with a joking twist of her hips.

'I've never seen anybody like you,' he said sitting up in the bed. 'And that's the honest truth.'

She picked up the wine again and they sat in bed and drank it, her left hand lolling in a friendly way around his naked shoulder, his right hand on her damp thigh. 'I've only seen this in books and on the pictures and television,' he said conversationally. 'I wondered if it would ever happen properly.' He turned his full eyes on to her.

'Let's carry on now,' she said taking his glass. 'But we're going to need a little something on there.' She tapped the head of his penis like a pet. She regarded him seriously. 'You wouldn't want to make me pregnant would you, Spike?'

'God, no,' he breathed. He grinned helplessly at her. 'Me, a father.'

'You'll hardly notice,' she promised as she performed a sleight of hand. 'There. You wouldn't know.' Professionally she eased herself across the bed and opened her thighs.

'Okay. It's time now,' she said.

He hardly knew how. Clumsily he climbed between her legs and she took him and guided him into her. A great smile of relief, bliss and achievement came over his face. She regarded him as a teacher might a promising pupil. 'That's very good,' she said seriously. 'Now let's both enjoy it.'

Toby scarcely needed the elevator. He felt he could have easily flown down to ground level. Out into the hotel lobby he floated winking at the girl in reception so that she said: 'Cheeky little devil.'

He was intending to go out to the bus stop but he saw a taxi discharging passengers outside the hotel. The doorman held the cab door open. It seemed to Toby that he skipped over the ground. 'I'll take that, please,' he announced beamingly. The doorman looked surprised but held the cab door open for him. 'Yes sir.'

'Where to, son?' asked the driver.

'Bedmansworth, if you please.'

'Where?'

'Bedmansworth. It's the other side of Heathrow.'

'Oh blimey,' the man grumbled. 'You'll have to show me . . . It's pitch dark out there. I thought you wanted to go to London.'

'Don't you worry, I've got cat's eyes,' boasted Toby. He felt he had eagle's wings too, and the gift of prophecy, the singing of angels, and the powers of Don Juan. 'I'll show you.'

Grumbling the driver set out into the hinterland. 'Hope I can find my way back,' he called.

'Sure you will,' returned Toby blithely. 'I get fed up with London, don't you?'

He sat in a warm dream. Remembering how, when they had finished in the room, as he was going, she had said: 'I had a good time too, Spike. It made a nice change.' She handed him fifty pounds. 'Let's split it.'

Staring at the notes he mumbled: 'I used to get half price in the pictures once.'

'But not now,' she assured him. 'You're a man, Spike. You're a full grown man.'

She had seen his name 'Toby Richardson' on a label sewn into his pullover by his mother. But she still called him Spike.

Thirteen

Sergeant Morris crouched almost double in his accustomed seat at the roadside outside St Sepulchre's, his face thrust forward, and tried to ascertain how far he could see into the distance. From the age of sixty, he had set himself minor tests as a gauge as to how far and fast old age was gaining. It pleased him that he could still, fifteen years later, touch his nose unerringly with his finger, stand on one leg, either leg, for half a minute, balance the Bible on his head, hit a lightshade with an orange pip once in three shots, and remain unsplashed while engaging only one hand at the urinal.

The winter days, however, helped neither his vision nor his comfort. Despite his overcoat and woolly balaclava the cold crept in, and fields and sky had become one glum curtain. He wondered if it were really there or if it were a mean trick of his failing eyes; a shroud, a harbinger.

The taxi pulled up almost at his feet. He had long ago learned in his military days, despite his training, that it was a mistake to react too quickly to an unexpected event. Alacrity often led to trouble. Now there was added to this philosophy an element of idleness and he remained composed, upright and seated, while Pearl Collingwood left the taxi and asked the driver to return in forty minutes.

'Well, hello,' she said to Morris. 'We've met before.'

He surveyed the old lady as the taxi departed. 'When?' he inquired bluntly. 'I try not to remember the past.'

316

'It's not too far in the past,' she returned sturdily. 'At the barbecue, remember?'

'That lot in the tent,' he recalled. He allowed himself a grim grin. 'I bet their feet gets cold these nights.'

She decided not to provide him with further ammunition. 'I've come to visit St Sepulchre's,' she announced briskly. 'Mrs Bollom invited me to come anytime. Is she at home?'

'She's at home,' he sighed vigorously. 'Wish she wasn't. Fussing around, do this, do that, don't spill your custard, you've got tobacco in your bed. Never stops, that woman.'

He stood up, however, as if having said his piece, he was willing to be cooperative. He even smiled. 'You're that Yankee lady,' he said. 'I remember now.'

With the familiarity that the elderly enjoy with the elderly, Pearl hooked her arm into his, and they began to progress sedately along the path to the front door of St Sepulchre's. An Air India Boeing seemed to graze the house-top as it took off.

Pearl covered her ears. 'What a helluva row!' she exclaimed. 'It's very noisy here. More than the village.'

'Indian.' He sniffed at the sky into which the plane was diminishing. 'Air India, they call that. See the tail. To think I helped to subdue that lot. Well, my regiment did. My grandfather was in the Seventeenth Slashers. And here they are flying right on top of us. And the Krauts, the Eyeties and the Fuzzy-wuzzies, and all ruddy sorts. All got their aeroplanes even if half of them can't afford to run them. I don't know what the world is coming to.'

'An end, eventually,' she mentioned.

'It is for us,' he agreed. He glanced at her as though they shared a truth. They had walked through the meagre trees and now she stopped and took in the house, its once white exterior walls stained with damp, its window frames peeling, its roof tiles like irregularly shuffled playing cards.

'The Americans were here once,' she confided to him. 'In this house. During the war.'

317

'Here and everywhere else,' said Morris relentlessly. 'Over here, over the girls.' He had the grace to look embarrassed. 'Oh, sorry, missus. I forgot you're a Yank yourself.'

At the front entrance, like someone performing a ceremony, Sergeant Morris rang the bell. 'In general we have to use the back door,' he told Pearl. 'But if there's a visitor you can come to the front with them. She reckons we muddy the carpet.'

Mrs Bollom herself opened the door. 'Ah,' she said taken off guard. 'Ah . . .'

Sergeant Morris was abruptly silent, merely wafting his hand towards Mrs Collingwood as though vaguely exhibiting her. The American stepped swiftly into the breach. 'Mrs Bollom, I do so hope you'll remember we met. I'm Pearl Collingwood. At the barbeque.'

The matron's expression cleared. 'Of course. You're the American lady from the Swan. Come in, come in and see us.'

'She's not *all* bad,' whispered Morris leaning towards the visitor's ear.

A heat like a desert wind was emerging from the house. 'My goodness,' Pearl said as the stepped into the hall.

'It's hot,' said Mrs Bollom familiar with the reaction. 'They like it like that. Nobody wants to be cold.'

'Getting ready for hell,' commented Morris. He had crept in beside the American woman and, at a motion of the head from the matron, he wiped his feet extravagantly on the doormat. He caught a second sharp glance from Mrs Bollom. 'Sorry,' he said. 'About that thing I said about hell. Didn't mean it.'

'Of course you didn't,' Mrs Bollom agreed firmly. They walked further into the house. 'It's not something we talk about here.'

'It's just I like a bit of fresh air myself,' said Morris inhaling with a snort. 'That's being in the army for you. That's why I go and sit on the seat.'

318

They walked into a large and polished room where four frail ladies were sitting on chairs and bouncing a huge, coloured-striped beach ball to each other.

'Harlem Globetrotters,' said Morris dolefully. He was busily cleaning his ear with a matchstick. The great, bright ball bounced towards him and he pushed it disdainfully back with his hand.

They went further into the lounge. There was a rank of chairs facing a wide French window. 'Our private viewing gallery,' said Mrs Bollom quite proudly. A Boeing 747 floated into view at the upper edge of the window frame and landed lightly before roaring along the runway. Polite applause sounded from several of the old ladies and another old man watching. 'They're on special strings, you know,' proclaimed the man knowledgeably nodding towards the airliner.

'So's he,' grunted Morris. He took a place on the end of the row. A United Airlines plane came into the frame. 'Yankee!' called Morris and there was a round of polite applause. Mrs Bollom brought Pearl a cup of coffee. A British Airways Trident followed onto the runway. A ragged cheer went up. 'One of ours,' Morris said helpfully to the American.

'Mrs Richardson, the social worker lady, suggested we might take them on a visit to the airport,' said Mrs Bollom doubtfully regarding her charges. 'But I couldn't risk it. They ran amok in a fairground once.' She rolled her eyes.

'I have an ulterior motive, I'm afraid, in visiting you,' whispered Pearl to the matron.

'Oh, and what is that?'

'I wanted to see this house. You see, my husband was stationed here in wartime. In this area somewhere. I understand that this house was used by US Air Force officers. I just thought I would like to look around.'

'Your husband . . .'

'He died some years ago. But I had an itch just to come see.'

'Is that why you came to Bedmansworth?'

Pearl hesitated. 'I'm not *sure* this is the place,' she said not answering the question. 'I just think so.'

A concerted booing came from the old people at the window. Raspberries were blown. 'Lufthansa,' sighed Mrs Bollom. 'Sergeant Morris makes them boo the Germans.' She tutted towards the old soldier. 'He's a terrible man, you know,' she said as if glad to have someone to tell. 'He's promised to marry at least three of the old ladies here. One of them is making her bridal veil. Nothing but trouble.' She led Pearl from the hot room. 'Well, you're welcome to look around, Mrs Collingwood,' she said. 'I don't know how many changes there will have been. The house is more or less the same, I suppose, but when it became a home for the elderly I know that some of the bigger rooms were converted into smaller bedrooms.' She appeared thoughtful. 'I had heard that the Americans were billeted here but it was so long ago. Strangely enough I had a letter only a couple of months back, from a chap, some sort of military historian, asking me if there was anything left from that time. He was putting together a local story about the Americans. But, of course, there was nothing I could do to help him.'

Pearl took her time. 'Would you by any chance have the name of that gentleman and his address?' she inquired.

Mrs Bollom said: 'I'm sure I could find it. I file everything away.'

The small, yellow cottage was almost obscured by the combine harvester parked in front of it. 'Excuse the lawnmower,' said Bert Trouton. 'There's nowhere else I can put it.'

'Looks like a prairie mower,' Pearl offered, surveying the massive machine.

He was a big man and patted the battered red front of

the harvester carefully as though to avoid damage. 'She's my baby,' he said fondly. 'Bought her for a song and she's my living. I've got a mechanical digger too, a JCB. I'm an all-rounder I am.'

She liked him at once. He led her into the low cottage. 'This is the good wife,' he said with the air of one who might have one not so good. A round and shiny woman shook Pearl's hand. 'I'll get you a cup of tea,' she said. 'Coming all that way from America.'

'I've only come from Bedmansworth,' laughed Pearl. 'Today that is.'

'Good job I was home when you phoned,' said Bert. 'Having a bit of a snooze this afternoon. I have to keep my strength up.'

'He has to keep his strength up,' confirmed Mrs Trouton as she went from the room. She returned at once. 'Is that your car out there?'

'It's a taxi,' said Pearl. 'He's waiting for me.'

'I'll take him a cup too,' she said. 'While Bert shows you his papers.'

'They're all in here,' said Bert. He led the way into a front room. The furniture and the floor were almost buried below files, boxes, bundles and books. 'I'm getting around to sorting it all out,' he said waving his hands above the chaos. 'It might look a mess but I know more or less where everything is.'

He cleared a staggered tower of books from a table and some ragged documents tied in string from a chair which he brushed briskly before inviting her to sit. His wife brought the tea. 'Kettle'd just boiled,' she said. She looked around the confusion half in dismay, half admiration. 'He knows where more or less everything is,' she confirmed. 'Though I don't know how.'

Pearl accepted a spoonful of sugar and sat down at the unsteady table. 'It looks fascinating,' she said.

There were some metal files piled like squared stones on

top of each other and Bert sat gingerly on them. 'Eighteen stone, I am,' he said. 'I could be crushing history.'

He was eager to tell her about it. 'By accident I started this,' he explained. 'I'm not a historian or anything, as you can see, I drive that harvester out there. But, see, I was always told that my father was an American, a soldier who was over here in the nineteen forties. He just vamoosed and my mum died a couple of years ago. But I set about trying to find out about him. Eventually I tracked him down to a town in Iowa. Bliss, it's called. The Americans, the authorities over there, were very helpful with it all. But when I tried to contact him I got nowhere. So I went over. I just went and got straight to this little place, Bliss, which was in the middle of nowhere. But he'd died too. All I was able to do was stand by his grave.'

'That's pretty sad,' said Pearl. 'But I guess it happened a lot.'

'Don't I know it. There's hundreds of cases. Especially from the War.' He looked at her anxiously. 'I'm not blaming the Yanks,' he said hurriedly. 'Some of the marriages lasted years.' He paused and picked up a sere sheet of paper from the top of a pile. As though he were reading from it he went on: 'But it was while I was going about this that I came across all sorts of relics of the Americans in this country. Stuff just left around, documents, photographs . . .'

'You have photographs?'

'Hundreds. So I sort of got interested and took it up like a hobby. When I wasn't working I went around gathering up stuff. Mostly, people were only too glad to get shot of it. It was in cellars and basements and old camps. I had to concentrate so I just did west of London, and there was plenty there, believe me.' He extended his hand. 'Well, you can see.'

Her eyes went around the crammed room. Bert's wife reappeared, as if anxious to keep in touch, and said: 'The driver's got his tea. I asked him if he wanted to come in

322

but he says he's quite comfy, thank you.' She looked around the rubble. 'You couldn't take some of this away could you?'

'Not yet,' said Bert warningly. He nodded towards his wife and said to Pearl: 'She wants her room back.' He moved one pile of boxes a few inches as if making a token effort. 'It won't be that long before it's all sorted.'

Mrs Trouton went out with Pearl's cup after offering her more tea. Pearl declined. She said to Bert: 'I think the whole thing looks wonderful.'

He seemed appreciative. 'Well, I'm not a scholar or anything, but I'm quite logical, you have to be with machines. So I've been spending my time off going through all this, sorting it out as much as I can. And all sorts of people have got interested. There was a bit in the *Sunday Express* about me. I've had two blokes from the Imperial War Museum here and the American Embassy rang up.' He looked at her shyly: 'And now you.'

His attitude made her smile. 'Just like I say I think it's wonderful,' she repeated. Then carefully: 'Is there anything from Bedmansworth?'

'It was the officers' mess of the 44th Tactical Support Group, US Air Force,' he said. 'I checked after you phoned. But if they left anything it's been dumped long since.'

Her disappointment showed. 'I understand. I just wondered if you might have *something*. I don't know what. My husband was there during the war and I'm trying to piece together his story. He died a few years back and as I was in England I thought it might be a good idea, it would occupy me.' She looked around the confusion. 'But it looks as if it's the needle in a haystack.'

He appeared to have caught her dejection. 'There was quite a bit at West Drayton, and stuff from Northolt. If it had been Kingston or Bushey Park then we might have had a chance. But Bedmansworth. There was nothing left.'

Pearl rose apologetically. 'I've been taking up your time,' she said. 'Not at all,' he assured her. 'I wish there might have been something. I'll look through any stuff from other places that might be connected, but unless I can pinpoint it, cut it down into Air Force units or at least place names, it's the needle in the haystack all right.'

'I'll leave you my telephone number if you should find anything,' she said. She wrote her name and the number of the Swan and gave it to him. 'I'm there with my daughter. But we must be going home before too long.'

As he and his wife showed her out of the cottage the full sense of disappointment came over her. She looked at the huge, unwieldy agricultural machine and shook her head. Some things were certainly difficult.

The taxi took her back to the Swan and she went to her room. Rona was out, sketching. How strange that after being so close after their arrival in England, they were now drifting apart, almost as they had been in California. Perhaps it *was* time they went home. Mrs Durie brought her a tray of tea. 'You must need this after all you've been doing,' she said enigmatically.

'I've been busy,' agreed Pearl. The other woman poured her a cup of tea. 'What's the royal news today?'

'Coming up for Mausoleum Day on December fourteenth,' sniffed Mrs Durie. 'Death of the Prince Consort, eighteen sixty-one, and Princess Alice, died eighteen seventy-eight same day. And the Abdication's on December eleventh, nineteen thirty-six. Did Jim tell you there'd been a phone call?'

'For me?' She almost spilled her tea. 'No. When was that?'

'Just before you got back in the taxi.' She shook her head. 'He told that Randy to tell you I expect, because Jim's had to go to Slough about the darts presentation. He was wondering if you'd like to go. It's early next month. That Randy. Thinks of nothing but what he wants to think of and that's not much.' She turned. 'I'll see if there's a message on the pad downstairs.'

'It's all right, I'll get it,' said Pearl anxiously. She followed the Englishwoman out of the door. Mrs Durie turned as she went down the curve of the stairs. They reached the closed bar and Mrs Durie handed her a note from the pad below the telephone. 'There, that's it. Can you see? It's a bit dim in here.' She turned on the bar light. 'That's more like it.'

Pearl looked at the message. It was from Bert Trouton. 'Thank you,' she said as calmly as she could. Randy appeared. 'Did your dad tell you to give Mrs Collingwood a message?' said his grandmother.

The youth tugged his pigtail defensively. 'Yeah, well I was going to, wasn't I.' He looked at each woman in turn and turned out of the room again. 'Little swine,' muttered Mrs Durie. 'I'll leave the light on so you can ring.'

Pearl dialled the number carefully. Bert Trouton answered at once. 'When you'd gone I had a good idea,' he said. 'I had a think about it and I went to a book I've got about US Air Force movements. It turns out that the 44th Tactical Support Group, those at Bedmansworth, got shifted. The whole lot went to Reading in nineteen forty-five. I've got a whole pile of stuff here. Photographs as well.'

Within an hour she was back at the cottage. As though in deference to her he had moved the gargantuan harvester a few possible yards, so that at least the front door was exposed. She told the taxi to wait and hurried along the garden path to the opening door. 'I should have thought about it before,' said Bert ushering her in. 'I ought to have looked in the Transfers Book. Obvious. Anyway that's what 44th Tactical Support Group did. Moved to Reading.' He led her eagerly into the front room.

'Like some tea?' inquired Mrs Trouton almost anxiously appearing at the door. The American thanked her and said she would not. 'Where are they, Bert?' Pearl asked.

He nodded at a bulging cardboard box. The string had already been untied and the sides sagged with the contents.

'It was in the Reading Council offices, masses of it,' he recalled. 'They were only too glad to see the back of it.'

Pearl sat at the unlevel table again. Almost as soon as she started to turn the pages, she saw her husband's name: 'Captain Michael Collingwood. . . . Instructions: Captain M. Collingwood USAF will be in charge of . . . Mike Collingwood to organise basketball. . . .'

'You . . . said there were photographs,' she said not looking up from the document in her hands.

Bert patted her arm. 'They're in the other lot,' he said. 'Here.' He lifted a heavier box from the floor and placed it on the table. 'They're a bit yellow, as you'd expect, but some of them are all right. It's amazing. Kept in the dry, I suppose.'

Pearl began, slowly and full of pain, taking out the faded photographs. She could scarcely keep back her tears now. There he was, young and tall, with that smile she had known so well and for so many years. Groups of officers, photographs on the base. The Christmas party. . . . the Christmas party . . . dated nineteen forty-four, December eighteenth. . . . There he was with the others below the decorated tree, loaded with lights and presents. Mike with a glass askew in his hand, with his fellow officers, all cheering and smiling, toasting away the last months of the war. And at his right hand with her hand on his shoulder was a girl. *That was her!* The shock rendered Pearl Collingwood speechless and still. She would have known that face anywhere.

When Rona went into her mother's room Pearl was sitting up in bed against the pillows, her early tea brought by Mrs Durie untouched on the bedside table, her *Daily Mail* folded on the bed, and in her hand a letter. Beside her, on the quilt, lay a small rectangular box, its edges worn, its lid put aside.

'You got some mail?' said Rona. She touched the side of the teapot. It was only warm.

'Written a long time ago,' said her mother still looking at the tight writing. 'It's one of your father's love letters.'

'Mother!' Smiling, Rona sat on the bed and put her arm around Pearl. 'You've been hoarding them. . . . You never told . . .'

'It's not *from* your father. It's to him,' she corrected slowly. 'And it's not from me.'

Rona frowned. 'Oh . . . well who . . . ?'

'Who wrote it? Well, I know now.' She turned her face and Rona saw with alarm that her eyes were wet. The old lady went on: 'But it's so long ago that it doesn't matter, probably not anyway. Only to me. And now I know.'

Slowly her daughter sat on the side of the bed. 'Mother, what are you saying . . . ?'

Pearl sighed. Her eyes returned to the letter. 'Your father and I were married for just a year when he went overseas in the War, came here to England. To this very part of the country.' She raised her head as if facing up to a difficult reality. 'To this place. To Bedmansworth.'

'So that,' said Rona slowly, 'is why we came here. Is that so?'

Pearl smiled seriously. 'I made sure we would, didn't I just. All that acting up, kidding you I was sick . . . but it worked. This is where we got.'

'Why didn't you just *tell* me?' asked Rona seriously. 'If you'd wanted to come to Bedmansworth then there was no reason *why* we . . .'

'It was just something, I guess, I had to keep private,' said the old lady as if she were telling herself. 'It was something I had to do alone. Nobody could help.'

Rona felt the teapot again. 'You haven't had any tea yet,' she pointed out. 'Would you like some now?'

'Sure,' said her mother smoothing out the letter on the quilt. 'This memory game is thirsty work.'

As she poured the tea Rona said: 'Tell me.'

Pearl took a deep, elderly breath. 'Sure. When your father died five years ago I discovered this.' She nodded at the worn cardboard box. 'In a strange way I suppose I was *looking* for it. I felt guilty, like most widows must do at those moments, just going through his private stuff . . . almost prying. The box was hidden away among some old, old papers, fifty years old most of them, in a corner of a trunk in the garage. I had the feeling I shouldn't be looking through it at all. He was dead and maybe I should have just got rid of the whole trunk, thrown it out without looking. But I didn't. I did look and I found these letters.'

'So they're love letters,' said Rona pursing her lips. She kissed her mother's hair. 'But from a long, long way back.' She had given her a cup of tea and Pearl was about to take a sip. But she replaced the cup into the saucer and handed both to her daughter. 'A good many years, Rona,' she agreed. Her voice descended to a whisper. 'But the *passion*, the sheer passion, lives on. The amazing, overwhelming, love and *passion* she had for him. It was an all-sweeping, all-engulfing affair. Me, I was just married to him, that's all.'

'It happened to a lot of people,' Rona pointed out carefully. 'It was the War that did it.'

'Not in this case. Not the War,' said the old lady slowly, firmly. 'You only have to read them and you'll see that. It shines from every page.'

'Oh, Mother.'

'I felt ashamed. Ashamed of eavesdropping on them, odd as that may seem, even though he was my husband, even though it happened so long ago. I felt ashamed too that our marriage had been just a marriage, a good marriage, I guess, but nothing special. Not a big romance, never passionate, not like this.' She tapped the letter.

'Mother, affairs are different from marriages. And letters

328

are different from real life. Who was she? What was her name?'

'That was my burning desire to know. None of the letters have any address. She was married later. The only name I knew her by is Elizabeth. But I know her now.' She dabbed her eyes. 'Call me an old, foolish woman, if you like. Maybe that's what I am. But I just wanted, I *needed* to know, before I die, who was this person who was the love of my husband's life?'

'And now you do.'

'I did my detective work too well.' She dabbed her face. 'I would have made a swell private eye. I knew that he had been stationed in this area, and he had mentioned Bedmansworth a lot when he was reminiscing about it. It's not a name you forget easily. One day I went to the Santa Monica library and checked out a large scale map of this part of England and I found Bedmansworth, and it was so near the airport. From that moment it was on my mind to come here. To find out.' Her eyes had been lowered but now she faced her daughter again. Rona picked up the handkerchief and dabbed the old lady's face. She thought she might begin to cry herself. Her mother said: 'It may sound crazy, but old people do crazy things. They're entitled to that. I got so obsessed with it. I had to know who this woman was who gave my husband such romance and happiness.'

'But you don't have any of *his* letters to *her* do you? You don't know if he felt the same.'

'Oh, but he *did*. Reading her letters is plenty enough to see how much they had together, how much they felt about each other. She refers to things that he has said. And we had only been wed a little while and I thought I had just lent him to the country to help with the War. It was at the back of my mind that he might have an affair – or more than one – not many of those boys didn't. But this, this Rona, was real, true, *passionate* love. That's what I find so

329

hard to face. All through Mike's life, whatever he showed, he must have thought of what might have been.'

'Okay,' returned Rona firmly. 'But you don't *know* that, do you. If they both felt that way why didn't they get together?' She realised abruptly how the advice applied. 'Two people . . .' she slowed. 'If it was as strong as you believe . . . why didn't they . . . ?'

'I've tried to comfort myself with that thought,' said Pearl. 'Don't ask me why but she stayed and married her husband and Mike came home to me. And we lived happily – or did we? – ever after.' She peered through her glasses at the letter. Just reading what she has to say, I just doubt it. These letters are over a period of five years, long after he came back to the States. After she wed. And then they ceased, as far as I know. There may have been others.'

'So you know, you've found out, who she was.'

'She's dead now,' said Pearl. 'I not only know who she was, I know what she looked like.' She reached to the drawer in the bedside table and opening it took out an envelope. 'Here she is. With your father. Don't they just look happy.'

Deliberately she slid out the photograph. Staring at her, Rona caught her breath. Pearl passed the picture across the bed. 'There she is. Recognise her?'

Rona's mouth dried. 'Oh my God, it looks like Edward's wife . . . it's Adele's mother.'

'There's a strong family resemblance,' agreed Pearl sagely. All at once she appeared calmer, relieved, now that she had shown the picture. 'You saw that portrait hanging in the Richardsons' house. Then only yesterday I saw this picture. She was my husband's lover.' She paused, idly studying the photograph, and then went on. 'The young boy, Toby Richardson, his middle names are Matthew Arnold. Remember how he was so embarrassed at telling us, in fact he *didn't* tell us in the end. Matthew, but not

Arnold. But he was christened Tobias Matthew Arnold in the church right here. I've seen the entry in the register.'

'You've really gone right through with it,' muttered Rona. She shook her head at the photograph.

'Elizabeth Hickman, Adele's mother, just loved the poet Matthew Arnold,' said Pearl. 'More than a century ago he stayed in their house. They were brought up on him. It was almost obsessive when she knew your father. This last letter describes how they went on Christmas Eve 1944 to Matthew Arnold's grave at Lalelam, quite near here. I've been there too. I went just the other day. Christmas Eve was the poet's birthday and apparently Elizabeth Hickman always visited there at that time. They – Mike and she – went to the churchyard and then walked along beside the Thames River. It's all described, remembered, in the letter. They knew they would be parting before too long.' She paused and gave a small wry smile. 'It is all *so* poetic I could almost feel sorry for them. And there was I, back in California, raising money for war bonds. He must have thought my letters were pretty dull.'

Rona's hand went slowly to the letter on the bed. 'May I?' she asked. She suddenly thought she should not. 'Do you mind?'

'If you like reading history,' sighed her mother handing it to her.

Her daughter read two lines of verse at the bottom of the page.

> 'And we forget because we must,
> And not because we will.'

'See, it's dated December twenty-fourth, nineteen fifty-one – Christmas Eve, Matthew Arnold's birthday – and five years after he came home. That's the last letter,' said Pearl. 'But they're all like that – none of them has a sender's address. Not even just "Bedmansworth".' The thin smile returned. 'Maybe to confuse historians and busybodies,' she said. 'But they're fine words. He was a good poet. I've read quite a lot of him now. And those sentences from his poem called "Absence" are repeated on Elizabeth Hickman's grave in the churchyard right outside this window. Yesterday when it was almost dark, I went in there and I read them to myself aloud.' Pearl was crying freely now: 'What a beautiful story,' she sobbed.

Rona put her arms about her. 'Now you know what you needed to know,' she comforted. 'There's nothing more.'

'But I'm so *jealous* of her.'

'The time for jealousy is gone. A long time ago. She's dead and so is Dad. Nothing will change.'

Pearl dabbed her eyes again and her daughter, with a sad smile, helped her and then wiped her own. Her mother, her head on her side, said: 'That house. How odd it should all have come from *that* house. The Richardsons'.' She touched her daughter's forearm and looking at her knowingly said: 'Isn't it strange, really strange, Rona, how life comes around in a complete circle. Even after almost fifty years.'

It was mid-afternoon in late November and the winter daylight was already drifting obliquely away. Barbara had a single lamp illuminating her cabin-bedroom. She woke from her doze and at once realised there was someone outside the window, the shadow of the head on the curtain. Her arm went backwards and made contact with Bramwell's face. 'Bram,' she whispered over her shoulder. 'There's someone trying to look in the window.'

'Mind the leg,' mumbled Bramwell blinking awake. His plaster cast was now replaced by a secondary support, but movement was still difficult and apprehension remained. He levered himself upright and turned towards the window.

'I can't see anything,' he said. He nodded at her like a signal. 'Take a look.'

Again he indicated his leg and reluctantly she left the bed, and pulling on her robe while she was still half concealed by the sheet, crept to the window. There she crouched and paused nervously. 'Take a look,' repeated Bramwell. She peeked through the curtains, shrieked and fell backwards. Her hand flew up and she feverishly tugged the curtains across and slid down to hide behind the bulkhead. 'He's out there, Bram,' she trembled. 'He's looking in.'

Bramwell manoeuvred his leg in its light cast out of the bed. 'The light,' he whispered. 'Put the light out.'

'*You* put it out . . .' As she said it she realised she would be quicker. She crawled along the floor and extinguished the light. Bramwell was trying to pull his trousers on, cursing his awkwardness. Finally getting them in place he comically staggered around the wooden wall and sidled to the window. He flung apart the curtains. There was no one there.

'Are you sure?' he said.

'Of course. Absolutely. Bram . . . he had an . . . Oriental type face . . . you know, the eyes . . . I saw him clearly in the deck light.'

'Moustache?' The colour slid from Bramwell's face. 'Did he have a long moustache?'

'Yes, Bram.'

'Lettie's brother. Oh shit.'

'He found us.'

'The bugger used to be a jungle tracker. So he says. Anyway he only had to look in the phone book.'

'What are you going to do?' She was pulling on her pants and trying to locate her sweater. 'We're right in it now.'

Bramwell tried to think. 'Just go to the door and have a peek,' he suggested firmly.

'Me? But . . . he may still be out there.'

'Look, I can't do it. He'll see it's me. I'll back you up. If the sod comes charging in, I'll get him. Have you got a bottle?'

'A bottle of what?' She was tugging on her sweater.

'Of what? *Anything*. Empty. I want to hit him with it not drink!'

'Don't shout at me, Bram. We should keep calm.'

She had put the sweater on back to front and was attempting to reverse it. 'Sorry, darling,' he said trying to help her. 'We really ought to. I can't go to the door anyway, in case he sees me. I'd better hide.'

'Oh, that's right, *hide*,' she reacted scornfully. 'What if he attacks *me*? We should ring the police.'

'Yes, that's a good idea. After all they're not interested in what *I'm* doing here, but a Filipino with a moustache, crawling around in the dark on the canal bank – that's something else. I'll ring nine nine nine.'

He did. 'It's a houseboat along the canal,' he reported. 'And there's a Filipino chap looking in the window. How do I know it's a Filipino? Oh God. I just do. Will you please send somebody along . . . and quick. These people run amok, you know.'

'That's Malays,' said Barbara thoughtfully when he had put the phone down. 'Malays run amok. I know because I've been out there. Something sends them mad.'

'Listen, don't let's split hairs. Lettie's brother is quite capable of splitting ours, believe me.'

'Oh Bram, I love you but this is terrible.'

'It means Lettie knows, or she's pretty certain. When the police get here I'd better hide because maybe he's still out there. Then he *will* recognise me.'

She acknowledged the logic. Then she said: 'If we ever get married, don't ever do this sort of thing.'

'I won't,' he said. 'I've had enough. Broken leg, broken nerve, broken marriage.'

They sat nervously in the dark and waited. After ten minutes a blue light was reflecting through the gap at the top of the curtains onto the ceiling. 'They certainly take their time. We could have been massacred,' Bram grumbled. 'I'll hide.'

He went into the bathroom and Barbara went tentatively to the hatchway door and called through. 'Is that the police?'

'Police,' confirmed a light voice.

She withdrew the bolts and turned the key. Two thin young policemen stood in the light of the deck lamp. 'Having trouble?' asked the first. The other was whispering into the radio attached to his tunic.

'There was a man out there,' said Barbara. 'Looking through the curtains.'

'He would have had to climb on board,' said the officer. He looked pleased at the deduction. 'He must have been quite agile, don't you reckon, Jonty?'

Jonty concurred. 'He was a Filipino,' Barbara told them.

'Ah, now they're quite agile,' said Jonty. 'We'll take a look around.' He gave her an anxious glance. 'Did he have any arms?'

'Arms?' she said astonished. 'Oh, guns. I don't know.'

The policeman gave a wide grin. 'You'd be amazed at the answers we get to that one.' He repeated it in a pleased way. 'Did he have any arms?' He looked at the other officer. 'Don't we, Rollo?'

'I'll say,' agreed Rollo. 'Amazed.'

They appeared to be debating the wisdom of looking around. Jonty walked to the end of the barge one way and his companion to the opposite end. They returned within seconds. 'Not a sign,' said the first officer.

'Vanished,' said the other trying to sound disappointed. 'We'd better take some particulars.'

She opened the door for them and they stepped heavily into the spacious area. 'Very commodious,' said Jonty as if he were thinking of buying.

Bramwell decided to come out of hiding. His entrance was more forthright and sudden than he had intended and

335

both policemen were facing the other way. They jumped as a pair and turned pale faced, Jonty almost knocking over the low table. 'You gave us a start,' he admonished. He put the table in its correct position.

'This is not the man, I take it,' suggested Rollo examining Bramwell.

'No, this is, my . . . fiancé. He's got a broken leg,' Barbara told them. 'Otherwise he would have been out there like a shot.'

'I'd have got that peeping Tom,' confirmed Bramwell.

'Yes, exactly,' said Jonty. 'Is it all right if we sit down?'

'Oh sorry, please do,' invited Barbara.

'These uniforms get very heavy,' said his companion.

'Would you like a drink?' asked Bramwell.

The officers faced each other. Jonty said: 'It's against the rules, but nobody's looking.' He glanced around.

'Nobody's looking,' corroborated Rollo. 'Any scotch?'

Barbara went to the cabinet, took out a plastic bottle and emptied three whiskies from it, then another plastic container from which she poured gin, adding tonic from a conventional bottle. 'Looks like it fell off an aeroplane,' said Rollo conversationally. 'You in the trade?'

'I'm a steward and Barbara's a stewardess,' intervened Bramwell. Jonty regarded Rollo severely as if he had abused the rules of hospitality. 'It tastes the same, I expect,' he said.

'Oh, I'm sure,' agreed Rollo, a little shamefaced. He accepted the glass but peered into it as though it might contain clues while Jonty took a quick swallow with the attitude of someone sportingly destroying evidence. 'The bottles were broken, unfortunately,' said Bramwell primly. 'I dropped the supermarket bag.'

'I'm always doing that,' said Jonty.

'You do,' said Rollo. They each took a second drink. 'They sell some good stuff in Safeways now,' Rollo continued. He looked up. 'Do you know a lot of Filipinos, sir?'

'Some,' said Bramwell guardedly. 'I'm married to one.'

'Ah, then it's domestic.' The policemen both nodded knowingly. 'Now that's different.'

'This Filipino could have murdered us,' pointed out Bramwell, his tone hurt. 'He was a jungle tracker.'

'Don't come across many of them around here,' agreed Jonty. 'Occupation "Jungle Tracker",' he said wistfully, pretending to write in a notebook. 'Trouble is "domestic" puts it into a different category. If it's a house . . .'

'This is a boat,' pointed out Barbara. 'And it's very isolated.'

'You're right there,' he agreed.

'Must be difficult for the shops,' nodded Rollo. 'And the supermarket.' He examined his empty glass. Bramwell picked up the plastic bottle and poured two more scotches. The action appeared to inspire Jonty. 'I'm not really empowered to give you this information,' he said inclining his head. 'Officially. But . . .' He studied his companion.

'Yes?' prompted Bramwell.

'A group of Filipinos were observed . . . at least the bloke thought they were Filipinos, although he wasn't sure. They were from that direction, anyway. He used to do a lot of travelling.'

'He was a train driver,' pointed out Rollo.

'Where?' Bramwell prompted again. 'Where did he see them?'

'The Crazy Kat Café. Know it?'

Bramwell exchanged glances with Barbara and they shook their heads.

'Sort of Stanwell way . . .' Jonty consulted Rollo. 'It is Stanwell there, isn't it.'

'Just,' said Rollo with the pedantry of an expert. 'Other side of the road is Bedfont.' He paused. 'West Bedfont.'

'He's red hot,' said Jonty admiringly. He continued: 'The Crazy Kat Café. They spell the kat with a K, can't think why. It's not a posh place.'

337

Bramwell took a deep breath. 'And these Filipinos . . .'

'Oh yes, them,' said Jonty as if he had lost his train of thought. 'Four. Three women and a man. The bloke that owns the place thought they was up to some illegal entry scam at Heathrow, you know getting another hundred or so sneaking in without passports.'

'He thought they were suspicious,' said Rollo. 'He thought they were plotting something and he feels there's enough of them in the country already, not just Filipinos either, and he was only doing his duty. So when they had gone he notified the police . . .'

'Us,' blinked Jonty. 'But by the time we got there they'd gone. Apparently the Filipino bloke had been in there before, and the good-looking woman. There was another older woman and a girl who didn't seem to know what was going on and didn't say much. Just moved her hands around. He thought she might be deaf and dumb.'

'Dumb,' said Bramwell dolefully. 'That's our Pauline.'

The policemen placed their glasses with finality on the coffee table. 'We had a peek around but we couldn't spot them,' said Jonty. 'And it's not something you can put an all-cars alert out for. We'll have another look on our way home. We're off duty now.'

'In twenty-three minutes,' said Rollo checking his watch.

They stood and replaced their hats and went towards the door. 'Thanks for everything,' said Bramwell sarcastically.

'Yes, thanks,' agreed Barbara misunderstanding him. He glanced at her. 'Domestic's very difficult,' Rollo said apologetically. 'There are things we can do and things we can't. If he'd murdered you then it's a different ball game.'

'You've got to be dead then?' said Bramwell.

'Or injured,' amended Jonty. 'Injured's all right. But not just domestic.'

'If we acted on every domestic then we'd have no time for anything else,' said Rollo. 'For a start, half the time

338

we'd be breaking into other coppers' houses. They're the worst for domestic.'

'I'll say,' said Jonty. They had reached the deck. 'It's got ever so dark,' he said.

'It gets dark early now,' confirmed Rollo.

When Bramwell had gone Barbara picked up her drink and then pushed it aside and instead made herself a cup of coffee. She was contemplatively sipping it when she heard a sound at the cabin door. The coffee slid into the saucer and out onto her lap. She glanced at the splash but apprehensively returned her eyes to the door. 'Yes? Who's there?'

Georgina's voice came faintly. 'It's me. Georgina.'

Barbara had pushed the bolt home and now she went to the door and withdrew it before unlocking the Banham. 'Don't you believe me?' whispered Georgina through the widening crack.

'Sorry about that,' said Barbara opening the door. Georgina stepped in. She was carrying an overnight case. She looked around in an amused way and inquired: 'What are you up to? Have you got company?'

'Had,' corrected Barbara moodily. She carefully secured the door again. 'Bram was here, but he's gone now.' She looked in alarm at Georgina. 'Georgie, there was a man looking through the curtains.'

'What!' Georgina turned and looked towards each window.

'Not now. We've had the police, everything. It was Bram's brother-in-law. He's a Filipino.'

'Ah, that explains it,' said Georgina. Lightly she held the other girl's hand.

Barbara said: 'He scared the hell out of me.'

Georgina released her fingers and went towards the drinks cabinet. She glanced backwards at Barbara's swamped coffee cup and saucer. 'You look as if you need something more than that. I'm having a vodka.'

'I had one, but I left it,' admitted Barbara. 'I'll have one now you're here.'

When Georgina had poured the drinks they sat on the long settee below the window on the river side. 'Do you think he's got a frogman's outfit?' asked Georgina peering over her shoulder. She smiled: 'Poor you.'

'I know it's silly but it was a scene believe me. Bram was here but he's still got a broken leg.'

Georgina made a wry face. 'Still? He did that weeks ago.' They both realised that they had not seen each other often.

'It's a difficult broken leg. He's out of the main cast but he still has a secondary cast on it. He's more or less immobilised. . . . Well, as far as getting about is concerned. And, of course, when he realised who this peeping Tom was, he couldn't show himself because the game . . . our game that is . . . would be up.'

'So you called the police?'

'Next to useless. They said it came under the heading of "domestic". They have pigeonholes and they just slot them into whichever is the most convenient. For them, that is. One was called Jonty. It *could* have been nasty. This chap was a jungle tracker.'

Georgina leaned forward and embraced her fondly. Barbara wiped the final tears. 'It's all so stupid really, isn't it. Life never seems to be easy.'

'It isn't,' agreed the other woman carefully. 'Are you and Bram . . . is that looking serious . . . permanent?'

Barbara nodded but not certainly. 'It's going that way. He's been a so-and-so in the past. Women . . . he's had a weakness. He's known for it. But I think he's sort of retired. This leg's given him a lot to think about.'

Georgina grimaced: 'He can't chase anything for a start.'

'I know. But I'm in love.' She looked up with embarrassment. 'I didn't think it could happen, not with his type, and a steward as well.'

'You're lucky to have got a straight one.'

'There are a few. He's been making up for those who aren't. Anyway, for better or not, it's become serious. I think the to-do this evening might make something happen. He's gone home now but he doesn't know what he'll find there.'

'She's from the Philippines,' said Georgina. 'One of those off-the-shelf wives?'

Nodding a touch shamefacedly, Barbara said: 'He bought her in a weak moment.'

'And you're sure he's not playing you along? Until his leg gets better?'

Barbara shrugged. 'Who knows?' she sighed. 'No woman can be sure, can she? All I know is that it's all going to come to a head. Her relatives are over here. The police said they were plotting in a café near the airport.'

'Plotting in a café! That's dramatic.'

'I think it's become like that. Anyway, *something* is going to happen, perhaps it will be for the best. It will bring it all out in the open.' Georgina's expression became thoughtful. She rose and went towards the vodka. 'Have another?' she asked.

'I ought to keep a straight head in case of another crisis.'

'Better face it with vodka.'

'Oh, all right. Not too much though.' She watched the other woman pour the drinks admiring her slim form, her backside, her legs. 'All I've done is talk about my own troubles,' she apologised. 'What's been happening to you? We've hardly seen each other. Have you been on a lot of stopovers?'

Georgina's shoulders lifted in a sigh. She returned with the glasses. 'No,' she said decisively. She sat down next to Barbara again. 'No, I've quit.'

'Good God, when? I'd no idea. . . .'

Georgina smiled tightly. She had planned to lie her way through this. 'It's been some time,' she said vaguely. She revolved the drink in her glass. 'I'm a kept woman.'

'*You've met someone!*' Barbara's eyes lit. 'Ah, the Porsche. I knew it wasn't your father.'

'I haven't got one,' said Georgina looking down at her drink. 'I've got a Porsche but not a father.'

'Who? Who is he then?' Barbara was excited. 'Somebody famous?'

'Oh, no, he's a businessman. French. He wants me to go and live in Paris.'

'How wonderful!' Barbara blinked. 'Then you'll be leaving.'

'I'm afraid so.'

Barbara recovered. 'That's all right. French! Is he . . . young . . . ish? What's he look like, Georgie?'

'French . . . Lebanese actually.'

'Dark . . . then.'

'A bit. Very good looking though. And masses of money.'

'I can see that by the Porsche. Do you think it will be . . .'

'Permanent?' She shrugged. 'Who knows? He's nice to me. All I have to do is to sleep with him.'

'That's all most of us have to do.' Barbara looked reflective. 'When will you be going?'

To her surprise the other woman said: 'Tonight. Now. I just came back to tell you and to collect some of my things. Perhaps I could send for the others later if I can't get back myself. I'll give you a month's rent if that's all right.'

Her words slowed and it seemed they would be overcome by tears. Barbara regarded her mournfully. They held hands. 'Are you sure you'll be all right tonight?' said Georgina. 'I ought to go, but . . .'

Barbara gave a sniffle. 'Don't worry. I'll keep the door bolted. Anyway the jungle tracker must be gone now.' She became thoughtful. 'I hope Bram is going to be safe.'

'Men usually are,' said Georgina her lips hardening.

Barbara regarded her oddly. With an abrupt turn Georgina went towards her room. She refused Barbara's offer to make coffee and reappeared almost at once with a medium-sized suitcase. 'The rest is in the wardrobe, and the dressing table,' she said. 'You're sure that's all right?'

'No problem,' Barbara told her sadly. She brightened a little: 'Bram may be moving in. If things get too hot.'

Georgina was ready to go. She still wanted to say something. Instead she said: 'Now don't forget, keep the curtains drawn tight.'

'Oh, I will.' Barbara puffed her cheeks: 'You've no idea what it's like to realise that a strange man is staring at you . . . when you're naked in bed.'

Suddenly Georgina stopped and faced her. 'I think I do,' she said.

Barbara saw the other girl's face falter. She was wet eyed, her lips quivered guiltily. 'Oh, Barbara,' she sobbed. 'I'm on the game!'

Barbara stood, aghast and transfixed, her eyes widening. Then she cried out and threw her arms around Georgina. They hugged each other and their tears mingled on their cheeks. 'Oh God,' howled Barbara. 'Don't say that . . .'

'I've said it,' stammered Georgina. 'I am. Honestly.'

Barbara searched her face. 'What's it like?' she asked, breathless.

Georgina took her hands and they returned to the settee below the window. 'Well, it's . . . it's like you'd think it would be. You meet interesting and . . . varied people . . . and . . .'

'Like being a stewardess.'

'To a point.' She sniffed her tears back and they dabbed their own cheeks and each other's with handkerchiefs. 'But the money's better.'

'Homelea',
Anglia Road,
Hounslow,
Middlesex,
England,
Great Britain

29th November

My Dear Father and My Dear Mother,

Your news was interesting although I cannot remember most of the people you tell me about. I am glad Asif at the Pavilion café could help you. Tell him Croydon is still there. Ask him if he knows what 'bottle' is for they say here that a person has lost his bottle. Answer – next time.

My great news is that I have a new, better job at London Airport (Heathrow) with much more space to work. Now I am responsible for a big part of Terminal Two, which the porters call Terminator Two because of a film which is showing. Every hour I must make a sweep of the area, checking on bins and under seats which is all part of the security. So that I do not look suspicious as I carry on these investigations, I carry a broom and a long-handled dustpan.

It is very cold here now. Brass monkey weather, and I have had my first flu – sneezing, quaking, throwing about in my bed. The Brits get it all the time. But I stayed in bed and sweated it out. These things you have to do.

Uncle Sammi is teaching me to drive a car. Everybody has cars here like they have bikes there in India. He has begun the minicab business which is another feather in his cap. My colleagues the porters say a minicab can go without brakes! I will help him with this business. Asif will tell you about minicabs.

Your loving son,

Barry (or Nazar)

Fourteen

When her mother, her brother and their Pauline had gone to the airport, taking her luggage with them, Lettie wandered around the compact house, surveying for the last time what had once been her future. She had always loved Christmas and it was drawing near. She would not be spending it in this house. Her slender, crimson-tipped fingers kept touching things; she unnecessarily dusted ornaments with her handkerchief, and tried not to cry. It was difficult, for to be bought and brought as a bride to England had been a wonderful thing and, contrary to most people's expectations, it was possible to love someone who had purchased you, and she had loved Bramwell, and not only for what he had done for her. If husbands had been for sale in the same manner as wives, he would have been the sort she would have bought for herself.

To come to a far country had been hard; the winds blew cold and most people regarded her just as coldly. But it was something she had been expecting (women who had been purchased as wives but had returned to the Philippines had told her). Another country she could cope with, but another woman in another country was different. She knew she was defeated. There was, nonetheless, a healthy instinct for revenge in her. Her brother, who was familiar with arson, had come up with the plan. Lettie, drinking her way through her final bottle of Ribena, had listened to him intently and then agreed.

There was a flight to the Far East that evening but the timing had to be precise. Her family was despatched in

345

good time by minicab and another minicab was ordered for an hour after they had left Bedmansworth. She spent much of the hour regretting and walking slowly and gracefully around the house of which she had been so proud, her Ribena glass tipped slightly tipsily in her slim hand. She put on her favourite compact disc and swayed to the softly spreading music. But, romantic as she felt, she kept one eye on her tiny gold wristwatch, a present from one of Bramwell's foreign journeys in the days when they believed he loved her.

On the hour the minicab drew up outside the house. She waved to the driver and he acknowledged the wave; then she finished her drink and placed the glass in the dishwater. Her eyes moist but with determined step now, she went to the rear of the house and down a flight of steps into what the builders of the houses of Bedwell Park Mansions had called a wine cellar. It was scarcely bigger than a cupboard and had never been used for wine. Sitting among the lumber there now was an oil stove with which, in the cold of winter, she had reinforced the warm-air heating.

She was familiar with its workings since she had often used it to prepare the house for Bramwell's late return from a flight. Now she checked the paraffin, the wick, and the tin chimney before taking a box of matches from the shelf above and lighting the stove. The wick glowed and enlarged suddenly, as though glad to be of use. She watched it fondly spreading its friendly light around the confined space. Then she turned the flame up fractionally, retreated towards the door, and leaning back extended her shapely foot to push the oil stove onto its back. Swiftly she went out of the door and shut it. She waited but then saw fingers of smoke sifting out. She turned, went in through the back door of the house, through the kitchen where she had spent so much time making exotic food, and to the small front hall. Her face was now expressionless, her eyes dry. Briskly she opened the door, and putting her handbag below her arm, stepped out into the dull November evening. The minicab was waiting. Her neighbour Mrs Hilditch was standing observing her from the window, clearly outlined. As she got into the car Lettie waved to the woman who had scarcely ever spoken to her.

The neighbour waved a surprised half-hand. Lettie told the driver to take her to Heathrow. She allowed herself one final look back at the life she was leaving before the car headed down the hill on the first few yards of her journey to Manila.

The first fire engine passed Bramwell's minicab as it was turning onto the Bedmansworth Road. There was little traffic but the driver pulled the car well to the left to allow the blaring, light-flashing truck ample room to pass.

'He's in a hurry,' he said over his shoulder.

'Cat caught up a tree, I expect,' muttered Bramwell.

'I expect,' echoed the driver. 'They just do it for a bit of excitement. Funny thing, excitement. I could do with a bit myself.'

As they turned towards the village and then took the road to Bedwell Park Mansions they saw the glow bruising the sky. 'It's a real fire, all right,' enthused the driver. 'A real good one too by the look of it.'

A heavy feeling invaded Bramwell's stomach. He tried to pinpoint the glow above the housetops. A second fire engine passed them. The cab driver repeated: 'Looks like a big one. It's on the top of the hill there.'

'I live up there,' moaned Bramwell. 'It looks like it might be my house.'

'Oh no!' exclaimed the driver. 'I'll get a move on.'

From the bottom of the hill Bramwell knew it was true. They had to stop halfway up because a police car was across the road and an officer waved them down. 'Can't come through. Due to a conflagration.'

Bramwell opened his mouth soundlessly. His jaw felt like a heavy sack. 'It's . . . it's my house,' he managed to tell the policeman. 'My wife . . .'

'Nobody in there,' the policeman assured him. 'Empty. Neighbours saw a lady go out.'

The cab driver was fussily helping Bramwell from the vehicle. 'And you with a leg and all,' he said sympathetically. 'Never rains but it pours, does it.'

Bramwell stared at him uncomprehendingly. He began to move on his crutch around the end of the police car.

'Sorry, sir,' the cab driver reminded. 'Six pounds twenty-five.'

Bramwell turned blank faced again. 'How much?' he asked. He turned to the policeman. 'Will you settle it?' he pleaded. 'I'll pay you back.'

'If I've got enough on me,' agreed the policeman. He produced a wallet and fumbled in it. 'Had to pay for the milk and the papers this afternoon.' His face brightened in the red glow of the blaze. 'It's all right. I've got it. Just. Seven pounds.' He glanced at Bramwell. 'You'll be wanting to give him a tip, won't you.'

'Anything,' said Bramwell. He returned his stunned expression to the house. The fire was past its peak but the windows belched smoke mixed with an orange glow. The roof had fallen in and the smoke rose like black hair above the walls. The firemen were pouring water from their hoses through the windows; none had attempted to advance towards the heat. There was no wind and the neighbours' houses stood untouched. He hobbled forwards.

'There he is!' exclaimed a female voice. Mrs Hilditch advanced, her finger pointing, her face puce in the fire. 'It's him. Mr Broad.'

A police sergeant and a fire officer came towards him. 'Are you the occupier?' asked the sergeant.

'I was,' mumbled Bramwell. 'I gather my wife was not at home.'

'No sir. Your neighbour saw her go out.'

'By minicab,' put in Mrs Hilditch. She glanced at the authorities. 'Not long before we saw the flames.'

348

Bramwell looked about him and made himself calm. 'I didn't know we had so many neighbours,' he mentioned looking at the crowd on the other side of the road, in the gardens and in the windows of their houses. A clutch of excited children were clapping hands.

'It's well under control now,' said the fire officer as he summed up the house. 'You won't have a lot left there,' he said. 'Just as well the next doors are a decent distance, well detached.'

'My potting shed's gone,' said a complaining voice from the crowd. 'The sparks started that.'

'Fuck him and his potting shed,' muttered Bramwell.

'Where do you think your wife is, sir?' said the sergeant.

'Gone,' said Bramwell more slowly. He looked up quickly. 'Gone to London. To . . . see a friend.'

'Well, you're in a bit of a state, sir,' continued the officer sympathetically. The fire chief went away as though this was none of his business. 'Broken leg is it?'

'Was. It's getting better now. But . . . look at my house.'

'Did you have a lot of valuables? Apart from the missus, I mean.'

'Oh, only the odd Rubens, a couple of Gaugins,' Bramwell remarked bitterly.

'There's always the insurance.'

'Yes, there's always that.'

'Would you like to go off by ambulance, sir? You look a bit shocked and there's that leg. The ambulance boys haven't got anybody else to take. They'd be pleased.'

'No, thanks. I don't need to go to hospital.'

'But you've got somewhere to go tonight? A friend or something?'

'Yes,' sighed Bramwell. 'I've got somewhere to go.'

Low, slow cloud hung over the flat country, grey, almost resting on churches and tree tops. Airliners leaving Heathrow vanished into it almost as soon as they had left the ground;

those arriving talked anxiously to Air Traffic Control and then came tentatively in, their trust in instruments and computers.

But there was little wind and it was mild for the time of the year. Sergeant Morris, his greatcoat collar extended, peered from the hole in his balaclava like a sniper hiding in a hollow tree. It was not a day you could see far, at least he could not, and he did not observe Anthony Burridge approaching until he was two hundred yards away.

'Can't spot you this weather,' said the old sergeant. 'No sun to shine on your bowler.'

'Haven't seen you for a long time,' returned Anthony. 'Are you all right?'

'Not bad. In December she stops letting us out, not till the outside is aired, I suppose. A lot of them have coughs and not many of them want to risk it. How's living in that bivouac?'

Anthony laughed. 'Oh, we had to give up. It got too cold and my wife's expecting a baby.'

'Is she now. Never had any myself. Not officially that is. Although there could be one or two around I s'pose.'

Anthony was unworried about not being on time now. He sat on the seat beside the old man. 'No, we've got a little flat in the village. Not much but we'll be moving out soon, anyway.' He smiled expansively at the elderly sitter. 'I'm going to be a publican.'

'That was always my ambition,' said Sergeant Morris quietly. 'One of them.'

'Mrs Mangold, the old lady at the Straw Man, is retiring and I'm taking over as manager in the New Year. I have to go on a training course.'

'Basic training, eh. Well, that's good. Time spent in training is never wasted. If I can get down there, if somebody gives me a lift, I'll come and have a free pint.'

Anthony patted his overcoated shoulder. 'We had to get

out of that tent,' he said. 'The weather got bad and one night the bloody horse came in.'

'Which horse was that?'

'Remember that old scruffy horse up there? We called it Freebie. It was raining and windy and it pushed its way in about three in the morning. Brought the whole tent down.'

'That must have been a sight,' said Sergeant Morris with a rare wrinkled grin. 'I'd like to have seen that.'

'It seems funny now but it wasn't then. The wife went mad. The bed collapsed and the horse panicked. That was the end.'

Sergeant Morris sniffed. Another airliner disappeared into the clouds. 'Women are so unreasonable,' he said. He nodded over his shoulder. 'I've been in terrible strife here. They nearly threw me out.'

'Why was that?'

'Said I'd upset three of the old girls. Said I'd proposed to them, like to marry them, and the silly old cows believed me. I was only making conversation. Trouble was two of them was sisters, never married either and you can see why, and they fell out because they each one reckoned I was going to marry her. Ended up throwing jam tarts at each other.' He leaned forward confidingly. 'It's not as though I can *do* anything,' he whispered. 'I had my last you-know-what when Harold Wilson was in. All that I did was hold hands. And the third old woman, she made her own veil for the bleeding wedding. I said she should save it for her funeral. It'll be sooner.'

'Are you all right now?' asked Anthony. 'I mean they're not throwing you out.'

'Oh, no they won't do that. Not with Christmas coming on. I'm the only one who can climb the steps to put the lights on the tree.'

Anthony rose. 'I'd better go. I've only got till Christmas in the City, then I'm behind the bar. I'll look out for you.'

'See you in the spring,' said Sergeant Morris. 'I like the bloody spring. It means I've made it through another year.'

Mrs Durie had already been in with the tea when Rona knocked quietly. Outside it was raining, patterning the windows, but Pearl's room was warm; over the months it had become homely with oddments that she had bought, prints of Middlesex, an old stoneware jug, a carriage clock, winter flowers in a brass jardinière, and a pair of cushions, petit-pointed with royal heads of George the Fifth and Queen Mary, especially for the Silver Jubilee and a gift from Mrs Durie.

When Rona entered Pearl was sitting on her quilted bed, drinking her tea sedately. Her daughter smiled her pleasure. 'You always look so comfortable,' she said.

'I feel just like I was born here,' said Pearl firmly. 'In this room, in this bed.' Rona sat at the bedside. Pearl's eyes moved sideways, her cup held, half tipped. 'But you've come to say that we've got to go home.'

Fondly Rona touched her forearm, just below the lace sleeve of her nightdress. 'I have,' she sighed patiently. 'We really have to, Mother.'

Pearl nodded. 'I guess you're right, Rona. I've done what I came to do here. Not that it's made any difference.' She looked shrewdly at the younger woman. 'And you think it's time you went too. Is that right?'

'Right,' said Rona looking directly at her. 'It's time.'

'They *do* have divorces in England,' said the old lady bluntly.

Rona told her: 'It won't happen. It's just one of those things in life that comes too late.'

'Nothing comes too late.'

'I don't think that's true. You know it.'

The old lady looked thoughtful. 'I guess I do.'

'So we really should be going back to the States.'

'Would after Christmas be okay? In three or four weeks?'

Rona smiled broadly. 'Christmas in Bedmansworth should be fun.'

'A whole lot better than in Los Angeles. I know more people here.'

Rona kissed her on the side of her head. Her hair was grey and soft. 'We'll go back in January,' she said. 'We'll fix a day. It's been wonderful but . . .'

'It's been wonderful,' said her mother with finality. 'Maybe on Christmas Eve I'll take a trip to Laleham Church.'

'If you think that's the right thing to do.' Rona looked doubtful.

'I must think about it. I'd need to sneak in at a different time to Edward's wife. She'd wonder what the heck I was doing there.'

Rona straightened from the bed. 'You know what's going on tonight,' said Pearl.

'The darts championship presentations,' smiled Rona. 'I know.'

'Sure is. The Swan, Bedmansworth, champions of the Heathrow League, Second Division. What a night this is going to be!'

She looked suddenly and seriously at her daughter, the lines on her face in the lace patterns. 'I've just loved being in this place,' she said quietly. 'I'm going to miss it.'

Rona said: 'So am I.'

Pearl had her hair coiffeured at Elaine of Hounslow and Rome and wore a trailing silver gown for the evening. The Bedmansworth Band played 'Yankee Doodle Dandy' and everyone joined in to sing to it. 'Learned that specially, they did,' said Dobbie Dobson proudly to Rona over the clapping. 'It takes somebody special to get this lot to get something right,' he said surveying his nondescript musicians sweating and smiling with the achievement. The girl with

353

the violin was regarding it with awe as if it had produced unheard-of magic.

Two hundred and three were there. Long white-clothed tables had been set down the room. There was prawn cocktail, beef and vegetables and fruit salad or cheese, wine and a lot of beer.

Rona still could scarcely understand how her West Coast mother had become so involved, so swallowed, by this nondescript and, in itself, displaced English community, a village which scarcely knew where it belonged. Her stride along the street, her bonnets, her voice, her kindness and funniness, and her forthright ways had been seen, heard, and admired in Bedmansworth; her fame had reached even Stanwell, Bedfont and Cranbrook.

'She's brought a new sort of life,' Dobbie confided to Rona. 'Made us realise that there's more in the world than Bedmansworth.' His tuba was leaning against his leg like a dog and he patted it. 'Still don't understand, mind, why she wanted to read the lesson at the harvest service. I'd practised and had my suit cleaned and was all ready, but she wasn't going to be stopped. Never mind. I'll read it at Christmas. She will have her way, won't she . . . ?'

Rona smiled and nodded. 'She certainly will. It was only her determination that brought us to Bedmansworth at the start. She wasn't going to be denied.'

'Why did you come?' inquired Dobbie as if he had been waiting long to ask. 'There's a sort of rumour that you had ancestors in the village.'

'Something like that,' said Rona. 'My mother wanted to research the church records. She found what she wanted to find.'

Dobbie would have liked to inquire further but he did not. Instead they watched Pearl as she was led up onto the rostrum. Rona put her fingers to her chin. Even the darts players from outlying suburbs and villages knew Pearl. So did the airport teams. She had become the mascot of the

Swan, Bedmansworth, and this was her, and their, great night.

The presentations were made on the stage by the overseer of the Heathrow sewage farm and Miss Aviation Maintenance 1992. The sewage farm was famous because it had been accused of stopping airport development and emitting smells, unmovable and unsociable. 'We don't mind what they say,' asserted the overseer in presenting the trophies. 'They might say we're blocking the way for their new terminal and what not, but where would they be without us?'

Ribald suggestions flew from the room, wives put restraining hands on the more outrageous husbands. Jim Turner from the Swan, blushing in the lights, went up to receive the cup, and made a little awkward speech. Then he introduced Pearl, and the band, scattered to various parts of the room by now, managed to get together for 'Yankee Doodle Dandy' again and everybody sang.

'Mrs Collingwood, Pearl as we call her, has become very dear to us,' said Jim into the stage microphone. 'She's our mascot and she can throw a nifty dart too. I wonder if we can ask her for a demonstration.'

Loud cheering was stemmed by Pearl saying into the microphone: 'Just try and stop me, Jim Turner!' Laughter rolled over the room. Rona sat shaking her head, wondering again at this woman who was her mother.Within herself she was deeply sad because although they were leaving, they had to leave, there was much they would leave behind. She tried not to think of Edward Richardson. One day and night by the winter sea was all that they had known together. For a few hours she had loved him and that was that. It was almost as if it had been her due.

Jim Turner handed Pearl a glistening dart. The girl drummer wtih the Bedmansworth Band even managed to summon a drum roll. 'Okay,' said Pearl. 'Show me the board.'

Jim manoeuvred her to face the dart board illuminated

355

on the wall. Rona watched with anxiety. 'Dart one!' Jim called. Mrs Collingwood hitched up her long, glittering skirt, and threw the dart. It missed the board altogether and struck the wooden wall.

'Who moved the board?' Pearl demanded, while they all applauded.

'Dart two!' exclaimed Jim. He handed it to her. She threw again. This time the aim was even wider. It bounded against the wall and plummeted to lodge in the floor. 'Nervousness!' exclaimed Pearl.

Everyone roared again but Rona could see she *was* nervous. The hand holding her skirt shook so that the material shimmered.

'Dart three!'

Pearl took a pace back. 'I can see better from here,' she called and again the audience responded, urging her on, but falling to silence as she poised with the dart. She drew back her arm and threw.

'Double top!' exclaimed Jim. A great roar went up through the room. Everyone laughed and applauded. It was as it should have been. Pearl turned, her face flushed with triumph and excitement. Jim helped her from the platform and, amid the faces and clapping, Rona went to meet her and kissed her.

Her mother's face was glistening with happiness. Her eyes were wet. 'What a wonderful, wonderful day,' she almost whispered. 'I swear it's the best day of my life.'

When they left it had begun to rain thickly. 'Don't you ever have snow in this country?' asked Pearl as Jim helped her into the mincab.

'Come back in April,' joked Jim. Pearl insisted on sitting in the front next to the Indian driver. 'And where in this world are you from?' she asked him affably.

'Hounslow,' he smiled.

Rona got into the back of the car. Dilys got in beside

her. It creaked as they sat down. Jim shut the door and walked back to the small bus that had brought the rest of the Bedmansworth villagers. The two vehicles set off through the heavy rain.

'Now,' announced Pearl from the front seat, 'we can go back to the States knowing that the Swan, Bedmansworth, are the champions at darts.'

'We all hope you'll be coming back,' said Dilys. 'We'll miss you.'

'Oh, we will,' asserted Pearl. 'Nothing's going to keep us away.'

'Nothing will,' smiled Rona in the dark.

They were tired and happy and eventually silent. The cab went across the main roads and into the winding lanes, black and rushing with rain, then entering the village. 'We're here. We're home,' said Pearl.

And at that moment Bernard Threadle rounded the wet corner on his small motor cycle.

'Homelea',
Anglia Road,
Hounslow,
Middlesex,
England,
Great Britain

15th December

My Dear Father and My Dear Mother,
This time my letter to you brings news of sorrow because Uncle Sammi is unexpectedly dead. It was an accident when he was driving his minicab late at night and the road was wet and a motor bike came around a corner. Uncle Sammi's minicab skidded and unfortunately hit a tree. An old American lady, who was sitting with him in the front, was also killed in this sad accident, although two other lady passengers were OK.

357

We were very proud at the funeral of Uncle Sammi because it was one of the finest seen in Hounslow or even Southall for more than one year. With Marika he was building up his business here over many years and he was well known among the Indian people. It was difficult to say how many there were to mourn him but afterwards we considered it must have been more than three hundred.

I have left my career at London Airport to take over the shop with Marika although we are no longer to have the minicab business and the social club register is also no longer because the lady who operated it has gone.

Now I have a camera and I have taken some photographs of Uncle Sammi's funeral. I will send some to you when they come back from the chemist.

Your loving son,

Barry (Nazar)

The single bell of Bedmansworth church rang out, neutral and inevitable. It was tolled by Mr Henry Broughton-Smith, wearing his brown tweed suit and his Military Cross. His hands were as solemn as his face. When it was all over Rona thanked him and he merely said: 'It's my sad duty, madam.'

Although it was only a week to Christmas, it was a day of summer-like sun, bright and widespread, with birds in the churchyard, the air mild. Bare trees spread their branches like cracks across the surface of the blue sky.

The grave, vivid with flowers, was against the old wall. Rona, her face white in the bright daylight, framed by the rim of her black hat and the black collar of her coat, stood just outside the lych-gate with the vicar and shook hands with the villagers. They seemed reluctant to leave, standing inside and outside the churchyard, conversing of other things as people do when released from a funeral; the lovely day, the plans for Christmas, the local gossip.

'I felt she was with us,' said Rona to Henry Prentice. 'Perhaps looking in at the window. Smiling that smile of hers.'

He smiled. 'Yes, I felt that too.'

'So many people,' said Rona. The crowd still occupied the whole of the churchyard path, standing, waiting on the grass to speak a few words to her. She could see Edward and Adele standing near the church door, moving with the people slowly towards her. Her heart was full.

The villagers came to shake her hand, some saying a few difficult words, some speaking of the flowers. Rooks began to caw to each other from the trees where they sat clearly outlined, looking down at the walking people.

Sergeant Morris, Mrs Bollom and three slow ladies from St Sepulchre's shuffled along the path, looking determinedly ahead, with not a glance at the tombstones. Sergeant Morris blew his nose in a big blue handkerchief, so loudly it scattered the rooks. Mrs Bollom looked at him reprovingly. 'Oh dearie me,' she said.

'I saw your grandson crying,' said the vicar to Mrs Durie. 'Tears streaming down his cheeks.'

'Randy, yes. He had to go home,' she said. Her eyes were red rimmed. 'I cut his pigtail off.'

She looked at Rona as though apologising. 'I couldn't stand it any longer, Mrs Train,' she said simply. 'Thinking of your mother and everything, and seeing him sitting in front of me. I've always got my scissors in my handbag so I took them out and snipped it off. That's why he was crying. That's why he's gone home.' Rona and the priest regarded her with plain astonishment. As if she thought they did not believe her she opened her handbag and produced the braided pigtail. 'There it is,' she said.

Others came, Jim and Dilys, Anthony Burridge and the hugely pregnant Annabelle. Rona had to stretch to embrace

359

her. Mrs Mangold haltingly said it had been lovely, and so did many others whom Rona scarcely recognised but whom her mother had known. Dobbie Dobson had read the verses from the Book of Ruth, repeating the words that Pearl had spoken in the church only weeks before. Rona thanked him for this and he stood searching for words of his own. Eventually he said: 'I'm very sorry. She was a nice lady.' Turning to the vicar with a sort of embarrassment, he asked: 'I can still read the lesson at Christmas, can't I, Mr Prentice?'

All the time Rona could see Edward and Adele Richardson coming step by slow step down the path from the church door. They reached her eventually and she turned and looked at them, two people with whom she knew she had kinship, the man she loved but from whom she was parting, the woman who, almost, might have been her sister.

As Edward and Adele came through the gate Henry Prentice was taken aside by a big woman who, Edward realised with surprise, was Mrs Kitchen. He and Adele and Rona stood together, the hands of all three intertwined. At first they found it difficult to say anything. 'Your mother made a lot of people in Bedmansworth realise the possibilities of life,' said Adele sincerely. 'I'm sure it's almost as sad for them as it is for you.' She leaned and kissed Rona on her white cheek.

Edward said: 'That's true. She was quite unique.' Still holding her hand and feeling its warmth and need in his, he asked: 'How long before you will be leaving?' Their faces were only inches apart, her eyes and her mouth before him and his before her. Adele watched them.

'I've decided to go very soon,' said Rona. 'The day after tomorrow, Thursday. I am on your company's flight to Los Angeles in the afternoon.'

'I'll make sure everything is done to make you comfortable,' he said. 'Any problems, please call me. I'm at Heathrow that day, unless something untoward happens, so I'll come and see you off.'

360

'Thank you, Edward,' she said. 'I'd appreciate that. And thank you both for coming today and for your flowers.'

Edward and Adele walked from the church. The large form of Mrs Kitchen was heading towards Bedwell Park Mansions.

Eventually the vicar and Rona were left alone. For the most part the people had gone over to the Swan. As though it were a reminder that it was a December day a sharp touch of breeze came through the lych-gate. The priest's vestments ruffled. He turned and held Rona's hands. 'I haven't said my piece,' he told her. 'And, in truth, I hardly know what to say.'

'You said it in the service,' said Rona quietly.

'I don't think I have ever felt so sad at a funeral,' he said surprisingly. 'It's part of a vicar's life, funerals, and if we believe what we try to teach others then the parting from loved ones is only temporary. But I was . . . so sorry. I was only glad in that I had known her.'

He took her arm and they walked across the silent and sunny village street towards the Swan. 'Your mother arrived in this village as a stranger,' he said. 'But it was almost as if she was meant to come here. Everybody . . . so *enjoyed* her. I know I did.' He looked soulful as they paused outside the bar. It was dim and full of people's voices. 'Who will I smoke with now?'

The house seemed emptier than ever when Edward returned on the evening of the following day; void and chill. The thorny rose climber was knocking metallically against the window. There were Christmas cards distributed through the house on shelves and bookcases, their colours and jollity mocking the sombreness of the rooms and his feelings. Even turning on the lights and lamps did not lend it much comfort. Edward lit the fire in the sitting-room and, after pouring himself a whisky, sat down moodily watching the flames spluttering from the dusty logs. It had been a long time

361

since it was last lit. There had been a sheaf of letters on his desk, left there by Adele. He had no idea where she might be. He shuffled them like a dubious hand of cards. Two had handwritten addresses. He opened the first:

Not In Air

> Halifax Villa
> Bedwell Park Mansions
>
> 18th December

Dear Edward Richardson,

I had hoped to speak to you at Mrs Collingwood's funeral – what a sad occurrence – but there was no opportunity. I did not know her but I felt it my duty, my last duty, to attend on behalf of the Residents' Association.

You will ascertain from the foregoing that we are leaving. You have won your battle. It often seems to me that the people who struggle least are often the winners. There is apparently some deficiency in the 1937 covenant which, according to the Residents' Association's legal advice, would make it doubtful in a court of law. I would have liked to fight but other circumstances have dictated that this will not be possible. We are quitting Bedwell Mansions forthwith, the Halifax Building Society having taken out a repossession order against us. There appears to be no room in this district for people who are prepared to act for their conscience. Perhaps I should point out that the reason that Bedmansworth village is preserved as it is today is because people, and perhaps you were one – when it suited them – fought the authorities. Otherwise it would now be part of Heathrow Airport. We would have liked to stay and support the campaign to prevent the monstrous plan for the new terminal on the site of the sewage farm but this cannot be. My husband has been made redundant and we are going to try our luck at Kilmarnock.

On a more personal note, may I just say that I like you. You are a gentleman which is more than can be said for so many round here who only think they are.

> *Yours sincerely,*
> *Kathleen Kitchen (Mrs)*

Richardson shook his head wryly. It did not seem to matter now. He opened the second handwritten envelope and saw, with surprise, that it was from Toby. He had forgotten his son's handwriting. It was addressed from Old's Antiques, Windsor:

18th December

Dear Dad,

I will be over to see you at the weekend (if you're in) and I have to collect some of my stuff. I will ring beforehand. I think Mum will have already explained that Mr Old has let me take over the flat above the shop. As I told you before, it is not really a flat, just one room and a shower room, but it's great. He is only charging me twenty pounds a week because he does not want to come into the shop so early from now on. He wants me to open up in the mornings and to run things a bit more. I hope this is all right with you. I know it's earlier than I said.

See you when I see you.

Love,

Toby

He read the letter twice. His sadness lay on him deeply. They had lost a son – it was *their* fault. It was *his* fault. He finished his scotch with one gulp and walked through the house, along the corridor, past the dim portraits of Adele's parents, touching familiar pieces of furniture. He looked up the shadowed staircase towards his study and the closed door to his observatory. Slowly he went up there, step by single step. There was the familiar desk and the deep chair. His books, the fine astrolabe and there, along the wall, were the old celestial charts with their rich colours and their fabled animals. He switched on the desk lamp and its light warmed the room. Then he took the further short staircase to the observatory and opened the door, with care, as if conscious that he would not do it often after this. The pale glow of the sky was like an open umbrella above him and he lifted his face and gazed up at it. Good old sky. It was a cloudy night but with lakes of clarity through which he could see the stars. They, at least, remained the same. Blinking.

He switched on the diffuse light and climbing the metal seat, began to work the eye of the telescope across the sky. Winter was the best time to view the stars. Polaris, the polar star, Ursa Minor which had joined Ursa Major, and Orion were all on display, shining and unconcerned. The Milky Way beamed through Cassiopeia. He settled back into the seat and touched the button for the music stereo.

Adele's voice filled the domed room. Startled, he sat upright and looked about him. 'Sorry to have to replace Holst or whoever tonight,' she recited steadily from the tape. 'But I thought this was the only way of being sure I would catch you and have your attention.' His hands drifted wearily to his face.

'Edward, I think that we both have realised for some time that our marriage is a failure and now I think it is time to bring it to an end. I have gone away for a while. I am with a man whom I have known for several years. I think you will guess who it is – because you have been so derogatory about him – Peter Rose. He is not now the successful person he once was. His business has gone the way of many others during the recession, in fact he is facing bankruptcy. His marriage is over and his health is also broken. I am with him because I believe that I can help him to regain at least something of what he had, what he was. He was a winner once and I know he can do it again. This time *I* want to be with him. As for you, I don't think you need me any more than I need you. So let's make the break as decent as we can, a compliment to the memory of the good times we had once. Toby has written to you to tell you that he is going to live over Mr Old's shop and I am happy about that and I hope you will be. I will expect you

364

to vacate the house within a reasonable time since I want to go on living there as my family have done for so long. I am sure you will be able to make other domestic arrangements, wherever they may be, here or abroad. Now, I will leave you to get on with looking at your stars. Goodbye, Edward.'

Rona had packed her belongings and her case was lying open on the bed when Mrs Durie knocked and came into the room. She regarded it with damp eyes. 'We'll miss you,' she sniffed. 'It's all been a bit too much.'

Rona comforted her and smiled. 'I'll certainly miss everybody here,' she said. She could see that the Englishwoman wanted to say something. After picking up the morning tea tray and putting it down again, Mrs Durie said: 'I'll look after the grave for you.'

'Thank you,' replied Rona. 'I was hoping you would.'

'I'm glad you left her here.'

'This is, I think, where she would want to be.'

Mrs Durie sat on the side of the bed. 'Isn't it funny how things work out,' she said. 'A few months ago we didn't know you and you'd never heard of us. And all the things that have happened since.'

'They certainly have. My mother did what she wanted to do by coming here.'

The Englishwoman looked up with her reddened eyes. 'It was something to do with her husband, wasn't it? Your father.'

'It was.' Rona folded the top of the case down.

'What time is your plane?'

'Oh, I've got plenty of time. I'm just going over to the churchyard.'

'Yes, you'd want to. I'll keep an eye on everything there for you. When the spring comes I'll take some pictures, I've got a camera, and I'll send them to you.'

'I intend to come back,' Rona told her. 'Some time.

Perhaps in the summer. I may even get around to see all the tourist sights next time.' She smiled reassuringly at Mrs Durie. 'No royal dates today?'

'Not much. Duke of Kent, the one who was killed in the war. His birthday's tomorrow, December twentieth. Born nineteen hundred and two.'

'You really should go on a television game show.'

'Oh, I don't know. I'm losing interest in it a bit. All these royal divorces and separations. Makes you think they're just like everybody else. And I've been thinking a lot, like you do when things happen like they've happened, that I ought to do something a bit more. I might get myself a bike. There's a new cycling club started. I might meet a nice man and get married again. It's been ten years. You've got to look forward in this life, not back.'

They went together down the curling stairs. Rona left her case in her room. Her mother's was packed and in the room that Pearl had occupied so happily. 'I won't be a couple of minutes,' she said to Mrs Durie. Dilys Turner, her face ashen with deep black rings dark as bruises around her eyes came into the bar and said: 'We'll be so sorry to see you go, Mrs Train. Jim will be back in time to see you off. He had to go to Slough.'

Rona kissed her gently on the cheek. She said: 'But I'll be coming back. I'll come and see you.'

She walked out into the bright sky of the forenoon. The air was sharp and the sun lemon coloured. It filtered through the stripped branches of the trees along the church-yard wall. The vicar was sweeping up in the porch. He laid his broom down and came towards her, his hands stretched out. 'You're on your way then,' he said.

'In a few hours,' said Rona. 'I just thought I would come over . . .'

'Yes, of course. I'll be here sweeping up for a while. I have to change the notices too. And the numbers of the hymns for Sunday.'

'Do you always choose them?'

'Naturally, that's one of the perks. That's why we have the same hymns so often. The organist complains because he thinks people believe he can't play anything else.'

She went under the dark yews along the old stones of the church path. Vivid flowers, wet with dew, shone on her mother's grave, a patch of brilliance in the dull grass. Rona stood there and closed her eyes, keeping her tears in check. Then she walked a few steps along the ancient wall to the white stone of Elizabeth Hickman with its two lines from Matthew Arnold. She read them aloud to herself:

> 'And we forget because we must,
> And not because we will.'

How strange that two women, divided by an ocean, united by one man, should now be lying there almost side by side. She shook her head and walked back towards the porch. Henry Prentice was pinning a notice on the board. 'We're giving it another try,' he announced standing back and regarding the pamphlet.

'Footballs for Africa,' read Rona aloud.

They walked together down to the lych-gate, now in silence. Then Henry Prentice said: 'Your mother certainly made her mark on this place. She was unique, quite wonderful.' He regarded her carefully. 'Wasn't it strange that she wanted so much to read the lesson that Sunday, at the harvest festival?'

'It was,' agreed Rona. Some geese flew over from the reservoirs, their wings sounding like drums. 'But not out of character with her.'

'She changed the verses around you know.'

'Oh? I didn't know that.'

'She read Ruth, chapter two, verse seven first – about Ruth gleaning in the fields, and then she skipped back to chapter one, verse sixteen. The lines go: ". . . where thou lodgest, I will lodge: thy people *shall* be my people." And then "Where thou diest, will I die, and there will I be buried." '

'How very strange,' said Rona slowly. 'As though it were a message.'

'Perhaps it was,' said Henry Prentice. 'I thought I was mistaken so I checked when everyone had gone.'

'And it was read by Dobbie Dobson at the funeral,' said Rona. 'I'm glad of that.'

'So am I. I don't remember a day like that. Not in this village.' Then he said: 'I hope you will come back to Bedmansworth.'

'I intend to,' promised Rona. 'I want to make arrangements for a stone on my mother's grave. And I feel I have so many friends.'

'You most certainly do.' They shook hands fondly. 'Well, if you need any assistance with the stone let me know. It's strange that she rests just below the wall your father may well have helped to rebuild in the war.'

'That's true. There are . . . so many connections.'

They said goodbye again and he watched her walk slowly along the street in the chill sunshine. She turned and waved and then he went back into the church.

Rona went into the Swan. The taxi was due. Her case and her mother's case were in the bar. Jim came through, shook hands with her and then, suddenly, embraced her, too full to bring out any words. Randy appeared, his hair projecting in short spikes, and shyly picked up the suitcases.

'You've got a new hairstyle, Randy,' said Rona.

'Punk,' said Randy, looking gratified she had noticed.

The car for the airport arrived. The boy insisted on putting the cases in the boot. As he did so Bernard Threadle came by on a pedal cycle wearing a black crash helmet. He waved awkwardly.

'He's got to face the inquest yet,' said Dilys.

'He wrote me a letter,' Rona told her. 'But he wasn't to

368

blame. I also wrote to the family of the driver. I thought it might be difficult for them to write to me. It was just an accident. They happen.'

She shook hands and embraced them again before getting into the car. They stood and waved quietly as she went away. Sad-eyed she watched the village go by. The Latimer twins were kicking a football, Major Broughton-Smith was walking staunchly along the street, eyes fixed, stick striking the pavement. Almost before she realised it Rona was staring at the broad oak, stripped of its bark down one side, the place where her mother had died. She turned her head away and the car continued to the airport.

Edward Richardson had remained observing the stars until the early hours. Then, before going down to bed, he played Adele's message once more, listening hunched shouldered. He closed everything up and went to sleep unpeacefully in the single room.

At seven he got up and made himself some coffee. The house was disconsolate, cold and unfriendly towards him. He avoided looking at Adele's parents' portraits. He went out of the front door and locked it with a sense of escape. A damp bird sat on the garden wall. It was still before eight o'clock.

There were some routine calls to be made at Heathrow. Bramwell Broad, Barbara Poppins and the steward they called Holy Holloway were crossing the concourse. Edward said: 'Beware of Arabs carrying pineapples.'

'We pray not,' said Holloway.

Bramwell said: 'I've got enough trouble as it is.'

Barbara moved away answering: 'I'm on a different flight this time.'

Edward went to his office at ten. He sat at his desk trying to rub the weariness from his eyes. That day he was going to write his letter of resignation.

369

'The word has it that Mr Grainger's going,' said Harriet with studied casualness from her desk.

He looked up sharply and said: 'Good God. Who told you that?'

She remained concentrating on her word processor screen. 'It's everywhere,' she said.

'It's probably a false rumour,' he answered. 'You know what this place is like for rumours.'

Harriet sniffed. 'He's cleared his desk,' she said.

Richardson shook his head. 'I thought he'd never move,' he said. He surrendered to the fact that she probably had the correct information. She usually did. 'How . . . how did that come . . . about?'

'You mean was he . . . or did he?' she inquired mischievously.

'Yes, I suppose so.'

'The word is that he was leaving anyway. He's landed some superjob somewhere. They reckon in America. And he was going to resign . . .'

Richardson completed it for her: 'But, not aware that he was leaving anyway, they made him redundant.'

She looked disappointed. 'Yes, more or less. Apparently he had his letter of resignation on him. Moira, his secretary, had typed it. He was going to deliver it to the Board when there was a call *from* the Board for him to go in and see them. When he went they said the usual business about reorganisation, rationalisation, and all that stuff, and said he was being made redundant. Very sorry, nice big pay-off and all that. And there he is sitting with his goodbye letter in his pocket. And, naturally, there it stayed. He's getting thousands and thousands.'

'Lucky Grainger,' said Richardson.

'The Devil looking after his own,' muttered Harriet. He glanced at her disapprovingly. 'Well, it is,' she added her voice subdued. She looked up. 'Are we going to apply?' she asked suddenly. 'We could get it.'

He frowned. 'I . . . I really don't know.' He regarded her across the space between the desks. 'It's possible I may not be here too long myself, Harri. I am thinking of making a change . . .'

To his surprise she did not seem shocked. Her phone rang. 'Yes, he's here, Mrs Train,' she said. 'I'll transfer you.'

Edward picked up the receiver. 'Yes, Rona,' he said quietly. 'Right, I'll be over right away.'

He replaced it and stood up. 'She's going,' guessed Harriet.

'Yes. I'll just go over to see her off. I won't be long.'

He went out. She shook her head sadly after him. It was a blank, cheerless day and he ran between his office and the terminal. The building was decked out for Christmas; there was tinsel and greenery, a tall decorated tree and carols were broadcast between flight announcements and security warnings. He went up the stairs and saw her waiting in front of the Departure doors. He held her hands and kissed her on the cheek. Desperately he wanted to tell her Adele had left but realised he could not.

'This is like one of those scenes you used to paint,' he said instead. 'But with Christmas trimmings.'

'I suppose it is,' she agreed with a sad smile. 'I still have some work to do on them but when they're completed I'll send one to you.'

'Will I recognise the figures?'

'It's possible.'

For God's sake tell her, his inner voice was demanding. Tell her that they were free, that they could be together. But his honesty, his decency, the very qualities that his wife had found so irritating in him, kept him back. As much as he wanted to tell her, to ask her, he could not. Not then. It would be too easy now that Adele had gone. Rona would have to stay because *she* wanted to stay, not because it was now convenient. She moved close to him. 'Edward, I have to go. One day I'll come back and things may be different. But now, I just have to go.' She shook her head. 'Some things happen too late.'

'The Copernicus Syndrome,' he said.

He held her for a moment. Tell her, *tell her*, his inner voice repeated. But there was more to it than that.

She made up his mind for him. He felt her relax against him. 'Goodbye,' she said kissing his cheek. 'Edward.'

'Goodbye, Rona.'

She turned decisively like so many of the departing people she had sketched, and without looking back went to the door, showed her boarding card and was gone.

Richardson watched the gaping door. Others took her place, turning and waving to those left behind, or going straight through as she had without a backward glance. He waited for a moment and then turned despondently and went down the steps and out into the December day.

Harriet watched him return from the window. She was back behind her computer screen by the time he came into the room. 'Don't forget you're going to Manchester tomorrow,' she said not looking up. 'And back to Australia on Friday. More trouble.'

'Ray Francis is quitting,' he told her. 'He wants to come home. His wife is having an affair with someone in the Sydney office. It started almost the day they got out there.'

He picked up a document from the desk, columns of figures which he hardly saw let alone comprehended. 'How's the cycling, Harri?' he asked suddenly.

'Oh,' she replied surprised. 'It's going well. Really well considering it's winter. We're expanding the club. We've sorted out PEDAL – "Pursue Energy Deportment And Longevity". It's a revolution against the engine.'

'Won't do us much good here,' he said. 'Try pedalling a Boeing.'

She had remained observing him. 'She's gone, hasn't she,' she said.

'Yes. She's just gone,' he said.

'Where's Mrs Richardson?'

'She's gone too. Everyone seems to be deserting me.' He laughed drily. 'What with Grainger as well.'

'I'm sorry. I'm still here.'

'Thanks Harri. I know you are.'

'You didn't tell Rona . . . Mrs Train . . . that your wife had left?'

'No.'

'Will she come back?'

'I don't know. I expect so. Her mother's grave is in the churchyard.'

Harriet's telephone rang. She looked up. 'There's a problem with the Los Angeles flight,' she said. 'The gate says that somebody wants to get off.'

'Oh hell,' he said. 'These people who discover a fear of flying at the last moment. It messes up security, the baggage – let alone everything else. And it takes a hell of a lot to persuade them . . .' Suddenly he realised. Slowly he looked up and across to her. She had realised before him. 'You'd better go across,' she said.

Richardson almost fell down the stairs. The receptionist jumped in alarm but he was out of the door before she could say anything. It was raining briskly now, but he ran head down, across the road and the pavements, dodging taxis and passengers with their luggage, scattering a group of gossiping sheltering porters, and hardly giving the sliding doors time to open for him. He knew where to go. He made for the Arrivals area. The familiar parade of waiting people lined the barriers, some holding up name cards, scrutinising the faces as they came from the customs hall piled with baggage.

He halted and watched the opening and closing doors. Rona came through at once, carrying her small hand case. She saw him waiting and ran towards him, tears glistening on her cheeks. He folded her in his arms and she put her wet face next to his. 'I couldn't,' she said. 'I couldn't.'

'I thought you had departed,' he said.

She told him: 'Not me. I've only just arrived.'